# FLOWERS FOR THE DEVIL

V. KAHANY

Flowers For The Devil

Copyright © 2022 Vlad Kahany

❀ Created with Vellum

*Dedicated to those whose shadows of the past
are the darkest,
but who have the courage to walk in the light.*

*"Shadows only dance when darkness fights light.*
*For when the light wins and comes in with full force, the only*
*shadow you see is your own."*

Harlan Krow, the gentleman-devil.

# PLAYLIST

*Devil Devil*—MILCK

*Play With Fire (Alternate Version)*—Sam Tinnesz, Ruello, Violents

*Lion*—Saint Mesa

*Devil You Don't*—CXLOE

*How Villains Are Made*—Madalen Duke

*Watch You Run*—ECHO, Tomer Katz, D Fine Us

*The Devil You Know*—X Ambassadors

*I Will Never Die*—Delta Rae

*Pala Tute*—Gogol Bordello

*Black Hole Sun*—SWANN

*Familiar*—Agnes Obel

*Lovely (with Khalid)*—Billie Eilish, Khalid

*Second (Skyrim)*—Mimi Page

*I Found*—Amber Run

*Oh Love*—Ane Brun

*Nemesis*—Benjamin Clementine

*Love story*—Indila

*Bottom of the River*—Delta Rae

*Heal*—Tom Odell
*Gems - Interlude*—Little Simz

You can find the playlist on Spotify.

# PROLOGUE

What does the priest do when the devil comes to confess?

What if the devil is a gentleman?

And, in fact, a beloved hero of the poorest of London?

What if his dark deeds eased the lives of hundreds? Perhaps, thousands…

You see, Reverend John Pearse doesn't have a choice. He hears the name that is so often whispered in the dark. He hears the voice that finally reached the light. He knows it shall be a story of darkness. And a thousand Holy Rosaries won't erase the crimes.

But Reverend Pearse is no stranger to darkness. Others' sins are his bread and butter. His lips are sealed.

So he listens as the low voice starts the dark story.

"Forgive me, Father, for I have sinned. My sins are too many to count. And, forgive me Lord, I would commit them again. My name is Harlan Krow, and this is my confession."

# 1

## VANITY FAIR

### AUGUST 1851

Countess Alina Bronskaya downed a glass of champagne and scanned the crowded ballroom. The chandelier lights were blinding but failed to erase the images of blood that still flickered in her mind like pictures in a horror book.

Blood.

A limp body on the ground.

And him—the dark shadow looming over her.

*"Are you all right?"*

Alina inhaled deeply, trying to calm the tremors in her body.

Adorned in gold and white and decorated with an extraordinary amount of fresh flowers, the ballroom was one of London's finest. Simmering in sparkling splendor and late August warmth, its floor-to-ceiling windows overlooked the crowded terrace, illuminated brightly by dozens of lanterns.

It was much too late, and the ball was already in full swing.

Alina hadn't had time to properly prepare for the party. No bath. No creams. Barely any makeup. Her hair had smelled of chloride and burnt coal when she'd gotten home, and she had to brush the so-hated pomade into it.

"The dress! Quick!" she had hurried her maid, Martha, who scrambled with laces and jewelry.

Alina had doused herself with perfume to disguise the traces of medication stench and rushed out of the house.

Her heart still raced at the memories, but champagne helped as she scanned the crowded room. So did the loud music, drowning the sound of the shadow's low voice in her head.

*"Are you able to walk?"*

Ladies and lords, stuffed into silks and feathers and excessive jewelry, were quite tipsy. Orchestra music laced with laughter and loud chatter vibrated through the ballroom crowded with powdered faces.

Lady Amstel's balls were jolly affairs even after the Season. But the wealthy could smell "poor." And Alina's work was cheap indeed—in St Rose's hospital on the edge of St. Giles, the invisible line that separated the very poor and the more fortunate.

Her mother, Anna Yakovlevna Kameneva, floated toward her with a well-practiced smile that hid disdain, her cold eyes sweeping up and down Alina's dress.

"You look like a merchant's daughter," her mother murmured with a thick Russian accent, the giant ruby necklace adorning her neck hissing with its devilish sparkle. "Could you not think of anything better to wear?"

She squinted in reproach at her daughter's modest topaz choker and shifted to stand next to her, facing the crowded room. Her lavish burgundy dress was like a bouquet of flowers compared to Alina's simple light-green evening gown, worn twice in a row in the last month. Anna Yakovlevna was the best example of true Russian nobility with its flair for chic and overbearing displays of wealth, be it jewelry or furs or golden goblets at their house parties.

"The Duke of Ravenaugh and Viscount of Leigh are here," she said in a low voice as she scanned the room.

*Old news.*

Alina rolled her eyes but made an effort to straighten her shoulders. "They only come to bask in the glory of everyone's admiration," she said indifferently.

She glanced at her arms to make sure there were no traces of blood. She couldn't quite remember the precise sequence of events back at St Rose's. Only the attack and then the dark shadow looming over her and offering his hand.

Shaking off the memories that had set her heart pounding again, she returned her gaze to the pompous crowd.

A gathering of vices and titles. Including her.

She despised how everyone bowed to the titles. How unwed women nervously clutched their fans and adjusted too-willing expressions as they put themselves out on display for potential suitors. How the wealthiest boomed with laughter and blinked slowly, not hiding their contempt, and the less powerful trembled in trepidation at their every word.

"They are something to aspire to," interjected Anna Yakovlevna.

"Pride and gluttony, perhaps," murmured Alina and snatched another glass of champagne from the tray of a passing waiter. The pleasant fizzy liquid made its way down her throat, soothing her nerves, and she opened her fan, trying to cool her burning face.

Her mother flicked her fan angrily and hissed, "If only you were interested in suitors more than homeless invalids."

"Mamá…" Alina waved her away in annoyance, having heard those words too many times.

"Quarreling again?" a soft voice came from behind them, making Alina turn to see her father.

*Thank the Lord.*

Nikolai Sergeevich Kamenev walked up to them. His lips were hidden by his thick mustache and beard, but his kind eyes smiled at his daughter. Her mother was a ferocious talker. Her father was a humble listener. It was a match made in heaven.

"Mamá is scolding me again. Papá, please, tell her."

"Oh, the advocate!" said Anna Yakovlevna with sarcasm, then added in Russian, "*Ostanetsia v devkah—budesh na starosti let plakat', chto net potomkov.*"

As usual, she grumbled at him for standing up for his daughter, who wouldn't give them heirs, he smiled kindly, met Alina's apologetic gaze, and winked at her. He was a shield between Alina and her mother, taking all the blows.

The exhausting notes of a waltz drifted across the room. Alina swept a glance at the self-important faces, gowns and suits, skirts and frocks. Alcohol slowly dissolved the noble manners. Lady Boarberry had gathered a number of men around her, cackling too loudly at the jokes as her young unwed daughter sweated away on the dance floor with the dozenth potential suitor. The ballroom was stuffy. The fans flicked with the speed of snakes' tongues.

The image of blood flickered in Alina's mind again. She closed her eyes just for a moment and shook her head, trying to shake it away.

"Sir John!" Anna Yakovlevna exclaimed, elbowing Alina in her ribs.

A short plump man with a red face and sweaty bald head approached, his sly smile aimed at Alina. His nostrils expanded, as if sniffing the air.

Could he smell blood?

*Oh, God.*

Suddenly, Alina was too aware of herself again. The images

of the night street and the dead body flashed in her mind. Panic rose in her like a tide.

She glanced down at her gloved hands, checking them for the dozenth time, though she'd changed the gloves for the ball. And as Sir John took her hand in his paw for a prolonged kiss, she had an urge to pull him away by his bushy sideburns.

A commotion at the door made the boisterous crowd turn their heads.

Samuel Cassell, the Duke of Ravenaugh, and Theo Van Buren, the Viscount of Leigh, entered the room. The two always seemed to show up together. One was sulky and indifferent as if there was no life inside his tall, impressive form. The other one was too talkative and deliberately attentive.

They could pass for brothers. Both wore their dark hair shoulder-length, slicked back and gathered by a tie, against the fashion. Both clean-shaven. Both tall, strong, and dressed impeccably. But while the duke's features were heavy but somewhat duller, the viscount's were sharp and cat-like, his eyes almost always squinting with a playful sparkle.

Alina had been introduced to them before but never gave them a second thought. One was a bore, the other a rake.

She exhaled in relief—at least someone would not pay attention to her.

Sir John Boldon stepped away, his eyes thinning on the two lords. The rest of the crowd whispered too enthusiastically, and a few débutantes straightened their shoulders. Fans in gloved hands started flicking more intensely across the room.

Alina studied her champagne glass with a tiny smirk.

The two titled bachelors in their thirties were the most anticipated catch, though no one had caught them yet. Van Buren, as per rumors, had caught plenty of fish in his net— catch and release. Cassell was a single heir, no family, no interests, wealthy enough to buy half of London but a quiet, boring man who definitely didn't interest Alina.

She wiggled her shoulders, the fabric sticking to her sweaty skin, and took another gulp of champagne that slowly eased her nervousness.

Suddenly, her mother's sharp elbow dug into her side again.

"Oh, my lord," Anna Yakovlevna whispered, lifting her chin and putting on a polite smile. Even her ruby necklace seemed to shine brighter at the sight of the two lords, who were making their way toward them.

Alina cursed in her mind and adjusted her posture, clutching her champagne flute with both hands.

Out of all nights, every man was suddenly paying attention to her while all she wanted was to disappear. Not once after their first introduction had the duke or his friend condescended to talk to her. They seemed like the rest of the ton— careful around the *immigrés* who'd appeared in London two years ago, giving plenty of reasons for gossiping. Fashion changed faster than the never-ending conversation about the Russian countess who had gotten rid of her husband and fled the country with her family.

Alina had heard all of it before.

*"Married at twenty. A widow at twenty-two. She must have poisoned him!"* sneered the women who loathed their husbands.

*"A Russian spy, perhaps?"* said those who dabbled in politics.

*"Such beauty often hides folly and bad taste,"* said those who scrutinized her dresses and jewelry and furs at every party, only to show up at the next one donning the same.

*"A black girl at her service. Savages, what else?"* said those who passed the laws to suppress the rights of the poor.

*"They brought an army of Russian servants with them. They must have been on the run."*

Oh, how right was the latter! It was the flight in the middle of the night, with the officers' guns pointing at them—a long journey from the suddenly hostile motherland to a land that looked at them with the suspicion and curiosity of zoo visitors.

And there was Van Buren, making his way through the crowd toward her, his too-intense gaze cutting her confidence down. Cassell followed him, gracefully nodding around and forcing himself to smile.

"Countess!" The viscount smiled, approaching and taking her hand in his.

"My lord." Alina curtseyed. "Your Grace." She attempted a smile at the duke, who kissed her hand without much enthusiasm, while her mother had enough for both of them.

The smell of cologne, polished leather, and cigars enveloped her.

The two men seemed larger than life. Their tall broad figures were like those of Spartans. They might be shallow men, but it was impossible to keep one's eyes off them.

Very few lords possessed true masculine beauty and strength, noble only in their titles. The wealthiest man in London looked like a baked potato with sideburns and a mustache so big and unkept they could hide a village. The famous Duke of Trent, who only months ago had married the prettiest girl, the daughter of an earl, no less, had a belly that could accommodate a brewery, bad breath, and an awful temper, which his new wife could not conceal with all the powder over her bruises.

But these two…

Alina took a deep breath and kept a smile on her face as the gentlemen exchanged pleasantries and well-practiced smiles with her parents.

They emanated power. This close it was intimidating.

The two lords were an example of well-bred nobility and truly aristocratic appearance. Their presence filled the room. No wonder they weren't interested in matrimony. Vanity was the sweetest drug. While mothers threw their daughters at the lords' feet at every function, these two only needed another fix. And the next one.

With exaggerated cheerfulness, Anna Yakovlevna poured compliments over His Grace and his friend. The viscount chuckled with well-disguised condescension while the duke stood like a statue, his hands clasped behind his back as if he didn't care to be here.

Neither did Alina. She wanted the men to leave them alone as the entire room pretended to carry on with their drinks and silly chatter though the women's occasional glances in her direction were as sharp as wasp stingers.

Van Buren's prowling eyes were on Alina again.

"Lady Bronskaya, you look stunning."

*Stunning?*

Had she misheard, or the lord had just given her a compliment? Was he flirting?

She managed another cold smile that didn't reach her eyes.

"Your eyes," Van Buren purred, gazing at her too intensely. "As if you ruined a man."

Her smile froze, and her heart lunged in her chest.

The two men nodded politely, but as they retreated, Van Buren's gaze stayed a little too long on Alina, his eyes glistening intensely.

Tonight had been the first time she hadn't brought Dr. Grevatt, Yegór, or Rumi with her to St Rose's. And then that atrocious thing had happened.

The images flickered in Alina's mind with new force.

The assault by the filthy man on the dark street by the hospital only hours ago.

An angry growl as his hand gripped Alina's arm, pulling her toward him.

The nasty words, "If ye' have no money, ye wou' haf' t'pay in some other way."

His vile face and malicious chuckle, wafting at her with the strongest stench of liquor and something rotting.

His one hand groped her despite her pleas and shouts. His other hand covered her mouth. She summoned all her strength and twisted out of his arms, shoving him away.

Then darkness…

Lost time…

She came back to her senses, realizing she sat on the ground against the fence. Looking around, she saw the attacker's motionless body, his head rimmed in blood, more blood soaking his chest.

*No-no-no-no-no…*

*How?*

Dark, almost black in the dark of night, the blood suddenly flickered bright red in the lamp of the passing carriage. Why his chest?

*No-no-no.*

And then the low voice came from the darkness.

"Are you all right?"

A shadow, like the devil himself, bent over her, stretching its hand.

A long black leather coat. A top hat with that signature red tassel that everyone in the poorest parts of London knew. Black hair down to his shoulders. The round tinted spectacles flickering like vicious glares.

"Can you stand up?" the soft deep voice asked, the black gloved hand still outstretched toward her.

Her stomach turned icy-cold. Her heart thudded so loudly that it seemed to rip through her chest. She gaped at him, trying in vain to discern his features in the dark.

He looked just like they described him in the stories whispered for years, hailing the hero of the poor, and in the headlines of the Gazette that detailed the gruesome crimes committed in the name of justice.

Alina swallowed hard and by reflex put her hand into his. He effortlessly pulled her up to her feet.

A head taller than her, he seemed like a giant. She forgot to breathe and forgot about the man on the ground, instead staring up at the darkness clad in black.

A killer.

A villain.

A legend.

"I am afraid I had to take care of your little problem," said the voice, deep but soothing.

The air seemed to still around them.

*Take care?*

Her heart thudded violently, making her knees weak.

No, she wasn't dreaming. This *was* the man who took care of the streets of the East End.

She stood, transfixed on the darkness and the tiny flickers of reflection in his tinted spectacles. She must have swayed, dizzy and confused, for he took her gently by her shoulders.

"Are you able to walk?"

She forgot to answer, staring into the face of darkness.

The West End knew him as the most elusive villain. The East End hailed him the hero of the poor.

The city called him the gentleman-devil.

He was the man Alina would get to know as Harlan Krow.

## 2

# UBUNTU

This story starts near the slums of St. Giles, Father.

Whitechapel. Spitalfields. Bethnal Green. Old Nichol. These sound like holy places, but they are the shades of darkness, the parts of London that one is lucky not to know.

The Devil's Acre—a name can't get more symbolic than that.

I knew the slums, its night terrors. Fires blazing here and there. Keeping some warm, burning the remains of unfortunate others. Sins festered in every corner. The air was heavy with stench and sounds of misery.

It didn't get blacker than the streets of Old Nichol by night.

The voices that moaned and grunted and begged for mercy.

The voices that echoed like thousands of ghosts in the darkest pit of London that never slept, cramped with tortured souls.

Anything that was too vile for the parts like St. Giles teemed here, in this tomb of existence. This wasn't living but surviving. And I felt like here, of all places, I could bring relief.

*One person at a time, Harlan.*

When I was in southern Africa, a local scribe taught me a word.

*Ubuntu* in the Nguni language means "humanity." But that is an English word. In the local understanding, it means, "I am because you are."

You see, Father, humanity is a reflection on itself. We don't act alone but rather with the consideration of others. Our acts are contagious. Wickedness sprouts like weeds, kindness like fresh grass. But weeds grow everywhere, and grass needs sun, water, and care. You don't change society suddenly but rather slowly, with acts of kindness—a trickle of them that might one day grow into a river.

I did what I did because it eased the lives of many, Father. Mine were not always acts of kindness, but they spared others' pain. Mine is a damned soul, but others can be saved. If one life is the collateral, would you blame me?

Oh, I see, Father. You do.

Well, think of it this way. You are a coachman who is driving a carriage. The horse goes mad. It won't respond to your reins. A whip in your hands is useless.

The road in front of you splits. Ahead, you have a group of five children on one road and a lone man on the other.

The horse won't stop, you know it. Which road will you take?

You say you don't have to make a choice? It's all in the hands of God, you say? I've heard that before.

What if I tell you that the lone man is a monster? Will God take the back stage then and let you make that choice?

I am not sure what drew me to St Giles that night. But I should be grateful.

How my angel ended up there was a mystery that I got to find out later.

Countess Alina Bronskaya.

The night I saw her, I thought she was lost. Only later would I realize that I was the one who was lost. Until she found me without looking.

*Ubuntu. I am because you are.*

I found my angel in the dark, Father. And she showed me the path to light. No prayers had ever accomplished that. No church had ever given me a home. No words of consolation coming from you had ever soothed the way hers would.

My story with her started with a murder. It would end with another crime. And it would end the most notorious villain that London had ever known.

Harlan Krow.

The gentleman-devil.

The shadow of the slums.

Who knew that death could be so sweet?

# 3

## THE KAMENEVS

"You are a bumpkin! I can't stand it, really!" The loud female shout echoed through the servants' quarters of the house on Birchin Street.

A door slammed shut somewhere followed by the sound of hurried angry footsteps.

Alina leaned on the doorframe to the kitchen, her arms crossed at her chest, and watched with amusement as another servants' brawl unraveled. She rarely stepped into the servants' quarters, but her maid and footman were the topic of constant entertainment on quiet dreary days.

The large kitchen reminded her of home. Trunks, boxes, chests, sacks with seeds and dry flowers and herbs, strings of garlic and onion. The shelves were lined with goblets and jugs of all sizes and colors. A large basket of apples spread the scent of a summer garden across the kitchen.

Prosha, the cook, had made sure her dwelling space was just like home. She minded her own business, the sleeves of her chemise rolled up as she sank her thick red arms into a tub of hot water.

Yegór sat at the kitchen table, his strong thick legs spread wide, his giant fists on the table. Even sitting down, the twenty-five-year-old footman was almost as tall as Prosha standing up. With a thick beard, unruly hair that pushed his cap off his head, and a mountainous body, he could eat a cow for dinner, drink a decanter of moonshine, read a prayer kneeling in the corner, cross himself, and fall into a deep healthy sleep. And the silly smile that beamed through his thick beard just now was no match to his intimidating form that scared passersby on the streets.

Alina studied his livery. It already seemed to come apart at the seams, the fabrics straining against his muscles. A loose chemise with a belt was what he preferred, but Anna Yakovlevna insisted on the proper Western attire.

The irritated female voice belonged to Martha, Alina's twenty-year-old English maid, a curvy girl with a pretty, almost doll-like face and straw-colored hair. Her voice grew muffled as she disappeared deep in the scullery, the annoyed chirping never stopping. Her curvy form reappeared with a stack of pots in her hands.

"And your ears are evidently dead," she rambled, not looking at Yegór but making him shift with the swing of her wide hips as she stomped by. "For if you opened them, you'd hear what I am telling you. And I told you a dozen times not to touch my belongings."

She came back to the table and struck a pose in front of him, putting her fists on her waist and glaring at him.

Yegór only smiled, looking up and down her hourglass figure and big bosom, constricted by her uniform.

Those two had quarreled almost constantly for the last two years since Alina and her parents had come to England.

"Why do you always smile? Answer!" demanded Martha, her eyes blazing.

Yegór's smile grew into a grin. His cheerful attitude was like a wall that Martha's anger hit all the time with no results.

She leaned on her hands on the table, bringing her face closer to Yegór's and narrowing her eyes on him. "You like being called a fool, don't you? Or you don't understand? You want me to say it in Russian?"

Oh, Yegór understood all right. The Kamenevs had hired a tutor to teach their Russian servants basic English. But the footman didn't respond, his gaze sliding to Martha's bosom, which looked even plumper as she leaned over. She noticed and straightened up.

"Gah!" She stomped her foot and clenched her jaw in frustration.

Alina cleared her throat, startling them.

"My lady." Yegór rose abruptly, bumping into the table and shaking it. Martha wiped her hands on her shapely hips and straightened up as Prosha continued the washing with her usual smirky expression.

"Anna Yakovlevna has been waiting for her tea," Alina said without anger, despite having to come here, for the bell hadn't been answered. Their servants were a mess but amused their household greatly.

"Those two will either kill each other or end up in a good tumble," Prosha often said, making Anna Yakovlevna gape in shock and Alina giggle.

Martha picked at her fingers, her eyes snapping up at Alina. "If it weren't for this fo—"

The words died on her lips under Alina's reproachful gaze.

"Forgive me, my lady. I'll send Dunya right away," the maid said quietly.

Alina walked back to the sitting room where her mother half-sat half-lay on the sofa, an herbal compress on her forehead.

"If they don't learn to lower their voices," Anna Yakovlevna said weakly in Russian, "I shall throw both of them out. They are like cat and dog."

Alina took a seat on the sofa across the low table from her mother and picked up the book she'd been trying to read for some time.

"Where is that insolent girl? I asked for tea an eternity ago," Anna Yakovlevna murmured. "One day they will kill each other."

*Kill…*

The word instantly tugged at Alina's mind with the memories from a week ago.

She'd thought the memories would be traumatic. But the weather was turning quickly. And as the last days of summer were gone, so was the dread at the memory of the night by St Rose's.

*Strange.*

The events from a week ago now felt like a distant dream. So did the summer. The leaves seemed to have changed color overnight. And just as fast, instead of summer jackets and parasols, the first days of September brought with them coats and umbrellas.

Rain started pouring relentlessly, draining the color out of leaves, turning them burnt ochre, gray, and knocking them off the trees one by one.

With the sun's cheerfulness gone, smiles disappeared, giving way to exhausted glares, grumbles, grunts, and curses as drenched feet stomped through mud and puddles.

Alina quite enjoyed it. People's eyes stayed down on the ground, searching for another puddle to avoid instead of burrowing into her with curiosity. The Season had been long over and the parties had subsided until they would pick up in December. She was glad there were fewer excuses for her mother to drag her to yet another function, trying to sell her off to some respectable bachelor. Preferably, a duke or an earl. A prince would be great, for Anna Yakovlevna thought her daughter deserved a king.

The fire crackled in the fireplace of the sitting-room as Alina tried to read, despite her mother's too frequent comments. Anna Yakovlevna had requested the fire to be lit, complaining about the early cold and the dreadful rain and her arthritis.

"This city turned from a glamorous lady into a shabby harlot in a matter of one week," her mother complained in Russian.

Anna Yakovlevna sulked, missing home like never before. She hated the monotony of cold seasons. She drank tea and *Nalifka*, sweet homemade berry liquor, idly picked out melancholic strains of music on the piano, and more often reprimanded their servants. She was restless one minute, another stood by the window, her arms wrapping the shawl tightly about her shoulders as she stared into emptiness as if waiting for someone.

The low rumbling voice of their footman sounded from the entrance. His disjointed English words with the thick aggressive accent cut through Martha's snappy replies.

The entrance door slammed.

The servants again—Anna Yakovlevna sighed in response.

Visitors rarely came these days. At first, when Alina and her parents had arrived in London, the entire ton had burst with curiosity. But there were few friends made. Alina preferred it that way, at least for now, feeling grief and bitterness take over her at the thought of home.

*This is our home now.*

Thank God for the servants they had brought with them. Anna Yakovlevna had insisted and had been right. The small two-story house they had acquired on Birchin Street was Little Russia, as Olga Kireeva had called it laughingly the last time she'd come to London. Prosha, the older, grumpy, but brilliant cook. Dunya, the young slender maid who had picked up on the English language and manners surprisingly quickly. And Yegór, the Viking of a man, who scared anyone who glanced at him.

There were three more servants who were English and in constant war with the Russians.

"Almost like back home," Olga had said jokingly and burst out in laughter.

Oh, how Alina missed Olen'ka! She couldn't wait until November when she would see her friend again.

Meanwhile, she was quite content with the foul weather.

Minus her mother's complaints.

Minus Doctor Grevatt's deteriorating condition.

Minus—

The dark man who she'd encountered a week ago.

She'd had nightmares for several days. But they'd subsided, just like the memories of him.

Now it seemed like a bad dream. She hadn't told anyone. Petty crimes were common. Lady Boarberry was said to have been robbed right in her carriage on Knightsbridge. Granted, it was in the middle of the night as she was coming back from seeing her lover. That part had been intentionally omitted in the story. And yet! This city was ridden with crime. But not many could say they'd met the man who was a myth and, according to some, didn't exist.

The sweet smell of baked dough seeped into the sitting room.

The English hated the smell of food in their houses.

"That is because it doesn't smell good," Anna Yakovlevna often said bitterly and thanked herself for bringing Prosha.

A round woman in her forties, their cook had a fiery temper, booming voice, huge hands that could knead a tub of dough in minutes, and a deep bark that scared the kitchen staff and even made Yegór straighten up. Prosha was reluctant to learn the English cuisine.

"Dogs have better taste than that."

Same went for the English language. The only words that had found their way into her vocabulary in two years were, "Sank you," "Good mor-r-rning," and "Br-r-rute." The latter she'd overheard on the street when someone snapped at Yegór. When she'd learned the meaning, Prosha cackled in that contagious way of hers and slapped the glaring Yegór on the forearm, saying, "Br-r-rute," bulging her eyes at him and rolling with laughter again. In her thick accent, that of a war-drum, the word sounded like the deepest insult.

"Prosha is making poppyseed pies," Alina said absent-mindedly.

"About time." Her mother started on the sofa. "I can't get used to the food here. Tasteless. Unimaginative. No wonder it dries out people's wits," Anna Yakovlevna whined in Russian as she played a dying swan.

Alina snorted. "You are being judgmental. You talk as if you are on vacation here for a short time." She answered in English, knowing it irritated her mother.

"I miss home, yes! Who can blame me?" Anna Yakovlevna answered in Russian, their conversations a never-ending war. "The fall with its bright colors. Oh, how beautifully Pushkin described it! Can you ever compare the golden fairy to this!" She motioned vaguely at the window as she half-lay on the sofa, shifting her feet on a pillow, a shawl over her shoulders, a warm compress on her head. "This country gives me headache. Dunyasha! Where is that insolent girl? Bring *Nalifka*!"

"Mamá, you are being melodramatic," answered Alina in English, not tearing her eyes off the book she was trying to read, stuck on the same page for the last half an hour.

She'd been trying to coax her mother to speak more English. But Anna Yakovlevna preferred French. Despite the wars, the close relationship with France had forged a flare for the French language among Russian nobility for centuries. "A love-language," she often said. "Unlike English. Br-r-rute," she mimicked Prosha, rolling the r-sound.

"The autumns are much the same in Russia," Alina argued now. "Your nostalgia is altering your memories. You used to hate Petersburg in the fall. You used to say it was dirty and full of rats, on the street as well as in its state offices."

Dunya walked in with a tray that held a teapot and a cup, a crystal cordial glass, and a decanter with dark burgundy liquid.

The thick, sweet berry liquor had become Anna Yakovlevna's medicine and now swiftly made its way down her throat.

Prosha was an expert in homemade drinks, tinctures, and liquors, vodkas infused with peppers and honey and apricot pits and sage and centaury, wines fermented from berries and fruit.

"Perhaps, you should drink more tea instead of strong spirits," Alina dared to suggest.

"Tsk." Anna Yakovlevna motioned for the maid to pour one more. "A wise man said, 'Tell me what you drink, and I shall tell you who you are.' Get rid of the tea, Dunya. I changed my mind." Anna Yakovlevna snapped her fingers at the maid but eagerly accepted the cordial glass with the second helping.

"E-ni-sing els-se, ma'am?" the maid asked with a willing expression and a strong hissing accent.

Alina pursed her lips to hide a smile.

Just like Yegór, eighteen-year-old Dunya tried to learn English. But unlike everyone who still quite often donned kaftans and loose knee-long shirts and bast shoes, she dressed like a proper English girl. Only late at night, running chores, she would answer the bell and show up in front of Anna Yakovlevna barefoot.

"Manners!" Anna Yakovlevna would snap, then complain to Alina. "By God, will they ever learn? You can put a dress on a scarecrow but you can't give it a brain, can you?"

The afternoon was rainy. Soon, the darkness would fall. Every day for the last week, Alina fell anxious by nighttime.

"I am taking a carriage and going to Dr. Grevatt's," she finally said.

"But dinner! Alina!" Anna Yakovlevna protested from behind the piano. "This family should be your priority."

"It is, Mamá." Alina looked in the mirror and adjusted her hat. "But I have other things to do right now."

Anna Yakovlevna theatrically shielded her eyes as if the reply pained her. "Take Yegór with you. A woman shouldn't be riding around the slums alone."

Alina was already by the doorway. "I am going to Dr. Grevatt's."

"And then to those sick."

"I shall be fine," she echoed from the hall.

"You are a respectable widow!" Anna Yakovlevna shouted into the ceiling. "And much too young to be fine on your own!"

And that was, perhaps, right.

"Yegór, you are coming with me," Alina said, changing her mind at the last minute.

Martha only scowled, fixing Alina's shawl and murmuring, "Get him out of my hair."

Yegór was called many names by the Englishmen. Prosha and the rest called him *bogatyr'*, a heroic warrior. Almost seven feet tall and strong like a bull, he was a marvel, making passersby start aside in awe and trepidation. He often hunched in a clumsy way as if trying to bend a little to the people he talked to. Alina used him as a personal guard when she made her weekly trips to St Rose's. They knew Yegór well there by now. Knew that despite his intimidating appearance, Yegór could crack a joke in English. He made children laugh, picking up three of them with each arm. His English was improving, mostly because he was quite fond of Martha.

It was a Friday, and the usual weekly day for the visit to St Rose's. Alina had made up her mind to not ever go there without her footman or at least Rumi by her side. Only blocks away from the worst slums in Central London, it was surely a dangerous place to be at night.

Alina's stomach twisted with unease as she stepped outside the house. Her giant footman followed. She turned to look up at him and met his ready smile. No one ever dared to come close when he was around.

She felt better, safer now.

She still hadn't told anyone about the night incident a week ago. She wouldn't.

And one thing she was sure of—the shadow man would not show up again.

# 4

## DOCTOR GREVATT

Two cluttered desks with battered edges sat on the opposite sides of a large dim study at Dr. Grevatt's.

"Tea, ma'am?" the maid asked, taking Alina's shawl, hat, and gloves.

Dr. Grevatt's study was in his flat that took up the ground floor of a brick house on Jermyn Street, about a ten-minute walk from St Rose's hospital where he practiced.

The study was a shabby but neat room with faded draperies and worn-out furniture. The carpet in the center was thin with a balding patch. The wooden boards squeaked underfoot. The room smelled of old books, medicine, and burnt paraffin. The place was like its owner—aging and gracefully, but nevertheless, falling apart.

Alina had gotten to love this place. But the monotonous routine would soon become hectic with the fast approach of the cold season.

Even the wealthy, simmering in the heat of the fireplaces, couldn't fight the cold. It penetrated the gilded walls, hitting even more ferociously when one left the warmth of the house. Bodies used to luxury were even more fragile in the English fog and rain that had no mercy. Sickness didn't spare even those wrapped in furs and thick woolen capes.

Soon Dr. Grevatt's workload would double. When it grew colder, he had to juggle the few wealthy patients and those who flocked to St Rose's in search of any cure for their never-ending coughs and ailments.

Dr. Grevatt tore his eyes from his desk and smiled at Alina, watching her enter the study. His wrinkled face looked unusually tired, his eyes reddened over the pince-nez perched on the tip of his nose. He lit his pipe and puffed out the first cloud of smoke, slumping in his chair behind his desk.

At the other desk across the study, Rumi was already arranging the previously finished papers of the essay with the fresh empty sheet set up in front of her. She straightened the quill and the ink bottle next to it, touching them for the dozenth time. Her meticulousness was astounding. As was her brilliant mind. She brushed her dark fingers against the white sheet and blew on it, as if to make sure not a single speck of dust marred it.

It was peculiar that the one person Alina could truly call a friend was Grevatt's protégé. A former slave girl saved from an auction in the Spitalfields. A black girl of Nigerian descent who could read Latin and Greek, spoke French fluently, and had a much wider education than most ladies of the ton. And poetry—oh, Rumi hadn't acquired her name for nothing!

Alina approached the desk, smiling at Rumi, then picked up the last page she'd narrated the previous day.

"All, right. We shall continue with the recent cholera outbreak and the mode of communication."

Rumi nodded and picked up the quill.

She treated writing like a ritual. The way she dipped the quill and dabbed it on the side of the inkwell. The way she made a barely noticeable circle with her hand in the air before bringing it down to the page. The high-neck dark-emerald dress brought out Rumi's full red lips and almond-shaped eyes, so dark, they made the whites even brighter, stark against her coal-black skin.

Rumi was beautiful. Looks. Heart. Mind. Only twenty-four and conjuring the poems that had made Henry Dorcer from the Literary Review bow to her.

Alina started narrating. She walked slowly back and forth in front of the desk, and as the words slowly left her mouth, she and Rumi settled into their usual work routine as Dr. Grevatt quietly carried on with his in the other corner.

Over a year ago, Alina had gladly volunteered to be Dr. Grevatt's assistant nurse in exchange for his mentorship. When she'd written her first essay, expressing her ideas on the cause of cholera, he had been stunned. That evening, he'd reread it several times, then walked around this very study, smoking and reasoning, then stopped and looked at her.

"Miss Alina," he'd said then, already on friendly terms with her. "You might be the most promising young person in the medical field I've met lately."

*Person.*

Not *woman.*

*Person.*

That was the biggest compliment she'd ever gotten.

He'd shared her theory with his colleagues.

"Dr. Schofield is impressed. Naturally, the ideas are too brave and need much more research and testing but enough to start a conversation. It is positively up for discussion, and, with enough persistence, it shall be published. There is just one thing, Miss Alina. Please, understand."

She knew the *thing* and what he was about to say.

"They will never accept the essay written by a non-certified doctor and"—he looked away with unease—"a woman." She saw a lump in his throat bob as he swallowed hard. "Miss Alina—"

"I know that." She nodded, a reassuring smile on her lips. "I know that, Dr. Grevatt. You don't need to remind me. And I am fine with that. If those ideas can further the medical research, it would make me happy. And if we can use your name to achieve that, then that is what needs to be done."

"Yes. Yes." He had nodded apologetically, the candlelight flickering at that so banal admission of societal inequality.

He'd always revised Alina's essays since then. She'd published four and was almost ready with the last one. The submissions to the Medical Gazette bore Grevatt's name, yet behind it was her research. Medical science had always been her passion. Her late husband, Count Andrei Bronskiy, had supported it and hired a chemist and a doctor to guide her in her pursuit of medical science. When she'd come to England, her arrangement with Dr. Grevatt had been the only thing that had kept her sane for some time.

And then there was St Rose's where she felt, for the first time, she could make a difference.

She kept narrating to Rumi, but her thoughts drifted toward the evening and the weekly trip to the hospital. But as soon as the thought of the hospital near St. Giles entered her mind, so did the image of the shadow man.

Her voice faltered, and she stopped narrating.

*A gentleman-devil.*

Her heart tightened. She stopped in the middle of the room. His image had cut through her mind like a ghost—a reminder of the awful incident.

She brushed away the images in her head and resumed narrating, but lost track of thought.

"Pardon," Rumi interrupted her. "The spelling?"

Alina stalled. She'd already forgotten what she'd said. The

darkness outside was taking her thoughts elsewhere, and her heart started beating faster.

"Look it up in *Vade Mecum* please," she said, slightly embarrassed.

Five minutes later, her mind was all over the place, mainly at the gates of St Rose's.

Rumi raised her eyes. "We are almost at the end of the second part. Three more pages, and you could do a revision, and I will make a clean copy."

Rumi waved the page in the air, letting it dry.

The floor panels squeaked as Dr. Grevatt shifted in his chair with his pipe in his hand.

Alina studied him as he slowly flipped through a thick folder of medical records, a cloud of tobacco smoke lazily rising in the air.

He was getting older day by day. But it wasn't age that was stealing away his sharp mind but something else—a bodily defect, a brain malfunction. As if parts of his brain shut down now and then. She'd seen it before, read about it extensively, and knew there was no cure.

"We received a large donation the other day," Dr. Grevatt said as if knowing she watched him and raised his eyes from the papers. Leaning back in his chair, he studied the room. "It seems to be one of the patrons of St James's Hill. Encouraging. Is that your doing, Miss Alina? Friends in high places and all?"

She didn't know what he was talking about.

St James' Hill was undoubtedly the largest social project ever undertaken in London. Boasting an orphanage, a hospital, a school, a factory, it was the first of its kind to provide care and education to the very poor yet with the quality far above cottage hospitals that the poor couldn't afford.

Money was the answer, of course. Unlimited donations were poured into it by its many benefactors. A mystery, in fact.

But the wheels of power had somehow been set in motion, and suddenly, St James's Hill was an example of the possibilities of reforms—something that the ton had never been keen on.

St Rose's was a far cry from anything remotely close to the establishment that got heavy funding from many big wigs and managed by a certain Mr. Nowrojee. The place known simply as the Hill was rumored to be acquiring another building soon, brand new, but built beside the rookery, as had been the other one. Mr. Nowrojee, the man in charge of the Hill, was known to be a man of many connections. Yet Alina had never met him. Neither had Dr. Grevatt.

"St Rose's needs much more than what we've got to keep up the quality of service." Grevatt exhaled exhaustedly. "We are just another cottage hospital, only a level above the poor law infirmaries in the workhouses. We do have trained personnel but not nearly enough."

"We don't get as many donations as some others," Alina agreed. "I tried to talk to Lady Whitshorn. But you know the elite. It only finances what would make a splash in the Gazette. A little dingy hospital on the edge of St. Giles is not it. We are not like St James's Hill."

"We should aspire," the doctor said.

"It is privately owned," Alina argued. "Surely, there is a purpose behind it all." She was skeptical of anything that had the involvement of wealthy lords.

"It is owned by a private individual, yes. That doesn't mean there are no good intentions. Lord, Miss Alina, if we could build a dozen of such establishments in this city, I wouldn't care if the money came from the royals or the devil himself—it saves lives and gives the poor opportunities!"

Ah, the devil.

And suddenly that word made an image of the dead body on the ground flicker in Alina's mind.

The gentleman-devil.

Unease washed over her at the memory of the night only a week ago. The attacker who had paid a heavy price that night. The villain London had been gossiping about for years.

She shook her head, trying to shoo the grim images away. This afternoon, they had been insistent, chasing her every other thought. It was her and Rumi's time for the weekly visit to the hospital, and the idea of seeing the crime scene made her heart race.

Alina walked up to the desk and changed the candle in the candle-holder, trying to distract herself.

"Perhaps you can put another word in, Miss Alina," Grevatt said, watching her and puffing on his pipe. "You are on good terms with the almighty."

She snorted. "An overstatement."

She'd heard that before. Dr. Grevatt had been pushing her to make an acquaintance with the very Mr. Nowrojee, but the mere mention of his name would raise eyebrows.

Rumi finished stacking the papers and put them into a thick folder with the rest, making a spreadsheet of chapters and notations. She tidied up and flexed her fingers.

Alina had tried to write herself. A year ago, she would show up at home with her fingers stained with ink to the alarming reaction of her mother.

"Like a commoner," Anna Yakovlevna had hissed. "Next thing, you will be lighting your own fireplace, cleaning your room, and cooking your own food."

And that had stopped it. Rumi was only glad to take on that chore, and Alina was grateful.

"Well, that is it for tonight, Dr. Grevatt." Alina glanced at the clock in the corner. It was six o'clock—time to leave for the hospital. Her heart gave a heavy thud at the thought. "Mrs. Clunn asked about you the last time you were absent, Dr.

Grevatt. She is back. Her shoulder is not healing properly after the surgery." She walked up to the desk and went through the annotation page as she kept talking. "I personally think that it won't unless she rests."

The doctor was quiet, staring at the pipe in his hand as if it were the most curious thing. His hunched figure in the armchair suddenly seemed old and fragile.

Alina flipped through the next page as she kept talking. "But we don't have spare beds for those in recovery. And Mrs. Clunn has to provide for her children." Not hearing an answer, she tore her eyes from the pages and looked across the study at the doctor. "Dr. Grevatt?"

The man raised his eyes at her and frowned, confused.

The air seemed to have been sucked out of the room. An icy prickle stabbed Alina's heart as she recognized that gaze and what would follow.

The doctor carefully set his pipe on the table and looked aimlessly around the room. "Who is Mrs. Clunn?"

# 5

## ST ROSE'S

"It is getting worse," said Alina as she and Rumi rode to St Rose's. The dimness swallowed the words, sinking the carriage into silence and the scary realization of Dr. Grevatt's condition. Alina stared at her gloves as if they had an answer. "I don't know what to do." She exhaled loudly and met Rumi's eyes, which matched Alina's submission to the grave thoughts.

"There is nothing you can do, Miss Alina. His mind is failing."

Alina shook her head and tilted it back against the wall. "This is the worst—when you dedicate your life to science only to realize that the one person it can't save is you. What wretched fate." She exhaled loudly.

The carriage stalled in the evening traffic of Central London. The streets behind the closed curtains were growing a shade darker and more dangerous. It was nothing compared to the East End, yet still swarmed with gambling dens and gin houses. That meant crime that spread its tentacles in all directions and the poor who found their way to St Rose's.

Panic was starting to seize upon Alina as the carriage moved closer to the hospital.

Questions had been asked by the Metropolitan Police, no doubt, though the police cared as much about vagrants in these parts as they did about homeless dogs. But the nurses would know about the accident outside the gate.

Somehow, Alina wasn't as much concerned about the now-dead attacker as she was about the other man, Harlan Krow.

He still seemed like a ghost—invading her dreams for the last week, his voice echoing in her mind throughout the day.

*It had to be done.*

She was saving lives at St Rose's. Could she justify a crime that had saved hers?

Rumi stared aimlessly at her hands, then raised her gaze to Alina. "What if this happens during his shift at the hospital," she asked, breaking the heavy silence.

It took a moment before Alina realized that Rumi was talking about Dr. Grevatt. The carriage stalled, and Yegór opened the door.

"I am not sure how long he has before he is not able to fulfill his duties there," said Alina, stepping out of the carriage onto the dark street in front of the hospital gates.

"And then?" Rumi asked almost with despair, walking slightly behind Alina.

"And then we shall deal with it, Rumi." Alina pulled the gates open a little too forcefully. She wasn't even sure why this building had the fence and the gate. There was no lock, no money to pay a guard, and in the warm seasons, often they found homeless people sleeping in the tiny garden at the back.

St Rose's was a small two-story cottage, with only nine rooms, a kitchen, twenty beds that were always full, and a small garden in the back. The front and back doors were locked from the inside after six every night. If someone wanted to break in, they certainly could. But this was the only refuge for the sick within a mile, and no one had ever dared an assault.

Except that night a week ago.

Right outside the very gates.

Alina squinted into the darkness. For a moment, her eyes paused on the spot where she'd been attacked as if it still held the traces of the attacker. But it was impossible to see much at night.

"It would be nice to have a street light installed here," she said, following Rumi, who lit the way with the dim gas-lamp around the building and toward the back door.

The wind rustled the tree canopies, sending a handful of leaves onto the ground. Alina looked around and shivered. The street and the garden were quiet as they always were at this time of night. September was unusually cold, and the shawl over her linen dress with high collar was much too thin for this weather.

"Except we don't have enough budget to cover the last medication bill," Rumi replied as she approached the back door and rummaged in her reticule for the key.

It would be nice to have a doorman, too, and another nurse for the night shift, and enough medicine and equipment to cope with the number of patients that was growing by the day, and fewer people getting sick!

Gah!

That was the trouble. Alina shed her jewelry and wore a cheaper dress when she came to St Rose's, for she'd noticed the patients' scornful glances before—her one necklace could pay for a month worth of coal and warm clothes and better food.

*"You can't save everyone. Nor can you give away everything you have for the sake of others."*

Her father was, of course, right.

A year ago, Dr. Grevatt had smiled the first time she'd come with him here. "One simply can't give everything one has for others. No matter how right it seems. You help them, Miss Alina, without a salary, on your own time, and conducting research that no person has done yet."

"Not to your knowledge, Dr. Grevatt."

"Yes-yes, of course." He smiled in understanding. "That is more than most people of your status can offer. If the patients knew you were a titled lady, they would be afraid to talk to you."

He was right. So, Alina had humbled herself and shed her jewelry and furs and pride.

And by God, did it feel good!

*Miss Alina.*

When her name fell off the lips of the sick and the dying, she felt close to the people. Every time she stepped into St Rose's, she felt like she was living rather than floating through life like an autumn leaf in the wind.

William's tired face poked out of the reception room as she and Rumi made their way down the dark corridor. "Cleaning up," the male nurse said in his usual nonchalant way.

Rumi went to check on the patients while Alina stepped into the reception room.

"Mr. Higgs asked to speak to the doctor. Mrs. Bleemly has fever again. Mrs. Clunn's shoulder pain is getting severe," William recited with boredom, refilling a lamp with kerosene as Alina studied the reception reports.

"Dr. Grevatt couldn't come today," she said without taking her eyes off the logbook as she took her hat and shawl off.

She heard Rumi's voice in one of the patient rooms, her soft but stern tone and the patient's whimpering.

Rumi was a legend in these parts. There were still occasional visitors who stared at Rumi in shock when they first saw her. A black woman in a fine dress and proper conversation in this part of town was unheard of.

"My dark angel," an old man had called Rumi once.

Rumi had snorted, telling Alina about it then. "There are no black angels in the Bible, but guess who is saving their poor arses now?"

Alina had burst out laughing. She could imagine their faces if they ever saw Rumi quote Aristotle, recite Shakespeare, or read her own poetry!

Alina had brought Rumi to one of the small dance balls a year or so ago. Oh, the stares she got—from the lords and ladies as well as ladies' maids who congregated in a separate room. But when Lord Chesterfield said something to Rumi, passing by, and she answered quoting Francis Bacon, whoever was around dropped their jaws in deafening silence and stared at the woman who was more intelligent than half of Alina's acquaintances. To think that she'd once been a slave girl, saved from the underworld of the East End!

It had taken two hours to go through the paperwork, check on the patients, and talk to William and other nurses. The one and only fireplace in the cottage would have to be used earlier this year and more often. The darn weather! That meant more money on coal, more candles, and more patients with consumption.

By the time Rumi and Alina were done with their usual Friday routine and walked out the back door, it was late into the evening. The lamp barely lit the way in the pitch black of the small garden.

The wind sent a rush of leaves to their feet, making Alina shiver and look around.

"Go on, Rumi," she said, passing her the lamp. "Wait in the carriage. I will only be a minute."

And as Rumi's footsteps grew muffled and the last traces of lamplight disappeared behind the corner, Alina stood like a deer in the forest, alert at any sound of danger.

She shouldn't have been here alone.

She shouldn't have been in pitch black.

This was stupid. Irrational. Against any logic and the mad beating of her heart. Yet something tugged at that very heart.

And there it was—the sense of some sick curiosity and strange excitement that overtook her for the first time in a while. It was the sense of danger and something new—something that jerked her out of her monotonous existence and the fake beguilement of the ton.

The shadows among the trees shifted. It could be a trick of her eyesight, but somehow, she knew it wasn't.

She didn't move, but her heart started pounding.

The shadow shifted again and acquired the shape of a man as it stepped from behind the trees.

Another step closer.

Then another, like a black crack in the air that was approaching and was about to swallow her.

Alina stood motionless, staring at it, able to discern the dark silhouette, the open coat, the top hat. Just not the face.

The shadow grew larger and stopped several feet away from her.

Alina stood facing it and holding her breath just like a week ago, the wind hissing with danger.

Until that same deep voice cut through the silence of the night and right into her hammering heart.

"So we meet again."

# 6

## THE GENTLEMAN-DEVIL

Alina had made acquaintance with Dr. Grevatt several months after her arrival in London. It was at a function, after a silly joke about the food and drinks, someone's words, "This function will provide food to the poor of Beldorf Parish," and Alina's murmur to herself, "What they need is clean water to prevent the spread of infections."

Anna Yakovlevna hissed in her ear, "Enough with this medical nonsense."

But while others kept laughing in their ignorance, one particular man cocked his head and slowly made his way to Alina. He'd introduced himself and inquired what made her say those words.

She waved it off, embarrassed.

"No-no-no, Lady Bronskaya, please. It is peculiar you said that, for I have a close friend who does public records on the epidemics outbreaks and—"

What started as a small talk turned into a conversation that continued for hours until the end of the function.

That was Dr. Grevatt.

Two weeks later, Alina met up with him in St Rose's for another chat.

A month later, she asked for his help writing an essay on epidemic outbreaks.

Another month later, she offered to assist him in his hospital.

He argued at first. "But Lady Bronskaya. Your status and—"

"It would make it much easier if you call me Miss Alina from now on and be done with it."

'But that is un—"

"That shall be the way." She cut him off. "In these parts"—she nodded toward St Rose's—"no one knows who I am. And in exchange, you shall help me with my research. If that sounds like a fair deal to you…"

That was the easiest deal she'd ever made.

Then there was sweet, wonderful Rumi—certainly, one of the most educated women Alina had met, who soon became the closest friend Alina had in this city.

She thought St. Giles was quite bad until Dr. Grevatt took her to the East End. That short journey a year ago had changed her perspective on poverty and England in general.

There was only so much one could see out of the carriage window. Those weren't the worst parts. But on that short ride, Alina had seen enough. St Giles might have been an outlier—a small district in Central London, ridden with poverty, gambling dens, and vices of all kinds. But the true poverty was several miles east.

Shoreditch High Street had once been the home of Shakespeare's Company and The Theatre. The streets were still sprinkled with theaters, little dingy pubs, and nighttime entertainment. But just blocks away from Shoreditch were the worst slums in London.

Amidst the dilapidated buildings and cramped structures, just on the edge of Old Nichol, stood what looked like a palace —St James's Hill. The fence with a gate wasn't much of a protection, for nothing prevented crime in these parts, as the building marked the border between sanity and desperation. But not a single attempt of any sort of crime had been made since the opening of the establishment six years prior.

Inside, the poor souls found relief, the juveniles found purpose, the promising ones got an opportunity. And outside...

Outside the gates slept the sick and the homeless who hoped to get saved in the moment between death and life.

St James's Hill was the largest project ever undertaken by the city of London to serve the poor areas. The wealthy benefactors never set foot into these parts, but the project was much rumored about.

"This"—Dr. Grevatt nodded toward the massive buildings as the carriage halted, not venturing to go any further into the slums—"is the epitome of progress." Alina studied the building with curiosity. "The fact that the wealthy contribute says something about our bourgeoisie finally taking notice of the failing societal structure."

"I doubt that," said Alina.

"Faith is a weapon." Dr. Grevatt smiled.

The carriage turned around and moved up Camlet Street. Alina felt unease just being in these parts, and they were still twenty streets out of the hell's depth.

"Do you see that statue, Miss Alina?" Dr. Grevatt pointed at something in the distance.

She furrowed her eyebrows in confusion. "Art? Here?"

On the corner of Old Nichol and Camlet Street, a simple iron statue had been raised. It was almost life-size—a woman in rags, hunching over a small child in her arms.

The *Weeping Mother*, they called it, though no one knew who'd given it such a name. A piece of art any other time stolen for the sole value of iron alone stood untouched. Its appearance had coincided with the first public act of brutal vengeance against the one who'd wronged the poor.

"It was a certain benefactor of a local Holy Trinity Parish and its orphanage only five streets from here," Dr. Grevatt explained. "It was a gruesome story. The crimes against the children had been committed for years. But the man had powerful connections. And, well, no one listens to the poor— their word against that of the man who provided for them for years. Until his brutal murder and the display of his body in public the next day. With the message about the atrocities he'd committed on all those children for years."

The story was quite dark, indeed.

Dr. Grevatt continued. "It made headlines in the Gazette. The Metropolitan Police got involved. And when the police came to interrogate the orphanage caretakers, dozens of folks showed up, telling their stories about the man and his abuse. It would have been swept under the carpet as it often happens in these parts if it wasn't for a certain journalist, who wrote those stories down and printed them in an independent publication. That was the first mention of the gentleman-devil. The article and those stories made a much bigger splash than the murder itself. The city council was called. Inquiries were made. And that, Miss Alina, was how the legend about the gentleman-devil started. That was his first crime. Many followed."

Alina listened with interest. "Surely, it could all be just a legend."

Dr. Grevatt laughed then and looked at her over his pince-nez. His eyes were playful. "Surely, legends are not made out of thin air, especially when you have bodies on your hands and police involved and witnesses."

He looked too cheerful for the gruesome story he'd just told. He nodded toward the window.

"They say St James's Hill installed the statue," he continued as they rode through the dim filthy streets, ridden with rodents and vagrants, rubbish and an overbearing stench that seeped into the carriage. "They would have the funds, certainly. Who else? They say it was more of a statement and support than anything else."

"Support for?" Alina didn't understand.

"Well, to put it boldly—to the cause of the man who committed those crimes. You see, in the eyes of justice, he is a criminal that they've been chasing for several years now. In the eyes of the locals, he is a hero. Only the ones out there"—he nodded toward the window—"tell the stories of the man roaming the streets at night. It could be that no such man exists. But the legend does. For the better or for the worse."

And so the statue of the *Weeping Mother* remained unharmed, for it was rumored to be in connection with the one name that started raising whispers among the poor and men of justice.

"Harlan Krow, the gentleman-devil," Dr. Grevatt said then.

That was the first time Alina had heard the name.

And then there were more Gazette headlines. Speculations. And more horrific crimes, though many argued that it was the Metropolitan Police's way to tarnish the reputation of the man who, in fact, did their job.

No one knew where he'd come from and where he disappeared. They said he drove a black carriage that held the monstrous men he captured. Others said he rode a horse—a black stallion with a white mane. They said one flower girl knew the name of the villain. They said the villain was her protector. One thing was clear—he'd done the right thing.

The *Weeping Mother* had been erected on the place of the murder, an ode to the childhoods ruined.

And just like vices in these parts, the name of the gentleman-devil started spreading around.

Another crime—a murder of a man who'd run the underworld slave auction, a dozen children saved from a dungeon, though the true criminals were the lords of the West End who could buy a favor, the darkest vice, or an innocent life.

Those were the best advocates—the children. In the darkest moments of their lives, they told stories of a tall, strong man, almost a giant, in a black leather coat and top hat, a red tassel hanging on its side. He had shoulder-length hair made out of black wire, with one white strand, like a swan feather. He wore tinted spectacles but not to disguise his eyes—for all they knew, he had no eyes—but to see into the souls and find the monsters.

The Devil!

At their side!

The children reeled with glee and trepidation.

In the West End, children were told fairy tales and magical stories. In the East End, they told the story of Harlan Krow, who came to the rescue of those who lived in hell.

A year ago, when Alina heard all those stories and shook her head with a smile, she could have never imagined that one day, the myth would come true.

In the worst possible way.

# 7

# THE FLOWER GIRL

They say the first kill is the hardest, Father.

Well, not when you are at war. Not when you are a soldier, only eighteen, the enemies' guns in your face, and the captain roars, "Fire!"

The lives are cheap at war. Enough of them taken and you might get a medal. They'll pat you on the shoulder, serve you ale, and say, "Next time you might get the Knights Companion."

You see, Father, you haven't been to war. At war, killing is an honor.

Was the countess afraid of this killer?

I wasn't sure, but I was curious. I couldn't let her go just yet. You believe in divine providence, Father, don't you?

Angels like her should never be around the ones like me. I doubted we would talk again. But I'd done research. I'd learned things about her. I knew what she did in St Rose's.

A lady of the ton helping the sick in St. Giles. Well-well!

It's not charity that draws people from the top to serve those at the very bottom.

It's trauma, Father.

Pain.

A dark past.

In some way, she reminded me of the flower girl who had started it all. Not the abuse, but something in the eyes that makes one push through grief and go on living.

Dark auburn hair. Thin features. Pale skin, almost translucent, making her look even more fragile. But the determination with which she marched through life and those dark streets in Central London!

I wanted her to know my story.

Do you know what is harder than killing a dozen? Killing one, standing face to face with him on a dark empty London street, knowing that the man is a monster feeding on the poor. The poor are used to hunger and abuse. They die of the silliest whims of fate.

And abuse…

That's how the story of Harlan Krow begins.

He wasn't a hero then but a broken man, having come back from years at war—the service, they call it—certainly not to humanity but to the grand plans of an empire that doesn't care for people but only its grandness.

It all started with a flower girl one day in July. I still don't know what made me talk to her. She was a tiny scruffy thing, barely out of her adolescence, in a blue print frock and an old black chip bonnet. Her eyes were wide with permanent trepidation. Yet she had the face of a saint.

She cried in the back alley that day I passed by, her basket of wallflowers and carnations still half-full, though the day was coming to an end.

I glanced at her with curiosity, then stopped and watched her from afar. Sorrows and tragedies draw more attention than displays of happiness.

I didn't approach her that day but walked that same alley the next day, looking for her.

And there she was, almost a child, her voice meek as she tried to sell her carnations. She wasn't cut out for the job. Perhaps, she would do better as a seamstress, sewing away her sorrows in the dull light of a candle in some dingy shop, quiet and alone.

Something drew me to her. Only later would I realize what it was—her eyes that reflected what I'd seen in so many men I'd served with at war. It was submission to the monsters that haunted their dreams.

She had beautiful eyes, but there was no life in them. Her basket was half-full. Her voice was barely audible. She looked into the indifferent faces of the passersby with desperation. Her tears were silent as she hung her head low and walked to an empty back alley and sat on a crate, her eyes closed, rocking slightly as if to some tune in her head.

I approached her then.

Harlan Krow was born the day the flower girl told me her story. The wildest stories come from strangers, Father. Hers was a story about a monster who stole innocent childhoods. A monster who should not be alive, not matter how your Bible reasons with it.

I hate summers. The blinding sun reminds me of the day I died. The day the flower girl told me her story, another monster came to light. They always do so on the most cheerful days.

"What is your name, sir?" she asked when she finished.

I sat dumbfounded.

You know what is more horrible than war, Father? Childhoods stolen by vile men. Filthy hands finding innocence at night and taking what is meant to be untouched for years yet to come.

"Harlan Krow," I said then without thinking.

The name was a lie. The given name was an alias I used during the service. The family name belonged to a boy, barely a man, who was my best friend. A joker, loud and at times annoying—we simply called him Krow. His military uniform was too big for him. And his heart was too big for the horror that was called war. He used to stare at the face of war with a naive smile, sang songs by bonfires, took care of the wounded. Exhausted after the attacks, he often wandered through the battlefields, closed the eyes of the deceased, and whispered prayers to our soldiers as well as the enemies. He made those who had no will to carry on laugh. And he was one of the hundred men from my battalion who were slaughtered that fateful day in the Hindu Kush mountains.

"Harlan Krow," I repeated, in that spur of the moment reconciling the boy who had died and the deadman who had come back. "And the name of the man you told me about?"

The girl said it then, almost in a whisper, as if afraid the monster would appear in front of her, then waved me away. "I am being silly, sir. We all live with tragedies. Never mind me, Mr. Krow." She smiled the saddest smile.

But I remembered that name.

That afternoon, I wrote down an address and told her to see a person for a different sort of job. I bought all her flowers but didn't take them.

And I decided to find the man she'd mentioned.

It took two weeks to learn the monster by heart—where he went, where he lived, who he was. A benefactor of Holy Trinity Parish and the orphanage she'd come from. It would be two weeks until the city got to know Harlan Krow.

The hardest kill is not the first one, Father. It is of the man who committed atrocious crimes but stood, one dark night, in front of me, shaking, saying, "My good sir, I have done nothing wrong. I have a wife and children at home."

The worst crimes happen on the most peaceful nights. When children are tucked away. When bedtime stories are read. When the night prayers are recited. Isn't it the best time for judgment too, Father?

That was the night that ended that monster, the first of many, his useless corpse the next day sending a message to the likes of him. Who would have known that the revenge would make it to the Gazette and the name would soon become a legend?

Killers shouldn't be worshiped. A crime is a crime.

Forgive me, Father, but he deserved it. And the children in that orphanage will not hear the bedtime stories anymore, for the monster was the one who used to read them.

## 8

## THE PROMISE

I f it were quieter, the silence would have made the meeting more tense. But the wind was tossing the garbage and the leaves around and banging the shutters on their hinges.

Alina shivered, staring into the darkness in front of her that suddenly had a shape, tall and broad.

He seemed like a passerby—a mere faceless stranger like any other.

Yet he wasn't.

Not in pitch darkness.

A gust of wind, suddenly too violent, threw a strand of hair into her face and whipped the shawl around her shoulders.

But Alina didn't move. Her heart pounded. She swallowed hard.

What did he want?

A thank you?

An acknowledgment?

"I know who you are," Alina said softly, shivering.

"But you know nothing of me, my lady." His voice was deep, just like she remembered, but not hostile. How was that possible?

"May we talk?" he asked.

*About that night...*

"Will you come inside?" She tried to trick him and felt goosebumps on her skin—this was an ignorant question.

"I can't."

*Of course.*

She almost laughed at herself and this silly invitation—a nervous laughter that she tried to suppress.

She looked around, but it was too dark, no moon, only tall trees surrounding St Rose's. The trees that usually protected the hospital now created a dark alcove. Inside it—she and the most talked about criminal in London.

Alina nodded, feeling like she was in some strange dark fairy tale. She walked toward the bench in the center of the small garden and took a seat, her body on edge from nervousness.

She felt rather than saw him take a seat next to her, his big dark form almost a head taller.

She owed him a conversation, she supposed.

There was no light coming from anywhere. And in that moment, Alina wasn't sure she wanted to see his face. As if by seeing it, she'd put herself in even greater danger.

"The night we met wasn't quite pleasant," he said.

*Pleasant...*

That was a strange choice of words. She swallowed, wondering if he would blackmail her.

His voice was low and somehow raspy, as if something choked him. But it was calming and quite young. It surprised her. She couldn't tell how old he was, but by the sound of him, in his thirties.

*Or twenties.*

*Forties?*

God, she was already guessing and wondering.

*Wondering* was a dangerous word.

All this—him—had been a myth until now.

Yet, she sat right next to his dark form in more awe and disbelief than actual fright.

"You understand, what I did that night had to be done," he said.

*Had to be done.*

He'd ended a life.

For her?

For fun?

That was what he did, wasn't it?

She saved lives. He ended them. A shiver ran through her.

"He could've hurt you," he said. "Men like him do unspeakable crimes every day and night."

She kept quiet.

"No one stops them," he continued. "No one dares. They get away with too much."

He was right. Yet the images of blood flickered in her head again.

"You can judge me, of course. But please don't put me in the same line with those who break the law out of fun or habit. You don't know what death is."

She smirked into the darkness. "You don't know me. Mister...?" She turned to look at him, though he was one massive chunk of darkness.

"Krow," he said.

Her heart skipped a beat.

*Of course.*

Coming from his mouth it sounded even more surreal. But she lived in a different world. How many in Old Nichol and the neighboring slums claimed to have seen him and know him and be saved by him? Yet, in the West End, he was still a tale told to scare the children or entertain the ton.

But the tale had a form and shape. It had a soothing husky voice. There was a man behind it, and she wondered what sort of man wandered the streets of the slums to serve justice. A burning curiosity to know him seized her at once.

"You don't know me, Mr. Krow," she said quietly, trying to keep her voice from faltering. "And I don't know *you*. But that night, you might have saved my life. Or dignity. I am not sure which is more important. I suppose I should thank you."

Was she truly thanking him?

"Don't thank me. I am doing the job the authorities should be doing—keeping the residents safe."

"Is that what you do, Mr. Krow? Truly?"

A dare.

He was a mystery. Some said he was a noble. Others said he was from the poorest parts of Old Nichol. Some said he was ageless. Others claimed he was a young boy but built like a Spartan. One woman said he had fathered her child. An actress from a small theatre in Shoreditch claimed he visited her by night.

There was no end to the rumors that surrounded the gentleman-devil.

And he sat right next to Alina.

She could ask him a hundred questions. And he would probably answer none. He was accused of numerous crimes he hadn't committed. And those he had, were made known, the rumors spreading like brush fires across London.

One of the Shoreditch theaters had a play named *Gentleman-devil*. Villains were more in fashion than heroes. And when a German councilman came to visit the Queen a year ago, he was rumored to have asked her at dinner, "What is the story of the dark angel in your poor districts who saves children and puts your law enforcement to shame?"

*He is here. He is here. He is here.*

Alina was amused by this fact.

"I could tell you what I do," the man said, finally breaking the windy silence. "But I am afraid my stories are much too dark for a woman such as yourself."

She wasn't sure why he talked to her. How many people had spoken to him? She wasn't in Old Nichol where he dwelled. What strange fate had brought them together!

"You don't know me, Mr. Krow. We all have dark stories." She wasn't sure what had made her say that. But she was curious. In the city of many and not a single person who even mildly entertained her, she sat next to the most talked about elusive criminal and felt like she had stepped out of a golden cage.

That was it.

Curiosity.

It had always been her friend. Her own motherland had shunned her for it. It had brought her to Dr. Grevatt and St Rose's. But it had also given her Rumi and the joy and satisfaction of helping others and the chance to give the world new ideas that were published in the most distinguished magazine, albeit under someone else's name.

And here it was again as she held her breath and dared another question.

"Why do you do it?"

It was such an abstract question that he could have brushed it off.

Instead, he said, "I met a girl once. She sold flowers."

Picked up by a cold gust of wind, his voice seemed like it came from nowhere. The door behind them slammed loudly. Alina shook at the sound. He didn't move.

Rumi's voice came from outside the gate, by the carriage.

"I should go," Alina said with surprising disappointment. For some strange reason, she wanted him to keep talking. "I would like to hear more of your stories," she said, cursing herself right away for it. "You are a mystery, Mr. Krow. How does one become so... dark?"

"It is a long story, I am afraid."

She shivered nervously. She'd just sat with a man in a dark garden. She'd talked to the man who the police had been looking for for years.

"Would you like to talk again some time?" the shadow asked.

And her heart thudded so violently in her chest that she thought she went deaf and misheard him.

Such moments in life were rare and often slipped unnoticed—the moments when life took a sharp turn, not so obvious but leading in a strange direction.

For the first time, Alina felt scared, if only for a moment—of what was to come, of what another meeting could lead to.

But she shut out the fear that lurked in the back of her mind and dared say, "That would be enlightening." *Dangerous.* "Though I don't come here often." *Liar.*

The man stayed silent for a moment, then rose slowly, a giant shadow looming over her, just like the night a week ago.

And yet that danger drew her in.

"You should not be on the streets by yourself," he warned her as they slowly walked toward the hospital gate.

Her boot heels clicked against the ground. His footsteps were almost silent.

"I know," she whispered.

"Please, be careful."

*Said the man who is feared by half of the city.*

"Thank you," she replied as the wind wafted in her face, almost knocking off her hat.

She reached the gate, Rumi's faint lamp illuminating the

silhouette of the carriage, the footman, and the coachman behind it.

She turned to say farewell.

But he was gone.

Poof!

In a split second, swallowed up by the darkness.

She frantically searched around in the darkness as she pulled the gate open. For a moment, she wondered if she was losing her mind—the man, indeed, was like a devil, born out of darkness and vanishing into it.

Rumi lifted the lamp, shining the way.

"Who was that?" she asked as they got into the carriage.

"Who?" Alina asked, trying to breathe deeper to calm her heart and straightening her skirt and coat intentionally too loudly. "Oh, that. No one, really." She waved it off and hoped Rumi didn't ask more questions.

And she was hoping to see the gentleman-devil again.

# 9

## THE INVITATION

Alina couldn't wait until the next week. She counted days that were spent in the usual monotony—Dr. Grevatt's, writing, her mother's melancholy, boring shopping, and an even more boring stroll at Hyde Park.

But her mind was galloping toward Friday and the weekly visit to St Rose's.

Would *he* be there again?

Did he know when she would show up at St Rose's? Did he watch her?

A hundred questions reeled in her mind as the weekdays trudged by.

On Friday, Alina woke up with a feeling of anticipation. All throughout the day, she felt like a conspirator, like she had something of her own, a secret that belonged to no one else. With it came confidence. And when she was at Grevatt's that afternoon, striding back and forth in the study, narrating the essay to Rumi, she would halt and smile occasionally, making Rumi suspicious.

When they finished, Rumi narrowed her eyes at Alina. "You seem happy today," she said.

Alina shrugged. "Things are coming together nicely, I suppose. The essay is almost done."

And when they rode to St Rose's, her heart started pounding in that familiar excitement mixed with nervousness.

*This is so very wrong,* she kept telling herself.

*He might not show up*—the thought tugged at her heart with slight disappointment.

And when the carriage pulled up to the gates of St Rose's, Alina held her breath and fumbled, then sent Rumi ahead with the lamp.

"I shall be in soon."

Rumi's footsteps disappeared around the corner. The sound of the back door closing sank the night garden into silence. Alina closed her eyes and stilled.

She was shameless and careless, standing in a pitch-black garden and waiting for a man, and not just any man.

"Miss Alina."

Shivers ran down her spine as her eyes snapped open.

He knew her name, yet didn't know her title. Or did he?

She turned around slowly.

And there he was. A tall dark shape in a black leather coat and top hat.

Did it have a red tassel like the legend said?

Several footsteps toward her—soft, soundless, like those of a predator in the prairie. Flickers of light reflecting where his eyes were—the spectacles.

She lowered her gaze despite not seeing his face—as if hiding.

What could she say?

They stood in awkward silence for some time before he took another step.

"I have to go," he finally said.

*Already?*

Her heart thudded in disappointment. A week of waiting and one minute of silence.

*It's for the better. For the better.*

Her heart was beating so fast, it was hard to breathe.

This was a mistake. He was a killer. A dangerous man. What if he jeopardized her reputation? What if someone caught them together? Rumi? Yegór?

"I wish we could talk," he said softly, "but I truly do have to go. I only wanted to see you one more time."

His presence was intimidating, yet his voice was magnetic. Husky. Smoky. Rich. Pulling her in like a drug. Like smoke, seeping into her.

No, she didn't want to part yet. She wanted to know more! How a man became what he was. What drew him to the lowest quarters.

*Please, stay a moment.*

"Write," she whispered, afraid of her own invitation yet stifling a chuckle at this absurdity. There was no taking her words back.

"Pardon me?" The surprise in his voice was unmistakable.

Her heart galloped at her bravery.

"Write," she repeated. "You can write, can't you?"

She held her breath, waiting. The idea that he—Harlan Krow, the man from the headlines—would write to her sounded insane.

"Write?" he echoed and laughed through his nose.

He could be illiterate, though his speech was most proper.

"You can write a letter," she insisted, her heart suddenly pounding everywhere. In her head, ears, stomach. Her legs. "And I promise I shall read it. One doesn't get a chance to hear the thoughts of a man who…"

She stopped herself.

*Madness!*

Yet this felt like a slap in the face of the ton. Lady Amstel. Sir John. Van Buren. Her mother, who despised Alina's work as it was.

For once in this boring English life, Alina felt like she was breaking the rules and breaking the chains that seemed to hold women captive in the society ruled by men.

Yes, this was a rebellion, dangerous but oh-so-sweet! That was why débutantes snuck away from balls unchaperoned to kiss the men they fancied. Why married ladies had affairs. Why Lady Whitshorn ran a secret literary circle of women.

This was why Alina, despite the nervousness shaking her knees and making her hands damp, had just invited the man for another talk. The man who most of the city feared.

*Yes!*

This was rebellion. That was why she worked with Dr. Grevatt. Why she came to this smelly hospital once a week. Why she had bonded with a former slave girl who wrote poetry. She wanted to feel like she lived in a world and not a gilded cage where she was fed and groomed so she could sing beautifully for the likes of her.

Alina's heart thudded like the first chords of a ball orchestra.

She pointed toward the yawning over the back door.

"There is an empty bird nest there," she explained. "You could leave a letter there. The rain wouldn't get there. Neither would curious hands. I wouldn't want anyone to know that —" She tried to come up with the right words.

"That you associate with the likes of me." He chuckled, and it was friendly, surprising her with its warmth.

*Associate.*

A gust of wind tossed an empty crate somewhere outside the gates.

"That was not what I meant," she said apologetically.

But it was. A smile forced itself to her lips despite the nervousness.

Another moment of silence passed between them.

"I shall wait until you get back inside," he said softly.

That was it. He was leaving. Alina nodded in reluctant submission.

"And please, be careful," he added as she started walking away.

The gentleman-devil told her to be careful—the absurdity almost made her laugh. The man who walked the worst parts of London by night was watching out for her.

And as she approached the back door, she glanced up at the empty bird nest, hoping that the next time she did so there was a letter in it.

## 10

## THE WHEEL OF FORTUNE

That was perhaps what drew me to the countess at first. A well-bred woman in these parts of the city is suspicious. A woman in the hospital is a sign of compassion. A noblewoman—well, that is peculiar, to say the least. Like me, the countess worked in the shadows.

Glamor beguiles many, Father. It hides misfortunes and unhappiness, broken souls and dying faith. That is why fabric is colored and gems are turned into jewelry. That is why, in its essence, we bother with looks at all—not as much to show off our wealth but trick others. Those who are truly intent on knowing others see beyond that. The nobles who despise the ton. The wealthy who don't bother with rules and etiquette. The true visionaries who hide in dark parlors and secret gatherings to freely discuss the ideas that might bring them to a guillotine.

That was what I wrote in my first letter to the countess. And the flower girl story. Perhaps, it was meant to scare her off. To me, it was a way to get the facts out.

Now there were three people who got to know Harlan Krow. The flower girl, the countess, and you, Father. It is a trinity, you might say, though not so holy. But where there are two or more, there is God, isn't that right? So please, listen to this story, for your deity had some plans for us.

Don't think for a moment that that encounter with the countess wasn't that of a man enchanted by a woman. The moment I saw her face the night we met, it struck me with awe —the face of an angel. Her small but regal figure. The elegant turn of her head. She was mesmerizing, no doubt. But behind that beauty was something else that I sensed right away. We predators are good at it.

There was a mystery about her, another side that I wanted to get to know.

I had to get closer.

They say I lived by night, but the day presented other opportunities—to get to find out all I could about her.

That is what the devil does. He lures the kind souls with the promise to save others. Did I want to lure her? I don't know. But she was so pure that I wasn't about to let her go yet.

Curiosity, Father, is a dangerous thing.

The Wheel of Fortune was already turning as I wrote the first letter.

Who would have known it would take me that far and take her with me?

## 11

## THE LETTER

"Oh, this dreadful weather," Anna Yakovlevna complained as she and Alina strolled through Hyde Park. "It shall be the end of me."

Alina didn't respond. It was indeed too cold for the middle of September, and her mother had already pulled out a dark brown shawl with sable trimmings. She dressed for any outing like she was going to a ball. She preferred dresses with low necklines and exposed shoulders. The current fashion wasn't much up to her taste. The high necklines in day dresses left no room for the elaborate necklaces and pendants Anna Yakovlevna liked so much. So she put on the purple alexandrite earrings and a giant matching brooch to clasp the shawl in place. The fur trimmings of the shawl matched the sable muff around her hands.

"It is not that cold yet," Anna had insisted. But there was no stopping Anna Yakovlevna who was fond of the display of wealth.

Her mother greeted the occasional acquaintances with an elegant wave of her hand that she pulled out of the muff to—

yes, for that very purpose—display the elaborate gold rings with impressive gems that decorated her fingers.

She was dazzling. Good thing it was the West End and the middle of the day, or they would be robbed. The current selection of jewelry on Anna Yakovlevna could feed a small village for a week.

Lady Anne nodded in their direction and exchanged greetings. And before she walked away too far, Alina heard the usual: "Her husband expired conveniently only two years into their marriage."

Anna Yakovlevna pretended she didn't hear. Her hearing was selective.

That was better than Mrs. Rugenford's famous remark, *"Rumor has it, they walk around the house barefoot, drink like sailors, and worship the devil."*

Alina only exhaled in annoyance.

Her late husband, Count Andrei Bronskiy, had died in an accident—that was public knowledge. Only the Kamenevs and Alina knew that it had been an assassination. For having thoughts about reforms that couldn't possibly exist in an empire built on absolute power and suppression of the poor. Russia was a great nation built on the idea that national spirit and military superiority made up for the lack of freedom. Andrei's death had preserved Alina's status. What a price to pay for a title! The title splashed with blood and humiliation...

There always seemed to be some sort of danger in Alina's life. Even now, walking with her mother and listening to her occasional remarks and complaints, Alina couldn't help but think of Harlan Krow.

She'd asked him for a letter. Would he write to her?

It had been three days since their meeting, and Alina was anxious.

"Mamá, you shall catch a cold in this weather," Alina finally said with feigned concern. "Perhaps it is better we return home."

When they got to the carriage, Yegór was arguing with the coachman and smoking tobacco rolled into newspaper as he spat now and then—another habit that irritated Anna Yakovlevna.

"*Ploot*," blurted Yegór angrily, calling the coachman a rascal.

"What was that?" The man glared at him.

"I said, good day," Yegór snapped and spat on the ground then saw Alina and her mother approaching and straightened up. "My lady."

Alina smiled and shook her head. Yegór seemed at war with anyone English, smiling and saying Russian curses right in their faces. Why her mother insisted on taking Yegór with them everywhere was obvious and quite annoying—Yegór's giant figure turned everyone's heads, just the way Anna Yakovlevna liked it.

"I need to go to Grevatt's," Alina told her mother as they reached Birchin Street.

"I knew it!" her mother exclaimed theatrically as she stepped out of the carriage. "You are leaving me all alone again. My husband is at never-ending business meetings. And my daughter prefers vagrants to her own mother."

Anna Yakovlevna produced a forced sob and stomped off toward the house as Alina rolled her eyes.

"Yegór! To St Rose's!"

"It is not the day, is it, my lady?" Yegór glanced at her in surprise.

Alina cocked her head in reproach, and he softly closed the carriage door. She ought to teach her servants some manners.

Thank the Lord no one knew how her footman talked about the people of the ton. But the thought was forgotten as the carriage rolled toward Central London.

Alina's heart thumped in her chest as half an hour later they approached the hospital. She hardly ever made it to St Rose's in the daylight. And when the carriage pulled up to the gates—open and with a line of people outside despite the cold —Alina felt too aware of her lavish dress and jewelry.

She pushed past the people and the glares as she walked inside.

William gave her a surprised look, and Dr. Grevatt in his office studied her over his glasses.

"Miss Alina! Is something the matter?" He motioned to the nurse who escorted a limping man out.

"No. I was nearby and stopped to say hello," said Alina, hating herself for the lies.

Rumi ran into the room, her skirt stained and hair out of place, and halted, seeing Alina.

"Miss Alina? Is something the matter?" Her gaze was suddenly too worried.

Alina chuckled nervously and shook her head.

"No. No. I was only passing by and decided to stop."

"Huh."

Rumi grabbed papers from the desk and hurried out of the office.

Alina bid farewell and, clenching her teeth in slight embarrassment, walked out into the hallway. But instead of going to the front door, she hurriedly walked to the back entrance.

Outside, the garden seemed deserted. Skeletal trees with the last leaves poked the gray sky and the clouds that hung too low.

Her heart pounding, Alina thievishly looked around, stood

on her tiptoes, and stretched her hand toward the abandoned bird nest above the door.

It took a moment before her fingers felt the paper, and her heart gave out a thud so loud that she thought the ground shook beneath her.

She pulled the letter out of the nest and looked at it in shock.

*AB*, her initials, stared at her from the cheap folded paper. She looked around again, then tucked the letter into her bodice and hurriedly started walking around the building toward the gates, a smile never leaving her face.

*You asked me how one becomes so dark. There is always a story behind acts of vengeance. Mine started a long time ago. Not one but many. It will take dozens of letters to tell them all. But the one that is most important is the story of the flower girl.*

The paper was cheap but the writing was immaculate and without a single ink blotch.

Alina read the letter in minutes, then re-read it again.

The story of the flower girl was so heart-breaking that when she finished rereading it for the third time, she sat in silence for some time, feeling an icy-cold grip in her stomach despite the burning fireplace. She remembered the newspaper article—the story of a benefactor of an orphanage and the way his body was found one morning in the most gruesome way— the place where the *Weeping Mother* was later erected.

One flower girl.

The birth of a villain.

A chain of events that unraveled in the city of London.

A knock at the door made Alina jump up and shove the letter into a drawer.

"My lady, a letter for you." Martha came with the news.

Another one! From Olga!

Alina smiled, shooed Martha away, and put her friend's letter onto the desk.

Harlan Krow's letter was back in her hands. She brought it to her nose and inhaled.

Smoke. Burnt coal. Dust. Leather. Something else in the smell seeped into Alina's nostrils. She cocked her head and studied the papers on both sides as if they held a secret. She caressed the handwriting, studying every letter, every curve.

Educated. Yes, the villain wasn't a pauper like some rumors stated. And though the paper was inexpensive, the immaculate writing was a sign of good upbringing.

*How odd.*

She wrote back right away. It was a simple reaction to his story, half a page long. And when she read it, she crumbled it in her hands and tossed it into the fireplace.

She wrote another one. Then another. Until she was thoroughly satisfied with her wording.

She asked why. She reasoned about justice. She had a hundred questions that couldn't possibly be answered in one letter.

*Would you like to talk again?* she wrote at the end.

There she was again, asking for a meeting.

Oh, that was a slippery slope, she knew. But she was tired of the perfect, seamless boring English life.

"Send Yegór here," she told Martha and paced around the room.

Yegór stepped into the room, hunching as always, as if he was afraid his head would hit the top of the door frame. His body definitely filled it completely.

"I need you to do something for me." Alina stared up at him, craning her neck. "But you have to promise you shall not tell anyone. Ever. Not Martha. Not my parents. Not a word."

His gaze hardened, but he only nodded.

She gave him the letter and explained where to deposit it.

He stared at it for some time, then looked at her from under his heavy eyebrows, shifting from one foot to another.

"Don't." She shook her head in warning. "Don't ask. Don't tell. Make sure no one sees you. If anyone does, you tell them I lost something at the hospital earlier."

"What?" he asked in hesitation.

"I don't know what, Yegór! Make something up. You can always answer in Russian and do that intimidating glare of yours."

She produced an amused laughter, though Yegór stared at her not a tiny bit amused.

"Do it now." She waved him away. "You can take the carriage. And let me know as soon as you get back."

He nodded, leaving in silence that was heavier than his seven-foot mountain of a body.

Alina paced around the room for some time, rethinking what she'd written. She ordered tea, came down to the sitting room, and listened for some time to Anna Yakovlevna plucking some melancholic tune on the piano, occasionally pausing to talk about the latest rumors and Lady Amstel's recent function.

The clock ticked the minutes away painfully slow, and when, two hours later, the front door closed with a muffled sound, Alina darted out of the sitting room to see Yegór come in, wipe his feet on the door mat, and drag his hat off his head.

"All done," he said quietly.

Alina felt like a conspirator, the familiar excitement starting in the pit of her stomach.

Before going to bed, she reread Harlan Krow's letter again and again.

Only when she was already in bed, staring into the dark ceiling, amused at what was happening, did she realize that she had forgotten to read Olga's letter—the one she'd waited on for months.

# 12

## RUMI

The next morning, Anna Yakovlevna beat away a happy tune on the piano as Alina danced around with Olga's letter in her hand, raised high above her head.

"Olga is coming the first week of November!" she kept singing to the faltering tune.

Nikolai Sergeevich sat on the sofa reading and smiled, watching his daughter's silly dance. She finally waltzed up, flung herself next to him, and exhaled loudly. She loved seeing her father in a woolen cardigan and house slippers—at home, without his usual seriousness.

Such moments of happiness had been rare since the tragedy back in Russia and their arrival in England. But life was starting to become more normal, and Alina was thankful.

"The lunch is served," Dunya announced in English with her perky accent.

Alina studied her with interest, wondering where the maid had gotten the purple dress that seemed too lavish for a maid and was in stark contrast with the servant's apron and cap.

They moved to the dining room where a *samovar* was set up in the center of the table, the white tablecloth and the porcelain tea set sparkly in the light of the candles. It was much too gloomy outside, and the candles were lit by early afternoon, the fire in the hearth blazing at all times.

Anna Yakovlevna took tiny sips of *erofeitch*, an old recipe of vodka infused with mint, anise, and other herbs. She was becoming a connoisseur of spirits.

Dunya served hot pickle soup with barley and freshly baked dark rye bread.

"Perhaps we can hire another cook to help Prosha learn English cuisine," said Alina.

Anna Yakovlevna gave her a reproaching look. "Next thing you know, you will be imposing fines in this household for speaking Russian."

Nikolai Sergeevich smiled without raising his eyes from his plate.

Alina couldn't quite figure out what was changing lately, but the house felt suffocating. She wanted to be at Grevatt's, writing, talking to Rumi, helping at St Rose's more often.

Such thoughts were sprinkled with the images of Harlan Krow.

"I am going to Grevatt's," she announced abruptly, rising from the table without finishing her food.

"But tea! Alina!" her mother exclaimed in despair.

"I have to go."

"You are pushing away from this family. Soon, you will be embarrassed to show up with us in public."

"Mamá! What nonsense!" Alina shook her head, suddenly annoyed with her capriciousness and wanting to be anywhere but home. "I shall be back later than usual today."

She kissed her father on the cheek and walked out, leaving behind her mother's complaints and the thoughts of Olga's visit.

She'd never talked to Rumi about Harlan Krow. The story had been discussed so many times in the newspapers and certain circles that everyone in the city seemed to know about the gentleman-devil. He was a legend and had become a part of the city's history.

Only half a year ago, Dr. Grevatt was reading an article about yet another crime. He'd made a comment, but neither Alina nor Rumi had been interested in that sort of news.

Now Alina wanted to talk about him. And when she got to Dr. Grevatt's, she met Rumi with more than usual cheerfulness.

She watched Rumi quietly set up the desk for yet another session of writing, watched her hands smooth the white paper. When Rumi sat down behind the desk and, picking up the last page of the essay, looked up at Alina expectantly, Alina studied her beautiful face with high chiseled cheekbones and full lips and sharp brows for a moment. Rumi looked like a lady, her bright dresses always in beautiful contrast with her ebony skin.

Where would she be now if it weren't for Dr. Grevatt?

Rumi had come from the darkness, too. If it weren't for the lords with dark intentions and a simple act of kindness that followed, she could've ended up dead, or worse. Alina had found out there were worse fates.

Wasn't that what Harlan Krow did? Besides taking revenge, he gave poor souls a chance for a better life.

Rumi gazed at Alina in silence. Their eyes locked. Not a word was spoken.

In moments like this, it seemed like Rumi could read her thoughts.

In moments like this, the story Rumi had told her months ago broke Alina's heart and then filled it up with hope again.

"I was six when my parents were killed in a rebellion in Niger," Rumi had told Alina one day. "I was sold to pirates, brought to the shore of Portugal, then transferred onto an English ship, and ended up in London.

"If you think that slavery was abolished—well, it won't be for the longest time, not until the dark underworld of cities like London cease to exist and the wealthy stop paying for their horrific indulgences. I should praise the gods for one wealthy lord who'd played a joke on his friend at my expense and Dr. Grevatt who saved me then. Though I believe it was a young Sikh man who had saved me all along.

"For some time, after we were brought to London, we stayed in a cage. Ten by ten, with a dozen people in it, all ages and ethnicity, cramped in some cellar, in the slimiest part of London, I am sure. A week or so—the darkest in my life.

"There was a young man with us. He barely had a beard. A turban. Blood-shot eyes. Ragged clothes that smelled of spices despite the strong stench around us. Kind eyes and soft smiles despite days of not being fed, exhausted and hopeless, awaiting our fate.

"I still remembered some native words that no one spoke but me and learned some English ones. So I would combine them into syllables that sounded soothing.

"You see, at a young age, I already had a love for poetry. I used the sounds to convey emotions.

"Iron bars like strands of hair of a giant.

"The floor the color of muddy water.

"The boy smiled at my words. He didn't understand a

thing but shook his head from side-to side. He did it often to anything anyone said.

"One day or night—it was impossible to tell—I lay on the stone floor, my arms wrapped around my knees, cold, tired, hungry, wearing only a knee-high tunic. I sang quietly to myself. I put the words together and hummed some tune that was a vague memory of my homeland.

"Someone touched me, and I opened my eyes.

"His smile again. A burgundy cloth covering my body. His hair, dark, messy, clumped, hanging loose down to his shoulders—he'd undone his turban to use it as a blanket for me.

"'*Kali roomi*,' he said, his head bobbing side-to-side like the upside-down clock handle.

"He coughed then, a strong fit that sprayed blood onto his forearm. Another smile, soft and apologetic. '*Gaao, gaao*,' he whispered, his head moving side-to side encouragingly, though his eyes were drooping.

"I knew what the Sikh boy wanted and resumed the singing, weaving the words I knew into the tune.

"He kept repeating those words, and that became my name, Rumi. Later, when a rich lord who bought me asked my name, he smiled. 'Rumi. Like the Persian poet.'

"My name was the biggest blessing, but I was too little to understand it then.

"*Black Rumi* was what that Sikh boy called me.

"The young man who gave me his cloth when I was cold.

"Who wiggled his head in a funny way.

"Who talked in his strange language and made me smile and feel less alone.

"The man who gave me his ration of bread—the only food we'd gotten in days—and by the next morning was dead."

Everyone had a history. Not everyone's was a story of slavery or a bullet in the head. Some were stories of an unwanted touch, a broken promise, a betrayal, a bruise, one too many.

Rumi understood such things better than anyone. Perhaps, that was what had drawn Alina to her in the first place—the past marred with a tragedy.

Rumi's was also a story of miraculous saving. Bought by rich lords at a secret auction as a joke, she was spotted by Dr. Grevatt and "acquired." Rumi called it "saving." The doctor never talked about that day. He insisted that she'd changed his life profoundly. Childless, he'd found joy in raising her and making her part of everything he did. Were it not for the color of her skin, she could pass as his daughter.

Rumi had been with the doctor for almost two decades. He'd noticed her affinity for words and had given her an education, taught her to read and write, hired tutors in French and Latin. Rumi read. And wrote. And helped at the hospital and with paperwork.

Oh, she was a marvelous woman! Alina found immense joy in their conversations that could last for hours when they'd first met. Rumi loved Rumi—the actual poet, a man at that. And she loved Catullus, who so tenderly spoke of love yet swore in Latin like the filthiest sailor. Omar Hayam had stolen her heart, of course. She'd learned from the best and was genius with words, weaving them like threads into beautiful fabrics that could bring to ecstasy the silkiest skin.

Alina had read many—Rumi had stacks and stacks of them.

"One day I shall publish them," Rumi said.

And Alina was determined to help. Poetry wasn't science. After all, anything that had beauty was allowed to have a voice. Alina's essays would have to stay under Grevatt's name for now. But Rumi's poetry had a future, she was sure.

"I don't feel like writing today," said Alina that afternoon, watching Rumi arrange the essay pages on the desk.

Rumi halted and gave her a curious glance. "That is fine. What would you like to do?"

Alina felt strange, indeed. She attributed it to the excitement about Olga's letter, but in truth, it was the upcoming trip to St Rose's and a chance to see Harlan Krow.

She called the maid for tea, and as she and Rumi settled in the armchairs by the low glass table in the sitting room, Alina stared absently at the window, watching it darken, waiting and waiting for the darkness to fall.

"What do you think of Harlan Krow, Rumi?" she finally asked, not looking at the woman who most definitely studied her in surprise.

Rumi set the teacup down and laughed through her nose. "He is a legend, a mystery." Alina nodded. She knew what everyone said. "A savior, one might say."

The words made Alina turn to Rumi and cock her head. "You truly think he is a savior?"

Rumi cocked her head to mimic Alina. Her raven-black hair, slicked back into intricate braids, reflected the light from the candles that the maid had lit. Her skin acquired a warm-brown tone, a shade lighter than usual. Kindness shone in her eyes that were focused on Alina and twinkled playfully.

"I think he makes an effort, yes," Rumi answered. "In his own way. More than anything, he brings the flaws of our justice system to light."

"To light," Alina echoed. "Is that what you call the display of his crimes?"

"The only person who brings the light is the one who comes from the darkness—it is peculiar, yes. But how else would you do it in those parts?"

Alina wasn't sure whether she was trying to talk herself

into redeeming the man or just wanted to hear his name again and again.

"You see, Miss Alina, I was one of the victims of this country's flaws. You know my story. Freedom is a misleading word. The day I was picked up by Dr. Grevatt was the day I was given what should have been mine in the first place. So the Bible says. So does the law. But the Bible-loving men sail across the oceans and enslave others, taking their freedoms away. I suppose, on those trips, their Bibles and law codexes stay locked in drawers."

Alina exhaled loudly, nodding.

"I was saved," Rumi continued. "But many are not so lucky. And still, many people have come back from worse, Miss Alina. When you've seen the worst of humanity, you spot evil everywhere. Every shade of it. Every shape. Every tiny speck. And you want to wipe it away in every way possible."

"But shouldn't justice be served in the proper way?" Alina looked at her in hopes of an answer.

"Look at the country we live in. This empire enslaved a quarter of the world and killed more innocent people than any other nation. What law or sense of justice could possibly allow them to do so?"

Alina didn't have the answer.

"They"—Rumi nodded upward—"live in their white, entitled world. They"—she nodded downward—"simply try to survive. And you are surprised that the one man who can do justice, even in his brutal way, is hailed a hero."

Rumi's smile was beautiful and kind, wrapping around Alina's heart that now beat calmly in acceptance.

They sat in silence for some time, the only sounds the ticking of the clock and the echoes of the maid's footsteps in the hallway.

"Will you read me some of your poems?" Alina asked Rumi finally.

"What would you like to hear?"

"Read something about darkness," said Alina, feeling her heart clutch with sudden sadness.

When they arrived at St Rose's, Alina sent Rumi ahead and stayed in the garden.

She shivered in the silent darkness, the unease and excitement twisting her stomach in the already familiar way. She had a feeling *he* watched her. The past two times she'd come to St Rose's, he'd been right there, waiting in the shadows.

Now, she walked to the stone bench and took a seat, clasping her nervous trembling hands.

This was unbecoming for a woman of her status. But so was nursing. So was publishing medical research under someone else's name. So was being married to a free-thinker. So was being called a traitor. Her life was a gradation of all things improper, it seemed.

The soft steps behind her made her heart race.

Closer.

Closer still.

She could be robbed or assaulted. The legend could be wrong. The man the slums hailed a hero and children told bedtime stories about could be only a criminal.

She didn't dare turn her head and stared straight ahead into the darkness. A sense of danger saturated the air around her. But the dark shape appeared in the corner of her eye and took a seat next to her. Like her own shadow.

Harlan Krow.

His presence was overpowering as they sat in silence, waiting. For what, she wasn't sure.

"I read your letter," she finally said quietly, her voice like an echo in the dark.

This sounded silly, but she didn't know what else to say. She felt they needed an introduction, being strangers and all. Yet, the ease with which they'd exchanged their first letters was astounding.

The first correspondence—she smiled at the thought. How many would there be?

And there was his story, coming back in all its details to her again.

A flower girl.

More importantly—the true reason behind the man whose name had become a legend.

The night suddenly seemed too cold, the chill running through Alina's veins, making her shiver under the shawl.

The silence was deafening.

"Those children," she murmured. "That is atrocious."

"But that is humankind," he answered.

Silence hung between them again.

"You judge me," he said, and there was a question in it.

"It is not that simple," she replied.

"It never is. Neither is humanity. Nor justice. Nor redemption."

"Isn't there a way to help instead of punish? A more... humane way to change things?

"Help..." He went quiet for some time. "I will tell you a story. You shall decide. Because it asks a very simple question. What if the hand that helps you is also the one that inflicts the most pain?"

## 13

## THE FINAL SHOT

What do you know about taking someone's life, Father? To what extent even the most virtuous soul will go to protect oneself, one's family?

They say forgiveness is a weapon. Leave it to God, they say. I've been to places that God abandoned. There are no churches in the wild, Father.

Afghanistan, 1840.

A small village just outside Jellalabad, ravaged by a military attack.

British soldiers who came to save it.

*We* came to save it—the glorious men of the British Empire, Her Majesty's Armed Forces.

It was a sunny afternoon, hot and dusty. Peaceful, too. The ruins always are.

I was walking around aimlessly, trying to come to terms with the place, the attack, the ashes we always left behind, despite calling it a victory.

I reached the last small hut on the outskirts of the village. Muffled screams wafted from the inside. I halted, slowly pushed the half-open door, and walked in.

A local woman was bent over the wooden table, her hijab askew, hair whipped over her face, which was contorted in pain. Her skirt was pushed up to her waist, a man pressing behind her, grunting threats and fumbling with the buttons of his breeches. His free hand pushed down on her back, keeping her in place. His scowl was that of an animal, rendering the face I knew—one of our own, the glorious soldiers of Her Majesty.

He didn't see me, but the woman did, her eyes wide in shock and desperation.

There was a meek cry—her baby lay in a heap of fabrics on the floor. Another meek cry came from her as the soldier kicked her legs apart and pushed into her.

I slowly pulled my loaded gun up. Its hollow click cut through the grunts and the buzzing of the flies.

The soldier turned and saw me, paused, then pushed away from the woman, his breeches around his hips.

"Mate," he said and smiled in surprise.

He was a friend, you see. Would you let your friend assault a woman, Father? What would *you* do, knowing that you could drag him away, but that dog would come back at night and finish what he'd started?

Anger rose in me.

Disgust boiled in my veins.

It rushed the pounding blood to my head.

The way I see it, there was no choice. I lowered the gun only inches and pulled the trigger, shooting the soldier in the leg. It was a small punishment for a beast. He screamed in pain and fell onto the ground, clutching his shattered leg. And—what do you know—whimpered the name of God!

They all call the name of God, Father. Your God is on good terms with everyone. He loves all his children, doesn't he?

As the soldier squirmed and whimpered, the woman

whipped around, pushing her skirt down again and again as if she couldn't cover enough of herself, then cried out in anger and kicked him as hard as she could and spat in his face. When she turned to look at me, I moved my eyes to his gun that stood propped against the table. Returning my eyes to her, I said, "It is yours if you want it."

She didn't speak the language but understood.

I walked out.

It was a fine day, simmering in summer heat and the buzzing insects.

The sun, Father, is the biggest illusion of happiness.

The soldiers were shooting for practice somewhere in the distance, drinking *doogh* and laughing. There was no way to tell who fired the guns where. But as I walked down the empty dusty street toward the garrison, one shot came from the last hut on the outskirts.

# 14

## STORIES

September grew into October.

The meetings and letters became regular, like clockwork.

Every week, Harlan Krow wrote to Alina. She read the letter and wrote back. And on Fridays, she came to St Rose's with her heart fluttering in her chest.

And he always waited in the dark like a secret lover.

His speech and manners weren't those of a commoner. His knowledge of literature and history was astounding. Yet, his clothes, from what she could gather in the dark, were fit for the slums. He smelled of burnt coal and fire pits and damp leather and rain.

And she never saw his face.

Only in the glimmer of the occasional reflections, she noticed a short beard. The tinted round spectacles he wore at times were orange, the flickers in them cutting like sharp steel through the darkness.

He was danger—in his form and the slick way he moved, in the swiftness with which he appeared and disappeared.

But his voice was low and smoky. A voice that you'd

imagine telling stories by bonfires. A voice that felt intimate at times.

In letters, they talked about people, sins, redemption, and salvation. He quoted famous scholars, and Alina wished Rumi could hear him. Oh, what pair they would have made!

And in person, he told her the dark stories of his past. The perils. The Afghan days. The war between the people who had no say in what games authorities chose to play.

Her questions grew more daring. "The dead girl a year ago, one of many—the authorities said it was you."

"It wasn't. I wish I could've saved her."

"What happened?"

He always answered as if in a confession.

"I found her in a dark alleyway. The lamp illuminated her malnourished body. She lay like a doll, porcelain skin, smeared with dirt and blood. A blue fall dress and a pretty face, almost angelic. A devil would have enslaved her. A monster would have ravaged her. No, that was banal in its tragedy—the hand of a man. She was one of many girls found like this in those parts. Some rich lords had wicked tastes. Her parents knew their names. But the men of law were paid off. And when the justice by my hand was finally served, that night the body of one of those men found its way to the slums again. But this time not for the horrific entertainment, but to be displayed for everyone to see—in its glorious death."

"Why such a gruesome display?"

"The poor need to know that justice exists. Those who commit the crimes in those parts need to know what awaits them."

His stories were dark. He was night. He was the fire pits that burned the sins away in the deepest slums. And he was the voice of the abused, whose stories made Alina's stomach churn.

And there were stories of kindness. Those were the ones that made her realize why children loved him so. Children didn't understand life or morality, but they knew acts of kindness and bravery when they saw them.

She'd seen a group of children once on the street, reenacting the legendary scenes. A little boy waved a stick in his hand like a sword, donning a bucket on his head instead of a top hat. He stood on an empty barrel, his little fists shaking in the air. "I am Harlan Krow. And I shall save ye, m'lady!" he declared to a group of children who stood around him. "I shall kill the bastard who wronged ye and sen' 'im all the way to hell."

She'd laughed then. But now the legend was reality. And she desperately wanted to *see* the man behind this disguise.

What was the color of his eyes?

Was he handsome or disfigured?

Did he have the face of a monster?

Would she care?

She couldn't tell his age but she'd done the math over and over again—he'd served in the Afghan war in his early twenties. So he was in his thirties now.

She dared to joke. "Do you ever come out in the day?"

He chuckled. "I like miserable weather. I pray for it, for when the sun cuts through the constant gloom and fog of this city, it shines brightly with the memories of war and one deadly day in the Hindu Kush mountains."

She bit back the urge to ask about it. His stories were dark. His scars deep.

They talked of monsters and saints. She told him of Russia, the cruel winters and beautiful souls.

The first time she'd told him about her footman, Yegór, and how he'd chugged three pints of moonshine on a bet, Harlan Krow laughed. The first time she'd heard him laugh, her heart tightened, the rich sound of his laughter so beautiful it startled her.

"I like your laughter," she said, smiling into the darkness, trying to imagine his smile.

He went quiet instantly.

"You should laugh more often." She didn't know what else to say.

"I shall. If you are around," he answered.

And the air stilled around them.

There was always that tipping point between a woman and a man—a slipped out word, a too-long gaze, a prolonged silence that told them they had a bond that was scary and exciting at once.

She shouldn't have been drawn to the shadow with no face. But behind it was a man. And he was magnetic, the power of his presence contagious, as if sitting on that stone bench behind St Rose's she was protected by the devil himself.

His stories scared her at times. She had an urge to cross herself, then remembered that he mocked religion. So she sat, shivering in the cold October wind, and pressed her hand to her chest where the little brass cross hung around her neck under the fabric of her dress.

He'd asked her about it then.

"We get baptized at an early age," she explained. "The cross is given by godparents. Mine were wealthy countrymen with more than humble beginnings. The cross is brass, simple and inexpensive. But I never take it off."

"Does it help you?" he asked. There was no mockery in his voice but curiosity.

"We all have our rituals, Mr. Krow."

"Please, call me Harlan."

She stilled.

"We all have our rituals." *Harlan.* "They help us keep the

routine that grounds us. The way we rise from the bed in the morning. The way we wash our face, then do our hair, and put on shoes, right then left. The way we go around the puddles on a rainy day and smooth our hair when upset. The way we say, 'Please,' in our minds, begging for the best outcome in hard situations, and exhale, trying to get rid of heavy thoughts. The cross is just that—a reminder that there is a power out there that might act in our favor. You don't believe in God. I understand that."

"I believe in angels." He chuckled, making her smile. "Does that count?"

And then he shifted. She wasn't sure what he was doing until she saw the dark shadow split in two and felt the weight of his leather coat on her shoulders.

"You've been shivering for a while," he said softly. "God doesn't protect in the cold times. Neither does faith. Coats do."

His scent on the coat around her shoulders was stronger. Rain. Leather. Burned coal.

She swallowed hard. "What about you? You shall be cold."

"Not if you stay for a while and talk to me."

And she closed her eyes, biting her smile.

His words felt like a caress.

## 15

# LADY AMSTEL'S

"I shall throw them all out and get new servants," whined Anna Yakovlevna one day when a door slammed somewhere in the depth of the servants' quarters for the fifth time in a minute.

There was something about the doors in Kamenevs' house. They were always opening and closing. As if there were dozens of people leaving and coming. It drove Anna Yakovlevna to insanity and frequent migraines. That, in its turn, was followed by sweet *Nalifka* or another herbal tincture and further transitioned into melancholy.

There was only one cure for that.

And that was a good suitor.

Alina's attitude was much too cold and unfriendly—on purpose, of course—and since their arrival to London, the number of suitors and men paying visits had decreased and finally turned to null.

But this time the cure came in the form of an invitation card for Alina, brought by Dunya and snatched by Anna Yakovlevna's authoritative hands.

"Oh, my," she whispered, reading it, and the melancholy disappeared off her face at once.

Attending Lady Amstel's ball with several hundred people was one thing. Attending her dinner party with only a handful of ladies and lords was an entirely different affair. And the invitation that came for Alina—the first one of such kind—was most surprising.

"Well, well. *Comme c'est gentil de sa part!*" Anna Yakovlevna smirked as she brought the perfumed paper to her nose and sniffed as if she could smell the true intentions.

The invitation, indeed, was nice and peculiar, for the lack of a better word. But Anna Yakovlevna's sarcasm was too obvious and was soon replaced with glee—Lady Amstel's dinner parties gathered a small circle of the richest and the most influential.

"I am not going," announced Alina. She sensed trouble.

"Oh, you most definitely are," her mother stated.

And that was how on a Saturday afternoon, Alina stood in front of the mirror, studying her dark-blue-and-pink silk taffeta skirt with plaid pattern. A matching evening bodice with a low but modest neckline and elbow-length sleeves was Alina's favorite. The colors were subtle but were in elegant contrast with the purple alexandrite gem that crowned her diamond-studded choker.

Alina had been raised by her parents in two drastically different ways. Her mother raised her for the ton, just like any wealthy girl. Manners, languages, hobbies, posture, the practiced politeness and calculated flirtation—the golden dust one blinded others with. That was all a good promising girl needed to find a great match. In Alina's case—a count.

Her father had raised her as if he needed a friend that he found in his own daughter. Books, hunting trips, science expositions, business meetings—everything that girls weren't supposed to be interested in.

The first upbringing had made a fine lady out of her. The second made her smart enough to know the power of it.

Anna Yakovlevna walked in and studied Alina with utmost scrupulousness. It annoyed Alina, but her mother seemed to be slipping into melancholy. If it gave her joy to oversee Alina's social life then that was one thing Alina was willing to sacrifice, being a dutiful daughter and a doll in her mother's hands.

Alina wrapped a dark-blue shawl over her shoulders when her mother walked to the wardrobe and pulled out a sable cloak.

"Mother, it's a dinner party," Alina argued, rolling her eyes.

But the blue shawl was already yanked off and the luscious sable was wrapped around her shoulders.

Alina stared at herself in the mirror—she looked enchanting, she agreed.

Anna Yakovlevna clicked her tongue in confirmation. "Just because others don't have taste in fashion doesn't mean you need to dress down for them."

Lady Amstel's house in Mayfair was the usual display of exuberant luxury.

There were eight guests in total. And as soon as Alina was led into the sitting room, she cursed herself—Samuel Cassell and Theo Van Buren rose from their seats to greet her.

*Oh, no.*

This was most unexpected. She had nothing against the two lords, except their presence always made others stiffen and act even more theatrically. They were like lions in a prairie. Van Buren—brazen and at times obnoxious. Cassell—silent and with a heavy gaze.

There was an older couple—a lord with a pear-like red nose who didn't let go of a wine glass and his wife of equally pear-like shape. There was a younger couple, the daughter of an earl who'd married down to a banker who nevertheless was rumored to have more wealth than the queen herself. Another banker, Henry Wadham, a bachelor in his forties with a sleazy smile that was directed at Alina almost constantly.

"It is so nice to have you here," said Lady Amstel as she led Alina away from the rest. The hostess with her dark-burgundy velvet dress and sharp black eyebrows was dazzling as always. A pink diamond pendant the size of a cherry around her neck was genuine. Unlike her words and everything she said in public. A small, brown Schipperke dog was tucked under her arm and looked at Alina as contemptuously as the hostess.

"The Viscount of Leigh insisted I invited you, Lady Bronskaya," said Lady Amstel in a half-whisper. She'd been drinking for a while, and her wine-sparkly prying eyes barely stopped on Alina but narrowed on the duke and the viscount. "You are not very fond of parties, but at his request, I made an effort."

Alina laughed. "How peculiar. His sudden interest and all."

"He is fond of beautiful women."

Alina smirked. This was matchmaking at its finest, though she wasn't sure what Lady Amstel was setting her up for, and she didn't like it a tiny bit.

"His friend, Samuel Cassell, the Duke of Ravenaugh," the host continued the hushed talk, "is not interested in much except donating to random causes."

Alina's eyes found the duke, dressed in an immaculate

gray suit, a waistcoat with intricate golden embroidery on emerald, and a gold chain across. His raven-black hair was slicked back, not a single hair out of sorts.

"I haven't heard much about him," Alina murmured, lost in studying him. Something drew her to him tonight, and she couldn't figure it out, finding it odd.

"Oh, it is a banal story. A sole heir. Parents passed. Very wealthy. Let me correct that—*extremely* wealthy. He traveled extensively. And many lost interest in him as he doesn't seem to be very interested in women."

"That is hardly a flaw. Perhaps a sign of integrity."

"Ah, but you see, Lady Bronskaya, women can sense that. If only you saw him at enough gatherings! He barely converses with anyone. I suppose Van Buren does the talking for both of them. But there are no stories—not even one—of any sort of"—Lady Amstel cleared her throat—"getting attention elsewhere."

"Elsewhere?" Alina frowned, scanning the rest of the guests.

"Establishments and circles that are more—how do I say it —libertine."

Alina smiled. "I see."

This was certainly the most open conversation Lady Amstel had ever had with her.

Alina shifted her eyes to the duke, and her smile froze.

He was gazing at her in a way that told her he'd been studying her for some time. He looked away, but the feeling lingered in her still—the feeling that the man was much more than what Lady Amstel and the rest assumed.

Quiet—he preferred to stay silent. Handsome—he had a look as if he didn't know that, absent and hollow. The realization creeped into Alina's mind—he wanted to be invisible, just like her, wished the attention wasn't on him when he entered the room, tried to avoid silly questions and taking part in irrelevant conversations.

Perfection was the word that described him. Yet his attitude made him look absent. His gaze was on his brandy glass again, then shifted slightly upward as if he knew she was watching him.

"Lady Bronskaya!"

She stiffened at the sound of the low but seductive voice that snaked into her ear and belonged to Van Buren, who walked up to them. His eyes pierced her with predatory curiosity.

"We finally have a chance to make a proper acquaintance." He nodded. "You are the subject of much gossip."

She'd heard all of it. She permitted a smile on her lips but didn't answer.

"And now that we have you, Lady Amstel takes you aside as if she has the sole claim on your attention."

Lady Amstel only laughed, and her dog yapped quietly as if in agreement.

Everything went according to the so-practiced for centuries etiquette. Enough chatter, and the guests moved to the dining-room, lit by a myriad of candles and beautiful sconces that pushed a faint glow through their ornamented brackets, turning the room into an intricate shadow pattern.

Alina stayed quiet, vaguely answering the polite questions. She should've declined the invitation, she concluded when Van Buren's voice was becoming the only one she heard. The man certainly knew how to draw attention to himself.

The duke seemed distant, observing the guests with indifference and an occasional sardonic tug at his lips.

And occasionally, he looked at Alina.

It startled her every time their eyes met. His gaze probed so deeply, she forgot about everyone around.

Another gaze.

And when their eyes stayed locked, suddenly he wasn't the indifferent shell of a man, a contemptuous duke who couldn't put a sentence together. There was a glimpse of a different man behind that gaze—someone who didn't let others close on purpose.

It mystified her. A current passed between them, but she forced herself to look away. The gaze had lasted much longer than appropriate.

Her eyes moved to Van Buren, who studied her with a cunning smile. "Are you lost, Lady Bronskaya?" he teased her. "We would love to know what amidst this dinner preoccupies the mind of the most talked about woman of the ton."

*Most talked about...*

Surely that was an exaggeration.

She flicked a glance at the duke, but he was again absently staring at the brandy glass his hands played with.

"Life, my lord. Surely, we all have things on our mind that preoccupy us even amidst the most amiable company."

"Surely, not all. And I only know one woman who pursues medical science." The words made her stiffen. "I hear you help out one certain doctor."

"Oh!" Everyone's curious eyes were on her.

Alina's heart gave out a heavy thud. How would he know that?

"It is admirable." Van Buren cocked his head, studying her.

Alina smiled coldly, meeting his narrowing glance. Her mother would never talk of this, considering it below her stature. Her father wasn't in the same company. How?

"Many find it below them," she answered. "Though there is nothing more humbling than to contribute to the wellbeing of the masses. Whether it is charity or fieldwork."

*Fieldwork.*

*Oh, Lord.*

Her mother would have killed her right now.

"Interesting." Van Buren was adamant in the way he pursued this conversation, as if he were trying to provoke her. "A certain villain London is talking about surely has a very hands-on approach to prove your own theory, Lady Bronskaya."

Alina froze at the words and raised her eyes to Van Buren.

His were smiling. At her. Again. Cunningly, if not knowingly.

The rest of the dinner passed with ohs and ahs at Lady Amstel's marvelous courses, quite boring in Alina's mind. Prosha's cooking would have made a better impression.

Afterward, as per the English tradition, the women were left to themselves. The men retired to the cigar room. This arrangement, so common in England, did not make sense to her. She would rather be in the company of men.

There was an established routine at all such gatherings—dinner, chatter, piano and singing, cards and discussions of rumors and latest news. Débutantes. Bachelors. Marital scandals. Latest fashion. An upcoming function. All that was accompanied by the annoying yapping of the pup in Lady Amstel's hands.

It bored Alina to death. Excusing herself, she walked out of the sitting room and crossed the hall toward the terrace to the garden.

The air was much too cold but refreshing. It grazed her neck and chest, exposed by the open evening dress. She should've worn something more discreet. Subtle color. Less jewelry. It annoyed her—the way she wanted to dress down in order to attract less attention in a world where the rumors about her already created enough talk.

She walked up to the terrace railing and gazed at the dark

garden, surrounded by already skeletal trees, the fence and the quiet street lit by the street lamp behind it.

The muffled footsteps made her turn around to see Henry Wadham walk out with a brandy glass in his hand.

"Ah, Lady Bronskaya!"

The arrogant banker with pigeon-like features and clumpy hair walked up to the railing next to her slowly as if approaching his prey. He'd been giving her looks the entire evening as if he knew a secret or two about her. Every stare made her shiver. Men like him thought they had power and their bank account made up for the lack of character or integrity.

Alina smiled coldly and turned to walk toward the door.

"Are you bored with us Englishmen?" he asked.

She turned to look at him. He leaned insolently back onto the railing, his legs crossed at the ankles.

"Not at all." She forced a smile. "Just getting some fresh air."

You, we, them—she knew that sort of talk.

"You don't seem to be cold." He cocked an eyebrow.

She smiled, wanting to turn and leave.

"Is it true..." He cocked his head and furrowed his eyebrows in utmost seriousness as if he was contemplating the right words. "Is it true what they say about Russian women?"

*I should leave.*

She could sense what was coming, though this was the last thing she would expect from Lady Amstel's guests.

*Go.*

But she stayed, raising her chin and meeting Wadham's arrogant gaze.

"Is it true that Russian women are as cold in bed as the brutal Siberian winters?"

It seemed like only a second passed.

A second when his sleazy grin lit up his face.

A second when her blood went cold indeed at the insult.

A second when the wind wafted into her face.

But it wasn't the wind.

Something swished past her like a powerful gust, a shadow, and the next second, someone lunged at Wadham.

The instinct and reflex in the person's movements made for a skillful fighter. He moved with fluid grace, danger in the way he easily grabbed Wadham and leaned onto him with all his weight.

The brandy glass fell over the railing, breaking with a sharp sound that echoed through the night air.

"How dare you," the words hissed in the wind.

Frozen to her spot, Alina held her breath, her heart hammering in her chest at the sight of the man.

The Duke of Ravenaugh.

She recognized him now, color rising to her face at the fact that he'd heard the insult.

He looked so much larger than Wadham, fisting his jacket and leaning so closely that the man with the pathetic face was bent backward over the railing.

The duke's quiet words hissed in the wind as he brought his lips to Wadham's ear and said something, then let go of him abruptly with a rough push at the chest.

"Apologize," he said calmly as if he'd been standing like this all this time.

Unease washed over Alina in one powerful wave. Blood pounded in her ears.

Wadham fixed his cravat, his beady eyes darting to Alina in fear. He cleared his throat, red coloring his face, matching his burgundy jacket.

"Forgive me, Lady Bronskaya. I was out of line."

She was trying to come up with a response when the duke

turned to her, his expression like a cold mask, only his eyes blazing like fire. "Shall we go inside?"

His voice was as calm as it had been every time she'd ever heard him speak. In fact, this was the first time she'd heard him speak around her. *To* her.

Her heart pounded in her chest. She nodded, fumbling, and started walking toward the terrace door. Stepping inside, she finally came back to her senses. She walked as fast as she could toward the music parlor and the sounds of the agitated discussion.

The warmth of the house suddenly felt nice and welcoming. She'd almost reached the open doors to the parlor when the duke's voice behind her stopped her.

"Lady Bronskaya."

It was soft and calming, somewhat strained as if he had difficulty speaking.

Alina turned to meet the duke's gaze.

He stood several feet away from her, hands clasped behind his back in his usual manner. "Forgive me for the scene. Please. I should've resolved it in a more appropriate fashion."

She managed a nod. "Thank you." She attempted a smile, which was anything but cheerful. "I've heard his words before."

"You shouldn't be hearing such remarks from anyone. Let alone a man. Let alone a man like him. But I do apologize for my reaction."

This was the most she'd ever heard him talk. There was concern in his words. An apology, sure. But also something else—holding back, as if it was hard for him to speak, as if he wasn't used to being around women.

*Odd.*

She was unable to think and realized she held her breath.

There was a mix of the elegance of a fashionable man and the quickness of a fighter in that moment on the terrace.

How?

He didn't follow her inside the parlor, and when he came back some time later, he came back alone.

Alina couldn't wait to excuse herself and leave this wretched party. Only one person held her back—Samuel Cassell. Her mind was preoccupied, trying to come to terms with what she'd seen earlier.

She couldn't help watching him as discreetly as she could. There was something predatory beneath his calm demeanor and reserved manners. The beauty of it was shocking and unexpected. And instead of feeling indignation at the insult of an insolent man, she was in slight awe with the duke.

Only sometime later did Lady Amstel look around, frowning. "Whatever happened to Mr. Wadham?"

Alina glanced at Cassell, who didn't take his eyes off his brandy glass. "I believe he had to leave urgently," the duke said.

"Without a farewell? How odd! And impolite."

The duke didn't answer.

Alina kept her eyes on him, and he smiled into his brandy glass as if he knew she was watching.

## 16

## OBSESSION

Obsession is like London fog, Father. It creeps up on you one day and envelopes you completely, sneaking under your coat and all the way down to your heart.

Not even an hour every day went by without a thought about Alina Bronskaya. To others, she was Lady Bronskaya, mingling at parties and functions. To me, she was my countess. But when she visited me at night, if only in my imagination, in those tender moments when I conjured the shameless scenes, she was Alina, my angel.

And here is the thing about men and women. Once you start falling for a woman, you can't stop lustful thoughts. You allow your mind to drift away in that direction, and you find yourself on paths unknown before.

I would lie in my bed during sleepless nights and wonder what she looked like in a gown. With her hair loose, brushing it before going to bed. I would imagine that it was cold, and her nipples got hard, poking the cotton of the fabric.

Were they pink and small like pebbles or darker and heavier with big areolae? I would see her in a dress but wonder what her hips were like, thighs, legs, the curves of her body.

And then I pictured her naked, taking a provocative pose on a bed, her limbs loose and leisurely, her legs open as if no one was watching, giving me a peek of her most private parts. And I thought of her sex. The curls that framed it, dark or perhaps lighter in color with a reddish tint like her hair. Her pink folds that I wanted to sink my tongue in, kiss them and caress them. That little nub that I wanted to touch with my fingers first then bring my mouth to it, making it tremble under my tongue. In my dreams, she opened up for me, showed herself in all her beauty, took my cock in her hand, and guided it to her well of pleasure.

How did she orgasm? Little gasps and mewls or unrestrained cries, suffocating and gasping as she reached her peak?

There was no end to such thoughts, Father. I lay one night and thought of her at length, stroking myself. I reached my peak fast, but a minute later, she was on my mind again, spreading her creamy thighs and playing with herself, opening her legs wider and asking me to touch her.

I stroked myself to the fantasies of her until dawn.

And that was the tipping point. Once she became familiar in my fantasies, that feeling transitioned into real life. And the next time I saw her, I couldn't help but want to touch the woman who became so intimate with me in my mind.

She was in my dreams at night and in my bed when I woke up in the morning, with her beautiful gray eyes, her chapped lips, and immaculately slick hair, coifed into a tight bun that I wanted to loosen up with my teeth like a naughty puppy.

When I saw her in those furs for the first time—oh, she was Venus, the classical beauty with pale skin, rosy lips, and a gaze that could send men to their death.

She was slowly replacing any other thoughts in my mind—a bad sign for a man like me.

I forgot my duty, Father. I forgot what had to be done—that monster, Hacksaugh, was still living comfortably, despite the things he'd done to you. Do you remember, Father? That day you confronted him, told him you would talk to the bishop and unveil what he'd been doing?

You tried so hard to make things just, Father. But you see, not all men of God follow the rules.

I came to see you that day. For all you'd done for me when I had come back from war as a broken shell of a man, I should have known what men like him were capable of. I told you then, Father. "Let me handle it. Go back to your parish. Trust in your God."

Oh, the look you gave me as if you knew in your heart that I was right.

That day I heard you cry, Father. And it wasn't a cry for help but of desperation. You can tell me that your faith didn't weaken then. And I will tell you that it's not the hand of God that will strike Hacksaugh soon. Sometimes, the wrong things can only be fixed by doing worse ones. It is a senseless argument, but oh-so-true. All your attempts were in vain. Getting you in trouble. Only making matters worse. Much worse.

But even Hacksaugh took the backstage as my letter exchange with the countess continued.

Stories. Memories. And the occasional encounters at St Rose's that weren't enough to feed my craving for her anymore.

Those became the best parts of my week—sitting next to her on that cold bench, in the darkness, hearing her voice, and letting my own thoughts out.

The days grew colder.

My feelings for her grew hotter.

And her mind! Don't underestimate the power of a person's mind when you realize it matches yours.

I asked her about Russia. She told me the story of her late husband.

"He was involved in pushing the reforms that would give the masses an opportunity to have more say in governmental decisions. It can't happen in Russia. We don't think freely there. My country has lived with the idea of greatness for far too long. But you can't be grand and imperial and let a notion of freedom make a home in people's heads. You can't control them that way. But if you have any compassion for your people, it is hard to be a privileged noble and dismiss the fact that your power is based on enslaving others. So you choose to keep people in the dark. You control the knowledge. You keep them poor. Because when they are miserable, they will cling to anything that will give them the sense of greatness. Even if it is their oppressive ruler."

That, Father!

She didn't know that her words mirrored mine. We came from different places but looked in the same direction.

Her mind hypnotized mine. My heart called out to hers. Our thoughts and words tangled in a way that makes a simple friendship grow into something else.

She'd warmed up to me, Father. And the night she told me about the party she was going to, she joked.

Joked, Father!

Humor is a deeper sort of friendship. Who knew that the angel would joke with the devil?

"If you could pull off your devil's magic and disrupt the party so that I don't have to go," she said, laughing. She said it was hosted by the Duke of Ravenaugh, and her mother insisted on her going.

Ah, the duke...

There are two types of men who really infatuate women. The powerful wealthy ones. They might lack character or wit, but the power alone draws women to them. The second kind are the tormented dark ones like me, who disregard the laws and everything that turns others into slaves. It is a power of its own, I suppose.

And that was how she found herself—between two men. That night, she didn't know it yet. She laughed so carelessly. And what happened at that party changed everything. She told me later that the encounter with the duke changed her opinion of him.

She smiled then.

My chest tightened.

That was the beginning of my end.

## 17

# THE BULLET

The days turned into piercing winds and low temperatures, early dusk and unforgiving pitch-black nights.

On such nights, yearning souls conjured tales—ones that stayed deep inside their heads, full of lustful fantasies and forbidden longings.

Alina sat in her room by the desk in the light of a candelabrum. She shivered in her house dress and wrapped a shawl tighter about her shoulders. For the third time, she tried to reread the completed first part of the essay, edited and corrected by Dr. Grevatt. Yet, her thoughts were elsewhere.

She replayed her encounter with Harlan the night before.

"Please, call me Harlan," he'd asked again.

*Harlan…*

As if they were close friends or more.

And how they had drifted to close friendship was a mystery. Dangerous but oh-so alluring. Was it possible to be attracted to a person without knowing what he looked like? She'd read stories like this. Beauty and the Beast. Princess Tatiana's letters to her betrothed.

She felt it in his presence—the unreasonable draw toward him that grew stronger day by day. His words hypnotized her. His stories fascinated her.

Behind the myth of Harlan Krow was a tormented soul. A man broken but strong. Dark but brilliant. She was drawn to him like a moth to a fire. She wanted his closeness so desperately that her heart burned with longing.

She tried to reason with him and his violent ways.

Oh, women! Always trying to save someone!

She felt she understood him now. His power wasn't something one saw but rather sensed. It came from his past tragedies. It was dark and destructive. It could save many, sure. But it was most definitely destroying the one holding it. Revenge was a short-term victory, eventually pointing its lethal end at the one holding it.

"There are better ways to help people," she said.

Next to the man who was slowly changing the way people looked at justice system and its pitfalls, her words sounded so primitive.

"Certainly." He didn't argue.

"Not a carrot dangling in front of them while their hands are tied, but something they can use. Tearing down the slums," she suggested. "Building better houses for the poor. What surrounds us makes us. Building schools. Curbing child labor laws. Women's rights. Access to medical care. Too many to count." She exhaled hopelessly. "Those people need an opportunity and an affordable one. But it has to be changed from the top. Only the powerful can bring social change. It is unfair, yes. But the people so desperately need our help."

They. Us.

Oh, God, she talked like Andrei.

Tears welled up in her eyes.

"There is a place," she went on. "You must have seen it many times. St James's Hill."

He nodded.

"They seem to do things the right way. But they have bene-factors, you see. Someone had enough compassion for one place like that. But this city needs dozens. Gah! Opportunities —this country has them. Where I come from, people don't."

They talked and talked.

No one talked to her like this—as if she were an equal.

One more minute.

One more second.

She dissolved in his low voice as they sat on that stone bench outside St Rose's—the two shadows in complete dark-ness. She cherished every word and dreaded the minute they would part.

Was that madness?

He was a villain.

And yet.

And yet.

"Your stories are always dark," she said. "Does anything bring you joy?"

"You," he answered, and her heart thudded at the word.

She felt at once happy. With Harlan next to her, it was as if the darkness was at his command. So was the night city. She'd never felt so safe.

Rumi had quoted Socrates once. "Those who are hardest to love need it most." Harlan needed someone by his side— someone to tell him there was another way, another life, another world to live in. Alina was a nurse by trade, hopefully a doctor in the future. And she wanted to heal him, take him in her arms, stroke his unkept long hair, and kiss his face, even if it was the face of a monster.

She constantly had to stop her thoughts that veered in the

directions too dangerous. They warmed her heart and seeped lower down her body. She yearned for his closeness, occasional brushes of his coat, the touch of his hand when, at times, he helped her into the carriage, the way he turned his face to her, and though she couldn't see it in the darkness, she wanted him to lean even closer so that she at least could feel him, touch him, taste…

*Oh, God.*

This was positively madness.

Alina sat by the desk, realizing that she'd pulled his letters out of the drawer. She aimlessly caressed them with her fingers as if she could get closer to him in this way.

Another man who wanted to change the world. What wretched fate!

In that instant, the memories flooded her.

That awful night leaving Russia.

The uniformed men with guns escorting them to the train station.

The piercing horn of the train.

The suffocating clouds of the steam.

No farewells, no tears.

Only the feeling of betrayal.

Alina had grown up on a country estate just outside Petersburg until she turned twenty and married Count Bronskiy. He was ten years older than her, gentle, educated, and quiet.

Still waters ran deep. Or, as they said in Russian, devil-men lived in the quietest ponds.

At times, Alina wished Andrei hadn't been so intelligent. She wished he hadn't cared about the people and the future of his nation. It would have made their life different. He would have still been alive.

They moved to Petersburg the same year they got married, and life acquired a faster pace.

She read the medical books that Andrei brought for her at her request. Already she was interested in science, and it made Andrei glow with pride when she talked about it. He hired tutors. She did home-practice with a doctor who'd taught in Austria.

And Andrei lived in his own world that was new and so foreign to her—late-night meetings, men coming to their house, smoking, talking, arguing late into the night.

*Ideas*, he called them.

Those were dangerous words. Alina knew from history that those could burn you at the stake or get you hung.

Then one day, men in state uniforms came knocking on the door.

There was a bruise on Andrei's face the next week.

Then a broken rib.

Then a three-day disappearance.

Upon his return, he sat her down one night and said, "If anything happens to me, I want you to leave Russia. Until it becomes a country for the people. And that is certainly not any time soon."

She laughed.

He was a count! Count Bronskiy! An untouchable!

But there came a night a month later when Andrei made her hide the most precious things, money and jewelry, in a small suitcase, and memorize an address in London. He talked to her parents, asking them to come to Petersburg and stay with them for some time.

And she laughed hysterically at the thought of it but one

night, she broke down and cried on his lap, murmuring, "Stop. For us, for our future, Andrei. Won't you stop?"

She looked at him with eyes full of tears as she begged.

But he only smiled sadly and stroked her hair.

She learned then that friends could betray. That Motherland could have a cruel heart. And the people you cared for never cared for you. Because they were a country of many and poor. And you were the titled and wealthy.

"This is our home, Andrei," Alina reasoned with him. "This is *our* country. *Our* friends."

She kept saying that day after day, trying to believe her own words.

Until one of those friends passed the word to someone almighty whose patience snapped.

One long week of Andrei missing.

Two bullets.

One in his heart. One in his head.

His body in the river.

The autopsy's official conclusion—an accident.

# 18

## SHE

I watched her for weeks, Father. It was obsession, though I tried to call it protectiveness. The way one takes care of a little bird, wondering how it managed to survive on its own. You know that it is perfectly capable. Yet you go on, day by day thinking that your care is the only thing that keeps it alive.

I watched my angel at night when she left Dr. Grevatt's. I found out everything I could about the doctor and the black girl who was a brilliant poet and a skilled nurse. An uncut gem, no less.

I watched the countess as she left the hospital with that monstrous footman of hers by her side. But she always paused and let him and Miss Rumi go ahead. And I made my presence known. At times, she arrived alone, as if she wanted more time with me.

Ah, the rare moments when we talked! We sat on the bench at St Rose's and shared stories in the darkness that had acquired a new sensation—the sound of her voice.

Her footman often lingered in the dark, loyally waiting for his mistress. He knew of our meetings.

I made sure she got to her carriage every time and often

walked behind it as it picked up the pace, carrying my countess away from me.

Days went by, weeks, bringing with them the first flurries and fantasies of her that became much darker.

I watched her in the daytime, wishing she recognized me, but she didn't. How could she? Mine was an unfair game. But can you blame a man smitten by a woman so powerfully?

I observed her clothes, those furs that she started donning, changing into the colder season. A shawl with intricate ornaments—Russian, no doubt. She liked fashion, though hers was simple and elegant, not screaming like the rest of the ton. Even her luxury furs looked like she was born into them. Second skin. I could never see her smile in the dark, but she smiled in the daytime at others, and I wanted to kiss that smile and press her close to me. Or have her touch me.

One touch.

The woman I could never have by day.

I know, I know, Father.

Soon, I knew everything about her. What she did in the hospital and at Dr. Grevatt's. How often she went shopping, and what pastries she liked. I found out her favorite flowers were peonies, but it was impossible to get them off-season. Her favorite author was Gogol, and I read every translation I could find. So she was into villains and folklore—I smiled as I read *Viy*—then ordered the books in Russian and put them in my library.

I learned what rumors said about her and how ignorant some of them were.

Her letters filled the gaps—the mind of a wise man in the body of a young woman. Unheard of! Who else could understand me if not her?

I wrote letters. Like a madman, they became my diaries.

And she responded the very next day, slowly turning into a close friend that I could share my deepest thoughts with.

She was lovely, Father.

She took my dark heart into her little hand and gently squeezed it until it swelled, unable to keep the even beat.

On those cold nights, sitting on that bench and talking, I wished I could take her hands in mine. Her thin fashionable gloves surely couldn't keep them warm. I wanted to cup her face and kiss those parched lips, healing them. When she told me why she'd run from Russia, I wanted to slay an entire nation for daring to raise its hand to my angel.

She made my heart sing, Father. Krow used to do that for us in those brutal war years. Young, kind Krow, who with his out-of-tune singing could heal the wounded hearts.

So did she.

She made my heart hum peacefully.

One day in the garden at St Rose's, she looked at me as if she could see through the dark.

"There is a real man behind all this. Isn't there, Harlan?"

I froze in unease, but she only laughed softly. That laughter made me want to scoop her into my arms, set her on my lap, and kiss her until she lost her mind.

"It's just…" She paused, and I didn't dare interrupt. "I feel like this is all a strange dream."

Except, if it were a dream, I could pull her to me and kiss her. I could take her home, strip her of her fancy garments, and take her with all the passion that burned me at night at the thought of her.

No, it wasn't a dream, though it sure felt like a fairy tale.

We'd met at a crime scene. We'd bonded through letters. One can fall in love with words, Father. I was falling in love with all of her.

With her mind that was unlike any other person I'd met.

With her sight—a beauty with hair of burnt amber, delicate features, and kind gray eyes.

With her scent, the way her letters carried the faint trace of her perfume. The way she curled the letter *H* when she wrote my name. The corners of her letters were always bent, and I wondered whether she carried them in her cape, or reticule, or tucked them under her bodice, hiding them from everyone.

I was falling in love because she was brave. While the city trembled at the sound of my name, she'd said that first night so simply, "Write a letter." Because she didn't see a villain or a powerful legend. She saw a man behind it, with all his scars and pain and tormented past. And she looked at me in a way that healed those scars, and breathing became a little easier day by day.

One night I wrote to her again. But that was a letter of a different kind.

*Would you come to a ball with me?*

It would not be like any ball she'd ever been to. I knew the proposal would torment her. The proprieties, the secrets, and all that claptrap that stops honorable women from getting what they want.

But, God, did I want to be next to her—anywhere else but that shabby bloody garden!

I wanted to talk and see her in the light, instead of writing and writing the letters and rereading hers, trying not to go insane with the want to be close to her every living moment.

That wretched letter paper had been closer to her than I'd ever been. And I had to change that.

I didn't know that it would happen so fast…

## 19

---

# THE PHANTOM BALL

S he was already flitting down the moral ladder. What was one more step?

That was how sinners thought.

*Ah, the devil!*

Alina couldn't help but smirk at the words. She paced around her bedroom, not realizing that she was pressing Harlan's letter to her bosom.

The ball! With the gentleman-devil!

Should she refuse it? Yes. Was it most unspeakable? Absolutely.

And her heart pounded like a hundred-pound drum when she took out a letter paper and wrote a reply.

*Yes.*

Yegór's lips were pressed so tightly that you could barely see them in his thick beard when he received the instructions to go to St Rose's and leave the letter in the usual hiding spot.

The next day, Alina sent Yegór to St Rose's again to check for a reply.

"What is it that you preoccupy him with these days?" Anna Yakovlevna inquired at lunch, her probing narrowed eyes never leaving Alina.

Nikolai Sergeevich answered for her. "Must you know every step your daughter takes?"

"Her life is my concern until she finds a proper husband."

Alina laughed in response. "It never fails," she murmured under her breath.

Alina's future marriage had become her mother's obsession, though Alina most certainly preferred science to men.

Most men...

She heard Yegór's low rumble at the door and darted like a rabbit from her seat and toward the main hall.

A letter! There was a reply!

She snatched it from her footman's hands and trotted up to her room.

Her lungs burned with heavy breathing when she read the instruction.

Tonight.

Fulham, west of the city of London.

How fast everything happened!

She inhaled deeply to calm her breathing and smiled, pressing the letter to her lips.

Later that night, Alina's carriage pulled down a dark country road and rode another mile, as per instructions, and stopped.

She peeked through the curtain and tried to calm her breathing as she stared at the darkness and the black blotches of carriage silhouettes parked on both sides of the road.

Yegór opened the door.

"My lady." His voice was a question and a warning.

"We shall wait for a moment," she said, knowing she sounded hesitant.

She didn't know where this was going and definitely wasn't going to leave the carriage on her own. But when the soft knock at the door jerked her up in nervousness and the door opened, she almost cheered in relief.

He was dark, but for the first time, the dim light of her carriage cast a glow on the man she'd been meeting for weeks.

And her heart fell.

Amidst the black garments and his long messy hair hanging like a curtain around his head, a mask stared at her, the top hat low over its forehead.

The mask covered his entire face. A black cravat was wrapped tightly around his neck.

"My lady." The voice she knew was muffled by the mask.

She couldn't take her eyes off him, wanting to find at least an inch of bare skin to hold on to.

Alas.

She'd never felt so disappointed. "I was hoping to have a better look at you, but…"

She'd only come here for this—to have a chance to be out with him, perhaps finally see his face.

Oh, the irony!

He didn't respond but stretched his gloved hand to her, in it— a jeweled Columbine mask that would cover her eyes and nose.

"Please, wear this," he said and watched as she put it on and adjusted the ties on the back of her head.

"Now you wear a disguise, too." A soft chuckle sounded from behind his mask.

*Just like you.*

She held his hand as she exited.

Yegór stood right there, his mountainous figure taller and

broader than that of Harlan Krow. But the gentleman-devil didn't turn to look at her footman.

"This way." He motioned and placed her hand around his bent arm.

Only now did Alina notice that the pitch darkness dissipated ahead, revealing a path lit by burning torches. Guards dressed in black and wearing masks stood along the length of it. Twenty or so feet up, another guard accepted an ornate invitation from her companion and opened the heavy door of the building. It was impossible to see the size of it outside, only the stone facade with lion heads.

Alina hated the mask that constricted her vision, for her eyes were darting between the unusual surrounding and Harlan, who was now shades lighter. And still the same—dark, all in black. Yet she could see the details of his hair, the crinkles in his old leather coat, the buckles on its sleeves. He seemed more real in the light of the torches. But with everything that surrounded them—certainly a dream.

A small stone hallway with a single burning torch and another masked guard greeted them when the guard opened the door and let them further in.

And Alina held her breath.

Candles and torches lit up the intricately carved stone walls and frescoed ceiling of a giant ballroom. Several hundred people mingled in semi-darkness. But there was no mistake—no proper ball or public masquerade would allow costumes like this.

Fauns with horns and tails. A medusa. Painted faces and half-naked bodies. Angels and demons. Mythological creatures of all kinds and the queens of all epochs.

Dragon-like painted women sashayed among the guests. A centaur with a real man, his visible half-body oiled and painted to match the sculpted bottom, stood in the corner like a prop.

"It's called the Phantom Ball," Harlan explained as he gently led her into the crowd. "This is where the almighty and deviants can truly express their love for extravagance. There."

He took a glass of champagne from the tray of a masked servant and passed it to her.

The orchestra boomed in one part of the room where ladies and lords danced.

Alina had heard of such gatherings. Yet this was the first time she'd stepped into a room that made her feel like the rest of the world didn't exist. A wicked fairytale.

A couple approached. A glistening sequined suit for him and a lavish Renaissance dress for her, her décolletage so low Alina could see her areolae.

"My good sir," the man said, addressing Harlan. "Your costume is most appropriate." His mustached lips below his mask stretched in a smile. "But I have to disappoint you. His lordship over there has beat you, I am afraid."

Alina looked to where the gentleman was pointing to—and there, in the crowd, stood another Harlan Krow, slick and fashionable, a wig, no doubt, in that rumored fashion—black loose hair with a bright white streak. The man wore tinted spectacles and donned a long beard.

She grinned and looked at Harlan then, knowing that his mask covering his entire face concealed a smile. And then her eyes paused on his hair. A white strand hung loose on the right side of his face—a strange detail that the legend mentioned that she'd never noticed in the dark.

"Now I understand why you weren't afraid to come here dressed as you are," she said, shaking her head with a smile.

"The lords seem to be fond of the concept," he said and pointed in a different direction—another man, shorter and heavier, but dressed like him, stood talking to his companions.

He could be just like those others—many who tried to appropriate the legend of the gentleman-devil. He could be a fake. It had never occurred to Alina before and made her shiver in unease.

But she dismissed the thought and took another sip of champagne. It tickled her dry throat and calmed her slight nervousness. The last time she'd had champagne was when she'd stood at Lady Amstel's ball, trying to calm nervousness of a different kind—from the crime she'd witnessed and meeting the legend of the East End.

And now she was here with him.

She observed the people. They stopped to listen to an aria performance by the actors whose bodies were painted, the intimate parts concealed by matching cloths. She had more champagne. They exchanged small talk. They veered among the bodies in the ballroom full of smoke and the heavy scent of liquor, chatter and loud laughter, open caresses and sensual kisses.

And all this with her hand wrapped around Harlan's arm. This meeting was different, and not because of the surroundings, but because she enjoyed his closeness, holding on to him, letting him lead her around as if they were an item. This was their first closeness of this sort. When they veered among people, she held on to Harlan tighter and felt his arm press closer to his body, as if he wanted to feel her touch there. He felt so much closer to her than ever before. Except for his voice, muffled, and somehow more distant than usual.

People came and left through the dark curtained alcoves, and Alina didn't dare ask what was happening outside this ballroom.

She tried to smile so as to push away the scandalous

thoughts about what she saw and what she felt. As if a curtain had been lifted, putting everyone's desires on display.

"This certainly goes against the morals and etiquette of the ton," she said.

"Morals are a fig leaf that covers our true selves," Harlan replied. "Except, no matter how big it is, you know what it is hiding. The whole world knows."

"But society needs that fig leaf."

He laughed, his laughter making her heart flutter again. "Isn't it peculiar that humans were banned from the garden of Eden for using that very leaf?"

"It is…" She couldn't find an answer.

"It is confusing, yes."

She was fascinated with him. And she wanted to see him. She desperately tried to catch any glimpses of the man behind the disguise. All in vain. His black coat and suit covered every part of his body. The black gloves never left his hands. His hair hung like a curtain around his face.

And his face was a mask.

She felt disappointed, tricked. She studied every scratch on his coat, trouser, and heavy boots. Behind that was a man. He had an appearance. He breathed. Talked. Laughed.

And then her attention was taken by the sea of people again.

Deep heavy silks in bright red and deep blue and emerald. Extravagant costumes with furs and feathers. Others donning what seemed like appropriate attire for a night with a lover in a bedroom.

A woman sashayed by, hanging on her companion's arm. A flute of champagne in her hand, she wore a mask with feathers that adorned her two-foot-high hair weaved into a grotesque chignon. A corset, tight undergarment, and a translucent slip made of a thousand golden beads let everyone admire her hour-glass figure.

"That is… very courageous," said Alina with a gasp.

Harlan's masked face turned toward her, but she didn't look at him.

"Not as courageous as the one over there." He nodded at a woman in the crowd who—

*Oh, Lord.*

Alina felt her face catch on fire as she studied a woman who wore nothing but a mask and a translucent chemise that put everything on display—her naked body, her heavy breasts, and—

Embarrassment tugged at her. Not at the display of nakedness but the fact that she was here with a man. She wanted to be with him, yes. Yet the presence of naked people made her feel ashamed. And aroused. And so libertine. And scandalous. Daring. Feminine. Free!

For a brief moment, Alina relished the thought that these men and women assumed she was accompanied by her lover.

"Why did you bring me here?" she asked softly, her thoughts scaring and exciting her at once.

"You wanted to see me in the light."

"But you still wear a mask."

"This is a compromise, I suppose."

She chuckled. Her arguments were useless.

"More importantly, I wanted to spend more time with you," he added.

Those words burned her all the way down to her lower belly. She caught sight of a man who kissed his companion sensually right in the middle of the crowd, his hand drifting up to her breast and palming it. And she couldn't look away. The more champagne she had, the hungrier she grew for this display of sexuality.

She wasn't sure how much time had passed. The smoke hung thicker in the air. The hall got louder. It was hot. Her head got dizzier from champagne. Yet all she wanted to do was follow the man she was with around, hold on to him, be closer than they'd ever been.

And that was when she heard the familiar laughter.

Her head snapped in that direction, and she halted, making Harlan stop at her side.

"What is it?" he asked.

Sir John Boldon wore a flimsy mask over his eyes, but it was impossible not to recognize him. His shiny bald head, his thick almost purplish lips, wide in that familiar sly smile. And his short body that was on display, only covered by trousers, a floor-length red robe, and a gold collar with a leash held by a tall, beautiful nymph.

Alina stared in horror.

*Oh, Lord.*

It wasn't the shock of seeing the lord like this, but the chance to be recognized, for her flimsy mask didn't conceal enough of her face either.

Only now, seeing a familiar figure, had she realized the danger of being in a place like this—being a woman, with a male companion, surrounded by half-naked bodies.

"I have to go," she whispered.

"Did you recognize someone?"

"Yes," she exhaled, pulling Harlan with her, trying to walk away.

"Come with me," he ordered and changed the direction toward one of those dark alcoves, hidden behind the burgundy curtains.

Glances followed them as they veered among the people— glances at him, smiling, nodding, appreciating the costume.

If only they knew!

Alina followed submissively. And when they stepped inside one of the alcoves, the curtains closed behind them, leaving them in complete darkness.

She felt Harlan turn to her, gently stepping into her, until her back hit the wall. She was breathing heavily, from panic or a sudden rush of excitement, she wasn't sure.

"Are you all right?" His voice was soft and husky.

They were in the dark again. Always in the dark. As if it were their safest haven. The sounds of the music and voices were muffled here, and Alina felt an urge to press closer to him.

"I shouldn't be here, Harlan," she whispered, though this was precisely where she wanted to be right now—with him, alone. "This place is…"

*So scandalous and so wonderful.*

"This is where men and women who create a facade fulfill their desires in secret," he said. "Everyone needs darkness once in a while, Alina."

She trembled at the sound of her name. She wasn't sure he'd ever called her that. His voice was lower and softer, his body closer to hers. They were in the dark, in the corner where the faintest light didn't reach. Only the murmurs and whispers of strangers slithered through the air. This wasn't an alcove, she realized, but a pathway somewhere else, the darkness stretching somewhere deep into the building, wafting with sighs and whispers.

Alina could always stop what was to come—Harlan was no scoundrel. But she wanted this, *him*, closer to her, his voice turning into a whisper, the words lost in the dizzying arousal from him being so close.

*Just one touch.*

"I want to see your face," she said quietly.

"You can't."

"Why?" she insisted.

"You will not like what you see, Alina."

But his voice was inviting, luring her into the darkness.

"I want to touch it, then," she whispered, her heart beating wildly at this brave declaration.

She felt him shift.

In a moment, his hands took hers, pulling at her fingertips, taking off her gloves.

She felt his touch—his bare skin, warm and rough, against hers. Bare of gloves, that touch was the most intimate yet.

She wanted to hold his hands, lace her fingers with his, explore his skin that was suddenly real and so human.

But he brought her hands to his face and cupped his cheeks with her palms.

No mask…

She took control then, feeling up his skin like a blind woman—his cheeks, then slowly tracing his thick eyebrows with her fingers, moving her forefingers down his broad nose and touching his lips just lightly. She felt the bristles of the mustache above his upper lip. The lower lip, full and soft. She could do it forever, she wanted to do it for the longest time, staring into the darkness wide-eyed and trying to paint his portrait in her mind.

His sudden movement made her jerk her hands away, but he caught them in his and pressed her fingers to his lips.

Soft kisses, on each fingertip, as if he were counting them.

She smiled in the darkness, though her heart was beating wildly in her chest.

He kissed every finger, then buried his mouth in her palm and kissed the sensitive skin in the center, then did the same to the other one.

"You bewitched me, Alina," he whispered, bringing her one hand back to his cheek, covering it with his.

He shifted closer and leaned down. His other cheek touched hers as his words seeped into her ear, "I can't stay away from you."

They were so close—skin to skin. His lips pressed to her cheekbone in a light kiss. Then shifted lower, his warm breath scorching her all the way down to her lower belly.

Another kiss on her jawline.

For a moment, there was an inch of warm breaths between them, their heads tilting at the tiniest increments, lips inching closer.

Another brief kiss at the corner of her lips—timid, like the tremor of butterfly wings.

Another one, brief and fleeting, the gap between them growing unbearably painful.

And she gave in, tilted her head to cover the last inch, and met his lips.

She held her breath to suppress a moan, feeling herself shake with need.

He kissed her again, softly, probing, molding their lips together.

The next kiss parted her lips, the moist tip of his warm tongue grazing her seam.

Another one, his tongue venturing into her.

Then again.

And again.

And again...

Like a tidal wave, he took her in a deep kiss. Desire washed over her, making her knees weak and her core throb with want. She moaned, but her moan was lost in his mouth.

The kiss erased her mind. The world around her dissipated until there was only this—their lips and tongues and warm breaths becoming one. Their hands bestowed the softest caresses. Their bodies yielded to each other. His big form pressed into her. Being trapped between the wall and the gentleman-devil was the most arousing experience she'd ever had.

The air was thick with their desire and the need to know each other with this intimacy. Darkness wasn't scary. It bore his scent that filled her, his tenderness that saturated it. It drowned with her soft whimpers that he caught with his lips and licked with his tongue. It whispered with the sounds of their garments brushing against each other as they gently pulled and grabbed and tried to find the curves through the fabric that took too much room between them.

If this was darkness, Alina didn't need light. If Harlan Krow was the devil, she wanted a lifetime of hell.

Blood simmered under her skin. Her entire body rose to the awareness of his arms around her, pressing her closer. She was breathless but kissed him as if his mouth were the only source of air. The one kiss turned into many that were love-making on their own.

They lost track of time, neither wanting to leave the darkness, pausing the kisses only to drown in the pleasure of each other's touch, coming back for more.

Did the devil ever lose himself in a woman?

She didn't know, for *she* was lost, the heat of his tongue swirling through her body, circling her heart, then going lower to her belly and lower still, between her legs, to the core that felt ablaze.

All she was aware of was him. There was no Phantom Ball. No guests of all classes as long as they could afford it, mingling in costumes and masks. No music that dissipated in the air with the smell of wine. No distant laughter and exclamations as the guests cheered for yet another performance.

Alina didn't need that. She'd come here for him. She knew it, and so did he.

And now he was all around her. His hands pulled her closer. His lips brushed gently against her cheek in feather-like kisses.

"I don't want to ever let you go," he whispered.

His scent—leather, and rain, and fire pits—took her away from the false splendor of the English ton.

There was only one thing missing—his face.

They drifted apart slowly, without words, their hands giving each other the last caresses, fingers intertwining, then sliding up to each other's faces to find more bare skin.

And just as slowly, they pulled away. In the darkness, she felt him glide her gloves back onto her hands. He shifted to put his mask back on.

Oh, that wretched disguise!

In that moment, she wanted to see his face like never before. And when he led her by her hand out into the hall, she cursed the light that pulled them apart again.

She wished they hadn't left the dark alcove.

But more than that, she wished she could see his eyes.

## 20

## THE KISS

That kiss, Father, said everything. That my angel wanted me. That her heart resonated with mine.

Mine beat for her like a mad horse galloping in an unknown direction. The world was suddenly brighter, and I'd never liked the light.

Until her.

What we had at the Phantom Ball, in the darkness behind the curtains, lasted for less than an hour but seemed like a gap that separated what I was before and what I would become.

She wanted to leave the ball then. I didn't stop her. And as we made our way among the costumes and masks and laughter and explicit caresses, I kept watching her face, hidden by the mask.

Her lips were pressed tightly together as if in regret. And mine tingled with her taste. How her lips had trembled under mine! How soft they had been seeking out my kisses! How her tongue had quivered the first time it touched mine!

Her lips were chapped from the cold. I wanted to kiss them, soothe them, soak them with my moisture. They begged to be healed. The image of them would scorch me for nights and nights to come. The one thing I got to find out, Father, was that a man could withstand bodily tortures—that sort of pain went away. But the ache for the lover that one couldn't have could make one go mad.

She didn't look at me until we were outside and I was helping her into her carriage. That monstrous footman of hers was watching me like a hawk, but I paid no attention to him.

"You shall get home safely," I said to her. I wanted to ride with her. But I couldn't. Not yet. I could ruin it. My desire made my blood boil and my sex throb with need. The animal in me threatened to throw away any sense of propriety and push her too far.

I stood by the carriage door and watched her adjust her cape—slowly, as if she were lost in her thoughts. She brought her hands to the back of her head and untied the mask, passing it to me.

Masks and disguises were my domain. My angel knew that too.

For the first time since the kiss, she raised her eyes to me.

I wish I were a brute, a sickened madman, so that I could kidnap her and keep her to myself for the rest of my life. In that moment, I wanted to pull her closer, take her face between my palms, and kiss her a hundred more times until she lost her mind and agreed to flee with me.

My angel was braver than me.

I couldn't shed my mask yet. Couldn't look at her and tell her what sort of man I was.

So she gazed at me, understanding, burning me with reproach, open in her acknowledgment of who I was. Her eyes sparkled as if in fever, lips unusually bright, the color of a ripe peach. Several auburn strands fell on the side of her face. She looked like a woman seduced by a lover.

*My* woman.

"I shall see you soon," she said.

And though I was the one who sought her out every time, her words were the sweetest promise.

"I wish I could say goodnight a thousand times. Until morning came," I said, hating the sound of my voice, intentionally lower, duller from behind the mask. "Then I would know you stayed with me until the next day and was with me again."

She smiled weakly. "And I still wouldn't see your face, would I?"

I followed the carriage on foot until it disappeared down the road into the dark. I walked for some time along the country road, my own carriage following me like a stray dog. I wanted to be outside. As if open air could bring me closer to her. My skin was icy cold, but my heart was ablaze. I'd never felt so alive. Being buried in my anger for years, only feeling a jolt of excitement when the monsters died at my hand, the feelings that were starting inside me spilled over, soaked my hardened heart, and filled every pore with ecstasy.

How do they describe resurrection in your scripture, Father?

Alina was life that suddenly rushed through my veins.

I made my way to my flat, surrounded by iron gates, hiding the secrets behind them.

In my empty bedroom that echoed with guilt and the monsters of the past, I stood in front of the mirror and studied the bitter smirk, the solemn face, the eyes that, for the first time, blazed with something new—hope.

My body was used to torments and pain, wounds and injuries, harsh weather and sleepless nights, fits of guilt and tremors of panic. But now it tingled with the sweetest memory of her kiss.

I closed my eyes, Father. I brought back that moment. The

countess in my arms. Her lips on mine. Her warm breath against my face. Her moans that I drank like the sweetest wine.

I hadn't had a woman in a long time. Despite the rumors about the gentleman-devil—conjured, no doubt, by the women in love with the ghost—I'd forgotten a woman's touch.

Hers was a revelation. My body burned with that long-forgotten tension, sweet and painful, seeking release. I wondered what it would feel like to be inside her, taking her as per my needs. I wondered what life could be like to have a woman like this by my side.

Dreams can be dangerous.

Did you ever think that the taste of a woman could change the world, Father? One world. Mine. It turned my life around. One single kiss, Father, and everything that happened afterward was changed forever.

In the course of events, it changed how one brutal crime would be committed.

Now that I think of it, it changed London.

The kiss of the countess changed the entire city...

## 21

# CONSPIRACY

P raises to God echoed through the Kamenevs' house in English, French, and Russian. They belonged to Anna Yakovlevna, who, with a look of utmost amusement, fanned herself with a perfumed card, then hungrily studied it again.

"A dinner at the Duke of Ravenaugh's mansion. Oh, Lord! Finally he heard my prayers!"

Nikolai Sergeevich peeled his eyes off the Gazette to meet Alina's gaze across the sitting-room.

She cocked an eyebrow and conjured the most bored expression as she sat in her armchair and feigned a yawn.

Her father lowered his eyes to the Gazette and straightened it with a slight jerk. "There is this genius, Mr. Anyos Jedlic," he said slowly, reading from the newspaper and ignoring his wife. "He showed this electric machine to the gentlemen at the Royal Society. It moves. A new sort of vehicle, they say."

"Anything goes these days," murmured the maid, who walked in with a tea tray.

"They say soon we might ride around in carriages with no horses," Nikolai Sergeevich added.

"Truly! Nikolai!" Anna Yakovlevna stomped her foot and

glared at him. "What can be more exciting now than an invitation from the duke himself? Your daughter might have enamored the most wanted bachelor in this city, and you are talking about witchcraft!"

"It's science, dear."

"And you!" Anna Yakovlevna turned to Alina, who right away put on the most obedient face. "You should be reeling with glee! But no! Just like your father!" She flung herself on the sofa next to her husband, but her irritated expression was right away replaced with a satisfied smile.

"You shall wear the best furs," Anna Yakovlevna said, dreamily studying the ceiling. "The best jewelry. And you shall take Yegór. Martha too, since your parents were not invited."

"I am a widow, Mamá, not a débutante."

But her mother didn't listen, already planning in her mind the wedding, the children, a mansion in the country, and the entire ton bowing to them.

"It is awfully quiet today," Anna Yakovlevna said after a moment, straightening up and cocking her head in confusion. "I don't like it. And I can't quite figure out what it is."

Alina smiled. "Yegór, Dunya, and Prosha went to Welbeck Street."

"Marylebone? Whatever for?"

"Tsk. To church."

"On a Tuesday?"

"Yes, early this morning. It is *Pokrov*."

"Oh!" Anna Yakovlevna gaped, surprised at her forgetfulness.

The feast of the Mother of God was the biggest Orthodox holiday. Prosha had cooked day and night. And the evening would be quiet as the servants would go to Whitechapel for a celebration among the Slavs.

But Alina didn't feel like celebrating.

Nikolai Sergeevich snorted from behind the newspaper. "One day you want to throw them out, and when they are gone, you miss them."

Anna Yakovlevna only waved him away. "You should've gone, Alina. Should've put a candle for a good marriage."

Dunya would no doubt put one for herself. That was a tradition on *Pokrov* for the young unmarried girls to pray for a good suitor.

"It's for young girls, Mamá," Alina argued.

"You are young, *ma chérie*."

"And a widow." Alina exchanged knowing glances with her father and suppressed a chuckle.

Anna Yakovlevna didn't give up. "The duke is fond of you."

Alina threw her head back against the chair back and exhaled in annoyance. "There is no indication of that."

"*Mon Dieu*, you are naive!" Her mother rolled her eyes. "He stared at you at dinner. You said so yourself."

"Nonsense. It was curiosity."

"Oh, sure. A man doesn't look this way at a woman unless she captivates him. You wouldn't have brought it up if it weren't significant."

Alina felt the blush color her cheeks. She wished she hadn't told her mother anything. But then, Anna Yakovlevna would have pried it out of her with a pair of pliers. Good thing Alina hadn't mentioned the incident. It was peculiar that only she and the duke knew about it. A secret between them. She smiled at the memory, then reproached herself.

"This is all very annoying, to be honest," said Alina finally.

"Oh! And working with the paupers is not?"

"I am talking about Lady Whitshorn and her invitation for an afternoon of shopping. It is the third such invitation. I am certain something is up."

"*Ma chérie*, it is all part of the game."

"It's a conspiracy," Alina argued.

"Well, you have to play along. Because when you don't…"

Anna Yakovlevna didn't finish, but Alina's father looked at Alina above the Gazette, and his gaze wasn't cheerful anymore.

*Right.*

*If you don't, you get a bullet.*

And just like that, Alina's mood was ruined.

Piccadilly was gray. Fog hung in the air, painting everything ashy colors. Rain had turned the mud into slush that now clung to shoes and the hems of dresses and coats.

"*Merde*," blurted out Lady Whitshorn when the carriage that drove too close to them splattered the bottom of her dress with mud.

Alina grinned. "Shit" wasn't exactly common in the ton's vocabulary. Lady Whitshorn was always frivolous with her language. That was one of many reasons why Anna Yakovlevna wasn't fond of the French countess who'd married an English earl twelve years ago. In her late thirties and child-less, Lady Whitshorn was certainly most entertaining and free-spirited.

Everyone seemed to be paying too much attention to Alina lately. You didn't have to be a fortune-teller to know that it had something to do with the duke and the viscount.

"Theo Van Buren seems quite interested in you," Lady Whitshorn said as they passed yet another shop Alina was hoping to go in to escape the cold wind.

*A-ha! The real reason for the meeting.*

"He's been inquiring about you." Lady Whitshorn leaned

over to Alina as if about to spill a secret. "That is inside information."

"He is on the hunt," Alina said, trying to suppress a smile until Lady Whitshorn burst out in laughter, making Alina grin openly.

The woman wrapped her gloved hand around Alina's arm. "That could be true if his friend, Samuel Cassell, wasn't asking questions too. And the duke *never* asks questions." Lady Whitshorn gave Alina a meaningful stare, but Alina suppressed the curiosity to ask about the nature of the questions. "You were at a dinner party at Lady Amstel's."

Every step she took in this city turned into an instant rumor. Alina only nodded.

"Anything of interest happened at that party to spike their curiosity?" Lady Whitshorn pressed on.

"No," Alina answered with as much indifference as she could master. "It must be the lack of prey in the city since many left for the country after the Season."

Lady Whitshorn burst in another fit of laughter and shook her head. "Lady Bronskaya, your straight-forwardness is most refreshing. Though you are very wrong. I've been around for some time and can tell you with certainty that when those two take notice, you should be careful. Or hopeful."

"Hopeful!" Alina snorted exaggeratedly.

"Tell me something. Were you invited to the duke's dinner tomorrow?"

Alina felt annoyed. Everyone knew everything in this damn city. "Yes," she replied reluctantly.

Lady Whitshorn nodded. "Of course."

They walked in silence for some time.

"I assumed you weren't a public person, Lady Bronskaya," said Lady Whitshorn as they casually strolled down Piccadilly.

"What makes you say so?"

"Oh, well, I suppose we have never attended many parties together. Next thing you know, you are at Lady Amstel's dinner. And now, the duke's. Do you see where I am going with this?"

Wherever this was going, shopping was definitely not it.

Alina stopped for a moment to watch a street boy play the harmonica, hoping that would silence Lady Whitshorn for some time. She fished a coin out of her reticule and gave it to him, and he grinned and bowed theatrically and followed her for ten or so feet, playing for her.

"Even children are mesmerized by you." Lady Whitshorn rolled her eyes theatrically.

Alina laughed. "This city is full of pretty ladies."

"Not like you. Yours is Slavic beauty. It has a certain charm. Men used to pile up at your door."

"No they didn't." Alina snorted.

"Oh, they did. Until the rumors made it clear that you weren't interested in marriage. Or men."

"Or that my dowry is an army of savage servants."

Lady Whitshorn chuckled. "Well, they surely still talk about you."

Alina inhaled deeply. She was tired of this talk. In fact, what she should do was politely decline the duke's invitation and stop all the discussions at once.

"Ma'am." A voice turned them around as a little boy stood holding a bouquet of red roses out to Alina.

"Oh!" Lady Whitshorn halted.

"What is this?" Alina stared in surprise as she accepted the flowers.

The boy bowed. "The gentleman paid me to give them to you."

"What gentleman?" Alina's heart thudded in excitement.

"There!" The boy turned to stab the finger at someone in

the distance, only for his hand to fall at his side. "Oh, he was right there just a moment ago. Good day, ma'am."

The boy sprinted away, leaving Alina dumbfounded and Lady Whitshorn with a cocked eyebrow.

"Fresh flowers in October…" Lady Whitshorn murmured with a cunning smile. "There are no flower shops on Piccadilly within ten blocks of here. And the flower girls don't work the streets this late in the season. You have admirers, Lady Bronskaya. Ingenious ones and"—she winked with a smile—"wealthy."

But as they kept walking, Alina kept searching for something—someone. She tried to hold back her smile and calm her racing heart that knew that *he* was somewhere in the crowd.

That night, Alina let Martha help her out of her clothes.

"You don't seem happy," Alina said, letting the maid brush her hair.

Martha's lips tightened into a line.

"So?" Alina watched her reflection in the mirror.

"That *krasavets*," the maid said, her gaze darkening. "He is twisting my guts every time he does something. It's as if he does things on purpose to anger me. Are Russian men all like this? Stubborn?"

Alina almost choked on suppressed laughter.

"What did you call him?"

"*Krasavets?*" Martha halted, meeting her gaze in the mirror and pursing her lips proudly at having learned a new word.

Alina had heard her perfectly well the first time. "Handsome" was the meaning of the word, so out of place coming out of Martha's mouth.

"Where did you hear that word?" Alina mused.

"I asked Yegór how to say *fool* in Russian."

Alina burst out in laughter.

"Forgive me, my lady." The maid's hands fell at her side. "But he is, is he not? So silly and such a brute."

*Handsome.*

Oh, the scoundrel!

Alina giggled, and Martha smiled, resuming brushing Alina's hair. "You don't mind if I call him that, my lady, do you?"

Alina grinned. "Oh, no! Keep calling him that!"

She let the maid go and took one of Harlan's letters out of the drawer.

It had taken all her willpower not to think of him in the last several days.

After the Phantom Ball.

After the kiss.

She went about her daily routine, but a simple walk with Lady Whitshorn ended up with flowers, and she knew who they'd come from. She listened to her mother's monotonous complaints, observed Martha and Yegór's Wars of the Roses, but all of it was done with almost forced attention. For when she didn't force herself, she thought of Harlan.

It scared her. It entranced her. It filled her with guilty happiness.

Around her family and friends, she felt like a criminal. But when she was alone, in her bed, conjuring images of him, she felt like a lover.

She couldn't tell precisely when her attitude toward him had changed. When her curiosity had grown into longing. When the fast beating of her heart had turned into butterflies in her stomach. When the anticipation of seeing him had become a pool of heat between her thighs at the closeness of him.

It had started before the kiss.

And then the kiss had unleashed the secret desires that had stayed bottled up in her for days.

The thoughts about him had turned into the late-night fantasies so scandalous they soaked her drawers and sheets and made her fingers restless against her throbbing sex.

Just like now.

Alina undressed completely, tossing aside the chemise and the drawers, and lay in bed naked, feeling aroused at the touch of linen against her bare body.

One of Harlan's letters was in her hands, and she reread it again and again, clinging to every word for meaning that might not have been there.

*Angel.*

She could hear his whisper as he said it.

*You bewitched me.*

The memory of his kiss made heat coil inside her. It spread through her body and simmered between her thighs.

She flung onto her back and pushed the blanket off, letting the cool air graze her nakedness. She closed her eyes and pressed his letter to her bare breasts. And as the memories of him slowly seeped into her mind, her hand started moving.

Holding the corner of the page, Alina moved it side to side, feeling the paper graze her hardened nipples. It caressed her in the most sensual way. His writing was so close to her skin. The paper he'd touched brushed against her breasts. She wished it were his hands instead. In her mind, they were, stroking her nipples as she arched her back to push them into the paper.

He'd touched this letter. He'd thought of her when he'd written it. There was a trace of him on it that now made her skin hum. Her hand shifted downward, between her legs that opened for the sensual invasion. Her fingers slid into her drenched folds and stroked with increasing intensity at the thought of him.

"Harlan," she whispered as if his name were a spell that would bring her sweet release. She arched her back, stroking herself, the letter grazing her hardened peaks, until she reached her climax, her mouth open in a silent moan as she pressed his handwriting to her heaving chest.

# THE INSIDE INFORMATION

A *ghostly palace.*

That was the impression Alina had when she stepped into the duke's mansion just outside London.

It didn't lack furniture or decoration—portraits on every wall, statues and antiques in every corner, mahogany and gold, marble and embroidered draperies. It was the vastness of the main hall and the emptiness of it despite the proper furnishings. The echo of footsteps against the granite mosaic floor. The stillness of the air. The silence with which the valets moved. The stone face of the elderly butler.

The place felt abandoned.

Occasional sounds echoed off the gilded walls. A giant chandelier the size of a carriage hung from the ceiling, but its lights shone with loneliness.

The host himself was serious yet graceful. A black jacket and matching trousers, a black shirt underneath the dark-blue waistcoat embroidered with gold. Amethyst buttons and gold chains across. Samuel Cassell emanated style and wealth, from his gold-threaded cravat down to his shoes, polished to a mirror shine. His black hair was slicked back perfectly as if it were made of wax. And his cologne—so exquisite and subtle, Alina felt like leaning over to get enough of his scent.

*Stop.*

"I am honored to have you here, Lady Bronskaya," the duke said, kissing her hand, and took it upon himself to take her sable coat and hat, his gaze on her the entire time. Haunted. Guarded. Piercing.

*I shouldn't have come*, she thought then.

Why had she?

But she couldn't stop thinking of the episode at Lady Amstel's. His quiet tone. His sharp movements when he'd pinned Whadham against the terrace railing. The danger in his eyes when he hissed something into his ear, the man's expression suddenly so cowardly.

Beneath the silk and manners of a true gentleman there lurked danger. She was curious.

As the duke led Alina into the sitting room, Lady Whitshorn gracefully glided toward her. She wore a sable shawl.

*Imagine that.*

Suddenly, all of London fancied furs.

"Lady Bronskaya, oh, dear, how do you always look so stunning?"

The lady's smile was so forced that Alina expected a forked tongue to poke out of the woman's brightly rouged lips. It said, "I told you so." As if Alina had a secret with the duke, and Lady Whitshorn was in on it.

"So, what do you think, dear?" the woman asked discreetly and with a playful smile. "Which one had the idea to invite you here. Cassell or Van Buren?"

Her smile was so cunning that Alina couldn't stifle a short laughter and covered her lips with her fingers.

"If there are any advances to come, Lady Bronskaya, I should like to be the first one to know."

Alina once again held back from rolling her eyes and gazed around.

Prying glances. Hushed whispers.

An older lady with sharp features and a contemptuous mouth narrowed her eyes on Alina's dark-brown dress with a modest neckline, the bodice threaded with golden stripes. Her gaze slid to Alina's garnet pendant the size of a plum and adorned with gold.

There were only ten guests.

The woman with the prying gaze turned out to be the wife of the commander of the Metropolitan Police. Her husband, Mr. Brootward, was a tall heavy man with eyebrows as thick as Yegór's and sideburns that could hide a dozen sins.

There was Sir William Nercer, the Lord Mayor of London.

Gray-haired Mrs. Rogerson-Frank, dressed head to toe in black and rings on every finger, hadn't yet uttered a single word.

This was an unusual gathering. What was Alina doing here? And Lady Whitshorn?

Van Buren, of course, was present. Alina stiffened as he approached.

"Lady Bronskaya, we meet quite often these days. And it is most delightful," he said with his usual prolonged gaze that made her too self-aware.

The viscount and the duke—there was a secret among those two, and she wondered what it was. They were almost like brothers, down to their meticulous looks and matching hairstyles and the mysterious glances they exchanged from time to time. But there weren't a pair more different.

Alina stayed close to Lady Whitshorn. The Frenchwoman could cushion a harsh joke and weasel out of a tricky conversation. Alina felt like the duke—taking the backstage and letting her friend by her side talk. She definitely was more comfortable observing.

The dinner was in the best English fashion. However many cooks the duke had—for the household of one—they had done a great job of ten courses. Roasted duck and mutton stew with oranges, truffles and pates, baked oysters and veal tongue. One of the chefs was French, and Lady Whitshorn paid a genuine compliment, which was certainly unlike her.

The wine was splendid, the brandy of the best kind but nothing compared to the liquors Prosha conjured.

Mrs. Brootward was too talkative. Mrs. Rogerson-Frank still hadn't spoken. The Lord Mayor was focused mostly on food. The commander constantly wiped his forehead with a napkin and drank more than he ate.

Alina was the youngest guest and wondered why there wasn't a single lady younger than thirty at dinner. Except for her. If either the viscount or the duke was looking for a match, there would certainly be someone besides her.

*Right.*

The realization again made her uneasy. She would have preferred to stay quiet all night, but the topic turned to a discussion of Russia.

Ah, how appropriate with her being here!

"No offense, Lady Bronskaya. This topic might get sensitive." Sir William smiled coldly without looking at her. "The hostility toward your nation is not toward the people. You understand."

*Lies.*

Van Buren interfered before Alina could reply. "There, of course, should always be a distinction between a nation's government and its people. But it's often hard to remember that, taking into account that people are the government's weapon and manpower."

Alina nodded. If Van Buren kept talking like this, she might start to like him.

"We are not hostile toward Russia," Van Buren continued, turning to smile at Alina, then back to Sir William. "We are simply intimidated by its military power. So is the rest of the world. There is savageness in the way they use it. In the way they are mute to brutality and hardship. Napoleon said just that after losing in 1812. Thousands of his soldiers died in the brutal winter before getting a chance to raise their weapons."

"Hmm." Mr. Brootward only shrugged and took a gulp of brandy.

"I'll beg different," contradicted Sir William. "I agree with Lord Tennison. He said that we, the British, can't put up with a regime founded on whips."

The loud laughter that followed belonged to Van Buren, who swayed a glass in his hand too leisurely. The duke smiled, gazing at him.

"Spare me, Sir William," Van Buren said cockily. "What was it that the British used to conquer a quarter of the world? Not whips, no. Ah! Extermination and enslavement. Right."

Alina was truly getting to like him now.

The Lord Mayor sucked his teeth but didn't answer.

Van Buren craned his neck to look at him along the table as if waiting for a reply. "And I dare say, we set a great example to individuals who then do exactly the same—announce their own laws."

"Who are…?" Sir William raised his disapproving gaze at the viscount.

Van Buren smiled and narrowed his mischievous eyes on Alina. "His grace and I were discussing a curious topic earlier today." Van Buren tossed a napkin onto the table and leaned back in his chair, a brandy glass lazily dangling between his thumb and middle finger.

The guests dropped their utensils as if it was a cue to pay attention. It was astounding and irritating how Van Buren asserted himself with others. But Alina couldn't help admiring his brazenness and quite brave ideas. She cocked her head and stared at him with interest.

"We were talking about a certain character that has made quite some noise in London in the past years," Van Buren said, tonguing his cheek.

"Charles Dickens?"

"Isambard Brunel?"

"Disraeli?"

The suggestions were blurted out with laughter as if it were a game until Van Buren produced a sinister chuckle and said, "Harlan Krow."

The table went silent.

"What is it?" He looked around with mocking surprise. "He is undoubtedly the most talked about person. That is, both in the West *and* East End."

"Are we discussing criminals now?" Mr. Brootward growled.

"We are discussing self-accommodating justice. And social issues. And yes, crime, too." Van Buren looked too proud of himself.

"Someone is writing a book about him, I heard," Mrs. Brootward said out of tune. "It should be a satire."

Alina felt her blood boil. She produced a cold smile, intentionally narrowing her eyes at the commander's wife. "A satire on poverty or the justice system, Mrs. Brootward?"

Anna Yakovlevna would have decapitated Alina right here and now.

Mrs. Brootward smiled but didn't answer. And the Lord Mayor narrowed his eyes at Alina.

Lady Whitshorn answered instead. "There *should* be

books about him. After all, the mind of a criminal, or a villain—whatever you might want to call him—is mysterious. The fascination with him in the East End is understandable and is growing exponentially. And the issues he brings to the table such as this"—she produced a mischievous yet obviously ironic laughter—"are something not to be overlooked."

"Lady Whitshorn"—Van Buren cocked his head at her with an approving smile—"I always knew I was fond of you for a reason."

She pressed her hand to her bosom with feigned gratitude.

"He is a man with a sick mind," said Mr. Brootward, his every word an irritated spit. "He conjures some"—his head shook in an attempt to choose the proper words—"sick acts of revenge. Makes them public." The brandy glass shook angrily in his hand as he spoke. "And makes the masses cheer to his gory display of so-called justice."

"You call him sick?" Van Buren cocked an eyebrow. "Surely, it would require close friendship to know the true mind of a person."

The duke's voice startled Alina. "We all have dark thoughts from time to time, do we not, Mr. Brootward?"

The duke spoke, and the table suddenly got quiet.

Sir William cocked an eyebrow and leaned back in his chair, studying Cassell with interest.

So did Alina.

Mr. Brootward didn't give up. "Just because one has a sick mind doesn't mean one needs to let it be public knowledge." He chuckled nervously and somehow cowardly.

The duke's face looked indifferent, save for a tiny smile that curled the corner of his lips. "The most beautiful and atrocious things happen in our minds. This"—he tapped his temple with his forefinger—"is where it all starts." His speech was slow, every word weighed. "Grand plans. Dreams. Fantasies."

"Oh!" Van Buren wiggled his eyebrows. "Go on, Your Grace, please. What fantasies possess you?"

The way he addressed him was so informal that Alina wished she could listen to the two men when they were alone, chatting freely and not with this well-polished pretense.

"Acts of brutal revenge," the duke added, drawing Alina to look at him with interest.

"Indeed…" Sir William nodded in agreement.

"Those who dare to bring them to life are brave outliers." The duke looked at the Lord Mayor almost as if challenging him to a word duel.

Mesmerized, Alina gazed at Cassell. This was the rare moment when the duke spoke at length. His face seemed to change sightly from an indifferent mask to that of deep intelligence. Hearing his voice made Alina's heart flutter.

"Well," the commander said, smirking into his glass of brandy, "calling Harlan Krow brave would be too generous. The man deserves prison. Or hanging."

Van Buren clicked his tongue. "Ask the poor. They beg different." He took a tasteful sip of brandy and hitched his arm over the chair back in the most informal manner. This was a peculiar stand-off of opinions, or a game—whichever one, Alina wasn't sure, but her father would definitely be entertained hearing about it.

"Are you playing devil's advocate, my lord?" Mr. Brootward narrowed his eyes on Van Buren.

Van Buren shrugged. "Feuerbach said, 'I would rather be a devil in alliance with the truth than an angel in alliance with the falsehood.' Harlan Krow did serve justice, did he not? The men were guilty but were never punished."

"And you, Your Grace?" The commander's eyes shifted to

the duke. "Surely you can't see anything noble in the way that scoundrel disposes of influential men."

"Of the men who escaped the law, you mean?" the duke asked, arching an eyebrow at Mr. Brootward.

*Bravo*, Alina cheered inwardly.

The commander glared at him, his lips pressed in a thin line.

The duke tapped his finger on the table as if taking his time to think. "I think the words villain and hero can be interchangeable at times. So can villain and criminal." He raised his eyes slowly at the man. "As to Harlan Krow, I pity him. He is a man sunken to the condition of a brute. He lives in darkness. Only a tragic past can set a man on such dark path."

*Pity? How dare he!*

Alina felt hurt by the words and suddenly protective of the man she knew. She was the only person at this table who knew the villain. Perhaps, the only one in the city! She couldn't stay quiet.

"Many things can," she said, speaking for the first time and already knowing this was a mistake. "A sense of compassion, for one. This is certainly something the privileged lack."

Van Buren turned to give her a lop-sided smile. "Women have a different idea of Harlan Krow. They love dark injured men. Do they not, Lady Bronskaya? Cheers!" He nodded and toasted to her in the air.

She avoided taking part in discussions for the remainder of the dinner. There were enough rumors. Those people meant nothing to her. Her opinion was surely an unpopular one.

Yet something about the duke drew her in. His words. His manner of speaking. She wished he talked more, but Van Buren seemed to talk for both of them. She observed Samuel Cassell with a sense of intrigue that was irrational. He grinned at one of Van Buren's jokes, and Alina froze. It was as if the sun had shone down on him. His demeanor changed. His gaze acquired a soft kindness that startled her.

And then he caught her staring at him.

Her amusement faded, flooded by sudden nervousness.

Oh, Lord, what was with the anxiety?

Men of power could be intimidating, sure. But she'd always considered the duke utterly boring. And that was changing, though she couldn't pinpoint when this change had started.

After dinner, the men retired to the cigar room while the women stayed in the music room. That was always the time when Alina wanted to leave the parties. And when Mrs. Brootward started plucking away on the piano, Alina discreetly walked out of the music room and strolled down the hall.

She was, perhaps, intruding, walking around the duke's house alone, but she was curious. There was much more to the Duke of Ravenaugh, she was sure, and she felt like a spy, walking the empty hall that echoed with the sounds of piano and occasional laughter from the cigar room.

She was at the end of the hallway that led toward the servants' quarters when she heard muffled voices from one of the parlors.

She would have kept walking. It was only appropriate.

She would have.

If the familiar name hadn't echoed from that room and stopped her in her tracks.

Harlan Krow.

There was a discussion of him, and she only wanted to hear part of it, just to know one more thing that others thought of him.

Quietly, like a thief, she walked up to the half-open doors of the parlor that shone a bright slice of light into the otherwise dim hall.

"The city will be at war soon," Sir William's voice hissed from the room. "His acts are bloody, but they don't scare the poor. They cheer for him!"

There came the sound of muffled footsteps and grunting— there was another person in the room.

"His retribution has stopped for now. There hasn't been anything for months. But there is something bigger simmering down in those quarters. Much. Bigger." Sir William's voice got more sinister. "And it's coming from there, from the bottom. Like the stench of the cesspools that threaten to spill over."

Alina cheered inwardly. So the conversation at dinner had bothered the Lord Mayor.

*Good.*

"Do you think tomorrow's arrangement is going to be a success?" The submissive voice belonged to the commander.

"We have to eradicate him."

Alina's heart thudded with unease.

"It's all in the slums," the commander agreed.

"It always starts from the bottom. And then there is no stopping it."

"He is a murderer. Yes."

"That's not what they say down there."

"We've pinned every possible crime on him!"

"Oh, but people know the difference. They always do. Those filthy rodents down there."

Anger stirred in Alina's blood and pounded in her ears. Anxiety spiked in her at the words that meant the Metropolitan Police was preparing a ride of sorts. She held her breath as she stood behind the doors, trying to catch every word.

"It can't go to the press," Sir William said quieter. "You understand? Those reporters who snoop around singing praises and starting conversations of the most inconvenient sort—they can't mention that. The Gazette shall get the official version. Independent press—send people to all of them, making sure they get the official version as early as midnight before they print the next day's news. If anything leaks—we were executing a cleaning."

"What cleaning?"

"Figure out what bloody cleaning!" the Lord Mayor snapped.

Alina almost jumped at the sudden loudness and started backing up, her entire body trembling at the words she'd heard.

A cleaning.

In the slums.

In search of Harlan Krow.

Her thoughts spun loudly as she turned to flee and ran right into the duke, his hands catching her by her shoulders.

"Your Grace." She gasped in shock and stepped away.

Embarrassed, she looked around as if something could explain why she stood by the half-open doors eavesdropping.

The duke studied her with interest. How he'd come so close to her without her noticing was puzzling.

"I am … I was…" Alina exhaled in frustration. "Forgive me. I got lost in your palace." She chuckled too theatrically and hated herself for this.

"Anything of importance?" He motioned with his eyes toward the parlor, and his lips hitched in a smile.

Was he being clever?

Alina took a step away, then another, slowly luring him away from the door.

"Politics, I suppose." She chuckled.

"And you are interested in politics, Lady Bronskaya?" He followed her.

Her heart was still pounding. "No. No. It's just…"

She didn't know what to say or how to excuse herself, tried to walk faster, but the duke seemed to walk slowly on purpose, his eyes never leaving her.

"Yes?"

"They were talking about some operation in the slums. I was passing by and got curious. And... I know, I know, that was utterly impolite of me. But I find conversations like those much more enlightening than Mrs. Brootward's singing."

The duke chuckled, and she felt relieved.

*Good.*

So this awkward little incident was over.

And then sudden awareness gripped her—the two of them walking down the hall, not a servant in sight, alone, again, in less than proper circumstances.

*Oh, Lord.*

Her mother would have found this story highly promising, no doubt.

The duke turned to look at Alina, and she looked up to meet his eyes and pulled the most charming smile.

"The men were probably discussing the manhunt in the East End," the duke said.

The return to the topic was so unexpected it wiped the smile off Alina's face.

"A manhunt?" She frowned.

She paused as they reached the main hall, wanting to hear more.

He nodded. Tall, handsome, his hands clasped behind his back—the expression on his face was that of utmost indifference. He turned slowly to face her. "There is inside information that the man will be at a factory gathering in the East End," the duke said.

Alina gaped, then turned away to hide her nervousness. Her heart started pounding with new force.

"At the factory gathering?" she repeated. "How would anyone know that? About a man who might not even exist."

"Oh, he exists all right." The duke chuckled.

She felt suddenly angry and raised her eyes at him. "And where is that meeting?" She was openly prying and didn't care.

"At the cross of Camlet and Old Nichol." He chuckled again and looked amused. "You don't need to worry about Old Nichol or criminals, Lady Bronskaya. People there play their own games."

She frowned at the words. "Do you find it funny?" she asked, cocking her head and staring at the duke, whose smile subsided. "Do you think there is something amusing in the fact that our justice system can't take care of crimes in the less fortunate quarters? That they leave it to a man who becomes so popular that they venerate his atrocious justice with a statue?" Her entire body trembled with anger as she spoke. She should stop. *Stop.* But there was no taming the feeling of hurt that festered in her heart. "Yes, Your Grace. There is a statue dedicated to the people who were harmed by those who *he* eradicated. And you laugh, thinking there is something funny in the fact that our glorious police don't care about the crimes in the East End but will send a hundred men to hunt down the one person who does."

A lump in her throat made her voice croak.

She should have stopped…

*Too late.*

The duke wasn't smiling anymore. His gaze was blazing now, shooting her confidence down.

*Oh, God.*

She'd embarrassed herself.

Alina looked around to make sure no one had heard, but it was only the duke and she in the empty main hall.

"Forgive me, Your Grace," she said quieter, casting her gaze down. "I was out of line, I suppose. I should go, really. I should… Yes. I'll leave." She started walking away when she heard his soft voice behind her.

"Lady Bronskaya."

She turned to meet his gaze.

"I am not amused by what is going on," he said with a sharp edge to his voice that was new to her. "I hope tomorrow proves that our justice system fails terribly and needs change."

She shivered at the words, held his gaze for longer than appropriate, unexplainable feelings colliding in her and making her regret she'd come here at all.

Without saying anything, or saying farewells, or looking back, she walked hurriedly toward the entrance, knowing that her abrupt departure would cause even more rumors.

But she didn't care.

She needed to warn Harlan.

## 23

## THE MANHUNT

I t snowed the next day.

The first snow lay thin like paper, concealing the mud. Another hour and it would turn into slush.

Alina wanted a lot of snow. It hid all the ugliness and the sins that festered in this city. But then the poor would then need better coats and shoes and coal to keep their hearths warm. You couldn't have the best of two worlds. Life simply was one or another.

Such were Alina's thoughts as she stared out the window, then moved to the piano, played some sad tune, then tried to read only to restlessly toss the book aside.

It was early afternoon when Alina gave up on trying to be calm. The night before, after returning from the duke's, she'd sent Yegór to St Rose's with a note for Harlan. But what were the chances he would get it on time?

Something had to be done, for Alina felt helpless. She changed into a dark gray dress, simple Hudson Bay seal coat and matching hat, and walked out into the hall.

"Yegór! We are leaving!" she called out, letting Martha fix the hem of her skirts.

The footman walked out into the hall wearing a thick sheepskin coat over his massive shoulders.

This wasn't the day for St Rose's, nor did Alina need her footman, but all the way to Dr. Grevatt's, she tapped her foot on the floor of the carriage with unease, kept jerking the curtain back and forth, looking for signs of trouble from the outside.

Had he gotten the letter?

There would be no indication of any turmoil here, in the West End, or in Central London. Yet she kept glancing outside.

The always warming and familiar study at Dr. Grevatt's was too quiet and irritating today. She tried to narrate pages to Rumi but didn't get past one page, realizing now and then she'd been staring out the window too often. It was already dark, and the glass now reflected her silhouette. The candles were lit, though she didn't remember the maid coming in.

"What is it, Miss Alina?" Rumi asked softly and put the paper and the quill aside. "I don't suppose we will accomplish much today. Would you like to go to St Rose's?"

The question was odd. Rumi's glances were too inquiring as if she knew something.

Alina realized she was walking back and forth in front of the desk lost in her thoughts.

*Harlan. Harlan. Harlan.*

His image flickered in her mind with ever-growing insistence. As if the memories of him were synced with the falling darkness outside.

*A manhunt.*

Dread creeped inside her, making her movements frantic, her hands restless as she grabbed the stack of papers on the desk, then put them down and tried to straighten the books.

Rumi crossed her arms over her chest and cocked her head in amusement as she observed Alina from behind the desk. A smile was spreading on her lips—too knowing and making Alina fumble with the books that fell onto the floor.

"Gah!" Alina tossed one of them back onto the table, then straightened up, her hands on her waist, and exhaled loudly, closing her eyes.

When she opened them, Rumi still watched her with an amused smile.

"Quit it, Rumi," she murmured.

"Are you going to tell me what it is about, Miss Alina?"

"I am going for a ride," Alina said sternly, calling for the maid to bring her coat.

"Where?" Rumi asked with suspicion.

"To St James's Hill. Yegór!" she called for her footman, who stepped out of the servant's door, brushing the crumbs off his chest and beard.

Rumi caught up with her in the hallway and gently stopped Alina with her hand. "Tell me you are not going to Old Nichol." Her eyes shone with worry.

Alina didn't answer. She most certainly was. Yes, it was madness. And it had become part of her life.

"I shall see you tomorrow, Rumi. When you see Dr. Gre—"

"I am coming with you," Rumi blurted, already pulling a cape over her shoulders.

Shoreditch was crowded with drunks and cheering crowds and flaring gas lamps and hawkers who lured people into the theaters and clubs. But several streets off the main road, and the tension hung in the fog that was suddenly too thick and edgy.

The carriage stopped. Yegór's face appeared in the open door. "We should turn around, my lady."

"Keep going," Alina blurted.

The lights around started fading, the dim windows changing into dark black holes and gaping doors. Occasional light came from fire pits and torches.

It grew quieter outside, but it was a different sort of quiet—dangerous, whispers and murmurs, silhouettes and shadows skirting the building walls.

The carriage pulled up to the tall fence around St James's Hill.

Yegór's face appeared in the crack of the door again as he hunched to look inside.

"My lady." He stared at Alina reproachfully.

Alina didn't know what to do, where to go. How would she find Harlan? Would she? No. This was the most ignorant idea.

Rumi stared at her expectantly, picking at her gloves.

"Up Old Nichol Street," Alina ordered, sensing her own hesitation.

"My lady." Yegór didn't move, and his gaze on Alina hardened.

She kept it. "You heard me."

He didn't move, as if staring at her could change her mind.

"Yegór," she hissed in warning.

He glanced at Rumi from under his eyebrows as if the other girl could intervene, then slammed the door, and in a moment, the carriage started trudging forward.

Alina pulled the curtain aside and pressed her face to the window.

Old houses, cramped together. Structures built over one another, towering into the fog like vultures. But it wasn't fog that was getting dense but smoke from the fire pits. With lack of coal, anything went. Whatever it took to keep warm or the empty stomachs satisfied.

For the first time, the slums weren't completely dark.

Rumi stared out the window too as the dancing light of the many torches illuminated her face. Something was starting outside. It wasn't a knowledge but rather a feeling.

A group of policemen on horses trotted past them, as if out of nowhere, guns and lamps in their hands.

The further the carriage went, the louder the streets became, contrary to the usual.

Alina spotted more policemen, who went from house to house, barging in, loud arguments bursting out.

Searching.

For *him...*

Alina's heartbeat increased a hundredfold. Her body was sore with painful tension.

"They can't possibly find him, can they?" Alina asked in desperation without looking at Rumi. "The man they are looking for." *Harlan.* "They won't."

She hadn't explained why they'd come here. She hadn't said his name. Yet Rumi didn't ask, her voice quiet when she said, "It is not a matter of luck, Miss Alina. It is a matter of betrayal."

The words stunned Alina as she turned to meet Rumi's edgy gaze that felt too knowing.

Who would betray the person they worshipped?

She stared at Rumi with so much desperation that the girl must have taken pity. "They won't betray their own though. Do you know why there are so many abused and enslaved in the slums? Because they are waiting for someone to come and save them. And it's not God. Whoever it is, they will be loyal."

No name was brought up, yet Alina felt that Rumi knew exactly who they talked about and what they'd come to the East End for.

The carriage drew abruptly to a stop. Several uniforms of

the Metropolitan Police checkpoint outside the window flashed in the light of the lamps. Yegór's raspy voice sounded too apologetic. The door opened, and a face atop a uniform peeked into the carriage, casting a sharp gaze around.

"Ladies." He touched the brim of his cap, pausing his eyes on Rumi a little longer. "You should not be here. It is not safe. Turn around."

"Of course. On the next street, sir." Alina nodded hurriedly, but when they started moving again, she stuck her head out of the window. "Keep moving," she threw to Yegór and the coachman.

Sounds of something being smashed came from the next street.

No, she shouldn't be here. They were on the edge of the poorest parts of the city, and the carriage wouldn't be able to turn into the narrowing streets, nor should. They could be robbed, assaulted, if not killed. Further into the slums, civilization fell away. And only the likes of Harlan Krow fearlessly skirted the night streets.

And now Alina was here, looking for him. She was silly, irrational, careless. And so worried that she felt like throwing up, her mouth dry with anxiety.

Whistles sounded up ahead. Someone shouted, others hooted, and the occasional, "Get him!" snapped through the quarters.

Doors slammed with eerie echo, and occasional shots pierced the air, followed either by a scream or sinister laughter.

As the carriage dragged for several more streets, the scene was changing still.

A small group of men with iron rods and wooden sticks possibly broken off from old doors or shutters rounded the corner, yelling something angrily at the coach, hitting the cab once or twice and spitting on the ground.

Curses and grunts of threats saturated the air.

Fires started flaring in the distance.

Something was already on fire, and the smoke enveloped the streets, spreading the pungent smell of burning trash.

Danger was contagious. It saturated the air around the carriage. The hissing of the boots against the slush and insane giggles and sharp grunts seeped into the quietness of the carriage like tentacles, wrapping around Alina's pounding heart.

Rumi sat motionless, transfixed on the outside.

A loud roar of dozens of men came from the neighboring street—the men were protecting their own. They didn't cower—they walked proud and tall.

"Ove' there. A dozen of 'em!" someone roared.

More uniforms flickered up ahead.

The streets were getting louder, brighter.

And suddenly, Alina saw *him*.

A tall dark shadow, cape and top hat, beard flickering in the light of the lamp as he was trying to tear away from the three policemen who smashed him with their truncheons.

*No-no-no-no-no...*

Horror gripped Alina's insides with so much force that the view started spinning.

"No," she murmured, pressing her gloved hands to the window, ready to jump out.

"Miss Alina?" Rumi whispered with chilled horror.

Alina threw the door open.

"Stop!" she shouted to the coachman as she stood on the carriage step, her heart ready to jump out of her chest.

"Take him with the rest!" one of the policemen shouted as the others dragged Harlan toward the commotion ahead.

Horses. Uniforms. Lamps. There already a crowd there.

"No. No," Alina kept saying as she climbed out of the carriage, afraid to take a step closer, her knees weak with fright.

"Get off me!" the shadow shouted and was thrown against the wall and hit with more truncheons.

*Harlan...*

Alina swayed in weakness, her heart ripping through her ribcage in an insane beat.

She wanted to run and kick the men.

She wanted to tear them off Harlan.

She wanted to stand by his side, staring into the face of the law that was barbaric and unfair.

Until her eyes darted just a bit ahead and she froze.

Tall, short, skinny, bulky—they stood, sat, leaned on the building wall in a long row.

More than a dozen of them.

All dressed in long black coats and top hats.

All donning beards.

All a spitting image of *him*.

"What is this...?" she murmured at a loss, staring wide eyed at the sight.

The shadow was dragged to the lineup and thrown at the end of it.

Dozens of Harlan Krows were lined up in front of policemen, who talked in angry murmurs, one of them shouting orders but with an unmistakable undertone—frustration.

Alina took a step forward, an absent smile tugging the corners of her mouth.

"Where did you get these clothes?" one of the policemen growled, fisting the last man in the lineup by his coat.

"Som'un paid me," the man growled back and spat on the ground. "Gave me these and tol' me t'show up."

"Bloody circus!" roared the man in charge, then saw the carriage. "You!" He started marching toward Alina.

But then the mountainous form of Yegór descended upon her, his huge arms yanking her off her feet and shoving her into the carriage. She almost fell and scrambled, on all fours, inside, catching her skirts as the door slammed shut behind her.

"We ar-r lost," Yegór's voice snapped outside at the policeman. "Par-rdon, sir-r."

The carriage jerked into movement and turned south on the next street as Alina sat slumped against the wall, panting, staring at Rumi, who stared back at her in shock.

A nervous laugh escaped Alina's throat. Her heart pounded. But she flung to the window again, a ghostly smile on her lips.

The carriage was leaving the dangerous streets, but the scene outside the window unfolded with new intensity.

People crawled out of their caves, the black gaps in the houses. And as they stepped out of their dwelling holes, they straightened their shoulders, spat out the tobacco, and lowered the dirty hats over their heavy brows.

Adults.

Young men.

Boys.

An army of many.

They found anything they could for a weapon and started walking, murmuring at first, then talking louder, soon stomping like a battalion, in a rhythmic manner that resonated with the slaps of the sticks against their palms and the dancing of chains that whipped in the air.

Fires flared here and there.

Shouts sounded behind the carriage, thickening toward the streets with the armed lawmen.

The carriage kept on rolling, but the dwellers of Old Nichol and the nearby slums kept coming.

They walked like ghosts through the smoke, rags and cravats over the lower halves of their faces like masks.

Bound for revenge.

Or defense.

High on the smell of blood and the promise of violence and pain that had kept them alive since birth, they were ready to protect what was theirs—the darkness and all that came with it, their sins and their dignity, whatever was left of it.

Someone ran past the carriage, hooting.

Others pushed and shouted into the night.

The brutishness of their existence was on their faces and clothes—ragged, old, patched. Some hatless, others in capes made out of rags. They all stomped toward the center of the rookeries, trickles of them turning into streams, soon to be a river.

Alina had never understood this until now.

They all were Harlan Krows.

In the dark pits of life, many of them had to do what it took to survive and take justice in their hands to simply go on living.

Pandemonium was soon bound to break out behind them. Crowds of men and boys ran in the direction of the checkpoints.

"This is madness," Rumi whispered, both her and Alina pressing their faces to the window as they watched the streets swarm with danger and anger.

"It might turn into bloodshed," Alina murmured, her heart beating fast like a drum.

"No," Rumi answered, craning her neck. "The Metropolitan Police will run with their tails between their legs. They don't protect these parts. They don't have power here.

They only came to flash their warrant cards and know that was a mistake."

She was right.

The police had no chance once the crowds poured onto the streets. This wasn't a random act of violence or entertainment. This was a war against those who tried to assert their power yet didn't have the right to step onto the territory they suppressed.

Alina pushed off the window and slumped in her seat, closing her eyes.

"There is no friendship in the slums," Harlan had once said. "Camaraderie does not exist there. But the survival instinct is the strongest. Like a pack of bees, people can bond to face the mutual enemy."

His words were always in her head.

*Where are you?*

She called out his name in her mind as if she could bring him to her by some magical force.

The carriage turned and started moving faster.

"Men are not born strong," Harlan had said to her. "They *become* strong. But it requires many hardships to temper a powerful character. Sometimes, it's atrocities not courage that make a hero."

The people down here, in the pit of the city, possessed a different sort of power. And it was coming to the surface tonight.

Despite the reasoning, Alina's mind reeled with the images of the men in black capes and top hats and beards—dozens of them willing to jeopardize their freedom for this strange game.

The distorted echo of an angry crowd and shots hammering into the air were left behind.

The carriage stopped. Yegór's figure hunched into the carriage through the door. "Where to now?" he rasped.

Alina glanced at the unsettled Rumi, then back at her footman. "To St Rose's."

When the carriage started moving again, she said as if to herself, "I can't be at home right now. I want to be with the people."

## 24

---

# COME UNDONE

Alina didn't know what to do with herself.

St Rose's seemed lifeless. Following Yegór and Rumi with a lamp that illuminated the dark path to the back door of the hospital, Alina kept listening and listening and listening for any signs of him.

Could he be here?

Was he in Old Nichol?

Was he among the men dressed like him, lined up in front of the officers?

The questions kept whirling in her mind with annoying insistence.

She didn't greet William or go to check on any of the patients. The fact that the hallway was crowded with makeshift beds, housing the sick, because the hospital was running out of room escaped her. She studied the charts just to occupy her thoughts.

But her heart would not rest.

At last, she told Yegór to help the nurse take the hot tea to the patients, told Rumi she would be back, and snuck out of the back door.

She always looked for him in the darkness. It whispered his name.

She walked out into the garden, pitch black and silent, shivered in the cold, and wrapped the shawl about her shoulders tighter.

*Listen…*

As if the darkness could tell her where he was.

*Listen…*

She closed her eyes, concentrating on the tiniest movements around.

*Please, please, please.*

Her mind whispered the plea into nothingness.

And when the sound of soft footsteps sounded behind her, she almost burst into tears.

Whipping around, she stared at the shadow, forming out of darkness. Her lovely ghost. Always so quiet as if he were molded out of silent nights.

"Alina."

That whisper, brought by the wind and the darkness. Sweet. Soft. Breaking her heart.

"Where were you?" she asked, hating the sound of desperation in her voice.

"There," he said.

"They arrested people," she said.

"I know."

"There were dozens of them, dressed just like you."

"I know." He laughed through his nose.

"How?"

"I paid them."

"But they will go to prison!"

"If they do, they will be released tomorrow and paid even more. They knew what they signed up for."

He laughed. A soft, deep laughter like that of a true villain.

"But I doubt anyone will go to prison," he said, his voice lacking the appropriate worry. "It's pandemonium there. Police are running. They should. People are finally awake."

That chuckle again.

So cold.

So unlike him.

So vain.

"Do you find it funny?" Alina asked, and he stilled. Only several feet away, he didn't move, didn't respond. Her heart was racing with worry and relief and the love for the man who had been in grave danger just an hour ago.

And he was laughing…

"I see it entertains you," she said even quieter, tears welling up in her eyes. "I should go. It's late."

She turned on her heel and started marching away.

"Alina."

She ignored him.

"Alina!" His voice was suddenly too loud and desperate.

But she didn't stop, her heart breaking into pieces with every step.

*Stupid. Stupid. Stupid.*

Oh, how stupid she was!

When she reached the back door, she paused and closed her eyes, trying to hold back tears and slow her breathing.

Her heart cried out.

*Damn you…*

He had laughed—there was vanity in it. It hurt. She'd gone like a madwoman to the place that many didn't go in the daylight. She could have been robbed or killed. And he could have been caught and shot.

And he was laughing as if life were a joke.

He couldn't do that.

*How dare he!*

Anger rose in her like a storm.

She whipped around and walked, almost trotted, back to where she'd left him.

His dark shadow was still there—just a shade darker than the night.

She flung at him like a bird and pushed him as hard as she could in his chest.

"How could you!" she shouted, then lunged at him again and pushed him, though he didn't stir.

"You are laughing." She pushed him again.

"No," he whispered.

"At me! At everyone!" Another push.

"Alina, angel," he reasoned.

But she didn't listen. Blood pounded in her head. Anger thudded in her heart.

"I went there to look for you." She faced the darkness and felt like roaring at it. But her knees were so weak. And tears were in her eyes. It was hard to breathe. To think. To talk! And he wasn't fighting back or saying anything. Something! A word! An excuse! "I was so afraid they would catch you," she said in a shaky voice, pushing him again, but much weaker this time—"and take you"—she sobbed—"and do something awful to you, and I won't see you again and—"

He stepped into her so fast that she didn't finish the words.

In a flash of lightning, he scooped her into his arms.

In another, he was kissing her madly.

And she was answering, pinning her frustration into that kiss, lips molding, teeth grazing, tongues twirling together in the passion that made the world around them disappear.

Her hands fisted his coat. But she wasn't trying to stop him —she wanted to hold on to him and never let go.

Deep, ravishing, the kiss was nothing like the soft gentle one they'd shared at the Phantom Ball.

This kiss was passion. It made her forget everything and only feel. How desperately she wanted him. The dizziness of merely being in his presence. How possessive his hold was, the arm around her waist getting tighter, almost lifting her off the ground, drawing her to stand on her tiptoes.

His other hand slid to the nape of her neck, pressing her closer for his sensual assault.

His kiss grew stronger and deeper. His tongue swirled in her mouth with deep powerful strokes. They went through her body with scorching force, making her moan and heat pool low in her belly.

She'd never known this before—passion that made her entire body pulsate with the need for a man. Her arms wrapped around his waist and slid higher up his torso, wanting to feel him. His warm tongue. His potent scent. His strength that made her feel so sweetly vulnerable.

She wished he would pick her up and carry her away somewhere where they could be completely alone.

Breathless in her passion, with only a flimsy shawl about her shoulders, she didn't feel the cold of the freezing winds but felt him open his coat and wrap its sides around her as he enveloped her in his warm embrace. Cocooned in it, she felt like the darkness was swallowing her.

Warm.

Erotic.

Making her weightless.

The kissing never stopped. It was desperate and hungry. She held on to him tightly as if they were free falling in an embrace.

The back door squeaked open.

"Miss Alina!" Rumi called from the gates, making them pause but not draw their lips further than an inch apart.

He bowed his forehead to hers.

"I was following you the entire time you were in Old Nichol," he said softly. "If your footman couldn't protect you, I would have."

Her mind was too blank to process what he'd said. "But—"

"I will never let anything happen to you, angel."

He dipped his head to kiss her. A touch of his lips, soft and tender, and the world was spinning again.

"I should go," she whispered, though that was the last thing she wanted.

"Stay a moment longer," he whispered back, his lips on hers again, his tongue licking like a flame into her mouth, making her forget that Rumi could find them.

The scorching passion was back. And the need to kiss him deeper. The desire to shed their clothes so that she could feel his skin against hers.

She wished that space inside his coat where she was held in his embrace were a different world—a world where she could disappear with him. She wished time would stop to keep them together longer.

Their kisses subsided slowly, like a tide, turning into whispers and caresses.

"I can't stay away from you, angel." His voice seemed to kiss her, too, his lips dragging in sensual touches across her cheek. His beard grazed her skin. "You take over my mind completely."

His mouth came back to her lips.

Another soft kiss. No tongue. Just his lips—taking hers, teasing, playing. Then his tongue gently swiped across her seam. Hers mimicked his. This game was turning so sexual she wanted his tongue in other places. She whimpered weakly.

*Stop. Stop!*

She buried her face against his chest for a moment, slowly coming back to her senses, then pulled away.

The cold licked her as he released her from his embrace.

She took a step back, not looking at his face—she couldn't see it. She never knew where to set her eyes on.

"You will be careful, won't you?" she asked softly, trying to calm her breathing.

*What a foolish thing to say.*

He chuckled in the dark. "I will, angel."

She shivered, suddenly too cold without his embrace. She wanted to say something else—anything to stretch this moment. "How are you not cold like this?"

His leather coat didn't seem to be of much use in this weather, though his body was like a furnace.

"I am all right."

She wanted to give him another kiss, or two, or a hundred. The silly thought made her smile. She shrugged her shawl off her shoulders and stood on her tiptoes to wrap it around his. "There," she whispered and chuckled nervously. "It shall remind you of me."

She bit her lip as she turned and walked toward the door, feeling his burning gaze on her, her heart aching with every inch that separated them.

# 25

## THE SHAWL

What happened that night in Old Nichol, Father, was a push-back against the law that picked and chose when it wanted to come to force. That night was a revolt against its flaws. There were victims on both sides. But it couldn't have happened any other way. The masses were starting to awaken. Whether it was my doing, it didn't matter.

To some, I was a hero.

To others, a criminal.

But behind that grotesque devilish costume was only a man.

You see, Father, when we shed our titles and forget morals and propriety, all we have left are those raw, animalistic selves.

My angel didn't know what she had done to me.

When she had gone inside, I hopped in my carriage and changed my coat and hat as a precaution. It was a miracle I thought of that in that moment, for my sense of reason had been slain by my countess's passion. She was a fire that had scorched me to my very core.

Her kiss was annihilating. I had kissed her like there was

no tomorrow. I had wanted to strip her naked and make love to her. Swiftly. Deeply. Roughly. Any way possible. All at once!

That kiss was a confession. There was no villain or countess. No saints or sinners. No titles or etiquette. Only a man and a woman bound by passion. And back there, in that dark garden, I wanted to feel that need of hers—a simple feminine need, a passion for a man and not her usual careful curiosity.

But she was suddenly gone, and the emptiness was unbearable.

On the ride home, I took off my gloves and gripped her shawl in my fists, bringing it to my face and inhaling her scent, the only thing tangible inside the dark carriage.

The images were vivid as day. Her auburn hair falling onto her face, her lips demanding mine, her hands gripping my back as she kissed me with the passion of a senseless lover.

My blood boiled with the need for her. And when, half an hour later, my carriage pulled up to the iron gate of my home, I rushed inside so I could be alone with my thoughts about her.

The noblest of men can't always hold back their need. And I was a wretched sinner. What did you expect?

I tossed the shawl onto my bed, undid my trousers and pushed them down. Still with my coat on, I flung myself onto the bed, burying my face in her shawl, pressing into it so hard I could barely breathe.

Her scent filled my nostrils. My long hair grazed the fabric that'd just left her shoulders. My sex was hard as a rock. And I took it in my fist with the passion that bore one name.

Alina Bronskaya.

I pushed my face into the countess-scented fabric. I stroked my cock like I had seconds left to live. I ground into the sheets, thrusting my hips into the bed in that desperate imitation of possessing a woman.

In the darkness, I imagined her body beneath mine, her thighs opening to invite me in, her sex begging for my assault, her soft flesh taking my cock. I whispered her name and some obscenities that should never leave a man's mouth but always linger in his mind.

My cock drove into the bed sheets.

My body was on edge.

My mouth, wide open, bit into that shawl as I imagined kissing her breasts.

I was an animal.

We *are* animals, Father. When we annihilate the humans in us, if only for that moment, all we have left are needs and reflexes. When we shed reason and morals all that is left are senses and instincts.

I wanted her like a man wanted a woman for the simple reason of claiming her, wanting her for myself, spilling my seed inside her.

I reached the peak too fast.

It's divine, Father. In that moment—one solid second of ecstasy—we all imagine our mates. For that brief moment, we are one with them, even if they are not there. That is the whole point of self-stimulation and ecstasy—not release, not some brainless discharge, but a chance of an ephemeral union with the object of our fantasies. It's not right or wrong. There shouldn't be shame or guilt. It's just that—a moment in time when we can be with the person we desire.

I climaxed onto the cold sheets so powerfully that I roared like an animal, knowing that the emptiness would come and there would be no countess in my bed when I opened my eyes.

That feeling is devastating—wanting someone so much that your body turns inside out.

Later, I sat on the edge of the bed in the cold dim room, not bothering with the fire, and thought of her again. There were things to be taken care of. There was another monster on the loose—Hacksaugh. You can't forget him, can you, Father? People suffered, and I needed to clean the streets of yet more human fungus.

But I couldn't think of anything without my countess whispering tender words in my ear.

That night I knew one thing—she cared in the most profound way. She'd gone into the slums amidst the upheaval to find me and warn me and—it makes me smile—*save* me. She was brave and kind and full of love. I could only hope that was the love for me and not some charitable cause.

A man's heart can withstand abuse, grief, and all sorts of evil, Father. But a simple act of kindness can undo it and make it beat wildly.

Mine beat for the countess so loudly it could drown the thousand feet stomping the ground that night in Old Nichol.

You see, Father, money comes with false promises. My countess lived through enough to know it. It offers opportunities but not success. It can bring a good match but not affection. It can buy you anything but not your life. It can cure anything but a broken heart.

True love is not prejudiced, Father. It transcends social barriers. It's the most free-spirited creature. It can't be bought, lured, or invited. This makes it so much more precious.

For a person who has traveled as much as I had, home is not a place but rather a feeling you get when you anchor somewhere that makes you content. The countess had become my home. My heart anchored in her.

I pulled her letters out of the drawer. I reread the first one, smiling at how far we'd come. I kissed the pages, catching her fading scent. I'd avoided the law for too long, yet realized that night that she was the only person I would ever surrender to. Even if she led me straight to death.

I wanted to go to her and tell her of my feelings that were spilling over.

I couldn't.

You see, here's the irony, Father.

The countess would never step into the light with a man like me.

But she could do that with the Duke of Ravenaugh. He fit the bill and everything that was expected of her. Yet, he would never allow himself to do what I could.

A smirk graced my lips at the thought.

Anyway you looked at it, for now, Alina was mine.

Only mine.

And as the thoughts of her spiraled out of control, her shawl found its way into my hands again.

## 26

## THE GUNSMITH

Alina couldn't shake off the memories of the passion that had flared in the darkness of the garden. She barely remembered how she'd gotten home, the thoughts of Harlan consuming her mind. She stripped off her clothes in her bedroom and stood naked in front of the mirror, studying herself.

Her auburn hair fell loosely down onto her shoulders. Her eyes glistened with the reflection of the candlelight and need—her need for him.

She thought of his hands, so strong but gentle, and started caressing her breasts, her nipples instantly turning into pebbles at the touch.

Did he imagine her naked?

She licked her lips, soft and velvety from his kisses. Her hand slowly slid down and between her legs. She leaned onto the dresser, pressed her cheek to her shoulder, and closed her eyes, stroking herself to the memories of him that were like a distant dream.

This was the thing about Harlan Krow. He was like a

dream. Everything that happened between them didn't exist in the daylight.

Only his letters were a reminder. When Alina felt like she was losing her mind, she opened the drawer of her writing desk and from deep inside it—that was where her life with Harlan dwelled—pulled out a stack of letters.

And there he was, her Harlan. His smell of burnt coal and tobacco, though she'd never seen him smoke. The immaculate handwriting, making her wonder where he'd come from. The cheap paper but not a blotch or spill on it.

His words inked her heart in the most profound way. In the daylight, they were the only proof that he was real. Those and her throbbing heart, longing for him.

He was her shadow. He followed her everywhere. By day, he was next to her when she was alone, and she had conversations with him in her mind. At night, he was in her bed when she closed her eyes and imagined him next to her, whispering those sweet words, kissing, touching her. She soaked her bed sheets with desire. She whispered his name when she reached her climaxes.

And when she woke up to the light of a new day, there was no trace of him.

Alina dipped her spoon absently into a bowl of hot buckwheat with milk and honey without taking a single spoonful yet in her mouth.

Anna Yakovlevna read the newspaper. "A cleaning operation in the slums!" she declared loudly.

Alina stiffened.

Cleaning…

That was what they called the manhunt. There was no

word of the failure, of the hundreds—thousands—who rose in silence to protect the villain who watched over the poor. She wanted to see the face of the commander when the raid was over, the anger, him spitting out curses.

She gloated.

"I am sure it had to do with that criminal, the gentleman-devil," her mother said, savoring every syllable as if it were an exotic taste, though there was no mention of him in the Gazette.

People were no fools. The authorities could call it cleaning, but the entire city knew the police had been looking for Harlan Krow and hadn't found him.

"I doubt they caught him," her mother kept talking as if to herself.

"I hope not," murmured Nikolai Sergeevich, finally voicing his opinion.

"Why would you care?" Anna Yakovlevna snorted. "He is elusive like all smart criminals are. But he is a killer, however noble."

Alina stopped playing with the spoon at the words.

"Funny you should use that word. Noble," Nikolai Sergee-vich said, pushing his bowl away and leaning back in his chair. "That is the rub. That half of the city considers him a hero yet the authorities deem him dangerous. That sounds very familiar."

"Oh, don't you start it!" Anna Yakovlevna tossed the paper aside in irritation. "That man has no political agenda. He is some madman who thinks he has the right to serve justice."

"*Who* has the right in those parts then, dear?" Nikolai Sergeevich cocked his head at her.

"Spare me. If you are implying it is anything similar to what happened to Andrei—and that *is* what you are doing, *dear*—you are simply wrong." Anna Yakovlevna exhaled loudly. "Andrei fought for high ideas."

"And achieved nothing." Nikolai Sergeevich picked up a teaspoon and started aimlessly stirring his tea. "This man could start a revolution, you know. Except there are very few like him. And you can't rise up without a group of like-minded people who hold some sort of power and can lead the masses."

"Where is he leading them?" Anna Yakovlevna spread her palms in question. "Toward chaos?"

"It's an idea, dear," he argued. "It is not about breaking windows or killing others. It is about understanding change and where it leads. It is about rights and freedoms." Nikolai Sergeevich's speech was getting faster. "Most importantly, it is about equality—judicial, social, economic. The equality in taking part in the governing process."

Anna Yakovlevna laughed bitterly. "Let's take the savages off the streets and put them in Parliament!"

"We! Are! Savages!" Nikolai Sergeevich exclaimed loudly, making both his wife and Alina wince. "Don't you see?" He leaned over the table, glaring at his wife. "They call *us* savages behind our backs. Despite *her* title." He stabbed the air with his forefinger, pointing at Alina but staring at his wife. "In this country, we are simply the *immigrés*. If it wasn't for *her* title, your furs and jewelry wouldn't let you come close to their ignorant gatherings, the silly balls that you so adore, or any of the houses you are so proud to attend. And back in Russia, they got rid of your son-in-law with the same swiftness as they would have of that Harlan Krow."

He slumped back in his chair, suddenly quiet, staring at the teaspoon that he still held limply in his hand.

Anna Yakovlevna stared back in shock, her lower lip trembling, then swiped her hand across her face and raised her chin.

Alina felt her stomach turn.

After a moment of silence, Nikolai Sergeevich spoke again.

"Your daughter, who helps in the cottage hospital you so despise, contributes more to the change in this country than any of the women you affiliate yourself with. But you still think that selling her off to a duke will be much more honorable."

"It is my fault entirely, sure." Anna Yakovlevna slowly put the napkin down on the table and rose from her seat. "Yes, taunt me, Nikolai. Taunt me! Throw a stone at me for loving my family!" She stood with her chin high, the expression of hurt on her face like that of an injured bird.

*The martyr act has started*, Alina thought but avoided looking at her.

"Yes. It is my fault for wanting the best for our daughter and this family." Anna Yakovlevna wiped her cheeks theatrically, blinking away the invisible tears. "For wanting her to have a happy life with a good man instead of running around the slums and asking to be robbed or killed."

The last words were intentionally accentuated as she turned on her heel and marched out of the room, producing a theatrical sob at the door.

"Well, that went sour," said Alina softly. She raised her eyes to her father, who sat tapping his fingers on the table, staring into an empty space. He looked suddenly older, sadder, as if what he'd said had aged him in minutes. "Thank you," she added.

He looked at her and smiled.

"She means all the best for us, Papá," she said apologetically.

"I know."

"She simply tries to forget what happened two years ago and make sure it doesn't happen again."

"I know."

"But you should go talk to her before she locks herself in the room and goes on a hunger strike."

Her father chuckled and pinched the bridge of his nose with his fingers, nodding. "I know, *dusha moya*. I know."

"The doctor is out visiting patients," the maid informed Alina when she arrived at Grevatt's. "But Miss Rumi is in."

Only now Alina realized that she'd been spending suspiciously too much time at St Rose's.

Rumi didn't say a word when Alina entered the study, only nodded in greeting as she sorted the documents on the doctor's desk.

"How is Dr. Grevatt?" Alina inquired.

It had become a common question as the doctor's condition was deteriorating. It was only a matter of time before his memory loss became worse, the lapses more frequent. Soon, they wouldn't trust him with the patients or even leaving the house on his own.

It pained Alina. One couldn't look without hurt at the brilliant mind failing to the disfunction of the body.

"He was all right last night," Rumi answered, setting up the papers on the writing desk. "He stayed up late, woke up early. It seems impossible to predict when he falters. Although he is becoming quite absent-minded." She exhaled and sat into the chair, staring at the desk for a moment, then raised her eyes at Alina. "I am afraid it will only get much worse."

Alina pressed her lips tightly together. "Well, we should

carry on as usual, and when the time comes, we will take action."

"What action?" Rumi looked at Alina in despair.

"I don't know what action, Rumi. He will need care." Alina picked up the pages of her essay, trying to focus on the words. "Where did we stop last time?"

There was no answer from Rumi. And when Alina raised her eyes, she met Rumi's gaze, probing and expectant.

She cocked her head at Rumi. "What is it?"

"You are friends with him, aren't you?" Rumi asked.

Alina frowned. "Dr. Grevatt? What sort of question is that?"

But her treacherous heart started pounding in her chest. She wasn't a good liar.

Rumi's smirk only confirmed that. "I am not talking about the doctor. I am talking about the man from last night."

*Oh, God…*

*Here it comes.*

"Who?" Alina asked, her words laced with obvious hypocrisy. They wouldn't fool Rumi. But this conversation scared Alina.

Rumi shook her head in disappointment. "Please, don't insult me, Miss Alina. I am not blind, nor am I ignorant. I saw you last night. Saw *him*."

Heavy silence hung between them for some time.

"And that was one of many nights," Rumi said quieter, her words sounding like a sentence.

The silence stretched for the longest minute when Rumi finally stood up and walked to the window.

"You know," she said quietly, staring outside, "people talk about Harlan Know as if he isn't real. Some don't believe he is. He is like a ghost, a legend. I thought so too for some time.

Men like him are something from dark tales. Until I saw you with him." She turned to look at Alina.

Alina stiffened. She couldn't possibly think that everyone was blind. But the people at the hospital had better things to do than pay attention to proprieties or gossip about strange encounters outside its walls.

Rumi was smart and observant. And, oh, how naive Alina had been thinking that her night encounters had gone unnoticed.

"Do you judge me?" Alina asked softly, meeting Rumi's gaze.

"Will you let me meet him?" Rumi asked, her eyes suddenly bright with hope.

*What?*

Alina stared in shock.

This wasn't what she'd expected. "He is a criminal, Rumi," she said, not believing her own words anymore.

Rumi's gaze turned hostile. "He is a hero!"

Alina swallowed hard. "For committing awful crimes?" She hated the desperation that came out of her mouth, wanting to hear praise and redemption for the man she admired.

"For serving justice, Miss Alina." Rumi shook her head. "You pretend that you judge him, yet we drove all the way to Old Nichol last night to look for him. We were looking for *him*, weren't we? Curiosity is not what drives a noble woman to the slums late at night and during a riot." Her smirk was too knowing. "You taunt him, yet you meet with him and seem to be on quite friendly terms."

Alina tossed her head and started taking slow steps around without much direction.

"Some rise by sin. And some by virtue fall. Shakespeare," Rumi quoted.

"He is an outlaw, Rumi," Alina answered. "A man who takes justice in his own hands instead of following the law." She didn't know how to explain this contradiction. She felt like she was the only one who knew him. The only one who *should* know him. And she wanted to keep him for herself.

There! She admitted it!

"The law…" Rumi's voice was like an echo. She smirked, crossed her arms at her chest, and took slow steps away from the window. "The law"—Rumi nodded several times as if conjuring the words in her mind—"protects the powerful. The white. The rich." She took slow steps around the room as if circling Alina.

"Yes. But pulling away from the dark ages and toward a civilized society is precisely that," Alina continued the thought, "enforcing law, gradually letting it control all parts of society. If society is to be equal, it has to start with law enforcement."

She was sure of her words. But how could she argue with Rumi who had come from a place where law was the last thing that ruled it?

"Harlan Krow," answered Rumi, the name making Alina's heart tighten, "is well-known not because he beats his drum the loudest, but because people do that *for* him. He is a hero, yes." Rumi stopped several feet away from Alina and turned toward her as if in a duel. "You might call him an outlaw. But who else will serve justice for those who live in its blind spot? We are invisible—the poor and those shades darker than white. When no one comes to the rescue, it is men like Harlan Krow who give us a helping hand."

That name again. Every time it came from someone else's mouth, Alina felt its warmth and slight jealousy as if he belonged to her only.

"Do we care for the nature of his character?" Rumi cocked

an eyebrow. "Not a bit. We look past morals, for they were burned in the fires when the nights were too cold. We forget about sins, for we were born or forced into them. We don't judge, for we can't afford it. The men of power, those above us, are convinced of their righteousness. They disregard God's rules that they so relentlessly preach about. The men below are led to believe that it's all in God's hands. And so they continue to suffer, taking the whipping with their heads low. Do you see, Miss Alina? It's a closed circle, vicious and nowhere close to righteous justice."

Rumi's eyes reflected the light from the window and sparkled with emotions. Alina loved seeing her like this—passionate about the people. Oh, how right Rumi was! And how desperately Alina tried to protect her man, even if that meant resisting others' praise.

Rumi slowly walked back to the desk, then looked up at Alina, who still stood in the middle of the room. "The people below live in the world of pain and loss but also incredible strength." Rumi's voice was soft now, her gaze sad as she took a seat behind the desk and deliberately slowly picked up the quill, setting her hand in front of the empty sheet as if ready to write. "Hope is a weapon, Miss Alina," she said as if bidding farewell to their conversation. "And in that world, you need weapons to fight for what is right. Harlan Krow gives people hope. To judges, he is a criminal. To the poor, he is a gunsmith."

## 27

# SAVAGE CULTURE

The last letter from Harlan made Alina's heart swell.

*I will gladly go to hell for all I've done. For now I know you, angel. And I will always have your image in my heart. No matter how hard life gets, I shall have the memories of us.*

She grinned like a fool and kissed the page. But of course, she had to entice a deeper conversation. So she wrote a response:

*What if there are no memories in hell?*

She would send Yegór to St Rose's later. Because today, there was a different agenda.

There came the most unexpected note from the Duke of Ravenaugh. Alina had thought that Cassell would not speak to her again. But to her surprise, a note from him had arrived the evening before, asking for a day out. At the Marylebone fair, of all places.

"Oh, how coincidental!" her mother exclaimed, for they were, indeed, planning on going.

"I don't understand," murmured Alina as she reread the invitation.

"What is there to understand?" Anna Yakovlevna mused. "The man is infatuated with you." She was already pushing the paper and quill into Alina's hands, urging her to write a response.

And so this morning, the Kamenevs' house echoed with footsteps and sharp orders from Anna Yakovlevna.

Martha seemed to be in a foul mood. Yegór had asked for a day off on account of the street fair and the large gathering of the Slavs. He'd asked Martha to come. She'd declined, saying something about her duties. Yegór had only smiled. And now Martha seemed irritated but asked to join the Kamenevs.

They were meeting the duke at the Spanish Place, a short walk from the fair.

Alina checked herself in the mirror for the dozenth time. Her woolen coat with dark brown Russian sable collar and matching hat were accentuated by elaborate sparkling ruby earrings.

"You are enchanting," said Martha as she studied her mistress.

"You are enchanting," said the duke when the Kamenevs and Alina met up with him later that afternoon.

As always, he was meticulously dressed and wore a gray wool coat, not a thread out of place, his dark hair slicked back under his top hat.

He smiled politely as he greeted the Kamenevs.

A bouquet of white roses for Anna Yakovlevna.

A single red rose for Alina.

His gaze probed her as she accepted the flower. But there was nothing in it to indicate more than usual courtesy. She didn't understand it. He seemed withdrawn despite this last-minute invitation for a day out, only days after that awkward dinner at his place.

The day was gray and foggy. More snow had fallen but was already turning into slush as they made their way up the street.

But the people didn't care, happy about another celebration, the humming of the crowd growing louder as they approached the small square.

It was filled with buoyant laughter, children and adults alike. Vendors sold hot food and drinks. Street performers gathered tight crowds on every corner. It was a small affair yet high-spirited despite the gloomy weather.

Alina's parents walked some distance behind, followed by Martha, who carried the flowers and looked around as if searching for someone.

It was awkward to start a conversation with the duke. He wasn't much of a talker, and Alina didn't know what interested him and what they possibly had in common.

This felt like courting. It made her uneasy and at once too aware of herself. Especially when Anna Yakovlevna laughed so cheerfully in Cassell's presence.

"Oh, Alina talks about you so warmly," she'd said earlier.

*Liar.*

Alina hated this forced matchmaking.

Yet the duke's smiles were disarming and more frequent.

She wanted to know more about him. Instead, he asked her questions, making her talk. His occasional smiles made her heart leap in strange excitement. He was handsome when he smiled. Light shone through his eyes that instead of probing and intense became warm, filled with a soft glow that she didn't understand.

He was mostly silent, if not overly distant. Yet every time

their eyes met, his gaze grew hotter, holding hers a little longer than permitted.

Oh, she was growing to like him. And she was glad that they were now walking in a crowd of people, the square busy, smoky, and loud, drowning her nervousness.

"Why do I feel like you already know so much about me, yet you yourself remain a mystery, Your Grace?" she finally asked, trying to coax him into talking.

"And I would like to know even more," he answered with a mysterious smile. "Mr. Nowrojee," he said, and the name suddenly made Alina stiffen, "the man in charge of St James's Hill told me you are interested in medical science."

Her heart leaped in her chest. Van Buren had brought it up at the party before. But how would someone like Mr. Nowrojee know about her?

"Indeed," she said and, after a prolonged silence, turned to look at the duke.

He only gazed at her expectantly. "Tell me more," he asked.

God, if a man could speak a word less, she would have thought he was mute.

But she talked. She told him about Dr. Grevatt and her time at St Rose's. Among the crowds of people who gawked and cheered, gathered in a big circle, their heads up at the tightrope walker, it was easier to talk about something that mattered to her but which could cause tension with the man. Any man, for that matter.

"Near St. Giles," the duke echoed when she told him about St Rose's. "Is nursing what you enjoy the most?"

Not a word of reproach or surprise.

"I enjoy other areas of science. But…"

Surely, it was too early to talk about it.

"St James's Hill," she changed the topic instead. "Are you one of the benefactors, Your Grace?"

She met his gaze and caught a flicker of a smile that was gone too quick.

"Yes," he responded. "I am very close with Mr. Nowrojee. He is an excellent man. It is thanks to him that the Hill is what it is now. We can only hope there are more places like that soon."

Realizing he'd said more than usual, he looked around as if distracted. A puppet show was happening in one corner of the square. A mime show gathered a small crowd of children in another one.

The duke nodded to a large audience surrounding a man dressed like a magician. "The sign claims he can read minds. Should we see what's on Lady Bronskaya's mind?"

Alina laughed loudly at this sudden playfulness. She shook her head, wondering if he was making fun of her or was truly serious.

"Come." He nodded toward it. "Let's try it."

She laughed again, stopping him with the soft touch of her hand on his forearm. "It's all right. We wouldn't want to shock the crowd, would we?" She feigned seriousness, then laughed again.

Her gloved hand was still on his forearm when his eyes dropped to glance at it.

She withdrew it, looking away and chuckling.

"I have a better idea, though," she said coyly, her heart fluttering for no particular reason. "Would you like to see a savage display of the best that Eastern European culture has to offer here, in London?" She looked at him playfully, trying to forget her inappropriate touch.

She felt foolish right away, regretted asking, when he said, "Absolutely. What else to do on a Sunday afternoon?"

He smiled wider, looking around.

"You are laughing at me, Your Grace," she teased him.

"Not at all." He turned to look at her, a smile on his face so broad that it took her breath away. "Savage and culture are the best words to use in the same sentence."

She laughed freely, glad that he was playing along.

They pushed their way through the crowd to a distant corner where the smoke was thicker, the smell of food more familiar, and the tunes of the panpipes, *balalaikas, volynka*, and *garmon,* a type of accordion, were like a cacophony of an orchestra gone mad.

There was a group of women dancing, their headscarves askew, coats flapping in the wind as they jumped around in a circle, young and old alike. A board was set up between two barrels where two men took turns arm-wrestling. A group of a dozen cheered, toasting mugs of *kvass* and *gorilka.*

"Welcome to little Russia," Alina said to the duke.

Bast shoes, sheepskin coats, headscarves and fur hats, thigh-long bass-belted chemises and embroidered linen dresses under their outerwear.

Alina's heart clenched at the sight. Her nostalgia had often been tarnished by the sense of bitterness toward her motherland. Except moments like this. When she breathed in the familiar smells, closed her eyes and let the folk music seep into her. When she heard the cheerful chatter in a range of Slavic tongues, grunts and shouts, women's laughter and the obnoxious wailing of the singer who picked up the popular traditional tune.

She breathed it all in, a bouquet of familiar sounds and smells lacing together and running through her veins. They tugged at her heart in a way that nothing else ever did. No exotic scents, no delicious tastes, no beautiful languages or melodies had such an effect. Nothing ever stirred one in the same primal way as the bits and pieces woven into one at birth and early childhood. And when one was ripped away from them, the mere echo in a crowd could jerk one dozens of years and thousands of miles back, making one's blood hum with the ingrained memories.

"Come." Alina nodded for the duke to follow, disregarding her casual gestures that of a commoner.

Her mother would kill her later for bringing the duke here. But Alina felt alive. Like back home. Surrounded by *her* people. And if she embarrassed herself in front of the duke— so better. He would stop his advances.

She pushed her way to the *kvass* vendor, a muscular bearded man in a Cossack knee-length gaberdine and no coat, despite the cold. A coin bought her two mugs of the traditional drink. She passed one to the duke with a mischievous smile.

He took a sip.

"Fermented bread drink," she explained. "You are not impressed." She laughed at his indifferent expression. "Our cook makes it in the summer."

"So the rumors are true, then," the duke said, a smile finally starting on his lips. "You do have an army of Russian servants."

"Hardly an army. Three." She nodded, a smile never leaving her face. "The cook, my mother's maid, and—"

She nodded to the center of a small tightly packed crowd spread in a circle around a man.

"Ta-da!" Alina announced. "Our footman, Yegór."

She laughed happily. She'd spotted Yegór only a minute ago—how could she not when he was a head taller than everyone else?

Yegór towered from the center of the circle like a giant. His coat, hat, and mittens had been tossed onto the ground, his sleeves pushed up despite the frost, exposing his thick muscular arms. A cloud of warm air out of his mouth looked like chimney smoke as he widened his stance in front of a giant stone, about three feet in diameter, on the ground.

"He is intimidating," said the duke, tilting his head up to get a better look at the footman over others' heads.

"He can be."

Alina's shoulders moved up and down to the rhythm of the *volynka*, a Ukrainian bagpipe.

"Do you dance?" the duke asked.

She tossed her head back in laughter. "Ha! No. Well, back in the country we used to." Her smile waned at the nostalgic memories. "My father used to take me to village festivities. My mother would refuse to go. But I used to love dancing with the locals. It was… humbling."

"*R-r-r-r-razojdi-i-i-i-is!*"

The roar to push back came from the two large men who appeared next to Yegór and motioned for the circle of spectators to widen.

Alina perked up again. "Come." She motioned with her head toward her footman and elbowed through the bodies closer to the circle where he stood. The hem of her coat and her shoes were already ruined by the mud. And she wasn't acting like a proper lady. But giddiness was making her feel adventurous. She wished she hadn't worn the fancy coat and jewelry and indeed could join the women dancing.

"There's my Yegór," murmured Alina proudly to herself, feeling, rather than seeing the duke right behind her, then turned to search for her parents in the crowd.

Dozens stopped to watch the giant man lift the impossibly heavy stone.

The circle around Yegór widened, opening to around thirty feet across, giving visibility to those watching from afar.

"Won't do it," a man next to Alina bet, his mate pulling a shilling out of his pocket.

Women gaped, covering their mouths with their palms in amusement.

Alina spotted her parents a short distance away, surprised that her mother had come so close to this *plebeian* celebration, as she would no doubt say later. And there, next to them, stood Martha, her doll face circled by a winter cap, her neck craning as she tried to have a better look at Yegór in the center of the crowd.

"*R-r-r-r-razojdi-i-i-i-is!*" roared the two men again, pushing the crowded circle even further from Yegór, who rubbed his palms together.

Children perched in the trees and dangled from the street-lights, gaping with agitation at the giant.

"Is he planning on picking up that stone?" The duke's voice behind Alina was etched with slight disbelief.

Alina feigned scorn as she turned to glance up at him. "Oh, he certainly will, Your Grace. He'd better. Or I'll send him away."

She laughed and turned her face toward her footman.

The two men called several people from the crowd to approach, then pointed to the stone. A woman couldn't move it. A young man squatted and strained, trying to lift it but only moved it several inches up. Another man approached, tall and quite muscular. He spat on the ground, then wrapped his arms around the stone, dug his fingers under it, and strained with all of his might. The stone lifted a foot. The crowd cheered. But as the man strained to lift it higher, his face turned red, the veins on his neck bulged, and he faltered and dropped the stone to the shaming booing of the crowd.

Yegór smirked, his arms crossed at his broad chest as he watched.

The two men called for attention and nodded to him.

"It is three hundred pounds, they said," a man next to Alina whispered.

"It's some trick," another one said.

"Go pick it up then," a woman snarled at him.

But the bets were already made in the crowd.

Alina pressed her palm to her mouth in nervous anticipation.

The old man started producing warning rhythmical sounds on the *garmon*.

The crowd stilled.

The warm clouds dissipated in the cold air as people held their breaths.

Legs like thick columns wide apart, Yegór squatted, bent over, and wrapped his arms around the stone. He dug his fingers under it and moved them around, his feet moving along as if trying to find a better side and angle or simply sizing it up.

When he stopped, his mouth straightened in a line, his thick beard jutting forward as his entire body strained.

The prolonged tense sound of the accordion was suspended in the air.

Yegór's body tensed. The muscles bulged. He dipped on his strong legs. His mouth opened, a guttural sound building inside him, as his trunk-thick arms started lifting the stone off the ground.

A low growl escaped Yegór's mouth as he slowly, inch by inch, was lifting the stone up—to his knees, thighs, waist, then stopped.

Whispers and cheers followed from the audience that the two men silenced right away.

Yegór's body seemed to sway back and forward as he suddenly jerked, ducking just slightly, and in a span of two seconds shifted the massive stone up to his chest, setting the flat part of it on his protruded chest like that of a cocky bird.

The crowd cheered again for a moment and stilled.

The man on the *garmon* produced a low warning tune.

Yegór's face was red, the expression the most savage Alina had ever seen. She held her breath but couldn't look away. Men and women in the crowd crossed themselves in awe.

Yegór shifted on his feet, his knees slightly bent, his head tilted back. His hands shifted around the side of the stone and toward its base, the heels of his palms creating the support.

The *garmon* picked up a higher prolonged tune.

Someone cheered.

Yegór strained with all his giant body. His one bent leg jutted forward, the other slightly behind, set on its toes, dug into the ground as he produced a loud roar like that of an angry animal.

His arms, their massive muscles bulging, started slowly lifting the stone. It was at the level of his head that was bent backward—then went up and up and up, inch by inch, his shirt slick against every muscle that strained to push the stone up. His roar grew deeper as his hands holding the heavy stone stretched above his head. And when his arms straightened up, the stone was proudly high in the air.

The *garmon*, accompanied by a disjointed orchestra, burst into a cacophony of sounds.

The crowd went wild.

Another roar, and Yegór tossed the stone onto the ground in front of him, the soil splattering around like an explosion under the weight of the stone hitting the surface with a dull thump.

Women squealed in delight.

The crowd burst into dancing and cheering and the arguments of sorting out the bets.

Yegór stood with a smile, arms spread out, his fingers wiggling. And as if on cue, women and children rushed toward him. He picked several children by the scruffs of their necks and lifted them, three at a time in each hand, into the air. The kids laughed hysterically and dangled their feet, hanging in the air.

Yegór only grinned proudly, then searched the crowd and, pausing his gaze somewhere in the distance, winked.

Alina followed his gaze, and there, next to her parents, stood Martha, her cheeks red, eyes blazing, her gaze on Yegór unblinking. But there was no trace of hostility in it. That gaze was a promise.

Alina grinned and turned to the duke. "So?" She cocked her head at him.

He nodded. "Impressive."

"Wait until the Butter Week at the beginning of spring." She grinned and nodded toward the crowd. "They go wild. Climbing the frozen pole naked. Fist-fighting dozens against dozens. Dunking into the ice-holes in the Thames. You should definitely attend that one."

The duke smiled.

The crowd started pushing and shoving and dispersing. Mugs of *kvass* and *medovuha*, the honey vodka, were passed around.

Alina glanced at the duke. With his pomaded hair and top hat and expensive coat, he looked as out of place here as she did. Yet, she felt like she belonged to this culture. And the duke probably thought it savage.

"We should go," she said, suddenly feeling awkward that she'd dragged him here.

He followed her without a word. And they walked out of the dense crowd slowly and in silence.

"How can you possibly tame these people?" she asked

without looking at him. "And how can you not give them freedom? They could do marvelous things!" Sudden bitterness washed over her. "And we just can't allow it, can we?"

She felt suddenly out of place, out of sorts, her mind rushing back to the same words spoken by her late husband.

"Forgive me, Your Grace." She put on a smile and turned toward him and froze.

The duke's eyes were on her—that same probing gaze as if he were trying to read her mind.

"Powerful people hold much pride in having these people under their whip," he said softly. "The powerful ones don't see much value in people if they give them freedom."

They stared at each other as they walked.

Yes, he reminded her of Andrei. Noble, intelligent, quiet, and talking about the people. This man was much more than what he led on to believe. There were secrets around him, hidden power that in moments like this took her by surprise. He spoke little, but every word meant a world.

And his eyes.

Good Lord!

When he looked at her like this, she felt that he looked right into her soul.

His eyes seemed to roam over her face, taking in every detail.

Her lips.

*Oh…*

She felt heat rising in her cheeks. She wasn't good at holding his gaze. And not when it was like this, almost intimate.

*What in the world…*

She wanted to look away but couldn't, the current between them too strong.

She could have loved him.

By God, she could fall in love with this man!

The thought was so sudden and surprising that she felt like her face caught fire.

She looked away abruptly.

"I think it is time to leave," she said quietly, trying to escape this odd moment of understanding that bonded them in the middle of the crowded street fair.

If only he spoke more.

If only she could get to know him.

If only another man hadn't taken over her mind completely!

She was lost.

One man could gaze at her for hours, drowning her with unspoken words.

Another one didn't have a face but seduced her mind with words.

Two men.

And her, caught in between.

## 28

---

# THE DUKE

Needless to say, Martha didn't return home with the Kamenevs the day of the carnival.

She returned after midnight, with Yegór, creating a drunk racket in the servants' quarters, both stumbling and laughing, his low grunts and sharp accent laced with her giggles.

Alina read late into the night by candlelight in the sitting room and only smiled when she heard them come in.

The whispers and giggling continued for a minute or two on the ground floor. Something heavy fell onto the ground. There came another burst of laughter. Then a loud reproach from Martha. And suddenly everything went quiet.

Alina sat alert for some time, her heart booming in excitement, her lips slowly spreading in a smile.

And then came the sound of the loud hurried footsteps of the two up the servants' stairs.

The Wars of the Roses seemed to be over.

The next morning, Martha was quiet and distracted.

"Did you enjoy the carnival?" Alina asked, studying her maid in the mirror as Martha was tying Alina's corset in a strangely disoriented way.

"Yes. Very much. Quite a celebration." She fumbled, then undid the laces and started again.

"With Yegór?" Alina asked, not taking her eyes off her maid.

"Yes." Martha didn't raise her eyes off the corset, still struggling with the laces as if it were her first time. Her mind was elsewhere, and Alina could bet the mountainous form of her footman was to blame. "We had *bliny* and *galushki* and something else that Yegór made me try. And then we danced, though I am pretty awful at it. And we had that honey-pepper vodka. Too much of it."

Alina smiled, turning around to face her maid. "Yes. I heard you last night. It sounded like you had quite a grand time."

She didn't intend to reproach her maid, but, oh, how marvelous was the blush that spread across Martha's face.

Alina's parents were already downstairs in the dining room when she came down for breakfast.

Anna Yakovlevna was extra-chirpy on account there was one day left—Olga Kireeva was arriving in London the next day. Alina couldn't wait. She needed to order Olga's favorite pastries. She wanted to shop for presents, knowing that Olga would only come for a week, most of which would be spent in Kent at the Tvardovskis' estate.

And Alina wanted to be outside. Despite the nasty weather, everything that was happening was making her restless.

Yegór seemed unusually cheerful. He hummed a song under his breath when Alina walked outside, sending Martha ahead.

"A good morning, isn't it?" Alina asked the footman, and he nodded eagerly.

"My lady." He stalled, shifting from one foot to another like he did in hesitation. He threw a glance at the carriage where

Martha was already waiting and spoke in Russian. "How do you call in English someone nice who you fancy?"

"Oh." Alina had to think about it for a moment. "There are many ways."

"Kind. Endearing. But… respectful."

"Well. You could call her *lovely*."

Obviously, it was a her. And Alina knew precisely who.

"Love-ly." Yegór repeated it several times, making Alina smile.

He walked her to the carriage, helping her inside. And when it was Martha's turn and she barked at him, intentionally strict, he replied, "Yes, lovely."

She gaped at him, then tossed her head. "I am not your lovely, *krasavets*."

"*Poka net*," said Yegór. *Not yet.*

Martha's gaze narrowed. His grin widened. He winked and shut the door as Alina burst out in laughter.

"What did he say, my lady?" Martha gaped at her.

"You two…" Alina shook her head and studied her during the ride, noticing how Martha brought her gloved hand to her lips and rubbed them gently, lost somewhere in her thoughts.

The day was spent shopping for pastries, stopping at a bookshop to get the latest books by Eugene Sue and Charles de Kick that Olga wrote about—she wanted to improve her English, she'd said in one of her letters. They bought silks in a new French shop. And after hours in the mizzling rain that threatened to turn into snow, Alina was exhausted. So was the fox stole, sadly sagging over her shoulder.

She ran into Mrs. Tritton, the wife of some banker she hardly remembered from a party several months back.

"Lady Bronskaya!" the woman exclaimed and rushed to take Alina's hands in hers as if they were on the best terms.

That was odd—that was, if Alina didn't think about the

duke, who, no doubt, was the reason why suddenly everyone was too nice to her.

The duke preoccupied Alina's mind more than she would like. Cassell was noble. Too quiet perhaps. But several meetings had shown her he wasn't quite like the rest of the ton. He kept friendship with the likes of Mr. Nowrojee from St James's Hill. And that was something.

She enjoyed his company, his rare remarks, the way he said things in a few words that could tell a novel-long story.

Most of all, she loved his eyes—his gaze so intense that it made her heart race at a single glance.

The rumors were already making their way to the Kamenevs' house—the Duke of Ravenaugh was courting the Russian countess. The ton was jealous of course.

She'd heard this so many times—rumors, stories, phrases said intentionally loud at parties and balls so she could hear.

"Certain Lady N was at their tea party. The tea was excellent, the Russian pastries divine, the decor overbearing, and the Russian footman the size of a mountain. He wore some sort of a sack and smelled of vodka."

Why Alina's mother insisted on keeping those ladies company was explained by Anna Yakovlevna many times.

"We have to make a life here. Russian expatriates and occasional visitors are not enough. You have to make a home here, *ma chérie*. A husband, children, status—"

"Please, Mamá." Alina would say, shaking her head in the never-ending argument.

For the last two years, Alina had succumbed to her mother's party-hopping. She did it mostly for her father, so that her mother didn't chew his ears off with constant complaints. Nikolai Sergeevich often smiled at such arguments, kissed Alina on the forehead, and occasionally came to her room to talk about the past and the future.

Just like this evening when Alina, exhausted by the day spent shopping, sat at the desk in her room and tried to work on her medical essay.

A knock at the door announced her father and his usual soft smile that could take away any worries.

She leaned back in her chair, studying him.

"*Vsio horosho?*" he asked, pulling a chair, and took a seat several feet away from her, absently playing with the pocket watch in his hand, asking her about her work and Dr. Grevatt.

She loved her father dearly—intelligent and wise in counteracting his wife's capricious and overly domineering ways. He did so with seeming submission that could fool anyone but Alina. She had seen too many times how he let Anna Yakovlevna have her ways, absurd and often whimsical, only for her mother to admit later that she was wrong and ask his forgiveness. He had his own ways of getting back at her, cunning and sweet, when he insisted on speaking English with her for days at times, making her curse in French and yell in Russian at the servants. He only smiled and winked at Alina.

He and Alina had their own secrets—the conversations they held in this very room, the discussions of the future.

"You know I am proud of you," he said after she'd told him that she was writing for the medical journal under Grevatt's name. And those words were the most important throughout her life. More precious than the constant, "You are beautiful."

She told him she was almost done with yet another essay—the research they'd done with the public water pumps and the outbreaks of cholera.

"Good, good." He nodded. "As a woman, back home, you wouldn't be able to do much with your knowledge and intelligence. You understand that, don't you?" He studied the pocket watch in his hand as if it held a secret. "Empowered women are dangerous, Alina. They threaten men's power, and that is the one thing men don't like to share. Women bear and rear children. They hold the power to change the mindset of an entire generation. Can you imagine what it would be like if an entire generation grew up with a clear idea of democracy, liberty, and equal rights?"

Alina exhaled heavily. "I am not doing much, Papá." She pursed her lips in disappointment.

"There is hope in this country, Alina. Reforms. Free-thinking is scorned and shunned. But it's not a bullet in your head."

"Papá!" She turned to cock her head at him in reproach.

"I happened to meet Mr. Nowrojee the other day."

Alina gaped at him. "You did?"

"Yes, yes. I know you are trying to keep it a secret. But there are people who understand gender inequality and can help you advance. He is a good man, with connections and all. And on good terms with the duke."

"Papá…" She held her breath.

"I was discreet. He was interested. If the duke doesn't agree with your inclinations, you don't have to look twice at him again. But he knows important men. It is time for your voice to be heard, Alina. Doctor Grevatt won't last long. And when the inevitable happens, you'll need support to be able to advance in a men's world. Mr. Nowrojee has connections to the medical journal. He is—"

"A free-thinker."

Silence hung heavy for a moment.

Her father nodded and glanced up at her from under his eyebrows. "Small steps, Alina. Small steps. At least, in this country you can walk."

"But I want to run," she said quietly, staring down at her hands.

"The next generation might. So do it for them. But unless you have children of your own—"

"Papá!" she exclaimed with sudden realization and glared at him. "You are bartering!"

A soft twinkle played in his eyes as his lips spread in a smile. "I am navigating through the storms in this family, dear." He grinned, rose, and came over to kiss the top of her head.

Oh, her father could melt her heart.

The one man who understood her was now walking out of her room, the door softly closing behind him.

Another one had died by a bullet.

And another...

Alina opened the drawer and pulled the several letters out. She opened the top one and smiled, looking at the signature.

*HK.*

The man who said beautiful things and sad ones alike.

The man who had a brilliant mind and was stealing her heart.

The man who was being hunted by the very lords who held the power in this country.

History was repeating itself.

Alina's smile faded.

## 29

# THE MOUNTAIN GIRL

This story, Father, precedes only by one day the brutal massacre that defined my life afterward.

Afghanistan.

January 1842.

The Hindu Kush mountain crossing.

That was a brutal day of traveling from Kabul. We didn't know that we were walking into a death trap. Freezing, starving, dying one by one, our column pushed through the Hindu Kush crossing.

At nightfall, eight of us ventured down a different path in search of wild animals to hunt and eat. Our muskets were frozen and useless, but this was an act of desperation.

Amidst the high rocks and the snow storm that was picking up, unusual and brutal in these parts of the mountains, we lost our way. The smell of smoke in the dark drew our attention. Thinking that it came from one of our camps, we moved toward it and stumbled upon a hut.

It belonged to mountain dwellers, a family of four, and smelled of animals, dirt, and mold. But nothing could spoil the feeling of the heat from the hearth, so welcoming and sooth-

ing. Two hens pecked the floor. And the soldiers' eyes lit up
—food!

There were two children wrapped in furs. A boy around
seven and a girl, perhaps of marrying age. Her eyes drew me
like magnets. On that brutal day, the moment I looked in them
made me forget the pain and the chance of dying in this hostile
land. Blue, luminous, the color of a summer river, they
warmed my heart amidst that harsh winter storm.

The family blurted something in their dialect but didn't
fight, didn't argue. They knew better than to anger the
strangers in the middle of the mountains. They stayed quietly
in the corner, their stares hostile, not trembling in fear but
glaring at us. Such was the temper in these parts. Those people
had brave hearts.

We ravaged everything we could find. And when our
appetite was quenched, one of a different kind arose as one of
the men slyly stared at the girl, then rose from the floor and
walked toward her.

"Stop," said Krow, knowing right away what was to
happen.

Oh, Krow! The innocent youth! He could do nothing, but
such was his fearless boyish heart.

The soldier only smirked with malice, closing in on the girl.

Another soldier stood up, grunting with anticipation.

You can't excuse brutality, Father. Not even on the verge of
dying. Our men could sense the end, were angry at the locals
more than at the defeat. War brought out the worst in us.

"They will answer for what their savages did to us," one of
the soldiers hissed.

The two men walked up to the girl and stopped at her feet.
The mother scowled at them, puffing her chest and
murmuring something in her lingo.

And that was when I stood up. My broad form was larger

than anyone's in the house. I probably could've taken all six of my men if needed.

But they stopped, sensing the danger.

"No, they won't," I said in a low voice, taking slow steps toward the family, Krow behind me.

"Then they can find another place to stay," one of the men scowled angrily.

"A snow storm is starting." I stared at him without moving.

"Not our concern, mate." The second man stepped up, raising his musket.

I could've argued, but the woman started murmuring, and suddenly the family rose abruptly and rushed out the door into the cold.

There was an empty chicken coop some distance away, barely big enough to fit them.

"They won't survive," said Krow, listening to the howling winds outside.

"But *we* will," chuckled one of the soldiers, spreading out on the floor in front of the fire in the masonry stove.

There is little compassion to enemies. There is none to those who slaughter two thousand of your comrades in two days.

I didn't care for revenge. This was an act of God, as you would say, Father.

But as the minutes ticked, all I could think of were the girl's eyes. And if I saw them in the morning, dead and void of that warmth, I would have never forgiven myself.

So Krow and I took whatever bread and dry meat that was left, a hide, and went to the coop.

The snow was already ankle deep, but the wild winds slashing our eyes with it were the worst. In the darkness, we could barely see the coop. We followed the rope that was tied between it and the hut so that when you went outside, you didn't get lost in the storm, step off the path, and fall off the cliff.

By the time we brought the bread and the hide to the coop, the winds were so bad that the ropes snapped. We had no choice but to stay in the coop. It was a musty little place, stinky and dark, save for a lone lamp.

"Sorry," Krow apologized to the family. "We are all trying to survive."

The family huddled around the dim lamp, the mother's gaze flicking up at Krow, then at me as she murmured something. There was no hatred in her eyes anymore, no fear, only strange intensity that lit her weathered face and those of her husband and children. And the mountain girl blew on her cold hands, her blue luminous eyes staring at me with curiosity.

"We need to stay warm," I said.

And when the lamp light waned and finally flickered off, all six of us cuddled together under that one hide, shivering but sharing the warmth of our bodies.

Krow started singing. I smiled into the darkness at the sound.

The mother started shaking, and only sometime later, I realized that she was rubbing her children's feet and hands to keep them warm. She didn't stop shaking until dawn.

When the first ray of light snuck through the wooden planks of the coop's roof, I could see my warm breath in the air. My body was stiff and cold. And as the woman rose, rubbing her children, murmuring something in her dialect, there was that strange look on her face—a half-smile, but with a devilish sparkle.

We were alive.

The storm had stopped.

The coop was snowed up.

And the woman still smirked.

Why? She knew something we didn't.

There were no voices outside when, shivering in the wind, eyes burning from lack of sleep, we made our way to the hut and cleared the snow from the door.

The house was warm and hazy inside. It smelled of some local liquor and tobacco. And something else that wasn't supposed to be there—death.

All six of the soldiers were dead, their bodies lifeless, exactly where they slept—on the floor, on the bench, at the table.

The unknown words came from the doorway where the family stood, the woman's spiteful gaze scanning the house without much surprise. Muttering, she shuffled to the masonry stove, wiggled the chimney damper on the side and pulled it. In a minute, the haze started dissipating.

You see, Father, when the weather was stormy like this, you had to open an additional damper. If the soldiers had let the family stay, the mother would have done just that and the men would have survived. They hadn't known that by condemning others, they had signed their own death warrants.

But then, in only one day, we would sign our own.

You will say that the reason Krow and I survived was because of the act of kindness. And that is a lovely story for the books, isn't it, Father?

But it wasn't compassion per se that drove us to the coop but the beauty of the girl, her blue eyes that drew me in, a human connection in that deadly time that I couldn't let go of.

Isn't it peculiar? It was the fascination with beauty that saved me and Krow. It was the mountain girl's beauty that saved her family too.

Why am I telling you this, Father? Because the next time I saw my countess, I found out something new about her. A kiss could be an accident. A second one—feeding the curiosity. But what happened next confirmed to me what I had hoped for since the day we became friends. That my beautiful angel's heart was burning for me just like mine was burning for her.

Carnal desires—you simply can't dismiss them in the grand meaning of life.

# 30

## OLGA

The Kamenevs' house was filled with the hurried footsteps of the servants, heavy boots against the floor, the sound of doors constantly slamming, and the smell of Prosha's elaborate cooking.

Olga Kireeva had arrived earlier this morning and spent at least an hour in everyone's embrace.

Alina had kissed her blond curls and non-existent eyebrows and coral lips and cupped her delicate face, then wrapped her arms around her and held her for minutes at a time, almost bursting into tears.

Anna Yakovlevna had indeed cried. Hours later, she still pressed the handkerchief to her wet eyes again and again, shouted at Dunya, called for brandy and tea, and ate most of the pastries that Alina had bought the day before.

Nikolai Sergeevich observed everything with a grin. "Olen'ka, do you not see that you are more welcome in this city than the queen herself? Those two will cuddle you to death."

Olga wasn't pretty, per se, but her piercing blue eyes and sharp contagious laughter changed her expression in the most profound way. She was only twenty and so full of life and careless mischief that her arrival was like the first rays of sunshine after a brutal winter.

This morning, Alina was happy, and for some time—the time she wished lasted longer—her mind was taken away from everything else.

"How was France? How is Count Nielson? How are Yasha and the Petrovskis?" Anna Yakovlevna chirped in Russian a mile a second while Alina wanted to have Olga all to herself. "And only one week with us? What is in France that we don't have in England? And Kent! The Tvardovskis! I love them to death, but they don't condescend coming to visit."

"They did in the summer, Mamá!" Alina interjected.

"Once! And that is only because of the Season!"

"Oh, I am tired of these complaints!" Alina exhaled. "Olen'ka! Let us go to the city!"

And despite her mother's protests, they whirled through the house like a tornado, changed their dresses, fetched Yegór, and left, laughing and grabbing each other and skipping like little girls.

There was so much Alina wanted to tell her friend! And as they left the carriage at Leicester Square, they walked the cold dirty streets and chatted without a glance around. If Alina closed her eyes, she could listen to Olga's voice, inhale the cold air, feel the hissing of the slush under her feet, and pretend that she was back home.

"Oh, how I've missed you!" she told Olga again and again, Olga's laughter making even the gloomy passersby smile.

"Remember the Great Exhibition?" Alina nodded to Wyld's Great Globe shaped like a coliseum. The square and the surrounding streets were much emptier since the exhibition was over. The last time Olga had visited was four months ago when the World Fair had been in full swing.

But the four months seemed like an eternity. And the two chatted about everything, forgetting the cold weather, walking arm in arm, smiling, noses red, eyes bright with excitement.

Olga tapped Alina's hand. "Those two are staring like we are the women from Covent Garden."

Alina laughed at the joke, turned to look in the direction of Olga's mischievous glances, and her heart jolted in surprise.

Samuel Cassell and Theo Van Buren stood by a carriage parked on the side of the street and stared in their direction.

"Oh, my. I shall tell you later what all this is about." Alina put on a polite smile and made her way to the men. "Please, no tricks," she whispered to Olga as they approached.

"My friend, Miss Olga. From Russia."

Olga smiled pleasantly, curtsied, and observed the two men with open curiosity. Alina made small talk with the duke. But any questions from the duke to Olga were answered with her smiles and glances in Alina's direction and short Russian words.

*Oh, the vixen.*

Alina knew Olga's playful ways.

Oh, to be so young and careless!

Only two years younger than Alina, Olga seemed to have never known any sorrows. It showed in her laughter and mischievous character and her cheerful attitude that smoothed any awkwardness.

It was contagious. And even the duke smiled at her responses in a foreign language, meeting Alina's apologetic gaze but smiling at Olga's every laugh.

Only Van Buren didn't seem amused. He kept throwing hostile glances at Olga, who only smiled pleasantly and nodded.

Alina was about to excuse themselves when Olga turned to

Alina and asked in Russian, "Is this gentleman always so arrogant?"

As if on purpose, she looked at Van Buren, then burst out in laughter.

Alina tried to suppress a chuckle and failed, cast her eyes down to the ground, then up at Van Buren. "I apologize. We should really be going."

But the viscount's eyes were blazing. Oh, he wasn't amused at all. "It would be convenient to travel when you learn another language," he said to Alina and glanced with a smirk at Olga.

Olga only grinned, openly staring at him.

"*Si seulement vous n'étiez pas un âne aussi prétentieux, monseigneur,*" Olga said with the sweetest smile. *If only you weren't such a pretentious ass, sir.*

The viscount froze on the spot as his eyes on Olga turned into steel bullets. "*Si seulement vous n'étiez pas si pleine de vous-même.*" *If only you weren't so full of yourself,* he answered, a haughty smile spreading on his lips, and added, "My lady."

Olga blushed and went quiet.

Alina gaped at the duke in apology.

Cassell only smiled. "Shall we escort you until the end of the street?"

He made a point of escorting Olga, just ahead of the viscount, who kept Alina company.

Van Buren was visibly irritated. "Perhaps your friend should vacation in France, since she is so fluent in French, and not in England."

Alina suppressed a snort, for the first time seeing Van Buren out of sorts with his usual confidence.

"My lord, you seem to be quick on judging," she replied. "She lives in France. But she speaks English better than I do."

Alina smiled at Van Buren, who blinked away and clenched his jaw.

Cassell and Olga seemed to be at ease. Olga laughed happily, and even the duke seemed to talk more than he'd ever talked to Alina.

Alina felt jealousy creep up at her, wishing she knew what made them so happy while she and Van Buren walked in silence.

They reached the street corner where Alina's carriage awaited. "We should be heading home," she said to Olga. "Miss Olga just arrived yesterday, and we have a trip tomorrow."

Van Buren coldly stared around while the duke bowed to Olga. "Perhaps the two of you would like to join us at a theatre tonight?"

Olga looked expectantly at Alina, who shook her head. "We would be delighted. But I am afraid my friend is quite tired."

"What is the play you are attending, may I ask?" Olga asked curiously in perfect English.

"Death by Candlelight," Cassell replied. "It is an aria by Cipriani. With a theatrical performance." His lips were spreading in a smile aimed at Olga. "And two thousand candles. And a magic trick. And the main performer burning to the ground at the end."

Oh, he was good at gauging characters, for he seemed to know exactly how to intrigue a young mind.

Olga's jaw was dropping at every word as she stared at the duke and then turned her wide eyes full of excitement to Alina. "Oh." Her eyebrows rose and knitted in that pretty begging face that Alina knew so well.

Alina laughed loudly, shaking her head in disbelief and meeting the duke's gaze. How had she run into him again? He seemed to be everywhere these days. And there was another invitation at hand. And how was it possible that he'd smiled so much today, his kind gaze on Alina expectant, knowing perfectly well that he was luring her in?

And her treacherous heart fluttered.

"This sounds intriguing," Olga whispered, her begging eyes not leaving Alina's.

Alina chuckled. "I suppose we could join you tonight. Yes." She met the duke's gaze. "It would be a pleasure."

And as Olga laughed happily, Alina could swear the smirk on Van Buren's lips deepened.

## 31

## DEATH BY CANDLELIGHT

Olga leaned on the windowsill, peeking out of the window that overlooked the front gate of the Kamenevs' house.

"They are here!" she exclaimed, her silk skirts swirling around as she waltzed into Anna Yakovlevna's embrace.

Anna Yakovlevna straightened Olga's woolen coat, slicked her hair with the attentiveness of a modiste, and exhaled. "If my senseless daughter doesn't find a good husband, perhaps you will. There." She touched Olga's fur hat, and as Olga waltzed away toward the entrance, crossed her in the air.

Alina and Olga walked outside to be greeted by the approaching men.

Yegór's eyes narrowed as he observed the duke kiss Alina's hand.

"*Vish ti, kakoi,*" he murmured a reproach, stepping aside.

"Yegór." Alina frowned at him.

Olga only laughed gayly and leaned to Alina as they walked. "Your footman is a character. I missed him."

When they reached the carriage, Olga halted next to Van Buren and waited until he met her eyes.

"My lord." She cocked her head in feigned pity. "Are you sure you still want to accompany us? I would hate to pain you with my presence."

Without an answer, she laughed so enthusiastically as she stepped inside the carriage that even Cassell let himself grin as he slapped the glaring Van Buren on the shoulder.

*Cipriani. Death by Candlelight*, the brochure announced when the four of them settled in the theatre box.

On purpose or not, the duke took the very corner seat, placing Alina next to him, making Van Buren sit next to Olga.

Alina leaned to say quietly to him, "Are you setting them up for a dog and cat fight?"

They grinned in sync, studying the hall.

It was a small theatre off the Strand, with only one box and the main hallway half the usual size, made even smaller by the large semi-circular space cleared in front of the stage.

"I don't believe I've heard of this place before. How is that possible?" Alina wondered.

Van Buren studied the attendees, leisurely splayed in his seat, his elegantly booted leg crossed over the other. "You have a reputation as quite an anti-social person, Lady Bronskaya," he said without looking at her. "Those who miss social life miss out on everything that is new and exciting."

Olga tipped her chin, a smirk on her lips. "Those who chase entertainment often do so to compensate for their lackluster existence," she said with a charming accent. "Or character."

The viscount turned to stare at her for a moment but didn't respond.

Alina glanced at the duke to meet his smile.

When the public finally settled, the hall was only lit by a handful of lamps.

A chubby elderly man with bushy sideburns wearing a red jacket with golden buttons walked out onto the small stage. He made a small introductory speech, concluded by the words: "Please, refrain from getting up and moving around. No refreshments shall be served during the acts. The public is not allowed to approach the stage."

The room sank into soothing dimness. The orchestra started playing. The curtain rose, and in the center of the stage stood a woman painted white, wearing a white gown. Her angelic voice seeped across the hall. And as she sang, the room started getting brighter.

Only then did Alina feel Olga's hand clutching hers. "Look," she whispered.

In the dimness, it was hard to make out the children dressed all in black, wearing black masks, who crouched on the floor around the stage, lighting the candles, hundreds of them, that sprinkled the clearing around the stage.

And as the performance progressed, suddenly the entire space in front of the stage was lit up with hundreds of candles.

Dancers in black body suits and masks appeared on stage, their shadows, conjured by the many sources of light, casting intricate flickers on the walls and ceiling and stage.

"What is she singing about?" Alina asked.

"It is a story of passion," the duke answered. "She is singing about her lover and a love so strong that it summoned the wrath of others. You see, it is her love that will burn her to ashes."

"How brutal," murmured Alina.

Olga studied the singer and the dancers and the space around the stage with utmost delight. "They must have an awful time with the wax on the floor."

Van Buren nodded toward the stage. "They built the floors specifically for this performance. They shave them with sharp metals sheets afterward." He turned to look at Olga.

She pursed her lips but didn't respond.

The entire performance, which lasted only an hour without an intermission, was conducted among hundreds of candles. And with time, the stage got brighter as more lights appeared —the torches on the walls, a chandelier descending over the stage that Alina hadn't noticed before. It looked as if the entire front of the hall was on fire.

"It looks dangerous," Olga murmured.

"It is," Van Buren replied. "That is the point. A flicker, and the entire room can catch on fire. Do you like danger, Miss Olga?" He turned to give her a mischievous smile.

"Huh." She studied him, amused. "In my motherland, we are quite attuned to the concept of danger. I was concerned about the performers, not myself."

The viscount's gaze hardened, and his lips hitched in a smirk. "There is a trench built around the stage to prevent an accidental fire from spreading. And they keep hundreds of buckets of water behind the curtains just in case."

Olga cocked an eyebrow. "Do you bring women to dangerous places to intimidate them, my lord?" She flashed a smile at Van Buren.

He smirked. "Usually my presence is enough."

"Oh, my!" She feigned distress, then rolled her eyes.

Alina grinned, leaning to the duke and nodding toward her friend and the viscount. "Who do you suppose will win that war, Your Grace?"

Cassell chuckled.

She liked when he smiled. His face was lit up by the bright light from the stage, and she studied him for a moment.

"Smiling suits you, Your Grace," she said. "You should do it more."

Perhaps, it was Olga's arrival or her contagious attitude—everything seemed to make Alina happy. She experienced the lightness of being that was too frequent lately, usually followed by moments of dread or panic.

The sound of violins sliced the air with sharp notes, and Alina watched the performance, transfixed. The dancers changed into semi-translucent gowns, floating in the air like wings. And the opera singer now looked like a bird, a phoenix, all in white, something white and bulky like folded wings hanging behind her. She looked like an angel. And her sad voice made tears well up in Alina's eyes.

She could feel the duke's gaze on her now and then, was aware of his every movement. And when the female performer showed up for the final act in the costume of an angel, pristine white, wings larger than her, now jutting out from behind her body, Alina looked at the duke in awe.

A tiny smile graced his lips, his eyes kind yet so intense that she immediately returned her gaze to the stage.

"Watch her," he whispered softly and so intimately as if they were watching something forbidden and all alone.

Alina felt hot. The heat and the heavy smell from the candles hung in the air. The entire room felt like it was on fire. It heightened her sense of danger, just like Van Buren had said.

Four men in black costumes with burning torches approached the opera singer.

Alina held her breath. Olga grabbed Alina's hand and squeezed it tightly, her wide-open eyes on the stage. The audience was mesmerized.

The angel hit the highest note. And when the four dark men touched the ground near the angel, the woman burst into flames.

The audience gasped.

A circular wall around the angel shot up with a blaze, concealing her.

Exclamations rushed through the room.

Someone's scream pierced the air.

Alina and Olga jumped to their feet, leaning toward the stage, their faces full of panic.

Poof!

The circle of fire was gone.

In the center of it—nothing.

No singer.

No angel.

No voice, as if it'd been cut off. Like she hadn't been there a moment ago.

A collective exhale rushed through the room, half of the audience on their feet, staring in shock at the stage.

The music died suddenly. And in that sudden silence, Alina thought she could hear people's hearts thudding violently in sync.

Thud-thud-thud.

The applause erupted like a volcano. And Alina joined, smiling at Olga, both with tears in their eyes.

"Brava!" the shouts came from different directions.

The applause was deafening, the cheers so loud that they seemed to make the candlelight flicker at the rush of air.

And when the violins started their post-performance humming, the actors walked onto the stage, among them the unharmed angel.

"How?" Alina turned to the duke, who slowly rose from his seat next to her.

He only smiled, clapping. "We can't give away all the magic, can we?"

"This is wonderful!" she exclaimed. "Did you enjoy it?"

"I've seen it before." The duke stopped clapping, and his smiling gaze turned to Alina. "I come here every month to watch the angel burn. It's a story of passion."

Alina's heart was still thudding heavily but for a different reason now. Because the words suddenly reminded her of someone else. Because her heart was tight with feelings. Because when Cassell looked at her like that, she felt like she was burning too. Their eyes stayed locked. She stopped clapping, though the rest of the theatre was still cheering.

"It's an allegory," the duke said, his soft gaze not leaving hers, his smile fading. "Passion is fire. The closer you are to it, the higher the chances of being consumed by it and then plunge into darkness."

Oh, the words. If only he knew how they affected her!

She blinked, not breaking their gaze. "But she survives. Right there." She flicked a glance at the stage and met the duke's eyes again.

He shook his head. "Not in the story, she doesn't."

"We all have the power to write our own story, Your Grace."

"You might be mistaken. More often than not, our stories depend on the power of others."

"Does yours?" Her heart fluttered at the words. She shouldn't be talking like this. They shouldn't be gazing at each other like they did now, unblinking and for far too long.

Olga and Van Buren were talking, but even that amusing fact escaped her, and so did the loud cheering audience, the whistles, the applause, the shouting, because something was happening between her and the duke—something she shouldn't have let happen.

"I used to think I was in charge of my own fate," he said softly, turning his entire body to face her. "Youth is arrogant." A smile flickered and disappeared from his lips. "And then someone else came into my life. And my story became not just my own."

A flutter hit Alina. She smiled nervously but couldn't look away, pinned by his powerful gaze.

"Lady Bronskaya," Cassell said softly and took a tiny step toward her, though it felt like he'd crossed the distance that had separated them in the last weeks. "My story is as much in your hands as it is in mine." The sound of everyone else around drifted away. "This is not the place or time, but I am afraid I can't hold back my feelings for you." Her entire body was a pulsating heart. "Will you do me the honor of being my wife?"

## 32

# THE PROPOSAL

"Proposed?" Olga gaped at Alina. "His grace? At the candlelight performance? Oh, dear, why haven't you said so?" She walked up to Alina and took her hands in hers. "Do you love him?"

Oh that was the question that Alina couldn't answer.

No.

But then…

She could.

If only.

If only…

They were both dressed in the nightgowns and robes, wanting to snuggle on Alina's bed and share stories like they used to back in Petersburg. And this was the news that Alina had just broken to Olga.

Alina hadn't answered the duke back at the theatre. She had gaped at him in shock, then muttered something incoherent.

"I shall give you time," he'd said. "Forgive me for this abruptness."

She didn't remember the ride back home, only knowing that she kept quiet the entire time.

And now the news crushed her with its full weight.

"It's... It's..." Alina couldn't find the words to describe how she felt. "Four meetings with the man, and he tells me about his feelings!" She stared at Olga in desperation. "He doesn't tell me what they are, only tells me he wants to marry me. How?"

She flung her hands in the air then ran them through her loosened hair as she started pacing around.

"Well." Olga took a leisurely pose on the side of the bed, leaning on her hand. "Sometimes it takes one glance. It is called falling in love. And it can happen instantly." She smiled, studying Alina, then stretched her hand. "Come here."

Alina sighed in frustration and came to sit next to Olga. Her blond curls hung loose around her shoulders, her blue eyes kind and so sympathetic that Alina wanted to cry.

"What did you say?" Olga asked, smiling with curiosity.

"Nothing. What could I say?" Oh, dear, the tears were welling up in Alina's eyes. She bit back a sob. "I couldn't utter a word. He said he shall give me time." She shook her head and bit her lip.

It was a disaster.

She knew what was happening and had hoped she had more time to figure things out.

But so sudden?

Now?

When she had other things on her mind.

Another man...

She felt so at a loss in that moment that she wanted to run away from this city, the choices, the feelings that didn't make sense yet were so obvious and contradictory and suffocating.

Olga frowned. "But if you feel he is the right man, you

should accept, Alina. He talked so fondly of you earlier today. He seems so noble and kind and attentive. And"—she wiggled her eyebrows—"handsome."

But Alina couldn't stop thinking about Harlan. Her eyes were pools of tears.

"He could be perfect," Alina said staring at the floor as if transfixed. "If it weren't now. If there wasn't…"

She didn't finish, knowing she was saying too much, feeling too much in this moment that made her chest shake with sobs. She covered her face with her hands and broke out into tears.

"Oh, dear," whispered Olga and pulled Alina toward her.

And Alina cried, weeping on her friend's lap who whispered, "*Gospodi*," crossed herself, and murmured something in consolation, stroking Alina's hair.

Except there was no consolation for Alina, who felt as if her heart was being torn into two.

The next morning, the house was once again turned upside down in preparation for the trip to Kent.

Alina and Olga sat together at the piano, trying for the fourth time to start a tune but faltering, laughing and getting distracted by memories about Petersburg.

Anna Yakovlevna walked in the sitting room and flung herself onto the sofa, leaning on the pillows and dabbing her forehead with her fingertips. "I have this horrible headache," she complained.

"Call for Dunya," suggested Alina. "Tell her to make you some tea before we leave."

"Oh, I've had enough of teas and this horrible weather. I wish there was a ball."

"Here we go again," murmured Alina, cocking an eyebrow at Olga next to her.

Alina felt more cheerful today. They were leaving London for a week, and she wished they were leaving for a month.

"How was the theatre, my dear?" her mother asked, looking at Olga. "Olen'ka, I hope you enjoy this wretched city. And the duke. Will you please tell my insolent daughter that he is a fine gentleman with great intentions that she refuses to admit."

"Oh!" Olga feigned surprise, staring mockingly at her friend. "Great intentions? Oh, my! How do you feel about his *great intentions*, Alina?"

Alina slapped her forearm, annoyed, as Olga only laughed in response.

Anna Yakovlevna covered her eyes with her hand. "Ah, Olen'ka, you simply don't know what it is like to feel the hostility of the entire ton. We will always be regarded as immigrants. Unless my daughter wises up and marries the duke."

"Mamá, please." Alina rolled her eyes and murmured, "Here goes her favorite song."

"Mamá"—Anna Yakovlevna sat up abruptly, glaring at her—"talks more to the duke than you. I would have married him myself if I didn't have your father. Much good that he does for this family."

She wasn't serious, Alina knew. Despite her mother's bickering and hot temper, her parents loved each other. Alina had seen it in the way they held each other that fateful night they'd left Russia. It wasn't fear in her mother's eyes as much as the despair of losing each other.

Alina still had the image in her mind as clear as day—how her father had held her mother's hands in his, whispering reassuring words. And her mother had clung to him as if he were Jesus. Her mother! The woman who could tell off the Grand Duke of Russia himself, was weak that night.

"Annushka," her father had whispered. It was the first time Alina had heard him call his wife so lovingly.

Yes, Anna Yakovlevna was bitter and eccentric. "My poison," Nikolai Sergeevich often called her with a tender smile. But the happiest her mother had ever been was when Alina married Count Bronskiy, tears in her eyes when she looked at Nikolai Sergeevich and said, "Our daughter. Look at her! We've done well, dear. You and I." As if Alina was the biggest proof of their love for each other.

Alina felt guilty. They'd all gone through tough times in the last years. Her mother deserved to be happy. And it seemed that her happiness depended on Alina's.

Alina ignored Olga's knowing glances and flicking eyebrows when she addressed her mother. "Would it make you happy if I married the duke?"

Her mother spread her fingers that theatrically covered her eyes and peeked at Alina. "Oh, Alina, how silly of a question is that?"

Alina could be happy with the duke, yes. He warmed her heart in the strangest way. Despite his seeming coldness, with time, she was sure she could get him to open up. His gaze told her so.

If it weren't for another man in her life. The one her heart beat wildly for, but the one she couldn't possibly have.

She pursed her lips and cursed herself.

What wretched fate!

Yegór walked in, his form almost too small for the doorframe.

"The carriage is ready."

Perhaps, that was what Alina needed—some time away from London so she could clear her head.

## 33

---

## KENT

A week felt like a month.

The Tvardovskis' Kent estate was marvelous—an old manor surrounded by vast gardens. The bare trees looked sad, thick trunks lining the driveway to the manor, the sharp branches scratching the gray sky. The snow here didn't melt so fast, lying like powder over the brown-gray fields.

A family of seven, the Tvardovskis had spent over a decade in England, loved it dearly, and were generous hosts. Their house was a different world with three little children running around, squealing with joy at the greyhound that was treated like a family member. There was a Ukrainian cook and a French governess, but the rest of the servants were English.

This was a much-needed distraction for Alina.

Mornings were spent at long breakfasts. Afternoons were spent in the music room or taking rides to the lake, cold and uninviting. Men shot guns and went for an unsuccessful hunt. Evenings were spent at the dining table, long conversations around a *samovar*, drinking tea for hours.

They had bonfires outside, in the cold, as they all sat wrapped in furs and had a tasting of liquors made by

Alexander Tvardovskiy from their garden's harvests. Until everyone was drunk. And tipsy Anna Yakovlevna blabbered again about the duke and London life. And Yelena Potapovna Tvardovskaya hugged Alina and asked her about the duke. And Olga was so happy, her trills of laughter made everyone laugh in response. The children played around, and little Emma sat by Alina's side one night, leaning on her with her little body and falling asleep, her soft brown curls splayed over Alina's lap.

It made Alina smile and almost break down in tears.

Alina was wealthy. The word alone seemed to be a conclusion on its own. She had a title—that was another badge of honor. All of it from her late husband, whom she'd loved but had never had passion for. And she felt she could easily trade this wealth for a quiet family life. But not with any man. The one she loved.

That word!

She'd never known the full meaning of it until now. The same with passion. She wanted a family. Children, yes. She wanted them to have the beautiful eyes of the duke and the magic of Harlan's voice.

She dreamt with her eyes wide open. That was what the old folks said when one was in love.

Her grand plans of being a doctor somehow had taken a backstage.

Everywhere Alina looked in the daylight, she thought of Samuel Cassell. She could have a happy family, children, a dog or two, quiet winters at a country estate, and noisy summers in London, filled with balls and trips with children.

Balls! Whenever had she dreamt of those?

But then the darkness fell, and she thought of Harlan. Somewhere, in a different world, they could be together. They could have a family, she could heal him, make him her home, have children perhaps. Family healed anyone. But when those thoughts preoccupied her, the people in her dreams were faceless, just like him. And it pained her.

She was a mess. Her life surely was, with all its dramas and secrets. And now she had these feelings that tugged her in so many directions.

And yet, every night when everyone was asleep, she stepped out onto the terrace and stood, wrapped in shawls, shivering in the icy November wind. She wished Harlan were here, in the darkness with her. She often felt so alone. The English always kept their distance—as if she were exotic or a curse.

But not Harlan. She wanted to talk to him and hear his voice. The absence of him was unbearable.

Only a week—a mere week that felt like an eternity without him!

The return to the city was filled with overbearing silence in the carriage.

"Would you rather live in the country?" Alina asked her mother.

"I would rather you married the duke and had a nice family," Anna Yakovlevna said, staring out the window.

There it was again.

A sense of mourning filled Alina as they approached London. Perhaps, it was slight envy at the Tvardovskis' family bliss. Perhaps it was the fact that in the country, in the absence of the English society that constantly reminded Alina of her status and etiquette, she felt more free. Perhaps, it was the week spent knowing that everything would be quiet and fine and boring. There would be no dilemmas, no villains, no proposals that she had to make decisions on. Perhaps, it was the fact that Olga was leaving, along with her contagious effortless happiness that kept Alina away from her grim thoughts.

But the closer they got to London, the more the thoughts of Harlan filled her mind. She stared out the window as if she could spot his shadow among the passersby. The city seemed to have his touch, his voice, his shadow. And she felt a sharp pinch in her heart.

London was gray and foggy and sinking into slush and mud.

Yet the Kamenevs' house was warm and welcoming.

Anna Yakovlevna started whipping out orders, her heels against the parquet floors sharp and assertive.

It smelled like a bakery shop, Prosha having conjured an assortment of dishes before they'd returned. Yegór grinned the entire time bringing in the trunks—no doubt having missed everyone. And Martha chirped away, giving him orders.

Alina stepped into her room upstairs, and suddenly, it felt like falling from the sky down to earth to the familiar ground.

In a span of minutes, her thoughts had become reality.

Her room was a reminder of Harlan. The desk with the candelabrum where she wrote to him. The books neatly stacked on its side that she'd bought to learn more about this country and its social reforms. The old clock in the corner that she looked at every evening, counting minutes.

She glanced at it again. Seven in the evening. She wanted to rush to St Rose's to see him or send Yegór to check for a letter, but shamed herself.

The bed…

She couldn't wait for the nighttime so that she could lie in her bed and dwell in the memories of him, *them* together, the obscene fantasies that she drowned in every night and that had grown stronger as soon as she was back.

"Are you all right?" Olga's bright voice made her turn around. Leaning on the doorframe, Olga smiled at her as Alina stood in the middle of the room, deep in her thoughts.

"Yes. I never thought I would say this, but I missed this house," Alina said. "It is peculiar how a foreign place suddenly makes home in your heart."

A person certainly did.

"Do you miss him?" Olga walked up to her and wrapped her arms around her shoulders from behind. She set her chin on Alina's shoulder and rocked gently.

*Him.*

Sweet Olga didn't know what she asked. And never would. No one would. And that made Alina so much more helpless.

## 34

## THE MEMORIES OF HER

Perhaps the night of the manhunt was the turning point. Perhaps, it had been the first kiss all along. Now that I think of it, Father, I can't remember a time without Alina in my life. It seems distant now—another life.

I was walking down the Strand one day, stomping through the afternoon slush, a man like many others. Not a villain. Not a saint. Just another coat and top hat among hundreds on that cold November day. Mine must have been the only smile around.

Soon there would be Christmas. Long nights, barely any daylight, fog and snow, piercing winds and starving homeless. That's why I liked the streets, Father. I sought out the lonely souls whose nightmares were worse than mine and tried to find a way to help them.

The rumor had it that Harlan Krow came out to the streets in those miserable times because he dwelled in the dark. The truth is, that was the time that reminded me of my past, that monstrous event in the Hindu Kush that was the birth of Harlan Krow.

But the day I walked the streets, a thought jolted me to a stop, and a grin spread across my face.

I was looking forward to the winter.

Yes.

Because now I had *her*. She was in this city. If not with me —somewhere. Houses, rooms, parties, cold months with her in them.

I'd never looked forward to the future before, Father. But I could survive another winter as long as she was in it.

That night, I went back to St Rose's and found my letter.

Two days later, it was still there, and it puzzled and upset me. A world without her didn't make sense.

I clung to the memories of her. The way she shook her head when she was confused or embarrassed. The way a breath caught in her throat when she was surprised. The way she touched her chest when she was nervous, feeling for that little cross under her garments. She kissed it often, she'd said. A cross! By God, I wanted to be a believer then. I wanted to be that very cross only to feel her lips on me, be close to her bosom, rest against her warm skin. Those little things were tormenting during the days I couldn't see her.

I went to her house one night. The place was dark save for the faint light in the servants' quarters. I stayed in the shadows for some time, but there was no sight of my angel. I looked up at her window. Oh, by then I knew very well where it was. I wanted to be in her room and see where the angel dwelled. I wanted to touch her dresses that I knew by heart. I wished I could lie in her bed, enveloped in her scent, touch the objects that were lucky to know her fingers, see her undress in the evening and take a wash in the morning.

I leaned against the tree, hands in my pockets, dreamy as I dwelled in the memories, when a sound came from behind me.

The monstrous figure of her footman stood only feet away. He was bigger than any man I'd ever known. His gaze was hostile as he stared at me in the darkness. Not dark enough, perhaps. I cursed myself. One thing I'd come to know from Alina about her servants—they were protective, secretive, and very perceptive.

"Yegór, isn't it?" I nodded, thinking that I could take him if he wanted to fight. I've taken ten at a time before. But he'd seen me before. Was that jealousy in his eyes? Suspicion? Threat? That footman of hers acted like a simple man but was the trickiest of them all. And he'd seen us plenty in that shabby garden.

He crossed his arms at his chest, raising his chin. "What you want her-r?" he growled, and by God, I thought his thick sharp accent could cut a man's throat.

Two more days passed. They moved with maddening slowness. My letter lay untouched at that abandoned bird nest. My patience was failing me. And if you tell me I was going mad, I won't argue, Father.

I needed my angel like air to breathe. If I could only see her, it would sustain me for some time. If not, I had to have something of hers. I'd reread her letters so many times that they acquired my own scent. She was only in the pretty letters and in the name signed on the bottom.

*Alina.*

I had to have more of her. And that shawl of hers served its purpose. I devoured the poor thing. I assaulted it more times than I can think of. It had lost its brightness, covered in the traces of my need for her. It started losing its scent that gave in under the assault of my obsession. Beneath the titles, frippery, and pungent perfumes, humans are equal in their desires.

And every night, I came to St Rose's, stood in the dark, and stared at the bench where we used to sit and talk. It was covered with snow, forgotten for what seemed like eternity.

Until one night when I made my way around the corner and halted.

It was dark, but the silhouette on that bench was unmistakable—my countess was back.

## 35

### THE FALLEN ANGEL

Cold wind rustled the fur of Alina's cape as she sat on the bench in the back of St Rose's and stared into the dark, Harlan's letter in her hands. She wanted to reread it again and again, but it was much too dark. So she sat, eyes closed, imagining talking to Harlan.

She so desperately missed him. She'd sat like this for over an hour, stiffening at the sound of every distant footstep, hoping it was him, though she knew that he was invisible and silent like a ghost.

She was in love with a ghost. The realization was ridiculous and at once frightening. She willed him to come to her so that she knew he wasn't a figment of her imagination. Nor were her feelings for him.

Surely, he would know she was here.

*Where are you?* her heart whispered.

And suddenly—a shift of air.

A whisper of the wind.

A crunch of the frozen leaves under the snow.

She didn't need to turn to know it was him, and her heart leapt toward him, her body trembling at his mere presence.

A shade darker than night, he came and sat next to her.

"I missed you," he said softly.

She smiled, opened her eyes, and turned to look at the broad-shouldered darkness. She wanted to wrap her arms around him and kiss that faceless man.

"We went to Kent," she replied, wanting to tell him what she'd done in those days, the people she'd met, how she'd missed him—all of it!

They sat in silence for some time.

She still didn't know his true name or his face. He'd told her so many stories from the past, and they'd painted an image of a tormented man. But how could she not admire the strength that came with it, respect the man who'd fought the war and now fought for others?

She felt utterly happy in his presence, aware of every shade and sound around her. And right away she felt scared of that feeling, the fright making her heart race, tears welling up in her eyes.

She knew what scared her—the feelings surpassing anything she'd ever felt before.

She loved him, the gentleman-devil, the dark angel of the night.

She had to talk about something—anything—not to burst into tears.

"Why can't you show me your face, Harlan?"

She felt like she was begging. If he could tell her all those dark stories, why couldn't he look her in the eyes? If it weren't autumn, if it weren't always cloudy and foggy, the moonlight could have given her a glimpse of what he looked like.

Perhaps, he was scarred, deformed. Did he think he was a monster? Would she care?

She felt a lump in her throat.

"Say something in your native language," he asked softly. "I'd like to hear you speak it."

Her toes were cold, so were her fingers. Her cape was much too thin for sitting outside like this. But she would have waited much longer for him.

She shrugged and smiled into the emptiness. "What would you like me to say?"

He turned to her. "Say: days were for others."

She chuckled in surprise. "*Dni byli dlia drugih.*"

"But the nights brought them together."

Her smile waned. "*No nochi prenadlezhali im,*" she said quietly.

"Days were unbearable without her." His voice was soft like a caress.

She swallowed, fighting the lump in her throat. "*Bez nee, dni byli nevynosimy.*"

"And the nights whispered her name."

Her chest tightened with a built-up sob, tears burning her eyes. "*Nochi sheptali yeyo imia.*"

"They were lost."

It was a confession, and she pursed her lips, keeping them from trembling, then took a deep breath and whispered, "*Oni byli poteriany.*"

"Until they found each other."

She closed her eyes, letting the tears slide down her cheeks, and held her breath, suppressing a sob.

They sat motionless amongst the snow and the silence, the words hanging in the air between them.

Alina wiped her cheeks, hoping that he didn't notice. She wanted to scream, drag him to light, and tell him she didn't care what he looked like. She would understand. Why wouldn't she?

She rose abruptly. "I should go."

He rose too, his figure blocking her way. "Let me take you home, Alina. Please."

*Alina.*

Her name on his lips sounded like a love word.

"Say it again," she asked quietly. "My name."

He stretched his hand and stroked her cheek, his gloves too thick to feel his warmth.

"Alina," he whispered.

She took his hand and pressed her cheek to it, closing her eyes and cherishing his touch. She didn't care for the voices outside the gate that got louder, heading in their direction.

But he did. The intimate moment was broken up too suddenly.

"Follow me." He took her hand and walked through the garden, the gates, and onto the dark street.

She followed submissively. He would put her in her carriage, bid farewell, and disappear into darkness like he always had.

But he led her away, toward his carriage that was right there, parked just ahead, the coachman a black shadow himself.

And when she stepped inside, he followed and closed the door behind him. And when the carriage jerked, she felt Harlan's hand cup her cheek—no glove, his bare skin scorching hers.

"My life is unbearable without you, angel," he said so tenderly that she forgot everything she'd thought a moment ago. "I can't stay away from you no matter how hard I try."

And without waiting for her reply, he pulled her toward him, searing her mouth with a kiss.

The desire ignited like fire.

One second their mouths met—the next one, their hands gripped and pulled, stroked and cupped each other's faces. Their hats fell off. He caught her hands and pulled off her gloves, then slid his hands under her coat and caressed her curves, pressing hard through the thick fabrics of her garments.

He engulfed her. Her hands frantically roamed his body, trying to find his bare skin, desperate to feel it under her fingers.

"I want to touch you," she murmured, not knowing how she wanted to touch him but wanting to be closer.

Days of being apart had brought them to this rare moment of intimacy that they seized with the desperation of new lovers.

Time ceased to exist. So did their bodies. They were one. Tongues. Fingers. Limbs. Senses.

His kisses deepened, making her dizzy. He seemed to touch her everywhere at once. But they weren't the silky light touches like those at the Phantom Ball. And not the slow burning of the kiss after the manhunt.

This was raw and carnal.

Their mouths fused together, then drifted away to find bare skin. She pushed his hair away and found his neck, kissing it, grazing it with her teeth, yanking away the cravat that hid more of him.

He grunted, grabbed the back of her neck, and brought her mouth to his again. And when the kissing wasn't enough and her hips bucked at him with need, she felt his hand lift up her skirts.

*I shouldn't...*

The thought was left unfinished, because the realization that he wanted her made heat pool between her legs.

She felt his hand on her thigh, the fabric of the undergarment too thick to feel his touch. He squeezed her flesh, and she moaned. So obviously. So inviting.

"You haunt me, Alina," he whispered as if afraid to scare her if he said it louder. "You turn me into a shameless man."

But she didn't need the words right now. She needed him. Everywhere. Inside her. Filling her up. Putting out the flames that coiled through her.

"You make me burn with desire that takes over my body and mind," he murmured as he kissed her jaw and neck.

His hand slid between her thighs and cupped her sex through the fabric.

Liquid heat coursed through her veins at his touch. If she'd ever known what it was like to truly have passion for a man, she would have recognized it at once. The way she burned for him. The way her body screamed and arched seeking out his.

"I do filthy things when I think of you, Alina. They bring the biggest pleasure. If only we could do them together."

*No. No.*

She should stop him, but she didn't want to. For once, she wanted to feel free in her desire. She wanted to let go and forget who she was, where she'd come from, and what was in the future.

This! This moment was what mattered!

"I can't be next to you without touching you," he whispered.

*He shall ruin me.*

But his fingers were so swift as if he'd done it a hundred times. Her body was so obedient as if she'd let him do it before.

He kept kissing her mouth, jaw, neck, coming back to her lips for more.

His seductive whispers made her tremble with need.

"I want your body and your heart. All of you."

His hand under her skirt untied her drawers—expertly, in seconds. And as if she knew exactly what he was about to do, she lifted her hips to let him slide the fabric down her hips, baring her for him.

"Harlan," she whispered and wasn't sure if that was an impulse to stop him or hurry him up.

"Yes, angel," he exhaled into her mouth.

His fingers found her yielding flesh, her opening, and swiped along her slick folds.

She cried out at his touch—his hand right there, where she needed it the most. His fingers moved slowly, tracing the shape of her sex. His arm around her waist tightened, pulling her down.

His hand between her legs slid to her thigh, pushing it lightly.

"Open for me, angel," he whispered.

Oh, she wished he would pull down his trousers and take her. But he wouldn't. She knew it. And so she obeyed and opened her legs, giving his fingers the full access.

"There, angel," he whispered, stroking her between her legs. His fingers pushed the lips of her sex apart and grazed her sensitive nub. She whimpered and rolled her hips against him, shameless in her need.

He grunted into her neck. His tongue licked her skin. And she moaned as his fingers slid down, then up her center, coming back to her most sensitive spot.

"I want you to feel me," he whispered, his caresses never stopping, sending her body into a sizzling pleasure.

She was melting in his arms, under his kisses, to the sound of his occasional whispers. Heat made her wet like an ocean. Her sex pulsated under his touch.

"I want you to fall apart under my fingers."

His hot tongue thrust into her mouth again and again to the rhythm of his strokes between her legs.

She whimpered, unable to hold back. Heat gathered between her legs and was slowly spreading throughout her body. Her hands wrapped around his neck tightly, holding him closer. Her body yielded toward his fingers that caressed her slick fold. Pleasure rippled through her in soft waves that were growing stronger.

"There," he whispered with the gentle thrust of his fingers. "Tell me that you think of me at night in your bed."

His lips moved along her skin as he talked and kissed her, all at once, his words like a strain of music.

"Yes," she exhaled and whimpered as his fingers circled her clit in rhythmic strokes.

They were finally cut from their bindings, letting each other closer, crossing that forbidden red line, though it was nothing compared to what they'd already conjured in their minds.

Alina felt the climax approaching, rolled her hips against his fingers, wanting more, harder, faster. He was all around her at once—his hot tongue in her mouth, his hard body flush against hers, his fingers in her wetness, the fire inside her growing into a blaze.

"There, angel. There." His words were like a spell. She went rigid, feeling the tension burst through her. "Come for me," he murmured into her mouth.

Her mind, body, and soul were wrapped around the man whose sensual touch was sending her toward a violent peak.

She cried out. A burst of heat dashed through her body like an exquisite torment. She arched her back as she climaxed, then went limp in his arms as her climax subsided, his hand cupping her sex, holding it until her hands' grip around his neck weakened.

"You come so beautifully, angel." His whisper grazed her cheek with warm breath.

And as the remnants of the climax licked across her body, a thought flickered in her mind: there she was, a fallen angel, in the arms of her gentleman-devil.

## 36

# LOVE

All the way back to my flat, I sat in a daze as the carriage rocked along the night streets. I reveled in the memories of what had happened—my countess soaked down to her stockings, her silky thighs opening to let me in, her little tongue twisting in my mouth with so much eagerness as I pleasured her.

My mind and heart were chaos.

We were bound by darkness. That was why she was drawn to me. She could let go, strip her title and furs and jewelry and be who she was—a woman. To simply be human and feel the power of it—what luxury that some of the wealthiest can't afford!

The scent of her femininity tickled my nose. I brought my hand to my face and inhaled her again and again. I licked my lips, savoring the taste of her. I felt the dampness of my cock, having climaxed inside my trousers in the precise moment she'd reached her peak.

I smiled into the darkness of the carriage.

My cock hardened at the memory, and by the time I got to my flat, it was throbbing with need again.

Desire, thick and hot, took over. That's what happens when you are in love with a woman, Father. It's tangible, like a magical substance flowing through your veins that clouds your mind, makes your heart beat harder, and your sex throb with need.

I rushed into my bedroom, dark and cold, and took her shawl out of my drawer.

Every cell in my body swelled with that magical substance. My hands shook as they pushed down my trousers. I pressed my forehead to the wall and rubbed my cock feverishly, pushing it into her shawl, fucking the fabric, unable to hold back my need for her.

Seconds were how long it took to reach that peak—and she was there with me, always was—her coral lips and gray eyes, her hair caressing my face as she kissed me and her words, "I want to feel your skin against mine."

My hand slick with my seed, I stood with my forehead against the cold wall for some time, trying to calm my breathing. But my heart was heavy.

I wanted to roar in disappointment.

I wanted to crash the walls that separated us.

Tears burned my eyes, and the grin of a madman was on my lips.

I loved her, Father.

She was everything.

Because she dared to be with a man like me. Because her every word was as if it were taken out of my mouth. And those that were different, shocked me, pierced me down to my very soul, making it ache. Because she gave me these precious moments of forgetting the pain and the nightmares, filling my entire life with herself.

Pain means you are alive, Father. That was all I'd ever

known. She brought a different kind of feeling, and it was ripping me from the inside in the sweetest torturous way.

I cleaned myself up, lit a candle, and stood by the mirror, staring at my reflection.

I had to tell her.

She would understand.

She was the only one who could.

I didn't know that in a matter of two days, it would all go up in flames. And the one holding the match would be a poor widow in St. Giles.

# 37

## THE REJECTION

A lina felt like she was swimming downstream, carried by a powerful current, and somewhere ahead was a high drop. Whether she would survive it, she didn't know. And it was petrifying.

When she stepped out of the carriage, she walked into her house like a ghost, ignoring Yegór, who'd followed Harlan's carriage and now stomped after her into the house. She disregarded his hostile stare as he took her coat and hat. She expected him to say something or growl.

He was silent.

She walked up to her room. Martha stood on the top stair, in a night dress and a shawl wrapped around her. "My lady, would you like me to get you ready for bed?"

"It's all right, Martha. You can go."

In her room, Alina took a seat on the edge of the bed, closed her eyes, and shook her head.

God! What sort of woman was she?

*There, angel. There.* She wished she could feel his touch on her aroused flesh again.

She tried to taunt herself but it was pointless—she would have done it again, wanted him *now*, in fact. She covered her face with her hands. And here he was again—his scent on her skin. She inhaled deeply until her lungs felt like bursting, breathing him in, holding that precious scent in her until it dissipated.

*You make me burn with desire.*

Her body throbbed again with the need for him. It didn't go away.

Not when she undressed, absently tossing the garments onto the floor.

Not when she got under the sheets and lay in the dark, caressing herself and wishing those were his hands.

*I want you to feel me.*

Not when her hand slid between her legs and stroked the memories of him into her flesh.

*I want you to fall apart under my fingers.*

Not when she climaxed, whimpering in ecstasy and clutching the sheets in despair, because he wasn't next to her.

Not when she woke up the next morning, hating the light that streamed through the gap in the curtains, for the daylight meant she wouldn't see him. The daylight dissolved the memories of him. Because the daylight belonged to a different man.

The Duke of Ravenaugh.

She felt like two different people. The Alina by night was brave, venturing into the dark quarters of London with a man by her side who was a mystery.

By day, she was the proper Countess Alina Nikolaevna Bronskaya.

And as soon as she was in the presence of the duke, her life seemed clear and straightforward—she could marry him and have everything a woman desired.

But she couldn't deceive two men. How could she live with herself if she chose one or another?

One was a ghost who had stolen her heart. He didn't offer anything. Like a shadow, he was always with her even when she didn't see him.

The other one was the perfect match yet didn't make her feel the way the gentleman-devil did. The duke offered everything. Oh, he would be a perfect husband, she knew. Her heart already ached for him in the most tender way. Behind his quietness was nobility, grace, and the wisdom that she wanted to know more of and could if she only let herself. If it were any other time in her life, she would have accepted his proposal in a second and would be happy. Oh, so splendidly happy!

She felt the familiar butterflies in her stomach when the duke's arrival that afternoon was announced by Yegór, who glanced at Alina in reproach. Her heart clenched with tenderness when Samuel Cassell stepped into the sitting-room, gracefully smiling at Anna Yakovlevna, who beamed so happily that Alina felt her stomach turn icy cold at the thought of what she was about to do.

"I shall be in the room next door if you need me," Anna Yakovlevna said, throwing a knowing glance as she left Martha in the room with them.

"My lady." The duke gazed at Alina with so much tenderness that it burned her to the core.

How could she shamelessly accept the noble man when part of her was with another, when what she'd done was far from noble? The memories of the carriage ride the night before flickered in her mind, and she did the only noble thing—the merciful killing.

"I can't marry you, Your Grace," she said quietly.

The words echoed in the silence of the sitting room as the two of them stood in the center of it. Only several feet from each other, their eyes locked. She didn't hide, didn't look away —the duke deserved that much.

"Forgive me," she added even quieter.

Nothing changed in him. He didn't move. Didn't raise an eyebrow.

"Why?" His voice wasn't angry but quiet and soft as if he wasn't surprised. This reaction puzzled her. She'd expected irritation, anger, disappointment, but not this—this calmness as if they were discussing a walk in the park.

She felt weak. The room was suddenly too hot, too silent. Alina's chest tightened. She wanted to shrug the shawl off her shoulders so she could breathe deeper.

"I am afraid I can't give you an explanation you deserve, Your Grace," she said in a weak voice. "But if we went through with this arrangement, I would be deceiving you, and I can't do that."

"Deceiving me?" His expression still hadn't changed, nor had his posture.

"About my loyalty to you."

*Oh, God.*

"Is there someone else?" His gaze burrowed into her.

"Not in the way you think."

"Is it too soon?"

"Not..." She swallowed hard. "I can't quite explain... It is..."

She went silent, closed her eyes for a moment to gather her thoughts and opened them to meet his gaze. "I don't deserve you or what you have to offer," she blurted out. "You want a woman who can make you happy. A proper society lady who will excellently play the role of a good wife and—"

"You," he cut her off. "You *are* that woman."

"But I am not," she said quietly, a lump in her throat. If he got angry, if he paced and reasoned with her loudly, she would have felt better. Instead, he stood motionless—the way he always seemed to be around others.

"Perhaps, you think my proposal was a mere calculation of sorts. It is not." He paused for a moment. "If I explain my feelings, would they matter in changing your mind?"

She raised her eyebrows in surprise.

He'd never talked of feelings. He hardly talked at all. His eyes seemed to hold a universe that told her what he thought.

*Feelings.*

Her feelings for him were what had made her come to this decision in the first place. "I am not what you think," she said, trying to choose the words that would be merciful. "And I wouldn't want to disappoint you if later on, you found out that the woman you praised was far from being a role-model."

"That will not happen, I assure you."

She shook her head and looked away. He was hard to say no to and hard to look at when the power of his gaze shot down her attempts to argue.

"I shall give you more time, Lady Bronskaya," he said. She looked up at him in surprise. "I shall not accept your answer yet," he said softly with what looked like a tiny sad smile that hitched the corner of his lips. "And not because I want to force you into something you don't want, but because you might want to tell me what this is truly about. The day you do, we shall decide together what we both deserve."

"But, Your Grace—"

"My lady." He bowed without letting her finish, turned, and walked out before she had a chance to stop him.

She heard his steps echo through the house. She met Martha's shocked stare at her across the room. She heard the fast steps and the rustling sound of Anna Yakovlevna's skirts as her mother trotted into the sitting room with an alarmed look on her face.

"What in the world are you thinking?" her mother hissed in anger as if she'd heard every word.

Alina didn't answer but started walking out of the room.

"Alina! Answer me!" her mother shouted into her back.

But Alina kept walking, lips pressed tightly together as she tried to hold back tears.

This was the high drop into the water that she'd thought about the other night. The words of a wise man echoed in her mind—*the worst part about having choices is not being able to make one*.

She'd just rejected the man who half of the ton dreamt of marrying.

And soon, she would say farewell to the man who held her heart hostage.

## 38

---

## THE TRUTH

She wrote to Harlan, seeking a meeting. The night of the meeting, she took the carriage to St Rose's. She left Yegór with the coachman and walked through the dark gates into the garden.

She moved with confidence, knowing that what she had to do and say was the right thing. She had to stop. *They* had to stop.

She rounded the corner and went to the back door.

*How times change*, she thought, not feeling afraid of the dark, knowing every curve and stone of the path around the building without a lamp, having walked it so many times to meet the villain who made half of London tremble in fear.

At the back door, she stood on tiptoes and checked the nest.

There was no letter, and hers was gone.

*He is here.*

She went into the garden and sat down on the cold bench. Her heart was heavy. She shivered, feeling the coldness seep into her bones.

*Where are you?*

She closed her eyes just like she'd done so many times, listening to the sounds.

Yegór's voice hummed in the distance outside the gates as he talked to the coachman.

*I am here.*

She was certain he'd come. He always had.

Yet there was no trace of him.

She didn't know how much time had passed. Too long. He couldn't have failed her. A strange thought occurred to her—he was a man with another life besides roaming the night streets.

Disappointment turned into worry.

What if something had happened?

There was no Harlan, no shadow that had become as familiar as if they were one.

A strange sound started humming in the distance. Voices. Many of them. Growing louder.

Alina rose from the bench. The awful thought of not seeing Harlan was like an ice pick in her heart. She turned around and started slowly walking toward the gate.

One step.

Another.

Yet another.

Every step—pieces of hope lost.

And as she neared the gate, Yegór's voice grew louder, and the shouts from somewhere nearby got more intense.

Yegór stood by the carriage as the coachman was crossing the street toward them.

"What is wrong?" Alina asked as the man approached.

"A fire two streets away," the man said. "Big one. Two floors. A widow's child trapped in the upstairs room."

She wasn't sure why the words jolted her entire body into panic. But suddenly, it all came together.

A fire. Shouts for help. Harlan, who was supposed to be here but wasn't.

Alina wasn't fully realizing what she was doing when she started crossing the street toward the block where the fire was.

"My lady! It is not safe!" Yegór shouted behind her.

But she didn't stop. Her legs carried her toward the place where someone was in trouble and another person made his life's goal sorting it out.

"My lady!" Yegór's voice sounded louder as he trotted behind her.

And by then, Alina was trotting too.

She started running, her coat open, flapping in the wind. Her eyes darted around the people she passed and others who were running in the same direction, suddenly too many of them.

The street ahead, usually so dark, was glowing.

The smell of smoke filled her nostrils.

Shouts were growing louder.

Someone wailed.

A thick crackling sound filled the air. A cloud of smoke shifted through the bright glow from around the corner. And as Alina rounded the corner of an old building, she shielded her eyes by instinct.

The blaze wafted into her face like a soft hot blow. Yellow-orange, the flames engulfed the two-story building. They were eating up the wood and stone. Sparkles zapped through the air like fireflies. Smoke enveloped the nearby buildings.

A crowd gathered around, but they just gawked. The woman closest to the blaze paced back and forth, her hands covering her mouth as she stared somewhere upward.

"Stay here," Alina ordered to Yegór behind her and approached the tight circle.

"A widow... match... hearth... oil lamp... three young 'uns... inside..."

The whispers here and there told the story, but no one moved.

"Why is no one doing anything?" Alina asked, staring around, her eyes burning.

An old man spat onto the ground. "Nothing here t' help wi', ma'am. Iz' ol' wood."

A woman next to Alina pressed the corner of a thick shawl to her mouth. "She has a child upstairs."

"A child?" Alina gaped. "But..."

Horror gripped her as the mother's wail pierced the air.

"There!" someone shouted.

"Ov' there!"

Fingers started pointing toward the upper floor.

"A fella crawled up to get 'im," the woman explained, craning her neck over dozens of bystanders. "There! He's coming!"

And then Alina saw it.

Her heart pounded to a still.

The air was sucked out of her lungs.

Because she would recognize him anywhere. The dark shadow that now glowed with orange around him like a halo.

"He is here!" someone shouted.

"Who?" someone asked.

"Harlan Krow."

Alina felt dizzy. Her heart hammered against her chest. It wasn't the worry for him, though she should have been petrified. It was the fact that, for the first time, she was witnessing what Harlan Krow did for the people.

He was smooth and quick, like a panther. His dark coat flapped as he scaled down the building. Flames licked at him. The smoke enveloped him. And he seemed even bigger, stronger, larger than life with another small body clutching around his front, shielded by his coat—a small child.

Alina stood watching in awe as he made it to the awning and jumped off onto the ground.

The fire raged.

The crowd cheered.

He stood, tall and intimidating, his head down as he untangled the child from himself.

The woman dashed toward him, ripped the child away, and flung down to her knees, cradling it and rocking, disregarding the sparks and the flames raging too close.

He turned and started walking away. In a second, he would be gone, she knew.

*My Harlan*, Alina thought as she gaped in admiration.

It was a child in the crowd who shouted his name first, whether the boy knew it for sure or didn't.

"It's Harlan Krow!" another shout came.

Then another.

Heads turned.

The crowd shifted.

The fire was abandoned. No one cared for a disaster when they had just witnessed a miracle.

Alina craned her neck, trying to see him, following the crowd that suddenly surged like an ocean wave in his direction.

He was running away.

He lunged in one direction, only to be grabbed by several men.

He jerked, trying to get out of their hands, but was cornered by several others.

They didn't want to hurt him, only to hold him, to make sure it was him—their hero.

"Harlan!" The shouts came.

"It's him!"

"There!"

"Hold him!"

More people were running in their direction, but not for the fire but the legend that was right there, among them.

He could have fought and fisted his way past them. He was strong, Alina knew. But this was Harlan Krow. He never hurt his own.

People started walking up to him from everywhere, and soon, a circle formed, twenty, then thirty, forty people as the circle tightened. He tried to lower his head, shield his face with his hand. But it was impossible to hide from the people who were in awe at the legend incarnate.

Alina pushed into the bodies ahead of her, craning her neck. She should have left but couldn't take her eyes away. Still hidden by the shadow, with his back toward the fire, Harlan's face flickered now and then with an orange glow. But that very moment that wasn't what shocked Alina—it was his humbleness. He was at the mercy of his followers.

The crowd, surrounding him, grew bigger. Soon, they were chanting his name. Women gripped his sleeves as if he were a miracle. Children touched his legs and the hem of his leather coat. They grabbed and pulled at him. They asked silly questions, thoughtlessly murmured his name, grinned, gazed at him as he tried to get away, gently pushing them away but not daring to apply more force to break through the human wall.

Alina was at the very back, ten or so feet away. She wanted to reach her hand and pluck him out of the crowd before they ravished him into pieces in their savage fascination.

Someone yanked off his hat, wanting to have a piece of him.

*Oh God.*

And suddenly, a loud cracking sound crashed through the

air and an awning collapsed, bringing with it a bright flare of fire.

The crowd gasped and surged to the side, distracted for a moment from their hero. By reflex, they turned their heads in the direction of the sound, their hands shielding their faces from the blinding blaze.

And so did Harlan, lowering his hand as he stared at the fire for a moment.

Just a moment.

A moment long enough—because Alina didn't look at the fire, she looked at *him*.

The orange glow illuminated his face bright and clear.

That face…

Alina felt her knees buckle. Everyone stared at the blaze, and she stared at the gentleman-devil, whose face was for the first time in full display.

Blood suddenly rushed into her ears.

"No," she mouthed, feeling it was hard to breathe, the world spinning around her.

"No," she murmured.

She felt a pit in her stomach.

And then she was free-falling.

No fake mustache or beard could disguise the face she'd seen so many times before. And that hair, ragged and hanging loose onto his face and not slicked back and held by a tie.

*My God…*

How had she not known?

She couldn't breathe. The pungent bitter smoke clouded the air. Her lungs burned. Her eyes stung.

"Can't be," she whispered, emotions unleashing in her all at once.

The truth was right there, finally in front of her.

He turned his head then, and suddenly his eyes found her

in the back of the crowd. The realization dawned on him, rendering his gaze with mild terror.

*No. No-no-no-no-no.*

She breathed harder, unable to fight the bile rising in her chest.

If only she had thought of it better, she would have noticed his posture before, his hands, his broad form, the slightly rendered voice but all the same, unmistakably belonging to the man she knew.

She stumbled, stepping backward. She tore her eyes away from him and, without knowing where she was going, darted away from the crowd.

"My lady!" Yegór's voice changed her direction.

She ran past him, down the street, the air burning her lungs, tears scorching her eyes. Her heart hammered in her chest. She reached the carriage and hopped in, slumping on the bench and closing her eyes.

Her hands were shaking as she covered her face and screamed into her gloves. Rocking, she tried to force herself to breathe, but the sobs were suffocating her.

She couldn't believe it. He—they—couldn't do this to her, but had, playing her like a fool.

Alina turned in her seat, sinking, curling up in the corner, sobbing and shaking.

"Oh my God. Oh my God," she kept repeating.

*Why can't I see your face?*

*You will be disappointed.*

The carriage rocked on the uneven road, and she felt like her entire world was spinning on its axis.

Samuel Cassell. The quiet, noble duke, who never said much, whose eyes always gazed at her as if he were trying to make her see the truth.

And the truth was right there. In the dark. In his caresses

and whispers and the life-changing stories he'd told. In the way he touched and kissed her, only to show up the next day in the daylight and pretend like he was someone else.

The despair clutched Alina's chest in a steel grip. Tears streamed down her face, turning her hurt into anger.

"*Liar*," she whispered with a sob.

## 39

---

## TWO LIES

Things were never supposed to get that far, Father. Oh, what a banal excuse!

*What's done in the dark shall come to light.*

For once, Father, your scripture was right.

After escaping the crowd that tried to tear me in pieces as if I were Jesus, I ran, and ran, getting away from those who tried to chase me, children shouting my name in the dark.

I'd come to meet Alina that night. But the fire had sidetracked me. A widow. A child trapped upstairs. I wanted to save yet another life, and it had become my own downfall.

I got to my flat. The dark iron gate hid the lifeless building that was a reminder of my double life.

A flat in London and an estate just outside it. A carriage that was stationed in the East End with a mute coachman who didn't know who I was but fulfilled his service dutifully for years. The lies that this place hid. The dark past. The memories.

Her letters…

I went into my empty bedroom, lit a lamp, and stood in front of the mirror.

A man with a smirk and tired eyes looked back at me. I picked at the corner of the fake beard and tore it off my face, then did the same to the mustache. I took a rag and wiped my ashy face. I smoothed my dark hair, pulling it back, and tied it, then picked up the coal powder and rubbed it onto the lighter strand of hair and its roots, gray and growing out.

I was taking off my disguise and covering up the traces of the gentleman-devil. But in the cold light of the oil lamp, the man who stared at me from the mirror wasn't a duke or a villain. He was simply a lost man.

*Will she listen? Will she understand?*

Her eyes in the back of the crowd—the despair in them, the pain, the shock.

*Dammit…*

Forgive me, Father. Sinners don't always intend to sin when they step onto the wrong path. Murderers don't always want to kill. But once you try the sweet poison, you come back for more. Retribution is a curse. It wraps its hand around your neck and squeezes softly but surely, watching life drain out of you.

I didn't need to prove anything when I avenged the flower girl. I simply wanted to show the world what monsters were. Truth is a weapon. That's why so many hide it in the wrong hands. And I simply handed it to people.

And then I met *her*. How could I have known that she would engulf my entire existence? That she would become my lifeline. That I would fall in love so deeply that the further I fell, the harder it was to show her the truth. Because this time, the weapon was pointing right at me.

When we met, we didn't know where it would lead. We kept seeing each other because we needed it.

Two lonely souls.

Two dreams.

Two visions for the people.

And I let it go too far. I failed her, I know. But what could I possibly have done when she was the only hope I'd ever had?

That night, I changed into my regular clothes. Three-piece suit. Woolen coat with a fur collar. An expensive top hat.

The duke was ready, ladies and gentlemen. His grace was a disgrace. Van Buren would have loved this. And he would have been proud of me if he knew.

But I hated myself at the thought of facing what I had done.

Betrayal is the worst. Oh, that very feeling had started the revenge. It had given birth to Harlan Krow as the city knew him.

I couldn't lose Alina. But the sense of betrayal—nagging, like a festering wound—was there, growing stronger as I left my flat and took a carriage to the Kamenevs' house.

The closer I got, the stronger the feeling of failure grew.

I knew that feeling before, Father.

It had haunted me with nightmares.

It haunts me still at the sight of military men.

I faced it nine years ago on that dreadful January of 1842, in the Hindu Kush mountains.

The day I was buried alive.

## 40

---

## BETRAYAL

A lina paced around her bedroom.
        The desk, the bed, the window.
The window, the bed, the desk.

The memory of Harlan's words made her angry at the silent duke. And the thought of the duke's gaze and smile made her hate the man who so cunningly hid his face in the dark.

She noticed the gap between the curtains and snapped them shut.

Would he be watching her tonight?

She wanted to crawl under the bed and never come out. Instead, she kept pacing, arms hugging her waist as if in this way, she could choke out the sick feeling gathering in her stomach.

Martha knocked on the door and peeked in. "Would you like anything, my lady?"

Alina sent her away. But a minute later, another knock came—Yegór.

"What is it?" she snapped at him.

He nodded down the stairs.

"There is a visitor."

"I don't want to see anyone," she snapped, resuming her pacing.

"It's his gr-race."

Alina halted to a stop, and her heart started racing like mad.

*No. No-no-no.*

Panic rose in her. She stared at Yegór with so much despair that he cast his eyes down.

"He can't…" she murmured. "I can't… I won't see him. No, Yegór!" She shook her head, and if the footman hadn't nodded, she would have begged him.

But, oh, her treacherous heart! Just knowing that he was downstairs, he, Harlan Krow, in her house, in plain view! Her mind started spinning as she tried to make sense of it.

There came an angry row from the stairs. Heavy footsteps. A commotion behind the door.

"Not r-right now," came Yegór's angry words, unusually loud.

Alina darted to the door, flung it open, and froze, staring wide-eyed.

Despite the duke's tall broad form, Yegór looked so much bigger. They stood as if in a duel, facing each other. Martha stood gaping at the top of the stair, her hand pressed to her bosom.

Yegór glared at the duke. And the duke calmly stared at the footman, his voice suddenly low and raspy and oh-so-familiar and etched with danger. "Step. Aside," he said sharply, his words like bullets.

Alina wished she could see the duke's eyes, because Yegór —*her* Yegór, who would never disobey her or listen to anyone but her—drew in a breath and took a step away from the door.

Only then did the duke turn his gaze to her.

*Oh, God.*

She took a step back.

He took a step toward her.

She took one more, letting go of the door handle.

He followed, coming into her slowly, softly closing the door behind him but never breaking the eye contact.

She was terrified—looking in the eyes of a man who was not one but two.

"Alina," he said softly.

Just like Harlan said it, for the duke had never dared to call her by her name. The duke's voice was always sharp, almost strained. But how could she not have seen the similarity?

She shook her head. Her anger was gone again, leaving her weak with hurt and the memories of that voice. She swallowed hard, her heart beating a dozen times a second.

She retreated slowly, not looking away.

"How could you..." she whispered.

The room was suddenly too silent. She could hear a candle hiss as it burned to a stub. There was silence behind the door, Yegór no doubt waiting there, not leaving her alone with the duke.

But the room seemed a different world.

Because *he* was in it.

Alone.

Two men in one, standing in the dim light, his hands at his sides, his coat open, his immaculate suit and shirt and cravat all screaming, "The Duke of Ravenaugh."

But a different image suddenly flickered in her mind.

Her gaze slid down to his lips that she'd kissed.

*God, no.*

Yes, that was certainly Harlan—his assertiveness, the protectiveness of his broad form usually clad in a leather coat, those gloved hands that—

*No.*

The sudden desire to press close to him, to feel the comfort of his embrace was so stark against the image of the duke, the man she'd been so proper with, that she felt like she was losing her mind.

"You have to understand," he said softly, though his voice sounded lower, just like his, Harlan's, as if he'd finally dropped the farce. "It had never—"

"Get out," she whispered, wanting this mad illusion to be over. The room was suddenly suffocating her.

"Please, give me a minute."

"Get out," she said louder, tears welling up in her eyes.

He wasn't supposed to be here. Neither of them—Harlan nor the duke.

She wanted to scream.

To hit him.

To push him away.

To hold him...

She was going insane.

"Please," he said, taking a step closer.

"You betrayed me. You fooled me," she said, hurt and despair rising in her with every word.

"This is not true."

"I kissed you!" she shouted, not knowing who she was talking to. "And then in the carriage..." She covered her eyes with her palm, shame burning her like a blaze.

"That night was special, Alina. I can't tell you what it did to me—"

"Stop!" she snapped, shaking her head, then looked at his blurry silhouette, tears sliding down her face. "You looked at me during the day, knowing—*knowing* what I've done. Do you know how humiliating it is?"

Her chest shook with a suppressed sob. She couldn't look

at him anymore. She wiped her cheeks with her palm and went for the door. But he was like a flash—that quick movement of a fighter so familiar yet startling her—as he caught her in his arms, so gently, as if she were caught in a cloud. His form blocked her way. His arms were around her but barely touching her.

"Please, don't run from me," he said quietly, his soft low voice making her melt on the spot.

She whimpered in weakness, trying to push him away, her head low. But he didn't let go of her, his arms around her like a shield.

This was unbearable, making her head spin. She recognized his scent that carried the traces of fire. She lifted her eyes to his chest and broad shoulders clad in expensive shirt and waistcoat with a gold chain and jacket that she'd seen before. But the strength behind it was the comfortable protectiveness of Harlan Krow. She raised her eyes to his lips—the lips she'd kissed with so much passion. Another inch up, and there it was—the soft gaze of the Duke of Ravenaugh.

She trembled, trying to hold back the tears that ran down her cheeks anyway.

"I don't even know who I am talking to right now," she whispered and pushed away from him. "Liar." She couldn't look at him. She couldn't even look at herself right now.

"I am, I know. Call me anything you want, but don't push me away. Not now, angel."

*Angel.*

Harlan called her that. *Her* Harlan. And now he stood in front of her in the disguise of the duke who'd proposed to her.

"You broke my heart," she sobbed, turning her face up to gaze at him.

And those eyes—*oh, God*—they were the end of her. And

this time, they burned with hurt. "That wasn't my intention, you must know that."

"All those words and whispers in the dark," she said, trying to keep her voice from cracking. "All those gazes in the daylight. You watched me night and day, and I was a stupid girl caught between the two."

"Not stupid. I couldn't do it any other way."

"You could have told me any time!"

"There *wasn't* a proper time, Alina." His voice was lower now, deeper, just like the one in the dark. "Not after days, weeks, when I was falling so deep for you that I thought, 'Just one more day.' Not when every time I saw you, I wanted to take you far away from the city where everyone knew me, either side of me."

"Coward," she whispered.

He didn't blink, didn't move. There was an invisible force in his gaze that pinned her in her spot. "Perhaps." He nodded. "But when it was time, it was too late, because I knew you had feelings for me. I reveled in them, and mine were too strong to let you go. So I kept you with me in any way I could."

"Playing with me."

"I loved you!" he exclaimed, his voice louder then she'd ever heard it, his eyes ablaze, but his gaze softening right away. "Don't you see, Alina?" His whisper was in stark contrast with the words before. "I love you."

The words shook her. Her chest shook with a suppressed sob that was trying to escape. She lowered her eyes, feeling weak at the words.

"I tried to stop myself, told myself this was just an escape of two souls lost in the city of many. I was a criminal, and you were a lady. There wasn't a chance that first encounter would go further than one more. Then another. Then all those letters. You are..." He tried to smile. "You are the one who knows both sides of me. *All* of me. And you wanted me despite everything. Even though you are angry, I know you feel things for me. You are scared. *I* am. And when the devil is scared, the only one who can calm him is an angel. You are my world, Alina. You are part of everything good that has ever happened to me. And there wasn't much of it until you came along."

He went silent, but she still refused to look at him, shame burning through her like a hot poker.

"Look at me, please," he whispered.

She summoned her courage and looked up to meet his eyes. The two men gazed at her through them. The man she saw so many times and wished for him to talk more. And the man who talked in her head for months but whose eyes she'd dreamt of seeing.

And for the first time, she sensed weakness in the man who she'd thought to be the strongest of them all.

He reached behind his head and let his hair loose, the dark strands falling down to his shoulders.

"Oh, God, stop…" she whispered, and a sob escaped her. She blinked, and tears rolled down her cheeks with new force. His transformation was so subtle yet shifted in a direction she didn't want it to go, revealing, second by second, the man she had fallen in love with, spent evenings with, days, months, exchanged letters, kisses, touches, and poured her heart and mind into.

"I can't look at you," she whispered, closing her eyes, her chest tightening. "You are a lie. Two lies."

"You are my truth, Alina."

His hand reached her face and stroked her wet cheeks. His touch had started a fire between them before and was now burning her to ashes. His other hand joined, and he wiped her tears, but they kept coming, her heart ready to explode.

She pushed him away gently and stepped back, retreating like a cornered prey.

"Don't walk away, please," he asked softly, his voice weak like never before. "I know you can't bear to look at me right now. I might be a disgrace, a criminal, a killer. But you gave me a chance once. I can prove to you I am worthy of your trust."

"Trust?" She raised her eyes at him. "What *about* trust? How can you look at me, knowing that I was with another man while you proposed? That I allowed another man to touch me while you courted me? And when you were with me during all those dark nights, how could you love me when you knew I was proposed to by another man and contemplated marrying him?"

"But it was me all along."

"But I didn't know that!" she shouted. She bit her lip to keep it from trembling.

He reached toward her with his hand again, but she took a step back, shaking her head.

"How could one offer a hand to a woman and let another man seduce her in the shadows?"

"Because I love you, Alina," he said quietly, the words hanging heavily in the air. "I couldn't stay away. I took what I wanted before I could open up to you. I was selfish. Scared of the feelings that took over me. Scared that you would choose one or another, and whatever you chose, I wanted it to be me."

The silence was so thick that she could hear the rustling behind the door, knew that someone was eavesdropping. But she didn't care. This evening had wiped away any sense of propriety, opened the curtain to who she really was, and the man who'd been playing his wicked games with her.

"Do you not see now why it is easier to do things in the shadows?" he asked. Oh, how he was right, and she hated herself for that. "Hiding from our true selves, tucking the shame away into the night. We all have two sides. Dark and light. They are both in us. You wanted the dark seduction and the joy of being noble. I wanted retribution and the love of the woman who deserved the best. I can be a villain in the shadows and a lord by day. But I don't need the darkness if I can be with you, Alina. Give me a chance, and I will show you that I can come out of the shadows and be the man you want me to be."

She forced herself to look at him. "How can *you* forgive me? What I've done?"

He shook his head with a weak smile. "There is nothing to forgive, angel."

*Angel.*

The word was ripping her apart.

"I was selfish," he said. "I did this to you, but I did it for myself, blind in my love. The only one here asking for forgiveness is me."

"You should leave, Your Grace," Alina said softly, searching the room for something she didn't know what, only not to look at him. She couldn't. Not now. Not yet.

"Please, don't call me that when we are alone," he said. "In the shadows, I could be myself—a man, not a title. You called me Harlan." He took a step toward her, took her hand in his, and stroked her fingers. "You could touch me." Oh, how she loved his touch. Even now. The feel of his skin brought back the memories. "You could find joy in the things that this hypocritical world deemed disgraceful. Because when you are next to the pitch-black that gapes at you, being a shade darker is not that bad. And despite Harlan Krow being a killer, you looked at him with more desire than you ever looked at his grace with all his titles and wealth."

Her eyes snapped up at him. "That wasn't what drew me to *his grace*," she said bitterly.

"I know, Alina. I *know* that. And that is what makes all the difference."

"You should leave." She pulled her hand out of his. "Please, leave."

He nodded, his eyes never leaving hers.

Oh, how she wanted to make those several steps, take his face in her hands and kiss him, feel his lips on her, his touch, make sure that was the man she'd fallen for and fallen hard. But the betrayal tarnished everything she'd ever felt for him. Both of them. The two men in one. Her curse. The madness that she needed to get away from to know who she was again.

"Leave," she whispered and turned away before his gaze could change her mind.

## 41

### HINDU KUSH

I walked the streets for hours that night. The city I knew so well seemed foreign. Revenge had been the one thing that had always made sense. Then my countess became my reason. But once you know what love is, you can't return to darkness, unless to sign your death warrant.

The memory of her tears pierced me like a hundred bullets. I wanted to take her in my arms and kiss away every single tear. Would it be different if I had confessed to Alina earlier? Before the kiss in the carriage. Before the Phantom Ball. Before I knew that she already had a hold on me like nothing had ever had before.

This is the most peculiar thing, Father. A man can be a most ruthless beast. Yet his heart will cowardly flutter at the sight of his loved one. A man can slay a hundred enemies. Yet he will be slain and go down on his knees in front of the woman he loves. A lion is a king of the animal world, yet he bows to his lioness.

And I was on my knees.

I stomped through the slush as I walked toward the East End that night. November was merciless, but my guilt even more so. The cold wind ruffled my loose hair, whipping the strands across my face and sneaking under my coat. I felt like Harlan Krow, but in my woolen coat and three-piece suit I was the Duke of Ravenaugh. If Alina couldn't reconcile the two, neither could I. I might have been deemed a powerful villain, but my angel was the one who held all the power. And if she didn't have the strength to forgive, I didn't have the strength to fight anymore. She held my heart in her beautiful hands, and if she chose to drop it, it would shatter into pieces.

I didn't feel the tiny snowflakes prickle my face, only saw them—the ashes falling from the sky. The wind howled around, sweeping through the cemetery that was my heart.

*How could you?*

A sharp tug in my chest at the words.

I couldn't lose her, I told myself. Not her. Not my angel. My countess. The thought of the city without her made me feel empty. As if she'd always been there—with her outrageous furs, elegant garments, hair the color of burnt amber in a neat bun, her gentle hands, always cold, the smart mouth that gave the softest kisses, her beautiful eyes and kind laughter.

I didn't know where I was going that night. For the first time, I was lost in the city that I knew by heart. And the winds were growing brutal.

The homeless don't whimper in the weather like this. Did you know that, Father? Their survival instinct makes them conserve their strength.

But walking through the slush and the winds that were picking up, I heard it—a whimper, meek, like that of a kitten.

A small figure was curled up behind a stack of barrels and writhed wearily. I made my way over and pushed it gently with my foot. It mewled. I sat on my haunches and peeled aside the dirty rag that revealed a child's face. A boy. Five-six —it was hard to tell. It could be ten and malnourished.

"A penny, sir," he murmured, delirious from hunger or cold. "A penny for a wretched soul."

I remember one bloody shootout with the enemy in the East. I remember my friend, Krow, as vividly as if he were in front of me. I remember the deafening silence after the battle, and Krow, his shaggy, blond hair smeared with mud and blood, as he kneeled over a dying enemy soldier as young as him and tried to stop his bleeding. Others only shook their heads.

I said, "You can't save everyone, Krow."

He looked at me with that naive desperation of his. "One person at a time, Harlan." And smiled sadly through tears.

The reason I roam the city in the worst times, Father, is because the snow and the winds would forever remind me of being saved.

So that evening, I rose to my feet and picked up that home-less boy by the scruff. He fought in his meek attempts to run, though he was barely breathing.

"Quit it," I barked softly. "Come with me."

We started walking. The little fellow dragged his feet and stumbled against my side. But I finally had a direction. I was going to the already so-familiar place—St James's Hill.

This was what eased the pain, Father. The killings were the revenge against the oppressors. The Hill was the apology to those who were left behind.

*One person at a time.*

In those brutal Hindu Kush mountains, I couldn't save a hundred men, or Krow, or even myself. It was a child who had saved me.

January 1842.

The Hindu Kush mountain crossing.

Those were the horrible days. The retreat. The captures. The defeats, one after another. The lies. Thousands of soldiers killed. Thousands of civilians punished. Our numbers decreased by hundreds, by thousands on the third day.

And yet, and yet, there was always hope as several troops, a hundred of us under the command of Colonel Helbron, moved through the Western range, trying to avoid the slaughter.

Betrayal is a horrible thing, especially by one of your own. Colonel Helbron was no angel, but who would have known that he was a traitor? He was supposed to lead us out of that mess. He was the only hope, and hope was still there when he guided us along a narrow path through the frozen mountains.

What happened next was a massacre.

The mountain silence erupted with shots, shouts, moans, and screams. We were attacked from everywhere, all directions. We were trapped—an open target, cornered into a small space between the rocks that towered above us. There was nowhere to run.

Bullets rained on us. Men fell one by one, on top of each other, like cut grass under a sickle. It seemed to last forever but only lasted minutes.

Then everything plunged into darkness.

I woke up in that same darkness—heavy, slippery, and suffocating. It was a mass grave, Father. A hundred slain men, and I among them.

As I lay there dying—I was sure I was—I felt it, the feeling I would never forget—the warmth of a hundred soldiers leaving their bodies. The warmest spot, the darkest, was my own, for I had been crushed by their weight.

However much time passed, I came back to my senses and started pushing through. It was an animal instinct of fighting despite the weakness. I gasped for air, pushing through the dead limbs, stiff corpses, uniforms slick with blood, the pungent smell of sweat, tobacco, and everything else left after men when life leaves them.

My own wounds throbbed, piercing my body with excruciating pain. But soldiers are trained to survive. So I kept pushing—up, up, up, through pain and dead flesh—until my hand reached a cold emptiness.

Light!

Heaven!

But I wasn't so lucky. It was just an ordinary sunny winter day. And as I reached the surface, there was a sea of dead bodies around me.

I wanted to scream, cry, moan, but strength was leaving me.

Have you ever seen red snow, Father?

The mountains were burgundy. The ground was covered in red slush that surrounded the bodies that lay like ragged dolls. Those were my friends, my comrades. Wonderful, kind Krow among them—my best friend who would never sing again or put smiles on others' faces.

For thousands of days, Father, I wished I had died that day. To some, darkness is a relief. To others, light is a reminder of hell. There wasn't a man on this earth who hated bright days more than me.

Our brave colonel, you ask? He'd made a deal with the enemies and led us straight to death. Keep your enemies close, they say. He kept his closer and got richer. A hundred coins was the cost of our lives. A coin for one man. Months later, the colonel would be a national hero for surviving the slaughter, soon a general and a royal friend. I shall never forget his face. Or the Grand Cross of the Bath Order that he received.

Colonel Helbron was the only survivor.

And then there was me. But I was barely a man. I'd seen death, but the day I crawled to the surface, covered in blood, atop a hundred slain men, I knew what death was—losing faith in simple human values.

We are incredible creatures, Father. Fire and ice. Saints and sinners. Darkness and light. We can withstand hours of torture and years of abuse. Scars, wounds, broken bones, and fractured souls.

And yet, a spider bite can end us in hours. A snake bite—in minutes. There is a rare flower that can kill with its seeds. We are the world's marvel. Life with torture. Death by flower. And we like testing each other. Many of us die at the hands of our own.

That day, I was barely alive. I couldn't walk. Frost bit at my fingers that clawed at the stone path and slipped through the slush as I tried to crawl away from the slaughter. My bloodied uniform turned into hard armor, growing icy cold by the minute. I was losing blood and wondered how I was still alive.

Giving up, I fell onto my back and lay in red snow, asking God to take me. I could feel frost seeping through my veins. The cloud of my warm breath got smaller.

Instead, God sent an angel.

As my gaze drifted around the towering mountains, it stopped on a small figure, bundled in furs. It stared at me from one of the closer rocks as it cowered behind it. And I couldn't mistake it for anyone. Not those eyes—blue, luminous, the color of a summer river—that belonged to the young mountain girl who would nurse me back to life.

*Ubuntu. I am because you are.*

You see, Father, we've come full circle.

## 42

## THE CONFESSION

It had been days since the fire. Alina sat in her room for hours, staring out the window.

Another day of waiting, for what—she wasn't sure.

The light from the window sliced the room in half. Darkness and light. Day and night. Good and evil. Alina sat empty-eyed, trying to reconcile the events of the past months.

Tap.

She tapped the tip of the quill on the desk.

Tap.

Minutes ticked away hours, and she tried to make it to the evening so she could put out the lights and go to bed, only to lie there, stare at the dark ceiling, and think of *him*.

And during the day, every noise in the house, the slamming of the doors, the footsteps made her heart race at the thought that he would come again.

Martha brought her meals into the room, but Alina didn't touch them.

Anna Yakovlevna came to talk to her, complaining about the brutal weather and gloom and something about Prosha and another function, then pursed her lips in disappointment. "You should write to him."

"Who?" Alina frowned.

"Ah, his grace, Alina! Who else? It is about him, is it not?"

*Indeed.*

Nikolai Sergeevich came in the evenings, sat in his chair, and studied her. "You don't have to tell me anything. But I want to make sure you are all right. *Will* be all right. If you need advice or an opinion, I am here."

Martha walked around on tiptoes. Her usual bickering with Yegór turned into hushed whispers, strangely friendly, which stopped when Alina was around. Their glances were those of conspirators.

"About time you made peace," Alina said to Martha, who only tsked in pretended annoyance.

Alina missed him. Harlan, Samuel—did the name matter anymore? There was a hole in her life where he'd been, and she couldn't find anything that could fill it even for a minute. She'd told him to leave and now desperately wanted him back.

After five days, Alina forced herself to leave the house and went to Grevatt's.

Rumi met her with a solemn face.

"He is having one of those episodes," she announced, following Alina into Dr. Grevatt's study where the doctor sat strangely quiet and studying the pipe in his hand. He had a robe on, undone, house slippers and a shirt, half-unbuttoned.

He met her with a cheerful exclamation. "Ah, we have a visitor! Mary, would you bring the fine lady some tea and biscuits!"

He started clearing his desk as Rumi looked up at Alina with eyes full of tears. She stopped him with a soft touch of her hand. "Dr. Grevatt, I shall talk to Miss Alina. You might want to take a rest."

He looked at her in surprise yet didn't argue. "Of course, of course, I shall leave you to it," he murmured, looking around for something, then frowned in confusion and walked out of the study.

"He's been like this since early afternoon," Rumi said quietly as Alina took off her hat, coat, and gloves and took a seat in one of the chairs. She stared at the floor. The silence of the study was so heavy that the maid with a tea tray felt like an obnoxious intruder.

Alina covered her face with her hands and shook her head, rubbing her forehead. Everything was falling apart around her. This feeling was the worst—losing the people she loved. It drained the life out of her. In this confusion, *his* words were so vivid in her mind.

*I love you.*

Tears burned her eyes as she repeated them to herself again and again. She needed him like the air to breathe. Even guilt and shame subsided under the need to have him by her side.

If he were gone…

She thought of Dr. Grevatt, his brilliant mind that was fading away like the last summer sunshine. Soon, he wouldn't know faces, people, or who he was. Soon, his body would be there but his mind would be gone.

She exhaled heavily and looked at Rumi.

Rumi sat quiet in her chair. "We knew it would happen." Her usual confidence was gone, her eyes pools of tears. This was the man who'd raised her, taught her, gave her the freedom of pursuing her passion.

Alina lowered her eyes and studied her own hands. The memory of Harlan kissing her fingers flickered like a firefly.

She closed her eyes and tried to think of something else.

The maid knocked on the door, peeking inside. "There is a visitor for you, ma'am," she said, looking at Alina.

Who could possibly come in at this time? She looked at the clock. Seven in the evening. Could it be Yegór? They should go to St Rose's, but she didn't feel like doing anything.

She rose slowly and walked out into the hall.

"The gentleman won't come in," the maid said, shrugging her shoulders.

Alina nodded, opening the door and raising her eyes at—

The duke.

Her heart thudded so forcefully that she thought the world around her shook. The cold wafted into her face, catching her breath.

Samuel stood broad and tall, his hair slicked back, his eyes —myriads of feelings, burning the space between them.

His form was so dear to her that her entire body stirred in response. She couldn't breathe. She gripped the door handle so tightly that her knuckles turned white—anything not to run into his arms.

"Alina."

That voice, low and soft, enveloped her heart like a thick fog.

She closed her eyes to keep her head from spinning.

"Please, don't turn me away." His whisper came like a plea as he took a step toward her.

She opened her eyes and saw a ghost. His voice belonged to the nights, his face to the daytime. He'd brought with him the feeling of shame that colored her cheeks red and the feeling of home where her heart felt at peace. She needed to run from him, but her knees felt weak, for she wanted to run into his embrace.

This was torture. Another step and she could reach him with her hand yet did nothing.

"Can we talk?" he asked softly. "If this is the last time, so be it. But I need to tell you many things you don't know."

There had been many strange days in her life lately. And most of them had to do with him. This was yet another strange night as she led him through the entrance hall past the curious glances of the maid.

Rumi walked out into the hallway, cocking her head with interest, then saw the duke and froze, her eyes darting from Alina to the man and back to Alina.

Alina held her breath and looked away. She brought him to the small office where Dr. Grevatt took occasional patients and set the lit candle on the small wooden desk.

*Talk. Please, talk,* her heart whispered. All she needed to be at peace again was to hear his voice.

They sat down in the chairs, but instead of facing each other, they sat side by side, facing the desk.

She was scared to face him again but weak with the urge to touch him, hold him, press against him and know that everything would be all right.

They sat side by side like they'd done so many times in the small garden at St Rose's. Except this time she could see all of him, the light of the candle bright and clear on his ashen profile and firmly pressed lips. His eyes burned as if with fever when he took his hat in his hands, and Alina held her breath, waiting for his first words.

"My mother died when I was five," he said softly.

And she listened, loving the sound of his voice. That was how he'd pulled her in from the very start—she'd wanted to know more. Except she'd never known the story of a simple man—a man with parents, family, childhood.

"All I remember is her smile. Probably for the better." His words came slowly, but she had patience.

"My father was a typical duke, less concerned about me as a person but more as an heir. So when the time came for me to pick out a good compliant wife and take over the estate and the lazy indulgent life of a bourgeois, I ran. With the military, naturally. My father would never let me join, so I joined under an alias. My father died when I was in service. It wasn't a tragedy. He didn't leave many good memories, only money. Some fathers don't leave even that."

Alina turned to watch him as he talked. He didn't look at her but stared ahead at the desk with the lone candle, as if he tried to see the path that his life was taking.

"I've been to many countries. I have seen many atrocities. And the hardest thing to come to terms with was not what humans were capable of, but trying to reconcile the brutal reality of war that I chose and the glittering splendor of the ton where I belonged."

She swallowed hard. She understood. She'd never been to war, but she'd seen the silent fight back in Russia where you could get a bullet in your head for thinking differently.

"I suppose I dreamt of a better life. And on the dark streets, I found it the night we met—in your eyes, your frightened gaze that I'd seen in so many and tried to help them. That same night, I saw you at the ball. Your gaze was brave and indifferent as if you had no worry in the world. Pretending—I knew what it was like, for that was how I'd lived for many years. That night, I decided I wanted to know more about you. I tried to stay away, but an invisible force drew me to you. Again. And again. Night and day. I tried to find a reason but gave up trying to rationalize, for I was falling for you fast and deep, until I couldn't remember a time you weren't in my life."

*Keep talking.*

He told her about his time in the East, the Hindu Kush story. She wiped her tears but didn't interrupt. Her heart ached for him, hurt for his pain, but she needed to know more.

So he talked. And talked. He'd told her many stories in his

letters. Those had been glimpses. Now he took his heart and lay it on his palm for her to see.

Dark.

Bloody.

Beautiful and sad.

Her own heart beat in sync with his words as his life unfolded before her eyes. His words were a river, calm and deep, carrying her away from the room they were in.

"I was used to living in pain. It was inside me, dark and thick, slicing with memories through every day. It was around me everywhere I looked. And taking the pain of others helped me dull my own. Until the space where it used to be was filled with darkness instead. Only one thing made it all dissolve—the moments when I was with you. Something other than icy darkness found its way into my heart. It was healing. I lived by night, and you were dawn. When you came into my life, I couldn't wait for a new day as long as you were in it. I've never known true love, Alina. But if it means reliving the horrible past only for a chance to meet you again—than I would have done it again so it could bring me to the day I met you. If it means going through a hundred tortures just to hear you say my name, I love you. If it means to lay down my life just to see you smile, I love you, Alina."

She drowned in his words, not paying attention to the tears that streamed down her face.

"In the last year," he said quieter, "I felt like I was standing on top of a cliff, staring down at a massive dark abyss. I was losing the ground under my feet and falling into it. But then a hand caught me, pulling me back. A gentle soft hand that by no means could possibly have that much power. But it did. It was yours, Alina. I know I deceived you, but it wasn't my intention. You think that I tricked you, but it couldn't have happened any other way. I was a coward, trying to hold on to you, knowing that if you found out the truth, you would have pushed me away. You see, I relished the fact that you understood my dark side. Despite the rumors and the awful crimes, many of which didn't belong to me, you gave me a chance. But I knew you deserved better—a man noble and kind, a man who could give you the proper life you deserved. A duke, no less."

She took a deep breath and wiped her tears. "Would you have kept lying to me if you weren't discovered?" she asked softly. "Or would you have walked away?"

He cast his eyes down at his hands that still held his hat. "I got carried away, Alina. But one thing I know for certain—I would have never walked away. I am a shadow, remember?" He smiled to himself. "I could only hope that one day, I would come out into the light, and you would accept me the way I was. I didn't mean for it to happen in such a painful way."

He looked at her then, and she turned to meet his eyes. One's gaze had the power of persuasion much stronger than words or appearances. *His* transcended all her reason. It made the world around them go so quiet that she could hear her own heartbeat.

The candlelight shone softly onto his face. She'd dreamt of seeing Harlan's face. And it was the one she'd seen so many times in the daylight.

He smiled weakly. The man who fought monsters looked vulnerable facing the woman he loved. But who didn't when stripped down to his dark dirty soul?

He'd humbled himself before her. The duke. The gentleman-devil. Tears burned her eyes again at the thought. She brought her hand to his face and stroked his cheek—his stubble, not the fake beard and mustache. He closed his eyes and leaned into her palm as if her touch could wipe away all his worries, then took her hand in his and kissed her fingers, like he'd done at the Phantom Ball.

Tears rolled down her cheeks.

He opened his eyes, meeting hers. "You saved many people, Alina. And you saved me. The best moments of my life were with you. The most tender, too. I've never felt so alive as I feel next to you. If you tell me to leave and never come back, I will honor your wish. But it will kill me."

"I just need time," she said, pulling her hand away, though it pained her to part.

He nodded, his eyes burning her with something new —hope.

## 43

---

## THE SPIDER

Nothing was right that night. Father. That should have been the sign. The streets were a cemetery. The houses stared at me with dark windows like toothless mouths. The cold arrow of wind now and then made me shiver. The dark alleyways were my dwelling place, but that night, they felt hostile.

I had betrayed Alina's trust. The thought of her tears kept cutting through my mind like a sharp knife, slicing all the way to my heart and the pit of my stomach, making me sick.

I could only blame myself. Blind in my curiosity, I had fallen in love so deeply that I believed in magic and miracles, thinking that things would sort themselves out. If she didn't want me, I would stay in the city that held her presence, kissing the roads where her pretty foot stepped, touching the surfaces that her gloved hand touched.

I lied to myself, of course. After all I'd been through, losing the person I loved would be a sure death. I shouldn't be able to go on. I didn't want to. The thought of her not wanting me was the biggest pain I'd felt. Like a bullet that would strike my body, then pull back, and pierce me again, again and again, a hundred times. Could you survive that, Father? I wanted to weep at what I'd done.

Even the devil can cry, losing the one he loves.

*One more time*, I told myself that night as I skirted the buildings of the dark alleys, knowing precisely where I was going and where to find the monster whose time had run out. *One more monster…*

I was in Central London. My pocket watch showed nine in the evening. Mr. Hacksaugh would be leaving the building on Inn Yard at ten. I didn't have time to get to my flat and change. The circus was over. This was the last assignment. And it didn't matter if it was the gentleman-devil or the Duke of Ravenaugh serving justice. I wanted this to be over.

Do you see, Father? My mind wasn't in it that night. I should've known. I should've stopped. You never wanted this, I know, but I wanted to punish the monster that had hurt you.

The closer I got to the slums, the darker the night grew. My boots were wet, my fashionable woolen coat too thin for this weather. My suit underneath constricted my movements. Harlan Krow was swift, confident, and sharp. But I wasn't myself that night.

Dogs howled in the gutters. Men moaned in pain. Drunks bellowed. The shutters of the houses slapped loudly at their hinges in the wind, and the occasional footsteps and murmurs in the dark seemed like those of ghosts.

I was in Shoreditch, past the streets hawking with entertainers, when I had an icy feeling of someone following me.

I used to be good with guns, then became an expert with a blade. Guns could miss. They didn't see the person, only a target. A blade, though, let you get close and look the monster in the eyes. It taught you to feel the human presence next to you. That night, I felt the closeness of someone else, but it was confusing.

I gripped the knife in my pocket so tight the handle felt hot. Its blade would soon scorch the monster, sheathing into his flesh. I never thought of the pain the monsters felt. Nor did I try to inflict it. I simply wanted to rid this earth of one more piece of trash, to ease the pain of those who suffered. More importantly, to spare those who would in the future. Getting rid of a monster was like pulling a bad tooth. Plucking a weed. Killing a mosquito.

I kept hearing footsteps as if the devil himself was watching me. Ah, the irony! *I* was the devil, remember? Yet, something kept lurking behind me as if the shadows of all the killed men had come back to haunt me.

This is the dilemma, Father. That treacherous Hacksaugh was the man I wanted to end so badly. The man—one of many —who'd wronged you and many others. When you've seen what humans are capable of, when you've witnessed what is done to the weak and defenseless, when you've learned for over a decade that your purpose was to fight an enemy, how can you see the enemy and not strike?

Ah, your Bible teaches us to obey the law and the ever-changing moral code. But who will enforce it? What if those who establish it break it? The Bible teaches us to turn the other cheek. But what if your cheeks are so raw from abuse that there is no strength left except to strike back?

That evening felt wrong, though. My philosophy had taken a blow, and I couldn't figure out where the blow had come from. Something nagged at me. I tried to focus on the mission, but my mind kept returning to *her*.

I came up to Inn Yard and stood at the building I knew so well for some time, leaning on the wall in the shade, watching the door. My pocket watch said two minutes to ten. Two minutes until Hacksaugh appeared.

He came out, pulled up his collar, and started walking fast, hunching and in a hurry. I'd seen him so many times that I knew what street he would turn into, where he would stop to buy a bottle of gin. I gauged his pace as I followed him down the dark streets.

Finally, I made up my mind. Those minutes usually were the clearest. My focus sharpened. My hold on the knife grew stronger. I lowered my face and took deep breaths, controlling my breathing. The wind howled in sync with my heartbeat— that was how it always had been, the world around syncing with my entire body in the wake of the attack. I walked quietly but determined, increasing my pace, like a shadow, following the man silently, closing the distance rapidly.

I moved swiftly, unnoticed. I was about to pull my knife out.

In that moment, when I was merely feet away from my target, about to strike, *her* face suddenly appeared so vividly in front of me that I halted in shock, my feet scuffing against the ground.

Sensing me, the man whipped around and halted, staring at me.

Her image floated before me again. *Her* eyes. Not reproaching, no, but sad and disappointed.

Her voice as if in the back of my mind, *"To heal means not to become the monster that caused you pain in the first place."*

And her image was somehow marred by the proximity of this filth of a man.

I couldn't do it, Father. That moment was a revelation. As if the light had shone onto me, exposing all the ugliness of what I was about to do.

I stood immobile, facing the monster who was supposed to die. He didn't turn away, as if he knew, waited, ready to give an excuse. Monsters always had an excuse, if not on their tongue then in their eyes.

"What do you want?" he grumbled. And suddenly a waft of stench came from him, like that from a sewer or a ditch with a dead dog in it.

I took a step back, retreating, like a lion sensing a dying animal. Did you know that lions don't eat sick flesh, Father?

I was about to turn and walk away, the images of Alina in my head in stark contrast with this foul man.

But I was wrong, Father. He wasn't a sick prey. He was a spider. A spider that should have been dead that night.

And here is a thing about spiders, Father. They can attack within fractions of a second. They can kill with one bite.

I heard him before I felt him. A growl. A sudden swish in the air. A quick rustle.

I was filled with the thoughts of her, you see. I let myself get distracted.

And in those seconds as my angel's image still lingered in my mind, a sharp blinding pain pierced my stomach. The stench suddenly became overpowering, the man so close, pressing flush against me, his face merely inches away. His hand jerked, and another sharp stab pierced me, taking the breath out of me.

Pain spiderwebbed through my body, pulsating the strongest in that one spot as if a hole had been carved out of me. My knees were suddenly weak, my legs barely holding me as I tried to remain upright.

The monster pulled away and retreated.

There was a shout right behind me, and the man darted away.

But everything seemed hazy. The pain brought me down to my knees, into the slush. I'd forgotten how sharp and dark it can be. I pressed my hand to the source of it, sudden weakness overtaking me. I thought it was the end. And in that moment, I had one cowardly thought—I hoped I wouldn't die, for that meant I would never see *her* again."

"Oh, God…" the whisper came from behind me. A female voice, soft, murmuring, calling my name. Yes, Father, my name.

Another angel?

"There is blood," the voice whispered in panic. The bluest of bloods is red when spilled, Father.

I tried to look around to see her face, but the pain was so sharp that it blinded me. Only for a moment, before everything sank into darkness, I felt gentle hands take a hold of me to cushion my fall as my body sank onto the ground. A woman's voice shouted for help, and I saw the face that called my name.

"Hold on, Your Grace," she whispered, and I recognized her.

She had the face of an angel, indeed. And it was the color of the darkest night.

## 44

## THE GRAVE NEWS

"Alina, *ma chérie*, is it so trying for you to accept the noble man? What burden it would lift!" Anna Yakovlevna cooed half in French, half in English. She tried to speak more English on the account that she was enamored with the duke. Her accent was smoother but somehow too theatrical, and it only annoyed Alina.

Alina had cried going to bed the night before. She'd been so angry. So hurt. So bitter. And missing him so desperately that she felt like her body was turning inside out.

The world still didn't make sense. Harlan was the night. The duke was the day. Yet, they were all the same.

Yegór asked if Alina wanted to go to Grevatt's, but she waved him away. She took Martha and went to a French pâtisserie on Greek Street.

London was sinking into mud and misery. Horses splashed with mud to their very knees. People no better. Slipping and sliding. Shoes muddied. Skirt hems soaked and splattered. Faces hidden in the pulled up collars and shawls. Wrinkled foreheads. Lackluster eyes.

Alina had loved the miserable weather. Until now. She

walked into the shop, followed by Martha, and exhaled. It smelled of sweet pastries and burned sugar. The warmth enveloped her, making her cold face tingle at the temperature change.

"Lady Bronskaya!" A high-pitched voice belonged to Lady Agatha, whose wrinkled mouth was always curled into a contemptuous smirk but now was stretched into an overly-sweet smile.

*Another one.*

"London is gossiping, Lady Bronskaya." She slid a glance over the fox stole, wrapped around Alina's shoulders, the fox face peacefully resting on her chest.

"Oh." Alina smiled politely.

"You and the Duke of Ravenaugh," the lady said, then leaned a bit closer. "Did he propose?" She cocked an eyebrow.

Alina laughed nervously, noticing Martha look away. "Martha, please get the usual." She was about to take off her gloves, then changed her mind. "Would the ton be enraged if he did?" She smiled coldly at the lady, avoiding the answer.

"Oh, they would be devastated at the loss of such a man to a foreign lady. The English don't like to share, you understand."

Alina laughed at this pathetic attempt of a joke that wasn't a joke at all. Alina glanced at Martha and wished they could be done here.

"Did he?" Lady Agatha's voice was too eager.

Alina felt her heart tighten. "Excuse me, Lady Agatha, we are quite pressed for time. Perhaps we could meet for tea and chat some other time."

She pushed past her toward Martha and as discreetly as possible yanked her out of the shop without getting what they'd come for.

"What did you tell her?" the maid asked.

"My life is no one's business," Alina snapped, stomping through the slush toward the carriage.

"It wasn't. Until lately, my lady."

Alina stepped into the carriage and settled in her seat, inhaling the scent of baking laced with the damp smell of muddy slush and leather.

The thoughts of Samuel seized her suddenly. With a gust of wind that wafted into the carriage before Martha closed the door. With the murmur of the street outside the window. With the shadows that bore the traces of him.

One particular thought snaked into her mind, like a drop of poison—that for some strange reason, she would not see him again. Horror gripped her heart with its icy hand. The thought of the world that didn't have Harlan Krow or the duke in it made her hollow. Tears blurred her eyes. She would go to him, she knew then.

She inhaled like a drowning person, gasping for precious air.

And life made sense again.

And Yegór's mountainous figure at the house made her smile as he took her hat and coat.

"Will you be gentle with the furs, *krasavets*!" Martha snapped at him quietly, but there was no anger in her words, only a shiver as his big hands grazed her shoulders when he took the maid's coat next.

Alina chuckled.

The sounds of the piano trickled through the house.

"Mamá! You are playing Couperin!" She smiled, walking into the sitting room. Her mother hadn't played her favorite song since they'd left Russia. Nikolai Sergeevich, dressed in a house robe and slippers, sat on the sofa, sipping tea, a smile on his face.

Suddenly Alina felt happy.

Yes, she would talk to Samuel again! There was much more to be said! She'd thought she needed more time, but she simply couldn't go on without him.

And as the thought made her heart flutter, she settled next to her father on the couch and wrapped her hand tightly around his arm.

Yegór walked in. "There is a visitor for you, my lady," he said, looking at Alina and nodding toward the door.

Her heart fluttered in hope.

"The girl with the face the color of coal," he said in Russian, crossing himself as they walked through the hall.

Rumi's gaze was solemn as she looked at Yegór hostilely until he huffed and stepped away. "His grace is at Dr. Grevatt's," she said quietly.

Alina furrowed her brows. "Why would he be there?"

Rumi swallowed hard. "He was attacked last night."

The world starting spinning around Alina.

"We brought him there to treat his wounds, but..." Rumi lowered her eyes to her hands as Alina's heart started pounding against her ribcage. "He is unconscious. You should come, Miss Alina."

And the world collapsed around her.

## 45

---

## HEALING

The carriage wasn't moving fast enough. Alina tapped her foot on the floor as she listened to Rumi's story.

She didn't say the gentleman-devil's name even once. "The duke," was all she said.

"But how?" Alina asked in desperation.

"The night he was here, I followed him when he left."

Alina shook her head in shock. The police had been hunting him down for months. Rumi had found him in one day.

Alina felt a warm touch and looked down to see Rumi's dark hand gently squeezing hers.

"He will be all right, Miss Alina," Rumi said with a soft smile.

And Alina had to turn away so that Rumi didn't see the tears well up in her eyes.

The hallway at Dr. Grevatt's smelled of spice and mold. "What is this?" Alina asked as she hurriedly shrugged off her coat and rushed into the small patients' room.

Her knees buckled.

Smoke curled in the air of the room that sank into dimness with the curtains half-closed. A large woman with a scarf wrapped around her hair in what looked like a turban sat by the bed and muttered in an unknown language, waving her hands around.

Alina gaped in shock and swallowed, stepping closer, so slowly as if she were a witness to a sacred ceremony not intended to be seen in daylight.

The duke lay on a bed that wasn't big enough for him. Motionless. Asleep. His powerful body outlined by the thin blanket pulled up to his chest.

There was a glass of evil-smelling liquid next to the woman by the bed, the scent of it reaching Alina's nostrils.

A hand on Alina's shoulder stopped her from moving closer.

"What *is* this?" Alina muttered in shock.

Rumi pulled her out of the room.

"She is a healer," Rumi explained.

"What sort of healer?"

"A witch."

"A what?" Alina gaped at her.

Rumi swallowed hard and crumbled a handkerchief in her hands. "A folk healer. That's what we call them."

"We?"

"In Southern Africa."

"Where did she come from?"

"I went to the Mile End this morning to fetch her."

"The East End? But Rumi!"

"She is said to have herbs that can turn a devil into a saint."

Rumi attempted a smile that faded under Alina's horrified gaze.

Alina shook her head. "In times like this, Rumi. You are a doctor!" Blood pumped in her ears. "Maybe I should bring a whisperer from Whitechapel, too. We shall have all the herb-healers for the duke. Gah!"

She turned to see the healer-woman in the doorway stare at her. Her face was darker than Rumi's, the whites of her eyes red, earrings the size of a palm dangling down to her shoulders.

Alina stalled, felt embarrassed for her words. "Thank you." She nodded and rushed to grab her reticule for money.

And when Rumi led the woman outside, Alina finally stepped into the patients' room.

*Oh, God.*

She took a seat next to the duke, hoping he would open his eyes. But he was unconscious. He looked so peaceful that Alina felt like a spy, observing him in this unguarded moment. She pulled the blanket down and saw his shirt slightly spotted with blood that had seeped through the dressing under the garment.

Her eyes burned with tears. The most powerful man in London was here, unconscious and weak.

"We changed him into a clean shirt."

Rumi's voice behind her almost made her jump. She pulled the blanket up to Samuel's chest and looked around. She wanted to open the window to get rid of the strange smell. She wished it were warmer. She wanted more light. And she wanted him to be awake.

"He talked in his delirium," Rumi said. "He was awake for a brief moment, but Dr. Grevatt gave him laudanum."

Rumi's voice was imposing. Alina wished she were alone with him. Wished he were awake. And the strangest thought occurred to her—for weeks, she'd thought of the duke, had been in his presence, but only several times touching his hand, and now he lay half-undressed in the patients' bed.

"We changed the dressing several times," said Rumi, still standing behind Alina.

And Alina felt jealous for a moment that the girl had spent more time with the duke in the most important moment.

*Oh, how unfair!*

He was hers! She was supposed to be next to him, but her pride hadn't let her!

"Dr. Grevatt thinks that the wounds weren't too severe," Rumi continued quietly. "He said the knife could've been caught on the gold chain of his waistcoat and didn't go too deep. But he gave him enough laudanum to keep him from moving. Because, you know, he would probably insist on leaving."

*Right.*

Alina wiped the corners of her eyes and cocked her head, studying him.

Rumi shifted behind her. "Dr. Grevatt says he should be kept sedated for a couple of days."

"A couple of days," Anna repeated quietly.

"I am sorry, Miss Alina," Rumi said.

Alina finally turned to look at her. "For what?"

"For the woman I brought. I should have asked you. It's just… If science could cure a body, mind, and heart, people wouldn't be in need of God or women like her. If everything was in our hands, there would be no need for dreams and hope."

"Rumi…" Alina closed her eyes, inhaling deeply so as not to cry again. "Can I be alone with him, please?"

Alina spent the rest of the day by the duke's side, and in the evening, when she returned home, she went to her room and broke down in tears.

"He will be fine," Dr. Grevatt had assured her before she left. "It could have been much worse."

Those were the words that tugged at her heart, making her weep into the pillow.

It could have been the last time she'd seen him. She could have spent her life regretting her harsh words.

The next day she woke up at dawn and was at Grevatt's by eight.

"His grace woke up late last night," Rumi said. Alina cursed in disappointment. "He won't be awake until later this afternoon."

"And the dressing?" Alina asked.

"I was about to change it. Dr. Grevatt has gone to St Rose's. He shall be back some time later to check."

"I'll do it," Alina said sternly.

This was the closest she'd been to him, to his skin, seeing his torso naked, seeing him so defenseless and…peaceful.

She wished Rumi didn't watch her when she cleaned his wound, her hands slightly shaking. She'd done it so many times with other patients but this was the first time she'd touched the man she loved. This felt intimate. She studied every inch of his skin, wanting to touch him everywhere, run her hands along his limbs, feel their strength.

Rumi's voice cut through her thoughts. "I haven't gotten a chance to bring the news to his household. He has no family, they say. His butler, perhaps? Surely, he needs to know. Arrangements need to be made. He is out of danger. Perhaps, they would like to bring him to his house."

"Well, yes," Alina agreed reluctantly. She wanted him here, close to her, *with* her when he woke up. "I shall go to his house. Will you stay with him, Rumi? Don't take your eyes off him."

She rushed out the door without putting her gloves on, so eager she was to go to his place. She'd been there once. That had been the time when he meant nothing—another dinner party. The silent duke. The ever-prying Van Buren. The eaves-dropping.

*Oh, the irony.*

Alina settled in the carriage and closed her eyes, tilting her head back against the wall. Memories flooded her again.

That night at the duke's—the conversation with the commander and the Lord Mayor. The duke's knowing smirks and replies.

*"A manhunt."*

*"Oh, Harlan Krow is very real."*

His laughter.

He knew.

Knew!

He played games with the law and authorities, being right in the middle of it all and laughing at them!

Alina smiled and chuckled, but right away felt like crying.

This was impossibly twisted.

The way he'd gazed at her that night. Had he wanted to see if she would warn him?

And she had. She'd run right into the center of the riot, trying to find him.

She couldn't help thinking that he was marvelous. Oh, she wanted to hate him for what he'd done to her. But how could she not admire the man who so cleverly wrapped the ton around his finger?

*The devil.*

She smiled.

*Her* devil.

Her heart tightened with tenderness.

Suddenly, her life filled with a new meaning—taking care of him, being with him, finding the new connection.

His house looked different by day. It belonged to the man who dined and wined with the ton and played the most dangerous game behind their backs.

Admiration blossomed in her chest at the thought. With all the feelings that had collided in her at the news, the grief she'd lived with in the last two days, a new feeling was starting in her heart—pride.

The footman greeted her with the most politeness.

"I need to see his grace's butler. Right away. It is a matter of urgency."

The butler, an older man with graying hair and sharp features, softened by the sideburns and beard, now looked different than she remembered. His gaze was too intense, almost prying, as if he were in on the whole thing.

"Lady Bronskaya," she introduced herself.

"My lady." He bowed. "I know. There is quite a lot of talk about you in this household."

It startled her for a moment.

"It's his grace." She swallowed, studying the man and trying to figure out how much he needed to know. She could've sent a note, of course. Yet she wanted to be close to Samuel and every part of his life. She wanted his staff to know that she was the closest person to him. This unnecessary pride was quite...

*Quite so desperate and woman-like.*

She snorted to herself.

*That of a woman in love.*

Her heart fluttered again at the thought. "His grace is detained by some quite unpleasant circumstances, I am afraid."

"Please, tell me."

"He will do so himself soon. He wasn't able to write, you see. But he is all right, and he will send a note as soon as he is able. I didn't want you to worry that he disappeared without notice."

The butler stared at her like she'd just made it up.

*Oh, Lord.*

"Until his grace is able to write to you, you may send any urgent messages to my house on Birchin Street—"

"The Kamenevs. Yes, my lady, I know," he finished with a knowing smile. "Everything is in order. His grace doesn't have anything to worry about. Mr. Nowrojee was inquiring about him. In fact, he is here with his steward. I shall pass the message on to him."

"Oh!"

What would the manager of St James's Hill be discussing with the duke's steward? Unless it had to do with charity.

Alina was shameless in her curiosity, but such was life. It wasn't the right moment, but she wanted to seize the opportunity and perhaps help.

"May I see Mr. Nowrojee?" she inquired.

"Why, yes! I shall tell him you are here."

She should be back at Grevatt's, taking care of Samuel. Instead, she was at his house, and above anything—trying to make connections.

"Lady Bronskaya!"

Mr. Nowrojee was a short slender man in his fifties. Of Indian descent, his short-cropped hair and soft features with large kind eyes made him look overly friendly. He looked more like a writer or a doctor than the manager of the largest project in London. Alina studied him in amusement as he approached.

"Mr. Nowrojee." She smiled eagerly. "I am afraid we've

never met, but I surely heard a lot about you and, in fact, was hoping to be introduced to you one day."

He chuckled softly, studying her with curiosity as he kissed her hand. His smile grew bigger. "Well, your beauty is as charming as your accent. Just as the rumor has it."

She laughed. There it was—her beauty, accent, heritage. It all came first.

"You are a person of science, I hear," Mr. Nowrojee said, his gaze even more intense at the words.

That was a surprise.

"Ah, I am not sure what exactly you've heard." Her heart fluttered at the words.

"That you are very knowledgeable in the medical field, for one. In fact, the word *brilliant* has been used." He nodded with a smile and bowed slightly. "That you are a patron of St Rose's and a practicing nurse there, in fact." He bowed again, as if he were counting her every achievement.

She felt her face heat up at the words. If a man with such connections and power didn't look down on her for doing what she did, that was surely a promise.

"That you help Dr. Grevatt with his research in the issue of clean water and cholera outbreaks," Mr. Nowrojee continued. "I've heard of Dr. Grevatt for some time and know quite a bit about his practice, but, to be honest, never heard of his interest in sanitation. It makes me wonder."

His gaze was suddenly too intense, and Alina's heart jolted at the thought that this man was too intuitive.

She smiled nervously. "I am sure certain rumors can be exaggerated. I simply help him out. But I was hoping to one day have a talk with you."

Mr. Nowrojee chuckled, and something in it—a mischievous sparkle in his eyes as he did—made Alina feel like he knew more than he lead on to believe. "I don't think those are rumors, Lady Bronskaya, since they come from a trusted source."

She cocked an eyebrow.

"Samuel." He cleared his throat. "His grace," he corrected himself. "He was the one who told me about you. Quite a lot in the last month. We've been trying to arrange a meeting but never got to it. And I am most delighted. I understand you and his grace are very well acquainted."

"We've spent some time together lately, yes." She tried to stop herself from blushing. "He is detained by some unfortunate circumstances, you see. I've come to talk to his butler and steward. And"—she chuckled and smiled—"it is quite marvelous I met you here."

"I hope all is well with his grace." There was a question in his eyes.

"It will be," she said quieter.

"Well, Lady Bronskaya, as soon as I have a word with him, we will arrange a proper meeting. More lengthy and more on point. His grace wanted to give you a tour of the facilities at St James's Hill. And I was hoping to discuss the topic of sanitation, you see." His eyes glistened with that mischief again. "We are always on the lookout for new, brilliant minds. Perhaps, we can lure you over from St Rose's. We have facilities and manpower and certainly enough funding to do any research that would improve the wellbeing of people in this city."

Alina laughed cheerfully. That was much too easy for what she'd thought it would be—him accepting a woman of science.

"I am sure not everyone in the medical field will be as welcoming of a woman as you, Mr. Nowrojee. You understand." Her smile faded. "But your words are humbling."

She raised her eyes at him and halted.

The man looked at her with some sort of confusion as if she'd said nonsense.

"The only opinion that matters, Lady Bronskaya, is Mr. Cassell's. Well, and mine. I am a man of science and would like to think of myself as a man of very little prejudice. And as to his grace—"

She nodded. "He is one of the benefactors."

Confusion swept across Mr. Nowrojee's face once again as he stared at her. "Why, surely, you must know."

She furrowed her brows, not understanding.

"Know what?"

"St James's Hill—the factory, the orphanage, the school, and the adjoining properties." An amused smile appeared on his lips as he stared at her. "They all belong to the duke."

Alina slammed the door of her carriage so loudly that it deafened her for a moment. But it wasn't intentional, and it wasn't as deafening as the news she'd heard only a minute ago.

Samuel—the owner of St James's Hill!

As the carriage jerked into movement, Alina leaned back in her seat and closed her eyes, trying to calm herself. Astonishment wasn't as strong as the shock of the realization that she knew so little about the man she loved.

If God created a saint and a devil in one, like those two-faced masks in theaters, that would be this man. Samuel Cassell.

She felt tricked again. And so small compared to the man who seemed to run the entire city.

The thoughts preoccupied her all the way to Grevatt's.

Rumi sat quietly at the desk, writing something of her own when Alina walked in.

"Still the same. Asleep," Rumi announced.

Alina nodded and walked toward the patients' room. The room where Samuel had confessed to her. Where he'd told her more about himself than she'd ever known. Where he now lay at her mercy, and she still didn't know enough about him.

She walked in quietly. His big body under the blanket was motionless, his chest rising peacefully.

Alina took the chair and took a seat next to him.

She studied every inch of his face. His strong nose, his thick eyebrows, one of them cut by a tiny scar. More healed scratches grazed one side of his face. How had she not noticed them before? His two-day stubble was no match to that fake beard and mustache that he'd donned with his disguise. But his hair, loose and splayed on the pillow, was a reminder of his shadow.

She leaned over and picked up one strand of his hair. Her body stiffened like that of a thief. He wouldn't wake up, she knew, yet her heart thudded in excitement.

And then she frowned and traced a lighter strand with her forefinger. Just one—it stood out in color—and as her eyes moved up, to his scalp, she saw the gray roots.

They had talked about it—they said Harlan Krow had a white strand. She'd thought it was a made up detail, just like many others. But it wasn't. It was right here, her fingers weaving through it—the gray strand that the duke always covered up.

*Samuel.*

"Sa. Mu. El," she repeated the syllables, barely audibly, then repeated them again and again, cocking her head and studying him.

A man. A broken human. The one she loved with all her heart.

Two lies. One truth. And she, caught in the middle.

A devil was once an angel, the scripture said. And she wouldn't have him without his darkness, the scars, the outrageous courage and the pain that carried on through darkness in order to reach the light.

With all she still wanted to feel—betrayal, anger, hurt—what she felt now was overwhelming relief. He was alive. That meant her heart was still beating like mad for him. Forgiveness was what she preached. To forgive was to absolve one of the wrongs. What else was worthy of fighting for if not love?

Rumi was always right. Her wise words once again flickered in Alina's mind.

*The strongest hearts come from suffering. The brightest souls from darkness. The most captivating things are covered in scars.*

Her heart was pounding at the sight of Samuel Cassell. It whispered words of love. It tempted her to press her ear to his heart to make sure it was still beating.

She wanted to tell him that. She wanted to talk and hear his voice. She so desperately wanted to see a sign of life in him as if her own life depended on it.

She would tell him how she felt.

But for that, he needed to wake up.

## 46

---

## REBIRTH

I burned with fever. In the rare moments when I regained consciousness, I felt the soft hands put compresses on my head, the dull pulsating pain in my belly. But I fell into fever again, and in that dark delirium that wasn't new to me, I whispered her name.

It was on my lips when I finally sank into deep darkness. But she was in my dreams, her gentle hand catching me when I was about to fall off a cliff.

She was there at dawn again, the vision of her arriving with the faint light of the new day that managed to sneak through the gap in the curtains that didn't belong in my house.

She was dawn—innocence, light, a new beginning.

It was dark again, but my mind was alive. Lights flickered in it. Voices. They whispered. They purred. The images of her. At times, they danced around like an erotic muse. In other times, it was the face of an angel.

And when I came back to my senses, she was there again, like an apparition.

I inhaled deeply. Among the smells of chloride and medication and foreign spices, it was the scent of her perfume that entered me, like a breath of air into my lungs, filling me up with something I knew so well.

"Good day."

*Day.*

She'd never been so close to me during the day.

But there was light all around me. And it was warm. I thought it was a dream.

Seeing her smile at me felt like the walls that imprisoned me crash around me—all at once, but silently, making me stare in awe.

A crack in time.

A shift from what was before and what will be.

Her.

My salvation.

Redemption.

Rebirth.

How many sacred words are there, Father?

My body throbbed with pain. My head spun as I moved, trying to sit up, but right away slumping as I lost my strength.

My angel frowned with concern. "You shouldn't move."

Her voice was like a lullaby. I licked my parched lips, and she saw it, flung to her feet, and brought a mug of warm tea.

My fingers brushed hers as I took it. Her other hand held my chin as I drank. She touched me openly, in the daylight, knowing it too. It was in her gaze that was full of so much timidness and kindness that I wanted to die right there and then so that hers was the last face I ever saw.

"You were attacked," she said, studying me. She sat on the side of the bed, and I wanted her closer, much closer.

I looked around.

"You are in Dr. Grevatt's flat. Miss Rumi had you brought here when she found you."

Miss Rumi, then, the dark angel. But how?

"You can stay here until you get better. You will get better, Your Grace." She smiled.

"Samuel," I whispered. "It's Samuel."

She nodded, again and again, a mist of tears in her eyes. "Samuel."

My heart was ready to explode. This was the first time she'd said my true name. It was a new beginning, Father, don't you think?

I didn't care what she saw in me then. Harlan Krow. The Duke of Ravenaugh. I was close to death, weak, sedated, in someone else's bed, not able to run or even stand like a man next to her.

I was so very tired of hiding, Father. Changing clothes. Donning a disguise. Keeping check of my voice at all times. Two carriages. Two houses. Two lives. Cheap letter paper. Expensive quills. Fashionable garments that covered the bruises and scars. Being free at night and having to act indifferent in the day. Punishing those who used money and authority to enslave others and sitting with the same people at dinners.

Those on the run eventually give up. Not because they are weak—but because they are tired of running.

I wanted to be myself, whatever that meant, not knowing which part of me was my true self anymore.

"You haunted my dreams," I said, my voice unusually raspy.

I stretched my hand to her, then. I wanted to touch her. One touch—I could give my life for it.

She glanced at my hand and took it in both of hers, bringing her beautiful eyes to meet mine. They said a thousand words that were written in her letters and spoken in the darkness. And those that weren't spoken yet.

Her words came softly like a confession. "I was so afraid

I'd lost you." My chest tightened. "If you didn't make it, I would have lost not one but two incredible men. Who can say that?"

She chuckled, and my own eyes burned with tears.

Was this forgiveness?

She gave me more tea. I wanted to hear her talk more. But she shied away. I tried to keep her in front of me, but slowly, minute by minute, she was slipping away. The tea—it had laudanum. And I cursed medicine that took away the pain, but with it, her, as I slipped into darkness again.

# 47

## YOURS TRULY

Almost a week had passed since the morning Alina had come to Grevatt's only to learn that Samuel was gone, having sent for his butler earlier.

"He insisted on leaving, though he could barely stand up," Rumi had said then.

Astonished, Alina had returned home and waited for a message from him.

But five days had passed, and there was no word from the duke.

"Have you talked to him?" Rumi asked, standing in the Kamenevs' hallway one early afternoon. The fact that Rumi had come to Alina's house meant that Alina had disregarded her duties.

"You haven't been writing," said Rumi as if in reproach.

Alina didn't answer, didn't ask if Rumi wanted to stay for tea, and stood by the door for some time after Rumi had left, absently staring at the floor and lost in her thoughts.

Martha and Yegór's voices echoed from the servants' hallway.

"Say my name," Martha cooed.

"Mar-r-ta," the footman repeated again and again in that thick accent of his, with an animal roll of the "r" and a bullet-like "t" that made Martha giggle. The two walked out into the hallway smiling and stalled as they saw Alina.

Alina studied them for a moment. "Your job is by this door, Yegór," she said sternly to the footman and walked away.

Immediately she felt bad for being cross.

Theirs was a simple story of pride and prejudice. She felt envious at others' happiness, the simplicity of it.

Her story with the duke was much more complicated. She missed him desperately. It had been a week since he left Dr. Grevatt's and not a word from him.

It was late afternoon. Alina sat on the windowsill in her room, a book she was reading abandoned. She stared at the thin layer of snow on the trees. She loved snow. It covered all the dirt and misery of the gray fall. The lone snowflakes drifted in the air like moths.

She waited. For him. For what was to come. The crackling of the fire in the fireplace soothed her aching heart, but not enough.

She felt restless again, rose, and walked about the room, measuring her steps across the floor, when the hall downstairs echoed with a pair of heavy footsteps and lighter ones trotting along. They went up the stairs, approached her room, and there was a hushed sound of Martha's hisses and complaints behind the door.

Alina pulled the door open just as Yegór was about to knock.

"My lady." He nodded.

Martha jumped right in front of him. "My lady, he is not supposed to come up and bother you. But he insisted. For he never listens to me."

Alina put her hands on her waist as she watched the two with reproach.

Martha turned to Yegór and hissed, "I said I shall bring the message." She stepped into him with her palm stretched out, demanding he hand it over, then whipped right away toward Alina. "Tell him, my lady!"

*Like children.*

Alina watched in silence.

Martha turned to face him again. She was a curvy girl, but next to him, she looked tiny and barely reached his massive shoulders. "I attend to my lady," she snapped at the footman. "You only—"

Before she said another word, Yegór leaned over, put his hands on Martha's waist and, as if she were a feather, lifted her and set her down behind him, then took a step toward Alina.

"My la—"

"How dare you!"

"Quit it!" Alina snapped, making both her servants straighten up like soldiers. She nodded toward her room and let Yegór in as he shut the door behind him and cast his eyes down.

"What was so important that you had to anger Martha again?" She walked to the window and leaned on the windowsill, staring indifferently outside.

"*I* deliver your messages, my lady."

His loyalty was truly astounding but overbearing at times.

"What messages?" she asked, suddenly irritated.

"A messenger came from that fella," Yegór announced.

Alina slowly turned her gaze to her footman. "What fella?"

"The important one. The duke."

Her treacherous heart thudded like a drum.

"Fella!" She gaped at her footman and slowly pushed off

the windowsill. "Yegór! The nerve! *His grace* is what he is to you."

He cleared his throat and lowered his eyes, shifting from one foot to another.

Trying to conceal the excitement that had spiked in her, she came over and studied him with deliberate slowness. "Where is your livery?" she exclaimed in irritation. "And the hair! I shall ask Prosha to cut it. And this beard of yours, too. Right away."

"Martha shall do it."

"Martha shall do everything for you now, won't she?"

She met his gaze, surprised and submissive. A mountain of a body, a heart of gold, and the gaze of a lamb. But the hurt in them—oh, she was being harsh. Her mother could scream and throw tantrums, but it wasn't Alina's way. And now she shouted at him for no reason like a spoiled child.

She exhaled heavily. "What did the man say?"

"What man?"

"The duke's man!" she exclaimed impatiently. "Truly, Yegór, you are testing my patience!"

"Oh, that… He brought a note for you."

Her heart halted, and she stared at the footman almost ready to kill him.

"Where is the wretched note? Yegór!" she shouted, tears of irritation suddenly springing to her eyes. She ripped the paper out of the footman's hand and read it.

*May I pay you a visit? If you need time, I can wait for as long as it takes.*
*Yours truly,*
*Samuel.*

Alina's heart was beating like a trapped bird.

*Yours.*

She bit her lip, suppressing the feelings that whirled in her heart.

She darted to the bureau and picked up a piece of paper and ink well. Her hands shook. She made a blotch right away, cursed in Russian, and took another piece of paper.

She wanted to write a letter, or two, or ten, explaining to him all she felt. But she'd rather tell him in person.

*What took you so long...* was her reply that she gave to Yegór. "Send it right away."

"*Slushajus-s.*" With a lop-sided smile, Yegór motioned with his head toward the door. "The man was given instructions not to come back without a reply."

"Good." Alina said, hiding her smile in the corner of the shawl that she brought to her mouth.

"That fella is insistent, huh?"

"Yegór!"

"Forgive me, my lady." He bowed almost to the floor with a cunning smile.

"And Yegór!" She stopped him when he was about to leave the room. "Apologize to Martha." She cocked an eyebrow. "Nicely."

"*Slushajus-s.*" He nodded and stomped away.

Minutes passed as Alina paced around the room, then suddenly felt embarrassed at her reply, darted out, and trotted to the hallway, calling for Yegór.

In the dimness, she halted at the commotion, her footman and Martha springing away from each other like spooked sparrows.

Martha smoothed her skirt.

Alina stared in disbelief.

*That's some apology.*

"Where is the duke's messenger?" she asked impatiently.

"He left, my lady." Yegór straightened his waistcoat and glanced from under his eyebrows.

"Never mind," Alina replied, studying for a moment the two awkward servants, who stood with their heads bowed, and left with a smile.

How long would it take?

Until evening?

One day?

Two?

Alina wished she could speed up time as she walked up the stairs to her room.

The bell rang at the front door.

*He'd better get that,* she thought of Yegór with unusual irritation.

The slightest thought of this house upset her suddenly, as if it were a prison. She burned with the need to see Samuel. Her heart was ready to jump out and rush toward his estate or wherever he was.

She'd barely closed the door and tossed her shawl onto the bed when a knock at the door whipped her around.

Martha came in.

"What now, Martha?" Alina exhaled, irritated. "Have mercy. Everyone wants something from me today."

But the maid's eyes were wide with excitement. "He is here," she said, the corner of her lips hitching in a smile.

Alina's heart stalled.

*Couldn't be.*

"Who?"

She'd just sent the note only minutes ago.

"His grace." Martha curtsied. "He is downstairs and is asking to see you."

The floor seemed to drop from under Alina's feet. She rushed to the mirror, smoothed her hair in several jerky strokes, tugged at her bodice, then looked in the mirror again, caught Martha's nervous gaze, and stared at her with so much despair that the maid rushed to her and flung to her knees, hurriedly smoothing Alina's skirt and straightening the laces. She flung back to her feet and held Alina by the shoulders, doing a quick up and down check.

The two nodded at the same time, and Alina hurried out the door, slowing down as she descended the stairs, her heart rushing ahead of her feet.

Samuel stood in the sitting room, hands clasped behind his back, like he had so many times before.

But this time, Alina wanted to erase everything that had happened between them. The harsh words. The anger. The misunderstanding. The accusations.

He turned and watched her approach and stop several feet away.

They gazed at each other in silence—thousands of words and ninety days between them.

"How are you feeling?" Her first words were so banal that she cursed herself again. Her body was so tense, she thought it would snap.

He nodded. A tiny smile grazed his lips. "Well. Thank you. And thank you for letting my butler know I was all right."

She nodded, feeling color rush to her face.

"And thank you for taking care of me."

The room sank into silence again, every passing second booming in sync with her heartbeat.

He took a step toward her, their eyes never leaving each other.

"It took all my willpower not to write to you sooner, though I wanted to," he said and took another step. "I don't recall us not talking for so long since we've met."

She smiled nervously. "Yes."

"I wish we never had to again."

He took another slow step toward her as if he were afraid to scare her away. She could see the emotions in his eyes, a current between them full of feelings that would only take a moment to burst out.

"Every man needs a place to call home," he said finally, his speech slow and measured. "I never had one. You became my home, for that is where my heart is."

*Me too.*

Tears burned her eyes. She clasped her hands in front of her so tightly that it hurt, the pain suppressing the emotions that were about to spill over.

"I truly don't know how else to explain myself," he said, his gaze on her unblinking. "Except that my title had put a mile-long distance between us. And at St Rose's, we closed that distance as if we'd known each other for years. Forgive me. I was a vulnerable man around you. A man, that's all. Not a duke. Not a villain. Just a man in love."

She didn't move, didn't look away, and held on to every word he said.

"I can ask for your forgiveness a hundred times if needed." He took another step, only several feet separating them. "I can tell you every minute of every day that I love you." He swallowed hard. "But you know that already."

He smiled weakly, his eyes shiny with a mist of tears.

"You knew the dark side of me, yet you looked at me with understanding," he said, taking another step and stopping in front of her. His eyes searched hers for an answer. "For you, I will leave all that behind." She felt a sob shaking her chest. "I will surrender myself to you completely, Alina. For nothing matters as much as seeing your smile every day."

She was slain by his words—a man like him humbling himself before her.

In this moment, she saw what had drawn her to him in the first place—not the darkness or the righteousness or the power over others, but the unfathomable strength of a man who'd lived through hell and yet was eager to help others.

He wasn't a devil but a dark angel, if only with broken wings. And she wanted to give him his wings back, make him rise above all that had plunged him into darkness. She would take all the light of being and gift it to him to make him shine again.

He took her breath away.

And he had taken her heart.

He must have seen it in her eyes, for he took that final step that separated them. His hand rose to her cheek, brushing it with the lightest caress.

"I shall be the best man I can," he said softly, "so you can look at me with pride. I want to spend the rest of my life with you and make you happy. Because without you, Alina, there is no life."

She tried not to blink, but once she did, tears spilled down her cheek. A sob shook her. She nodded, not quite sure what she was nodding to.

He brought his other hand to her face and softly wiped her tears.

"I have asked you to marry me once," he said. "And you said no." He smiled weakly. "But that was an eternity ago, or so it seems. So I will ask you again. Will you do me the honor of being my wife?"

She smiled through tears. "If you haven't turned this city into mayhem yet, *this* will."

He chuckled, his eyes still searching hers for an answer. "Is that a yes?"

A myriad of emotions burned in them. And if she didn't see that gaze every day, her life would be a mere existence.

"It is a yes," she whispered. "Yes. Yes." The reply was both terrifying and liberating at once.

And before she could say anything else, he wrapped his arms around her, and his mouth was on hers in a kiss that was the sweetest but the most important yet.

Him.

It had always been him.

His taste.

His warmth.

The feeling of the world going still when he was next to her.

There was no familiar brush of his beard and mustache. The smoothness of his skin was new. But the lips had the softness of the dark minutes they'd spent together.

This was a kiss of surrender.

Confession.

The final answer.

His kiss grew deeper, his tongue dipping in slow soft strokes, making her head spin. She didn't want this to stop. Nothing else compared to his closeness, as if he shielded her from the rest of the world. She didn't care what face belonged to the man she loved. For when she closed her eyes, she knew him by his voice and his touch, the way he kissed her as if she were a source of life, and the way he pressed her flush against him as if without her in his arms he would collapse.

"I missed you so," she whispered.

"I can never let you go," he whispered back, kissing her temple, cheek, jaw. "I won't."

And she was lost again, like she always had been—in his

caresses, his soft lips that found hers again, taking them with slow-burning passion. He tore his lips from her again and buried his face in her hair, inhaling loudly, his hand on the back of her head, pressing her closer.

He didn't wear cologne. And he didn't smell like the rain and fire pits. Yet she knew the scent of his skin that she smelled only in moments like this when they were in each other's arms.

His scent filled her nostrils.

It made her skin hum.

It made her body go limp in sweet longing.

She pulled away and cocked her head, studying his face. "Your Grace…" she whispered.

A smile tugged at the corner of his lips. "Lady Bronskaya." He stroked her cheek with the back of his fingers, then lowered his forehead to hers.

"I am losing my mind with you, Alina," he whispered. "I am losing myself in you. I am not a religious man, but I was praying you felt the same."

She closed her eyes, dissolving under his touch. "We shall make it work, won't we?"

She wanted him.

This.

Them together.

"We shall have to make promises," she said. "There are things not easily accepted. Not in the daylight."

When she opened her eyes, his were so close that his feelings seeped into her heart, making it clench with tenderness.

The entrance door slammed. The sound of footsteps echoed at the entrance. Anna Yakovlevna's voice chirped at Yegór. His hushed voice followed. Nikolai Sergeevich called her from his study.

The entire house tried to keep Anna Yakovlevna away from the sitting room where Alina and the duke were.

But her footsteps were already approaching with astonishing speed.

Alina pulled away from the duke the very moment her mother flitted into the sitting room.

"Ah! Your Grace!"

Anna Yakovlevna grinned like she'd been just crowned a queen as she approached the duke. She shrugged her coat into Yegór's hands, who scurried behind her. Her eyes shifted to Alina.

"*Dusha moya!*" She halted in surprise, clasping her hands, noticing her daughter's tears. "What is the matter?" she whispered, her eyes darting to the duke.

"It's all right, Mamá. We were talking." Alina blushed and tugged at the hems of her sleeves.

"Mrs. Kameneva." The duke bowed gracefully with a smile.

God, Alina loved how he pronounced Russian names!

Anna Yakovlevna giggled like a young girl as he kissed her hand. "Won't you join us for dinner, Your Grace? Yes?"

He glanced at Alina and smiled, casting his eyes down. "I am not sure—"

"That would be nice," Alina blurted.

He met her hopeful gaze again. "Then I would love to."

"*Ah, merveilleux!*" Anna Yakovlevna threw her hands in the air. "Dunyasha!" she shouted for the maid. "Where is that insolent girl?" She flitted out of the sitting room. "Make arrangements—" Her voice trailed off then came back. "Oh, that is just splendid!" In a moment, she was back in the room. "Your Grace, what have you been up to? We haven't seen you in a while. Yes? Oh, how Alina missed you!"

*Indeed.*

The corner of his lips hitched in a tiny smile.

Nikolai Sergeevich walked in, assessing the situation with his usual kind smile. Alina looked at him with a plea, and he understood.

"Your Grace, what do you think of the latest changes in the Parliament?"

And as her father and the duke engaged in a small conversation, she at last started to feel at ease.

Finally, the dinner was set up in the dining room. Alina only wondered how and when Prosha had gotten time to prepare all of it—crepes with sevruga caviar, marinated mushrooms with thyme and cloves, grouse roasted with dried plums, mutton dumplings. What pleased Alina was the fact that the duke was having dinner with her and her parents. What amused her was that Harlan Krow was here, eating Prosha's dumplings. The aristocracy would have choked on their tongues.

"I hope you enjoy our humble cuisine," Anna Yakovlevna said with theatrical coyness.

Nikolai Sergeevich raised his eyes to the duke. "Now you know what all the rumors are about."

The duke chuckled but suddenly went quiet, then set his utensils down and looked at Nikolai Sergeevich. "Mr. Kamenev, Mrs. Kameneva, I proposed to your daughter," he said quietly.

The room sank into silence.

Dunya, who was serving Nalifka, halted like a statue with the decanter in her hand.

Alina swallowed as nervously as the first time she'd heard those words. "I said yes." Her heart tightened.

Anna Yakovlevna broke out in relieved exclamations and what looked like tears that she swept away with a napkin.

Nikolai Sergeevich smiled softly, gazing at Alina with curiosity.

Dunya darted out of the room to spread the news, and in a moment, Yegór's big form loomed in the open doors in the dimness of the hallway as he narrowed his stare at the duke.

And Alina met Samuel's eyes.

While her parents were saying something, the world suddenly went quiet as she studied her gentleman-devil.

His gaze on her was that of a saint.

## 48

## THE WEDDING

Anna Yakovlevna took an enormous diamond necklace in her hands and studied it with pride.

"I shall not wear it, Mamá! It takes up half of my chest," Alina tried to argue.

"Nonsense. This is our ancestral jewelry." Her mother was already wrapping it around Alina's neck.

"It screams wealth."

"What would you like it to scream? Orphans?" Anna Yakovlevna stepped back and took a look at her daughter with a satisfied smile.

Alina wore a simple silk wedding dress. The low but modest neckline was now accentuated with the lavish necklace of seventy-five diamonds. Her hair was slicked back and pinned in a bun as was always her fashion, a small white hat with tiny flowers pinned on the side of her head.

The two weeks leading up to the wedding were the happiest Alina had ever been. Days had been filled with Samuel's presence, walks in the city, dinners, conversations—a lot more of them. His gaze had been so openly tender that

Alina felt aroused just by being in his presence. And the days he had been occupied with business, he'd sent her letters—directly to the Kamenevs' house, on fancy perfumed paper but in that unmistakable writing that she knew so well.

She couldn't wait for the wedding day—to be alone with him, to finally *be* his. The ceremony was a mere formality.

"You are mesmerizing," Anna Yakovlevna said, clasping her hands at her chest as if in a prayer as she studied her daughter in the mirror with tears in her eyes.

Alina smiled nervously. Her heart starting to race at the thought of going down the aisle. If it were up to her, she would have married in a simple dress without jewelry. No guests. Only Samuel and her.

But it didn't matter.

For when, an hour later, she walked into the church, she didn't care to see the hundred guests who'd canceled their plans at such short notice to witness the most talked about union. She didn't pay attention to the whispers and gasps, the hungry eyes and intense stares.

Nikolai Sergeevich smiled softly as he led her down the aisle, the warm light of hundreds of candles sparkling and reflecting on every surface of the holy establishment.

All eyes were on Alina.

Hers were on the man who stood at the end of the aisle.

Her heart thudded at the sight.

Samuel's shoulder-length raven hair was let loose and neatly tucked behind his ears. The gaze of the duke. The shadow of the gentleman-devil.

This was a statement and a revelation, his secret only known to the two of them.

Two men in one.

Hers.

Their eyes were only on each other as her father led Alina up to her groom and stopped at his side.

Gently, Samuel took her hand in his, and she wished she wasn't wearing gloves so that in this special moment, she could feel his touch.

*Are you all right?* his gaze said.

Alina smiled.

She wanted everyone to disappear. She wanted his voice to be the only one she heard.

The clergyman started a well-practiced speech that was so mundane to others. His voice drifted away as she and Samuel stood in front of the pastor yet turned their heads to gaze at each other. Their vows seemed to have been sealed by some strange fate. They knew it. The man of the church was a mere formality.

They didn't break eye-contact when the pastor asked Samuel to repeat the holy words after him. He did, his lips lifting in a smile.

Her eyes were pools of tears as she repeated the same words.

*"Till death do us part."*

Death was what had brought them together. At times, the darkest moments led to the most beautiful ones. Theirs was a story of redemption.

Alina tried not to blink, for fear of tears spilling down her cheeks.

"You may kiss the bride," the pastor said.

Samuel stepped closer, cupped her face, and bowed his forehead to hers. "I don't like seeing you cry," he whispered.

"I am happy," she whispered back, the air between them burning with tenderness and passion that was hidden by their formal garments.

"As long as you are, my duchess."

His kiss was the softest yet.

But that was all the better.

She didn't want to share their love with others.

He was hers and only hers.

## 49

## DARKNESS AND LIGHT

The lit fireplace radiated warmth, but Alina shivered as Martha helped her into a lavish nightgown, white and semi-translucent, grazing her naked body in a soothing way. Alina was nervous and excited at once. She'd been looking forward to this night. But with Martha by her side, smiling intriguingly and caressing Alina's hair that she'd let loose, she felt like it was a ritual.

The duke's bedroom was large and cozy, with a big bed and plush carpets. But dozens of candles made it too bright for Alina's liking. Too bright for tonight...

A knock at the door made Martha's smile grow into a grin as she hurried toward the door and disappeared behind it, letting the duke in.

Alina held her breath.

Her heart fluttered as he approached, glancing over her gown. He smiled. His eyes searched her face as if trying to figure out what she felt. She cast her eyes down, a nervous smile tugging at her lips.

He shed his jacket. The room seemed too quiet. Every

movement whispered seductively and made her body tense with frightful anticipation. She'd known his closeness before. But when he came over and took her chin between his fingers, gently nudging her face up to look at him, his gaze burned her to the core with the mutual knowledge—they belonged to each other now.

He leaned down and pressed his lips to hers in a soft kiss.

"Finally," he said.

"It took a while." She smiled at him as he kissed her again.

His arms slid around her waist, pulling her closer to him as he studied her face. He seemed to be in no hurry, and she was grateful.

"How are you this evening, my duchess?" He kissed her temple, then her forehead, her brow, her cheek, making her chuckle. She slid her hands up his arms, feeling his muscles and feeling small and fragile next to his tall broad form.

"I am all right." She lifted her hands and caressed his hair. "And you?"

The words seemed useless, but they slowly pulled together everything that'd kept them apart.

"I am happy," he said, his hand sliding up her back in a soft caress.

Gently, she wove her fingers through his hair, pulling it from behind his ears and bringing it down the sides of his face.

The touch of her gentleman-devil. The face of the duke.

The two men weren't the same one.

Not yet.

Not in her mind.

She smiled meekly. And when she closed her eyes and buried her nose in the crook of his neck, caressing his shoulders, he was her gentleman-devil again, the scent undoubtedly his.

Yet, without darkness, he was like an apparition. And she felt dizzy at that disconnect. Her heart swelled with love but ached with that inner torment.

His fingers stroked her spine through her nightgown. As if sensing her unease, he pressed his lips to her temple. "Are you nervous?"

She nodded.

"You don't have to be, angel."

But she didn't want to open her eyes. All she wanted was to feel.

"Can we put out the lights?" she asked softly.

"The lights!

The lights, Father!

My duchess wanted to be in the dark!

Oh, the irony!

She married a duke but missed her Harlan Krow.

Who could blame her? I bloody did that to myself. And I wanted to kill myself that very moment for tormenting her so, for she still couldn't see the two men in one.

But that was all right. I could be whatever she wanted—a duke, a gentleman-devil, a monster, a villain, a sinner, a lover —all in one. I would heal her with my love. I had so much of it that it was tearing me apart from within.

She stood in her lavish cotton nightgown, embroidered with golden threads, a little brass cross hanging around her slender neck. Her auburn hair was loose—she was fire, her gaze so timid yet burning me to ashes.

I knew that would be the last time our eyes met that night. But I'd tortured her with that too many times before. The tables had turned.

My heart ached, but I walked around the room, putting out every candle, until the bedroom sank into the faint haze from the low fire in the hearth. In the darkness, I came back to her and took her in my arms.

Now I knew how she'd felt all those months—wanting to see my face, staring into the darkness only to hear my voice. I took her soft lips in a kiss, melting under the soft strokes of her tongue, sharing that painful realization with her.

But pain could be healed with love—she'd told me that once.

The warmth of her body was in stark contrast to the cold floor. I wanted to keep her warm, take her feet in my hands, and warm them with my breath. She was mine for the rest of my life, and suddenly I wanted to be immortal.

Her hands on my shoulders burned me with their sweet touch. My own hands slowly roamed her body, gliding up and down her, trying to relax her.

"Better?" I whispered, nibbling at her neck, careful not to go too hard and fast.

"Yes," she replied, gasping barely audibly at my touch.

I kissed her worries away, inhaling her and getting lost in my desire for her. I could barely hold back my need. My hardness strained my trousers. I wished she was as passionate as me so we could ravish each other.

Slowly, I shed all my garments, then picked up the hem of her shift, pulled it up, over her head, and tossed it aside.

There.

My duchess.

I wished I could see all of her. But again, darkness was a curse. The curse she used right back at me. We were two shadows in the dim glow of the fireplace.

I pressed her to me, reveling in the feel of her bare body against mine. My hardness pressed against her belly, and that was already enough to send me over the edge. But I wanted to make her lose her mind in pleasure before I reached my own peak. So I went about it slowly, like a serpent seducing Eve—caressing her skin smooth like silk, warm like morning sun. I found her mouth and seared it with a kiss, gentle but deep.

Her lips grew needy and in a matter of seconds. The kiss drowned both of us. My hands roamed her body, slid down to her hips, then back up, along the curves of her full breasts, grazing her hard peaks, up her neck, and into her hair.

I wanted to taste her everywhere.

I pushed her back on to the bed and got on top of her. My mouth trailed kisses down her chest and to her breasts. I palmed one of them, my mouth on the other one, lapping at her nipple that I wanted to lick off her skin.

She moaned and arched into me.

*My angel.*

She wanted me. It would take time, but the darkness was already unleashing her desire. The power of it was unmistakable, for we'd forgotten where we were and only had the memories of how much we'd wanted this.

I kissed my way down her body, my hands learning every curve on the way.

I left little kisses on her stomach, smiling at the way she shifted in pleasure under my lips.

My long hair brushed her skin as I trailed light kisses to her hips. I pushed her thighs apart and kissed the tender skin around her sex.

My hair slid along her slit and caressed the sensitive flesh there.

She sucked in a breath.

Oh, I knew what I was doing. The gentleman-devil was back. And while I kissed and licked her inner thighs, I made sure my long hair caressed her sex, readying her for my invasion.

She was wet—an ocean between her thighs. The strands of hair that brushed her sex were already soaked with her honey. And when my fingers brushed against her soft curls, she whimpered and whispered something in her tongue.

I let my fingers travel down to her sex and stroked her gently, barely touching. She moaned, rolled her hips, and pushed herself into my hand. I smiled—my lips hadn't even reached her most intimate part yet.

We were both burning with need. She was yearning for my touch. And I wanted to taste her everywhere, to mark her with my lips, to let her know that every cell of her body would soon be under my command.

I kissed her between her legs, then spread the lips of her sex with my fingers and swiped my tongue up her seam.

Women's moans of pleasure are beautiful, Father. Hers were like a sweet melody—gasps, whispers, whatever my angel was murmuring in her tongue as I kissed and licked her flesh.

*Mine.*

I took her clit between my lips and pulled it gently, again and again, then licked it slowly, feeling her body tremble under my tongue.

I wanted to learn what she liked. Wanted to know her taste. Wanted to feel the texture of her most private spots and invade them, knowing she was mine.

I'd begged your God for so long to let me have her, Father. I'd asked her so many times to give me a chance.

Finally, that night, I was a man claiming his woman. And with all the powers she had over me, I had that one—to bestow the pleasure onto her and make her forget everything outside our bedroom.

She had the body of a goddess. I stroked her silk skin. I pushed her slender legs wider apart. I dipped my tongue into her wet core, drowning in the sweet scent that filled my nostrils.

She moaned. Her fingers wove into my thick hair that splayed on her thighs. I feasted on her flesh, sinking my tongue into her slowly and rhythmically, swiping up and down, then circling that sensitive nub in the center. I played with it, dragging my tongue over it in long swipes, then flicking it, taking it in my mouth and pulling it gently.

I was learning her.

Slowly.

Patiently.

Touch by touch.

The darkness laced with her soft moans was most erotic. Everything swelled and heated. My cock was rock hard and seeping. I bucked my hips into the bed, and if I did it rhythmically, I would have come right there and then. It was a miracle I lasted as long as I did.

But that night wasn't about me. I wanted to please my angel. I worshiped her body, and she was loving it. Forgetting is not forgiving. But that night I made her forget her shame and worries.

I kneaded her sex with my fingers and kissed and nibbled at her flesh. I drank her in like a thirsty man. I was shameless. And she might have been new to this. But it was dark. And darkness strips reason and leaves only senses.

I made love to her sex like I had done to her lips before— carefully first, probing, then falling into a rhythm. Her moans grew heavier. Her sensitive bud swelled at my persistence. It would learn my tongue by heart. It would swell at the mere touch of it. I wanted every cell of my duchess's body to sing under my lips. I wasn't an expert, but she made me wild. And if I needed to coax a forgiveness out of her, I would use my tongue and lips and hands and my cock to do so and make her forget who we were.

She trembled in her first climax, rolling her hips against me. My sweet angel knew how to let go. I kissed her sex gently to sooth it, then kissed her silky thighs, my fingers playing with the texture of her soft curls, sliding to her folds now and then and building up her need again.

I kissed her hips and lower belly, growing impatient as I trailed my mouth up her body. I caught her nipples with my lips and made her gasp.

"Please," she whispered. "I need you."

My angel was begging me, Father.

She was so open to my love. And that night she was open to her man—walking flesh, no matter his past or present.

I brought my lips to hers that were loving me back as she kissed me demandingly.

Without her furs and skirts, she seemed so small under my large frame, and I hoped I wouldn't hurt her as I hovered over her, settling between her thighs.

Her legs opened wider. She bucked her hips, her sex grazing my hardness that needed a release so badly. Inside of her. Grinding into her. Making her mine.

Her hands slid to my hips, pulling me toward her.

"I am right here, love," I whispered.

I pressed the tip of my cock to her entrance, nearly spilling at the feel of it, and she pushed onto me.

My angel wanted my cock—my mind went dark with lust. I wanted to see her face, but it was too dark. So I pressed my lips to hers gently but not kissing her, so I could feel her warm exhale when I finally entered her.

She wanted me, and that was all I needed to know when I pushed inside her.

Are you blushing, Father?

You can hear atrocious confessions without a flinch. Yet the explicit descriptions of the most sensual kind shatter your sanity, don't they? They question your faith in celibacy. They chase you like demons that you toss your prayers at in hopes of them leaving you alone.

It's all right.

We are all human.

That night I was a man in love, hungry for my woman. I get hard just thinking of it. And I am a hard man to impress. Excuse the pun.

You talked about God, Father, yet never said that God was ecstasy. What do nuns feel when they lose themselves in their holy prayers? That word is from your scripture, Father. It only has one meaning. And God must be right there when two lovers lose themselves in each other.

I took my angel as slowly as I could that time. My thrusts were calculated. My passion contained. I palmed her breasts, kissed the skin around her nipples, took them in my mouth, and when she moaned, I shifted upward, catching her moans with my mouth, never stopping my thrusts.

"My Alina," I murmured, wanting to let her hear my voice.

"Yes," she whispered back, her hands roaming my body with sweet gentleness.

"My duchess," I whispered as I drove my cock into her, gradually increasing the rhythm. She knew my voice so well, and I hoped it helped her heal.

I drove my cock into her again and again. Her legs fell open more and more. She mewled. My long black hair swept across her skin, and she threaded through the strands like they were the finest silk she'd ever held in her hands. Her body yielded to me, and I reveled in the way she was taking me in.

I'd fantasized doing so many filthy things with her. I would soon, I knew. But nothing compared to being between her legs, my cock sinking into her warm entrance.

In and out.

In…and out…

In…

Out…

The sounds of our flesh coming together were soft and erotic. The cracking of the fire in the fireplace resonated with our gasps and grunts. I tried to stay focused, but my mind was going wild at the feeling of her warm tight sex clenching around my hardness, my hips coming into contact with her warm thighs, slapping and rubbing together. I drove deeper inside her and paused just to feel her grind into my shaft, then resumed the thrusts.

I'd thought before that she was my madness. Making love to her made me realize I didn't know a fraction of it.

I kissed her breasts. I licked her nipples. My mouth trailed up her chest and found the speck of cold metal. I flicked that little brass cross with my tongue, again and again, until the rope twisted, and it sank onto the pillow underneath her.

God and his symbols!

I drove harder into her to prove my point.

She moaned.

She was mine.

"I won't last long," I murmured, feeling my climax building up.

"Yes," she whispered absently, arching under my weight but not reaching that peak that I wanted her to reach.

I kept the rhythm, sheathing in and out of her, my cock ready to explode. I slid my hand down between our bodies and found her sensitive little nub. And when I started rubbing it softly, she moaned loudly and bucked her hips to meet mine.

"Do you like that?" I murmured, dizzy with arousal.

"Yes…" Her voice strained as she whispered. "Please don't stop. Don't stop."

And then there she was, my angel. Her hand fisted my hair, pulling me down to her. She sank her tongue into my mouth in the most ferocious kiss yet. And right away, she let go and cried out, pushing her sex onto my cock and my hand, coming undone most beautifully.

My desire was unleashed. I drove inside her more forcefully this time until heat exploded in my groin and I spilled inside her in one final thrust. I buried my grunt in her hair, having reached the climax just barely after she'd reached hers. And it was perfect.

*We* were perfect.

I sagged on top of her.

Our chests rubbed together as we panted. She raised her knees and wrapped her legs around me as if she wanted to lock me in her embrace forever.

"I love you," I whispered into her hair, not sure if she heard me.

The traces of ecstasy were subsiding in my body. Our hearts were beating in sync. There was nothing between us but our love. And that little brass cross dangling off her neck.

The devil. The angel. And that little silly cross.

I wanted to wait until she stirred. But she stayed motionless and nuzzled my hair. And I was as still as possible so I could feel that—her lips puckering to press soft kisses to my head, kissing those dark strands. Nothing felt better than being in her arms.

*Mine.*

And then her voice came, soft as if it echoed my thoughts.

"I don't want to let you go." Her thighs tightened around my hips.

My heart almost exploded with love. "Don't," I whispered, shifting to find her lips. "Ever." I kissed her slowly.

Her lips were moist and hot and wanting mine.

I'd like to think that I'd healed her that night.

Have you ever heard of the devil healing an angel, Father?

We finally pulled apart. I tucked her under my arm, keeping her close. I looked down at the soft orange glow from the fireplace that illuminated our bodies, and it was hard to believe that we weren't a dream.

I drank in her closeness, wanted the world to slow down so I could sink into this feeling—the soft stroking of her fingers on my chest, the warmth of her breath as she whispered, "I finally have you."

I couldn't stop touching her. I'd kissed her so shamelessly, licked her like a savage, and now I wanted her again. I was too aware of her body against mine, her hand on my chest, my own nakedness save the wedding ring. I smiled, deciding never to take it off. It was my new beginning, and it meant much more than the banal matrimonial oath in your church, Father.

We lay like this for some time, caressing each other.

"I so wanted you for the longest time," she said, her confession so arousing that I felt my sex hardening. "At night, I thought of us so many times."

Night. Us. I knew what she meant, and her straightforwardness gave me goosebumps.

I leaned over and kissed the top of her head, then tilted her face up to find her mouth.

Her hands were on me again. One touch and I was hard as a rock again.

"You keep talking like this," I murmured, "and I will have to take you again."

I shouldn't have said that. The first night, and I was already making my claim on her.

"I'd like that," she whispered barely audibly.

*Little tease.*

And the lustful beast was back.

I flipped her onto her stomach, making her yelp in delight. I climbed on top of her, blanketing her body with mine.

"You are making me wicked, my duchess," I grunted.

I pushed her hair to the side and kissed the nape of her neck. She arched and pushed her sweet buttocks up against me. My cock was hard, pressing to the crevice between her silky mounds, and the liquid heat of desire shot through my veins. I palmed her breasts and kissed her shoulders and back, rubbing my body against hers.

"Tell me what you did when you thought of me," I whispered.

She pushed her butt into my cock. My little Russian vixen wouldn't admit it.

"Tell me, angel," I insisted, pushing her legs open with my knees.

"Tell me," I repeated, shifting my hips to press the tip of my cock to her entrance.

"I touched myself thinking about you," she whispered.

And I sheathed into her in one swift movement.

She cried out. I grunted. And the world once again dissipated into that one blissful feeling of being inside her.

They say the first time is madness. The second is a chase. The third time is a revelation.

I took her again later that night and made love to her slowly, studying the sensation of being inside her, kissing and nibbling at her, and whispering the sweet filth that echoed on her lips.

But my sweet angel asked for mercy. She laughed when she did so, and I let go of her and kissed her to sleep as she cuddled in the crook of my arm.

We had an eternity together. And it seemed not nearly enough.

## 50

---

## HUSH

Alina ran away the next morning. In the faint light of dawn that snuck through the gap in the curtains, she slid out of bed and hurriedly put on her chemise.

She looked at the bed where her husband lay on his back, one arm still curled around the empty space where he'd cradled her.

Alina's heart swelled at the sight.

Sneaking away was wrong. But the thought of being naked with him in the daylight, for him to see all of her, made her panic.

Darkness was easy to get lost in. Last night, love and lust had coiled in them with astonishing force, tangling them like vines around each other in their lovemaking.

Yet, she was afraid that Samuel would take her in the daylight and see uncertainty in her eyes. She didn't want to ruin it. He could be awake, but if he was, he certainly didn't show it, lying still, her gentleman-devil perfectly peaceful in the morning haze.

She smiled and tiptoed out of the bedroom.

Martha was already in Alina's dressing parlor.

"Early morning?" Alina smiled as she sat on the banquette, waiting for Martha to mix the hot water for bathing.

Alina didn't want to bathe. She didn't want to wash off his scent or the traces of his desire that still coated her thighs and belly. She wanted to return to the bedroom, sneak under the sheets, and caress his strong body until he grunted so deliciously under her fingers and wrapped his muscular arms around her, opening her up in any way he found fit.

In the dark.

But it was morning, and she needed to face the reality.

"How was it?" Martha's curious gaze lingered on Alina now and then as Alina ran the cloth over her curves, thinking of him.

"Good," said Alina, blushing at the memories.

"How good?" the curious maid insisted.

"Hush," Alina silenced her, wanting to dwell yet for another minute in the memories of her and Samuel between the sheets.

Later, she walked the morning halls of her new house—the furniture so scarce as if no one lived here. She would change that, she thought with a smile as she walked room after room of the ground floor, nodding to the occasional servants.

She stepped into the library—a vast hall full of books, a floor to ceiling two-story window, letting in the abundant light that illuminated the three walls filled with shelves top to bottom, leaving a small opening for the door.

Alina walked around wide-eyed, breathless at the beauty of it, and traced the spines of the lower shelves with her fingers.

"I suppose this will be your favorite room."

Samuel's voice whipped her around.

He looked even more handsome, wearing dark-gray trousers and a simple linen shirt. No waistcoat. No chains. No pomade. His hair was once again loose but tucked neatly behind his ears.

Two men in one—he was letting her get used to him.

"My second favorite," she blurted without thinking.

*After the bedroom…*

She hoped he wouldn't ask and turned her gaze to the books, willing her blush to go away.

"There are Eastern European translations and the originals," he said, slowly walking toward her.

"Oh! Have you read any?"

"Gogol, yes," he said.

Her heart fluttered in surprise. "A Ukrainian genius." She produced an excited laugh. "He is my favorite."

Samuel walked up to her, and his hands lightly touched her waist. He planted a soft kiss on her cheek. The casualness of it made her aroused and left her breathless. How could mundane be so special?

"Do you spend a lot of time here?" she asked, raising her eyes to meet his smiling gaze that burned with all the knowledge of their night.

"Yes." He studied her face for a moment. "Breakfast is ready."

And breakfast was a big light-filled room, two valets, and a long wooden table of five feet that separated them. Too long. Occasional remarks. Smiles and glances chasing each other.

Alina couldn't think straight. She tried to calm her nervousness and get rid of the thoughts of him naked next to her.

"Samuel," she said, setting her teacup down.

"Say it again." His gaze was playful when she met his eyes. "My name. Say it again." His smile grew wider.

She laughed then, looking away and shaking her head, then pursed her lips and batted her eyelashes at him.

"Samuel." She feigned seriousness, though his smile grew into a grin as he leaned back in his chair, openly studying her. "Miss Rumi and I wanted to ask you if you would give us a tour of St James's Hill."

He nodded, mischief dissipating in his gaze. "I've already arranged that. This afternoon, angel."

*Angel.*

It took all her willpower not to drag him up the stairs back to their bedroom.

**51**

---

# THE HILL

Alina sent a note to Dr. Grevatt, telling him about the trip to the Hill, and burned with anticipation on the way to the doctor's.

She sat next to Samuel in the carriage and marveled at the fact that she was his wife.

His closeness was distracting.

"Mr. Nowrojee is extremely excited about your visit," he said, his voice calm and smooth. She wanted to hear him talk. More than anything, she loved watching him, observing his movements, the way he smiled and nodded.

"Wait until he meets Dr. Grevatt and Miss Rumi." She smiled.

"I am sure they will all be fond of each other." Samuel turned to look at her. His gaze roamed her face for a moment, making her too self-aware. "We should have dinner. Mr. Nowrojee and several other gentlemen from the Hill, Dr. Grevatt, Miss Rumi, of course." He smiled. "You and I."

*You and I.*

The words made her heart flutter.

She cocked her head, studying him. "Why did you wear the beard? So dark by night and so meticulous by day."

The question was out of place, but she had so many of them.

"The beard reminds me of the war and the past." He turned away and stared out the window. "We spent so much time in the deserts, with no people around, we didn't care for the looks. And Harlan—I've been called that half of my life. Just not here, in this city." He turned to meet her gaze. "I like to think that I was nobler in the days of war than I ever was as the Duke of Ravenaugh."

She narrowed her eyes at him as a sudden thought occurred to her. "What was your last name in the service?"

"Hill."

She nodded, confirming it. "And your best friend Krow's first name?"

"James."

"Harlan Hill. James Krow. You must have loved him very much."

Samuel's smile was ghostly. "He was a rare human who could heal others with a smile. It's a gift. You have it too, Alina."

He was so close. And that sadness was again in his eyes. And she was his wife, for God's sake! It was her duty to make him happy, and she so wanted this sadness to go away!

She leaned over, touched his face with her gloved hand, and kissed him softly on the lips.

She pulled back and looked away, embarrassed at this display of affection.

"Alina?"

She didn't respond, pursing her lips.

"Are you all right?" he asked.

"Yes." She smiled nervously. "The kiss... When you are next to me, I have a hard time focusing on other things."

She chuckled. There it was—her coy confession.

She felt his fingers take her chin and turn her face toward him. His eyes burned like those of a desperate lover. They darted to her lips. Hers to his.

And he kissed her.

His hands wrapped around her waist and pulled her closer.

Closer yet.

The kiss deepened.

God, how was it possible to want someone so much?

By the time the carriage pulled up to Dr. Grevatt's, Alina was ready to turn around and go back home, take her husband upstairs, close the curtains, and make him do shameless things to her.

She was flushed, fixing her dress, glancing at Samuel, who only smiled, not taking his eyes off her.

*Oh, God.*

This man would be the death of her!

This was the first such passionate kiss in the daylight, the kiss so unrestrained that when the coachman knocked on the door, she sprang away from Samuel and felt like the world was spiraling around her with astonishing speed. She was panting. Her undergarments were soaked. And she had a hard time finding an answer when Samuel said, "I like when you kiss me first."

She avoided his gaze though couldn't hide a smile when the doctor and Rumi joined them in the carriage.

Only a matter of weeks and everyone in her life was suddenly coming together.

Dr. Grevatt sat across from them and smiled. "It is an honor, Your Grace." He seemed unusually cheerful and energetic, and Alina hoped he didn't have one of his episodes today.

"Wait until you meet Mr. Nowrojee." Samuel smiled. "He is the true king of the Hill. Without him, our grand ideas wouldn't be possible. Money can buy a lot of things, but compassion and vision are the signs of true nobility."

Next to Dr. Grevatt, Rumi studied the man she'd saved with interest. She was one of the very few who knew the duke's secret yet had not spoken of it.

The trip to the East End was spent discussing funding and St Rose's. When they pulled up to the gates of St James's Hill, the streets were crowded and dirty, the fence and the gate lined up with vagrants and beggars. The early December snow was nonexistent here. All that was left of it was mud and biting frost.

"We won't get robbed here, will we?" Alina joked, stepping out of the carriage, and immediately regretted her words.

Samuel wrapped her hand around his arm and gave her a mischievous look. "I recall you've made a trip here in worse times and by night."

She suppressed her smile and the feeling of slight embarrassment at the mention of that night. What madness that was, indeed!

"And no," Samuel added as he led her and the rest through the gates, opened for them by the gatekeeper. "With me, you won't be robbed anywhere. Least of all in the slums."

Mr. Nowrojee was already in the hallway talking to a superintendent and several nurses. He cheered in delight upon seeing the visitors come in. He'd attended Alina and Samuel's wedding. Though she didn't remember seeing him there. Or anyone or anything, for that matter, the day completely absorbed by Samuel and what was happening between them.

Dr. Grevatt and Rumi were introduced. Though it was Rumi and Mr. Nowrojee who said at the same time, "I believe you were—" and chuckled.

"At his grace's wedding," Mr. Nowrojee finished.

"Yes." Rumi smiled.

"Though we didn't have a chance to talk." Mr. Nowrojee bowed to her slightly.

"No, we didn't, did we?" Rumi nodded in response, their eyes locked for a moment.

"This way!" Mr. Nowrojee waved elegantly toward the end of the hall. "Your Grace, you don't mind if I take over, do you? I will show you our hospital building, then our reformatory and the school. We have a parish on the premises, though it is a small one, and we are starting to accept more people from the outside. Then, if you are interested, we can take a short walk to the workshops. You see, the first three buildings are connected by walkways. The workshops are detached but are within the complex area."

And as they followed Mr. Nowrojee, Samuel behind them, Alina felt like they were submerged into a different world.

It wasn't the number of personnel, exceeding any other such establishment, or the number of beds in the hospital building, the rooms clean and smelling like medicine instead of sickness and decay, that impressed Alina.

It wasn't the number of children, poorly dressed yet clean and more or less healthy looking, or the order and discipline that seemed to rule in the place unlike any other school—three stories high, with a staff of five teachers and more to be hired, as per Mr. Nowrojee.

It wasn't the workshops, or the young men and women

who seemed concentrated and enthusiastic, or the elderly people who were occupied just like everyone else, or the sheer number of people in the building—a world in itself, yet organized and clean and spacious.

It was the overall sense of belonging, having a home, and moreover, having an opportunity that left Alina in awe.

It felt like a magical world where things were perfect, and if it weren't for occasional sadness or desperation in the eyes here and there that hinted at traumatic pasts, this could be, indeed, a fairytale.

"What we strive to do is work out the hierarchy of positions," explained Mr. Nowrojee. "Professional and trained personnel are all on payroll. Those who come from the streets and want to volunteer in exchange for food and shelter help out for free. Yes, we have shelters built in the back of the main complex. But they leave much to be desired. We shall not go there."

"This is amazing, Samuel," Alina said quietly when Mr. Nowrojee was exchanging words with Dr. Grevatt and Rumi, leading them to yet another hall and leaving her and Samuel alone. She turned to look at her husband with admiration and awe that she couldn't and didn't want to hide anymore. "You are a saint," she whispered.

Samuel chuckled, shaking his head. "I simply have a lot of money and nowhere to spend it."

"Oh, you are… impossible." She wanted to kiss him. "Why haven't you told me about this?" She motioned around.

He stroked her cheek with the back of his forefinger. "It is easy to seduce with kindness, Alina. Much harder to be liked for your true self."

She looked away. She was tired of this philosophy. She wanted to love this man for being himself. And his true self was mesmerizing. She loved him so before she knew of his title and this—she looked around and smiled happily.

An older man walked in through a side door, singing and dragging a heap of cloths or garments.

Samuel nodded toward him. "They say he used to be a talented soprano at the Shoreditch Opera Theatre. Then lost his wife. Lost his mind. Lost his job, then his place. He started singing on the streets, and whatever money he got, he used to come to Old Nichol where he had grown up, and walk around at night, passing bread to homeless children." Samuel smiled as he made several slow steps toward the man, Alina follow-ing. "He got sick one time and couldn't collect. Was almost dying outside the gates of the Hill. That was when one of our stewards picked him up. He never left the Hill. He is in charge of the reformatory. You don't need a sound mind for that. But music can heal, I suppose."

As if hearing, the man suddenly turned. His eyes widened at the sight of Samuel. By the time he shuffled over to grab Samuel's hands, his smile had turned into a grin.

"Samuel, my boy," he said, his almost translucent eyes watery, his gray hair down to his shoulders. "You are here! You have to tell them. They won't listen to me."

Samuel held the man's hands with a smile, blinking slowly. "Good day, Mr. Pagody."

"No-no-no. They don't listen to me. You have to tell them, Samuel," the man begged, clutching Samuel's hands insis-tently. "There are children outside the gates. At night." The man mumbled and looked somewhere outside the bright windows. "I can hear them at night. They sing to draw atten-tion. But bloody Jacob, pardon, ma'am"—he turned to Alina to apologize and continued—"he won't go outside! Talk some sense into him, will you? The children are always gone by dawn. Always gone," the man echoed.

"It shall be done. Sure." Samuel's kind smile grew wider. "Mr. Pagody, I want you to meet someone." He turned to Alina, drawing the old man's attention to her. "This is my wife, Alina Cassell."

The man froze, studying her as if he'd just noticed her. "But Samuel!" He turned to look at the duke. "An angel?"

Alina and Samuel laughed in sync as the man turned to look from one to another with a lost smile.

"He is a good man," said Samuel when they finally walked away. "His mind is getting worse."

"Mr. Cassell!" Another loud voice echoed through the hall. An old woman was making her way toward them. Then someone else stopped to greet them.

"Mr. Cassell? Samuel? That is what they call you?" Alina looked at her husband in amusement.

He chuckled. She loved that he laughed more often these days.

"Most of the people here don't know who I am," he replied with a coy smile. "Nor do they know my title, and they don't care. In fact, if they knew, they might never talk to me like they do. It is much easier when you bring yourself down to the same level, I suppose. For them and for me. It always is, isn't it?"

His gaze probed into her to the very depth.

God, how she loved this man! His humbleness, out of all things.

To her, he was her Samuel. To others, he was his grace. Yet, some of these people talked to him like he was a good friend.

One particular girl drew her attention. She caught Alina's gaze from across the hall and smiled, nodding, then saw Samuel, and her entire demeanor changed as if the sun had shone down on her.

"Who is she?" asked Alina.

The duke followed her gaze and smiled warmly. "The flower girl."

Alina's eyes snapped at him. "But she knows..."

He shrugged. "Faith can be a weapon too, I suppose."

He nodded at the girl, who grinned, staring at him as if she'd seen God, and Alina swore she saw tears in the girl's eyes.

"Does the Viscount of Leigh come here often?" she wondered.

The duke laughed. "He is not fond of such establishments. He is a marvelous man, just not cut out for helping the poor."

"I thought you are best friends with him."

"He is one of the closest, yes. Though not my best friend."

"Who is? I am curious to know the man who you cherish above all."

"John Pearse," he said, his smile slowly disappearing. "Reverend John Pearse."

"A reverend!" Alina stared at him in awe. "Did I meet him at the wedding? Forgive me. I forgot. I should like to meet him."

"Miss Alina!" Rumi's voice made her turn her head. Rumi, Dr. Grevatt, and Mr. Nowrojee were making their way down the stairs with smiles on their faces.

"It's most splendid! Most splendid!" Dr. Grevatt kept saying as Mr. Nowrojee led them all outside into the courtyard.

"Outside that fence is another property that is being developed," Mr. Nowrojee explained, his gaze almost always directed at Rumi, who smiled coyly. "His grace acquired it just over half a year ago. The old houses shall be taken down, the new development shall be built, and the residents shall be relocated to the new dwellings. It will take some time. Meanwhile" —he turned to give everyone a mysterious smile—"this year is the first time we are putting up a Christmas tree for the children and the workers of the Hill. Just at the example of his royal highness, Prince Alfred. We should aspire, yes?"

Dr. Grevatt flicked his eyebrows at Alina. "Even the grandest of them all always aspire to someone else."

Alina laughed happily, and her admiring gaze was on her husband again.

## 52

## THOSE TWO

It was yet another morning when Alina snuck out of bed before Samuel woke up, though she had a feeling he barely slept at night.

Martha was fixing Alina's hair in the dressing parlor.

"This place is like a palace," the maid said. "But it feels like an empty nest. Couldn't his grace have more servants?"

"We shall fix it," said Alina, studying herself in the mirror. "Give it time."

She smiled, remembering the night before. The reddened skin from Samuel's passionate kissing was visible above the high neckline of her house dress, making her blush and feel aroused.

"You love him, Miss Alina," said Martha, meeting her distracted gaze in the mirror.

Alina smiled coyly. "Yes, very much."

She studied herself in the mirror, wondering if he would like what he saw. Her hair was left loose, the front strands braided and pinned in the back. Suddenly, she felt like a young naive girl, wanting to impress a suitor. She blushed at the thought. The emerald choker seemed too extravagant.

The house dress with fur trimmings too lavish. Was it too much?

Martha's quiet sigh brought Alina to meet her solemn gaze in the mirror.

"What is it, Martha?"

The girl shook her head, trying to look positive. "I shall miss Prosha's cooking."

Oh, the vixen. The maid's sulking was of a different kind. She'd been the only one who'd joined Alina in their new household. But it wasn't the cooking or the Kamenevs that the silly girl missed.

"You can visit her any time you want."

The maid nodded.

"Is there something else you miss?" Alina narrowed her eyes on the maid, who didn't reply, only raised her chin in that little haughty manner of hers. "Someone?" A smile hitched the corner of Alina's lips.

"Nonsense," responded Martha, but her eyes were misted with tears as she forced a smile and studied Alina with too theatrical satisfaction. "You are ready, my lady."

Samuel didn't say anything about Alina's morning disappearances. But his gaze on her was smiling. And when she met it and blushed, he chuckled, blinking away.

He leaned back in his chair as he sipped coffee at breakfast and studied her for some time. "Would you like to have your footman here?"

She looked up at him in surprise. "Why would you ask?"

"You are fond of him." He shrugged. "I feel like he wanted to tear me apart like an angry dog when he learned that you were going to marry me and move away."

Alina laughed and leaned back in her chair, mimicking Samuel's pose. "He is a character, yes. He rubs off on you and becomes like that sibling that you love to hate. His presence annoys you at times, but when he is gone, you miss him terribly."

Samuel laughed through his nose. "He knew about us, didn't he?"

She'd noticed Yegór's hostile glances when she used to leave St Rose's after hours of talking to Harlan in the garden. Perhaps, she'd been blind in her love. Others hadn't been. Rumi certainly hadn't.

"I always thought so, yes," Alina said, casting her gaze down. "He delivered the letters. But he would never say anything, you know it."

"I am not worried about that."

"I think Martha is missing him terribly. I think they are very fond of each other. That's an understatement." She chuckled.

"Let's bring him here. I would like that. If your parents don't mind, of course."

Alina felt suddenly happy. Things were coming together in the most wonderful way. Only, she needed more time to come to terms with the two men in her life being one.

And she wanted Samuel again.

Oh, God, she should've stayed in bed!

She trembled at his touch when they left the breakfast room and he walked next to her, placing his hand on her hip.

"Would you like to do anything in particular today?" he asked.

She shrugged. "Anything, really. I am perfectly content staying in."

*And endlessly listening to you talk.*

He only smiled. "I shall send for Yegór, then."

"Oh, the rumors among the ton!" She laughed happily. "Next thing you know, they will be calling it a Russian invasion of the English *crème de la crème*."

Samuel laughed, making her heart flutter at the sound. "I would call it the English seduction of the Russian intelligence. And with what skills!"

His hand slid to her waist and pulled her toward him. In that laughter, their eyes met and locked in a gaze that brought back the memories of their love-making.

"I love you," he said so casually, leaned over, and kissed her softly on the cheek.

Yegór arrived that very afternoon.

The duke's older footman stared up at him in horror, nervously jerking the flaps of his livery.

Alina only grinned as she met Samuel's eyes.

"There will be another servants' war," she whispered.

He cocked an eyebrow. "We should place bets."

"It might end peacefully still. It will only take one night of Yegór drinking with your men, and they shall be brothers."

Or not.

Because that very evening, Yegór and Martha were having a row, in the dining room of all places, though the parlors were off-limits to the servants.

Alina marched toward the sound.

"You cannot behave the way you do back at my parents' place," she said sternly, approaching.

Martha and Yegór straightened up like soldiers.

Martha glared at Yegór. "Yegórushka," she hissed, "you shall have both of us thrown out of here." She then looked at

Alina. "He says he can't figure out his way around this place yet. Truly—*krasavets*, I tell you, my lady!"

Despite anger, Alina burst out in laughter, and Yegór's body shook as he tried to suppress a chuckle.

"We shall keep it quiet, my lady," he said, turned on his heel, and left with a grin.

"Forgive me, my lady." Martha looked defeated.

"What's with *Yegórushka*?"

Martha rolled her eyes and cocked an eyebrow. "I asked him how to call him when I am cross with him. He said there is a Russian ending for that. Everything in your language has an ending for a certain mood, doesn't it?"

Alina burst into laughter.

"But, my lady!"

"It is not a cross way to call someone, Martha."

"No?" The maid furrowed her eyebrows.

"No. On the contrary. It's very endearing."

Martha's eyes flashed with immediate anger. "That rascal! How endearing?"

"Very"—Alina cocked an eyebrow—"endearing."

The maid's chin ticked up in disdain. "That *krasavets*, he'll get it."

Alina held on to her stomach laughing. Those two were like two fires that flicked together at the slightest blow of wind.

The maid murmured angrily in the hallway as she walked toward the servants' quarters.

Alina followed, out of curiosity and to see the fight that might be started by the English girl and the Russian footman on duke's soil.

"Yegór! You tricked me!" The shout came from somewhere deep in the kitchen. There came the sound of heavy footsteps, a door slamming closed, a squeal, and Yegór's rumble, "*Moya anglijskaya chertovka.*"

Alina shook with silent laughter—he called Martha his English she-devil.

Then suddenly, everything went quiet save for a set of heavy footsteps going up the servants' stairs. It only meant one thing—Yegór was carrying Martha in his arms, undoubtedly to show her his new room, and her snappy mouth was certainly preoccupied.

## 53

# PASSION

Those two from the Kamenevs' place—it was a bliss to watch their love unwind, Father. Only being a bystander do you understand how lucky someone is to be in love.

That Russian Viking and Alina's maid certainly were a blaze. They turned the house upside down. Other servants complained at the racket. But one night, Yegór made them all drink *medovuha*, the honey liquor, until dawn, and the next day I noticed smiles around, my own butler humming some tune under his breath.

I laughed, knowing that it would all settle. Such are the Eastern people. Strong spirits are their magic potions. Once you share a drink, they hold your heart captive. For once, my house showed signs of life.

Alina's cook, Prosha, came one afternoon to teach my cook, Canderby, some ethnic cuisine. She raided the kitchen, cellars, and storage chests. She made Canderby scoff and whimper in pained frustration. She only answered in Russian, giving him instructions in her native tongue, and soon, he shouted and pulled the hair on his head. They had a huge row about the difference in pancakes and crepes—in what language, I am not sure.

On day three, Canderby asked to see me and threw his hands in the air in desperation.

"Your Grace! She is impossible! Rude! Obnoxious!" He paced back and forth in front of me. "She turned my kitchen into a battlefield. Flour everywhere like it's winter. No sense of order! Your Grace, please take pity." His face contorted in the most sorrowful expression.

I smiled as I listened to him. "The duchess wants you to learn the recipes. So clench your teeth and write down all you need. I am sure you don't need many words in the kitchen. You are the best French chef in this area. But I am sure you can learn something from someone else."

Canderby rubbed his forehead in frustration, his mustache twitching as he murmured under his breath. "I shall quit, by God, I shall finish myself!"

He didn't. That afternoon, the Russian cook seduced him with the recipe of a layered honey cake.

That evening, I told Alina what had happened. She only laughed.

I love her laughter, Father. It's like a trickle of water that suddenly appears through cracked soil in the middle of a desert.

Theo Van Buren stopped for dinner. He praised Prosha's cooking. You see, Father, Russian cuisine was beginning to seduce the elite.

Amidst the amiable chatter, Theo inquired about Alina's friend. "Is she coming for a visit any time soon?"

Alina narrowed her playful gaze at him. "Why, my lord? Are you suddenly interested? I thought you weren't fond of Olga's attitude."

"Oh, it's mere curiosity." He took a sip of brandy, his jaw hardened, a smile on his face frozen.

My wife glanced at me, and we both smiled.

As Theo and I smoked cigars later that night, he studied me for some time with that intrigued gaze of his.

"Marriage, huh? I never saw you as a family man, Samuel."

What could I reply to that?

"Whatever struck your fancy with her?" he insisted. "Although, I do admit, she is the most beautiful woman around. Her and that brazen friend of hers. Ol-ga." He pronounced it with the too obviously theatrical contempt. "And the most whispered about, certainly. But you were never into pretty looks." He cocked his head at me.

I didn't reply.

Theo chuckled and shook his forefinger at me. "There is something dark about you, my friend. I should've known, of course. The way you asked me to approach her at the ball months ago and ask Lady Amstel to invite her for dinner. Made me talk to her. Ask all those questions. Like a script. You —always in the shadows. Always silent. For a while, I thought you were playing matchmaker. And here we are."

I chuckled. "You enjoyed it."

"I did, I did. But couldn't help feeling you were playing some game."

"She was never a game."

"Oh! And look where we are now! I bet in your marital bed you play many games." Theo's gaze acquired the familiar sly sparkle. "Tell me, is she as cold as—"

"Stop," I warned him though failed to conceal a smile.

"Oh, sensitive, aren't we?" Theo laughed loudly.

Sensitive wasn't the word, Father.

I couldn't stay away from Alina. My body was exhausted

trying to hold back the need to touch her—those moments were reserved for the night. I hungrily looked at the clock every minute, waiting for the time I would snatch her away to the bedroom. And in the bedroom, it was a slow seduction into the dark.

That evening, in our bedroom, I pulled her toward me.

Her Grace the Duchess of Ravenaugh—the title would never do her justice.

"You run away every morning," I confronted her softly, stroking her hair, trying to be as tender as possible, trying to hold back my shameless lust.

Her cheeks turned pink and so lovely. I took her head between my palms and planted soft kisses on them.

She smiled and pressed her forehead to my shoulder, hiding her face, and I wrapped her in my arms.

I loved how she rubbed her cheek on my shoulder. How she kissed me softly on my jaw. How she intertwined her slender fingers with mine, rubbing her thumb over mine.

Yet, she never showed passion in the daylight, saving it for the man she loved in the dark.

"It is still so strange," she said, her fingers stroking the texture of my waistcoat.

"It feels like back then when I had to wait for the nights to be close to you," I said, the words paining me still.

I weaved my fingers into her hair. She let it loose in the evenings, turning from an angel into a lover, slowly unleashing her own desire.

"I need time to get used to you," she said.

I kissed her forehead, then hooked my finger under her chin and gently pulled her face up, bringing her lips to mine for a kiss.

Her breathing grew uneven. I felt it every time she gave in —her desire that was held back just like mine.

Yet, every time she opened her eyes, she looked almost surprised as if she hadn't expected to see me.

"Take all the time you need, angel," I said, hating myself for being the cause of this torture.

*Angel.*

She closed her eyes at the sound of the word. I knew the effect. "I love you," I said softly. I would never stop telling her that, though she'd never said those words to me.

And at night, in our bedroom only lit by the faint light of the fireplace, she was different.

Oh, my duchess was passion, growing braver night after night.

She let me have my way with her. She let me open her up in most shameless ways and use her body the way I found fit.

I taught her things. I coaxed her hands to bring me the biggest bliss. I took her quickly to get relief so that I could take my time with her after that. And then I sheathed into her slowly, studying the sensation of our flesh grinding together. I caressed her every sensitive spot, learning what made her moan.

I feasted on her body. There wasn't an inch of it that I hadn't kissed or probed with my tongue. But I would trace the same paths again and again until I knew them by heart.

In the two weeks following the wedding, we barely slept at night, making up for the days during which we kept our distance.

I became a scholar of her body. I knew how hard she liked it and when she needed it gentler. I knew where she liked my tongue and guided her hand to the sensitive parts of my body that she wanted to touch but was too timid. I knew what got those erotic little sounds out of her. The range of her little breathless pants when she approached her peaks. The way my name fell off her lips. The sound of that little brass cross slapping feverishly against my chest when she straddled me and panted away.

That naughty cross...

Finally, I'd gotten closer to her than it was. And every time I trailed kisses along her body, I made sure to flick that brass rascal with my tongue.

My angel could be like an ocean, calm and taking me in submissively, or stormy and taking charge in her wild passion. She'd never been as loud as she was in my arms, reaching the peaks of ecstasy as I took what I needed and made her shudder with need.

She moaned and whispered my name.

Samuel.

Harlan.

It didn't matter.

The love language was helping her stitch together the men she'd known before and the husband who was the two of them in one. We talked for hours during the day. And at night, stripped of everything but the wedding rings and that little cross hanging from her neck, we tore at each other with teeth and claws, grunting and moaning, then soothing those wounds with kisses and nibbles and the softest caresses that lasted into the dawn.

We were a mess.

Two aching hearts.

Many lies.

And the truth that could only be resolved with time.

*Angels, demons,*

*Saints, and sinners.*

*Memories define hell and heaven.*

Miss Rumi wrote that, Father. That woman is brilliant. I will have her poems published soon. One person can't possibly keep such poetic genius to herself.

And one woman couldn't possibly hold as much passion as my Alina did. We stayed up until dawn. Talking and making love.

Somehow, I felt like that was it—the past was behind me.

Until that fateful meeting at Willi's Rooms.

The night that put a crack into our bond.

And that crack bore one name.

General Helbron.

## 54

---

# NEMESIS

I t was a week before Christmas. And oh, how blissful life seemed!

The Kamenevs came for dinner to the duke's place. Anna Yakovlevna donned her best furs and pounds of jewelry. She smiled and laughed, and it made Alina happy. Finally, her mother was at peace.

"I love England," Anna Yakovlevna chirped at dinner. "I love its fall, and the rains, and the winter. And the food! Oh! How can you not love this! Splendid!"

"Mamá, his grace's chef is French."

Samuel smiled. Nikolai Sergeevich met Alina's eyes and reddened, suppressing laughter.

And when the men retired to the cigar parlor, Alina gave her mother a tour of the house.

"Oh, how beautiful! *Dusha moya*, I am so happy for you!" She pulled Alina into a hug but never asked whether Alina was happy.

The next day, they met at Willi's Rooms Restaurant. A familiar face at the table on the other end of the main parlor drew Alina's attention.

She leaned over to Samuel. "The commander of the Metropolitan Police is here," she whispered.

But Samuel had already noticed—the table of twelve men, some in uniforms.

"My interest in conversing with those gentlemen diminished lately," he said and met Alina's eyes. She cast her eyes down with a knowing smile. The events of the past seemed like an eternity ago.

But there was no avoiding the gentlemen. Alina and Samuel were leaving when the voice stopped them.

"Your Grace!" The commander made his way toward them, several others following behind him.

Alina smiled and looked at her husband.

And froze.

She knew his face by heart. Knew every little frown and smirk. Knew when he was irritated or displeased.

But what she saw in Samuel, who stared at the approaching men, were pain and hatred so profound that her insides turned icy cold.

She turned her eyes to the commander, maintaining a pleasant smile.

"Your Grace." Mr. Brootward took her hand and bowed. "Congratulations are in order." He nodded to Samuel, then turned toward his companions. "You are not acquainted, but my companions are very much eager to meet you. Mr. Hatchinson, the superintendent of the Metropolitan Police. A good man to know, besides me, of course."

His laughter boomed across the entire floor as the men shook hands. But Alina watched Samuel, whose face was frozen in an emotionless mask.

"And this is my dear friend, General Helbron, His Majesty's hero and most decorated military man."

*Oh, no.*

Alina felt the floor drop from under her feet.

She knew the name. She'd heard it from Samuel. There wasn't a person he hated more than the man in his fifties with a bald head, wide sharp mustache, and beady sparkling eyes. The entire city of London had been changed because of what this man had once done.

He stretched his hand toward Samuel, yet the duke didn't move. Awkward silence settled between them for a moment as the general's smile faded.

"Your Grace," Alina whispered.

"General," Samuel said coldly, his lips stretching in a cold smile.

His hand stretched slowly to meet the general's, who took it in his and shook with enthusiasm.

The men seemed to relax and cheered up again, chatting. Only Alina noticed Samuel clasping his hands behind his back, flexing the fingers that had been touched by the hero of the Hindu Kush battle.

They talked about the weather and London and the dinner with the Lord Mayor, all the while Samuel's face a cold mask and Alina's heart bleeding for her husband.

"Your Grace, would you like to attend the parade?" the general asked.

"The parade?" Alina echoed. She already hated his sleazy smile and the toad-like mouth and the way his spotless uniform crinkled and his boots made a squeaking sound against the parquet floor.

"The military parade at Victorian Square in three days," Mr. Brootward said.

The general nodded, his chest puffy like that of a pigeon. "We would be delighted to have you."

Samuel's lips pressed in a tight line. His jaw was set.

"I am afraid we are engaged elsewhere," Alina said with a nervous smile. "In fact, we really do have to leave. It was good to see you." She nodded to the commander, knowing—or rather feeling—that things had shifted in a dark direction again.

The ride in the carriage was silent. Samuel hadn't uttered a word since the restaurant. And in the dimness of the carriage, Alina felt like back then, the first time in the dark garden at St Rose's, when next to the gentleman-devil she felt danger. She hadn't known him back then, for when she got to know him, that sense of danger dissipated.

But she'd never seen him when he'd stalked his prey. She'd only heard the stories. Told in his voice, they seemed like bonfire tales about a dark legend. Not Samuel. Not her husband.

But the sense of danger was almost tangible in the carriage —in the way he wouldn't meet her gaze, wouldn't say a word, in the way he clasped his fingers on his lap and his chest rose and fell heavily.

"Samuel," she said softly when they approached the house. "Are you all right?"

He didn't answer.

At home, he retired to his study, and when she walked in two hours later, he was drinking.

A decanter of whisky stood next to him. The sweet smell of his cigar curled into her nostrils. The room was silent.

He turned his whisky-sparkly eyes to her as she approached.

She'd never seen him like this—drinking heavily, smoking.

So quiet but not for her—sinking in the horrible memories after facing his biggest enemy.

"You will let go, won't you?" she asked almost with a plea in her voice.

He didn't answer.

That night, he made love to her quickly, roughly. She liked it just as much. But there was desperation in the way he thrust into her with force, the impatience with which he fisted her hair, kissing her deeply. He flipped her onto her belly, then yanked her to stand on all fours as he took her from behind, his hand sliding around her thigh to pleasure her.

She let him do it his way.

She tried to sooth his pain.

"I love you," he whispered again and again, and she knew he used her to try to subdue the memories that suddenly were too vivid.

She lay in his arms afterward, in the dark and for what seemed like eternity, and knew that his eyes were wide open, staring at the ceiling until dawn.

The next day, when she woke up, Samuel was gone. She walked into the study, looking for him. He wasn't there but something else was—a flyer on his desk.

It was an announcement of the military parade at Victorian Square in two days, the festivities that accompanied it.

And the highlight—the speech by the honorable servant of Her Majesty, General Helbron.

Alina's heart thudded with unease.

The gentleman-devil was back.

"You promised me, Samuel," Alina said when she confronted him that very evening. There was none of the usual kindness in her husband's eyes.

His hair was loose and messy.

And it was a reminder that the villain was never gone. He was simply resting. He was preparing for something, she knew. His absence the entire day was a grave indication.

She reasoned with him.

He argued softly.

She raised her voice, reminding him of his promise.

"I have to do this," he said sternly, without looking at her. "I promised that he would get what he deserves."

"Death?" She shivered at the words. Harlan Krow was in the past. The Duke of Ravenaugh was the present. It had been much easier to accept the villain in the darkness. But darkness was again crouching up to her feet.

"I don't know, Alina."

"But can't you see?" She was desperate. "You can't become a monster like them, Samuel."

She stroked his face, hoping that her display of affection would change his mind.

He took her hand and pressed it to his lips. "Are you afraid of me now?"

"No. But the last time you took to the streets, you almost died. I am afraid to lose you, can't you see? I am afraid that you will never get enough of revenge, and it will destroy you."

"It won't, angel. Do you trust me?"

She looked away.

*Trust.*

She'd learned that word the hard way.

"I know what it is like to lose someone," she said. "I almost lost you." She felt a lump in her throat. "I can't go on like this, thinking that one day you will find another dark cause, another target." A lump in her throat was suffocating. She could only think one sentence at a time. "Won't you stop?" she asked with tears in her eyes. This was the second time in her life she'd asked a man dear to her to stop. "For me, Samuel. Won't you stop?"

And just like the time before, the man she loved did not answer.

## 55

---

## ONE LAST TIME

"**Y**ou are quiet," I said, caressing my angel in bed that night. She was growing cold, and I couldn't find the words to warm her heart. I could tell her of what was to come. She would try to stop me—I knew my angel—and that just wouldn't do.

I had nothing to offer but love words that night.

"I love you more than life, Alina," I whispered.

"I know," she whispered back, though my angel didn't know the value of life.

"Don't be cold with me, angel."

"When I try, it doesn't work."

Her soft accent was like a purr. She made me smile. My duchess was hot with need. Her body pressed into me harder with every kiss. Her hands got braver with my every encouragement. She shifted and rose on her hands, her face looming over mine in the darkness, her hair spilling down. I slid my hands into it, pulling her to me, taking her lips in a kiss, letting her straddle me.

She wasn't a kitten anymore. She was a leopard. Want

leaked out of her, smearing over my abdomen. She lifted her buttocks and sank onto me.

And as she made love to me, her hands were on my chest, pressing onto it as if she wanted to pin me down to that bed forever.

The next morning, she was gone again. Yet she wasn't at breakfast.

"She went to the Kamenevs' place," her maid announced gravely.

The note came only in the evening.

*I shall stay at my parents' tonight.*
*We had an agreement.*
*You broke it.*
*I can't go on if you don't stop.*
*Please, forgive me.*

That note was a stab in my heart. I wanted to go get her, bring her home. This *was* her home.

But here is the thing, Father. I trusted her with my life. And this time, she needed to learn to trust me, too.

I wasn't about to break my promise.

But justice had to be served.

One.

Last.

Time.

## 56

---

## THE NIGHT WE MET

My Alina...
    She was fearless, kind, noble.
She wanted to save me, Father.
It brought a smile to my face.
But she couldn't stop me, and she knew it.

What I was about to do, I did for myself, there is no denying it. But also for the hundred men who deserved better than some traitor basking in glory at their expense. And I did it for Alina. Don't smirk, Father. Carrying out the last act of justice meant to finally slay my own monster called hate. If I didn't do this, I would be a bitter man, forever looking for that revengeful splinter in my heart until it would fester with time and turn into an open wound, making me a miserable man. My duchess deserved a better man by her side.

There is one thing my angel never understood—a killing can be a crime, or a simple act of defense, or mercy. Those are not shades of the same. They are entirely different.

You see, Father, the night I encountered Alina on that dark street, I saw her before the attacker approached her. I recognized her, of course. Predators' eyesight is sharpened by night.

I'd never looked twice at her before—a stunning beauty with an alluring accent and an intriguing past but nevertheless only a pretty picture. I didn't know her then. Her presence at balls and parties was a mere decoration.

But that fateful night, I saw her slender figure march down the dark street too close to the parts that even men didn't venture to at night.

It made me wonder.

What would a lady be doing in these parts and on her own?

It raised my eyebrows. So, I followed her.

I saw the attacker then, his figure fast approaching, the intention obvious in his hunched posture and fast steps. Before I could react, he grabbed her, murmured something, his groping and her shouts too quick as I darted toward them.

She pushed the man, who stumbled, tripped, and fell backward. His heavy body thumped against the ground and suddenly went still. And the countess went limp against the iron railing and sank down onto the ground.

She was unconscious when I came over.

And the man…

Well, when I checked his pulse, it was barely there, his head rimmed with a dark pool of blood as it lay against a sharp stone. Fate can be swift when it deals its blow.

I looked at the countess again. A light from a passing carriage illuminated her face for a brief moment. Hers was the face of an angel. How had I not noticed that before?

Would you ever betray an angel, Father?

It is unbearable to live with blood on your hands. She was not used to it like I was. I'd committed many sins. What was another one?

You see, Father, if that monster had survived that night, he would have assaulted others, no doubt. He didn't deserve to breathe.

But if he died right then, he would have died at *her* hand.

I couldn't let that happen. I couldn't possibly know back then that she would change my life. But the decision was quick and spontaneous.

The attacker was still breathing when I took a knife out of my pocket and, with practiced quickness, sank the sharp steel into his heart.

No begging.

No excuses.

One decision.

One stab.

One life.

I pulled the knife out, wiped it on his chest, and put it back in my pocket.

It was done.

The monster expired.

By *my* hand, not *hers*.

Angels live in heaven, Father, but I found mine in hell. And, God forgive me, but if it took such a sin to carry her out of there, I would do it again.

## 57

---

## TRAITOR

Alina missed Samuel terribly. The night she spent at her parents' house was miserable, cold, and full of dark memories.

By morning, she tried to be calm but couldn't do anything besides pace around her room. She was hoping Samuel would come and tell her he wouldn't execute another brutal revenge.

He didn't. And so Alina walked about her quiet room, waiting for something. For what—she wasn't sure. The clock ticked away minutes, then hours.

Her mother didn't understand, of course, calling Alina a run-away wife.

Her father came into her room for a minute and studied Alina in silence.

"I feel like my life is going in circles," she said, staring empty-eyed out the window. "I feel like what happened in Russia is happening again. It's a curse."

Nikolai Sergeevich didn't know what was happening but was an understanding man. He stood for some time in silence, hands in his pockets, and finally turned to leave. But before the door closed behind him, he said, "In moments like this, Alina, despite hurt feelings and a sense of betrayal, one should always be next to the loved one."

And those words broke her.

In a minute, Alina stormed out of the house and was on her way to Victorian Square.

The gravest days were often marked with a sense of the most cheerful beginning. Tragedies often happened amidst the bliss.

Despite the gray skies and falling snow, the city was cheerful, unaware of what was to come.

*Where are you?*

Alina 's heart pounded as she rushed through the crowded streets leading up to the square.

A wooden grandstand was set up at the center of it.

An orchestra boomed.

The celebration was in full swing.

In the buildings on either side of the grandstand, balconies and rooms had been rented out for those who could pay for the privilege of observing the parade up close. Smiling faces stared through the open windows. Bodies leaned over the balcony railings.

By the stage, rows of benches were set up for those of military rank and public office. Uniforms and official garbs, medals and sashes, pomaded wigs and perky mustaches.

And the rest of the square around it belonged to the people who gathered as if for a big holiday.

Lemonade vendors, bakers, oyster sellers. Meats and corn were fried in portable stoves, the smell of it floating across the square. The smoke from the vendors hung like clouds, gray and alive above the heads.

Costermongers and street performers of all kinds, factory

workers and laborers, carriages and donkey-carts, street musicians and beggars, children, crying infants, dogs, cats—everyone gathered on this day to the square, pushing to and fro.

Thousands of odors tainted the cold air—from burnt coal, unclean bodies, damp coats, food. The air was thick with people. And though it was snowing lightly, the snowflakes didn't reach the ground, melting in the thousands of warm breaths.

Alina didn't know what was happening, or if anything would. Samuel said he'd keep his promise, yet she knew he'd interfere.

*But how?*

She veered among the sea of people, her fluffy dress suddenly too big, the hem soaked with melting snow threatening to trip her. But it was much too busy to get to the center of the square. People didn't care much for the parade or the officials. But why not celebrate? They'd brought food and wine and their children.

Despite the cold weather, the city seemed to be warm. And when the orchestra boomed with a merry tune up by the stage, the crowd halted and turned their faces toward it. No one could hear the officials who made a speech. But everyone understood that because of them—those courageous honorable men who protected their country and them—they had this cause for celebration. So they cheered for His Majesty's army and for the men who led the soldiers to victories.

Alina pushed her way toward the grandstand. Her heartbeat quickened. It was daylight. And Harlan Krow didn't strike by day.

And yet...

There were people in the windows and on balconies all along the main street. They stood on the roofs. Children hung in the trees. They were watching, and that was what Harlan Krow wanted.

Alina pushed among the bodies, craning her neck to see what was happening upfront.

The murmur and shouting came from afar. The voices rose by a notch. There were shouts of the boys, who zipped through the crowd here and there, swerving among the bodies and passing out leaflets. Suddenly, the air whispered with the sound of hundreds—thousands—of bird wings flopping.

Alina raised her face.

Those were not birds but leaflets. They danced and fluttered in the air, falling down like snow onto the square, the boys on the roof throwing handfuls of them.

People picked them up.

So did Alina.

A face she knew stared at her from the page. A bald head. Wide pointy mustache. A military uniform and an exaggerated medal on his chest. The man in the sketch stood proudly, legs wide apart, on a pile of dead soldiers.

*Good God…*

She didn't need to read the name on the sketch—General Helbron—to recognize him.

A sharp epigram followed.

> *Oh, his smile is a trick,*
> *And his honor a sham,*
> *Hiding the bloodied gold in his den.*
> *If you look in the light,*
> *The gold star shines bright red—*
> *With the innocent blood of his men.*
>
> *And so here we have it—*
> *The epitome of grace*

*Tucked warmly under the royal hand.*
*But as long as the dead men*
*Remain only ghosts,*
*This atrocious disgrace will not end.*

*Say a prayer. Or fifty.*
*They won't raise the dead*
*Whose lives cost just a coin or ten.*
*But the power of those*
*Who stand up for the truth*
*Shall bring honor to a hundred slain men.*

Below the poem was the name of the regiment and a list of a hundred names of the soldiers who had laid their heads under the command and betrayal of disgraceful General Helbron in 1842 in the Hindu Kush.

Who'd written the poem? A guess loomed in her mind, but she shooed it away.

She raised her eyes and scanned the crowd.

Soon, the leaflets scattered the ground, stomped, darkened in the slush. They kept dancing in the air as someone threw more of them off the roofs.

Hands shot up, catching them, hungry eyes reading them, and those who couldn't stared at the picture, frowned, and pointed fingers in the direction of the grandstand, then asked someone to read the text.

Alina grew weak. This was it—ousting the monster in front of the people and bringing him to light. For the first time, Harlan Krow brought the monster to public knowledge instead of dealing with him.

The angry shouting started somewhere in the distance. It grew louder like an approaching storm. They must have scattered the leaflets all over town, for there was a river of people coming—men, angry, brandishing sticks and stones, women, their eyes red with tears and blazing.

This was it. It was coming. Alina's chest tightened with panic.

That day, Alina would come to find out, men stomped out of factories and shops. They brandished fists and weapons. Women sobbed in grief. Widows raged.

They poured like a river down the streets, a thousand boots digging into the slush.

They made their way to the square.

"Punish him!" one shouted.

A child threw a stone in the direction of the stage.

It didn't take much to enrage a crowd, not when there were thousands of them, realizing their power in numbers.

The orchestra music burst into a cacophony of merry sounds, but the people kept coming. They pushed and shoved, filling up the square. They pushed past Alina, almost knocking her down. But she didn't notice, transfixed by this display of camaraderie.

Harlan Krow had given revenge to the people. And people didn't forgive, he knew. The masses didn't have mercy. There was nothing that could stop them—a sea, seeking vengeance for the death of their own.

The air was thick with anger. This had started as a celebration and was turning into an uprising.

Alina's chest was heavy. It was hard to breathe. Anxiety spiked in her, making blood pump through her body, in her head, in her ears. She watched, her eyes wide in shock, her heart thudding with astonishing speed.

People.

So simple.

So primal.

They wouldn't be merciful. There was no redemption for

the criminal responsible for the death of a hundred men, and how many more—who knew?

They began to push, shove, elbow each other, yet moved in one direction. Their anger united them in this march. Their feet stomped forward, sinking into the slush that turned brown under their feet.

Hearing the shouts, the military officials on stage scrambled. A man whispered something in the general's ear and pulled him aside, down the steps of the grandstand, and toward one of the carriages that waited behind it.

Running—the coward was running.

Alina's heart jolted in panic. In that moment there was still that flickering fright that Harlan Krow would strike. He couldn't, could he? He would never show his face.

And then the words were shouted somewhere at the front. It was just a shout, followed by many, and soon, it rippled its way through the crowds.

"Traitor!"

It got picked up and in a moment was chanted like a sentence across the square.

"Traitor!"

"Traitor!"

"Traitor!"

Like the stabs of a knife. Like the shots of a gun.

The crowd pushed and surged forward toward the stage where the general's carriage was.

Alina pushed through the bodies but had no chance to move forward. She saw the boys gaping and grinning as they climbed street poles so they could see. She picked up the hem of her skirt and did the same—climbed onto the elevated base, wrapped her hand around the pole and searched with her eyes for the carriage.

There it was. It tried to move. A dozen or so guards held

away the circle of the crowd that tried to push past them. The carriage jerked forward and halted, the horses held up by the men in the crowd. The coachman whipped the animals. They reared, snorted, squeezed but couldn't move through the human wall that stretched for a mile.

And suddenly, the human wall collapsed. The people broke through the line of the guards and lunged at the carriage. They pounced at it, grabbed at it, tried to open the doors—all in vain. The coachman was nowhere to be seen as the men crawled to the driver's seat, then the roof of the carriage. They banged their fists on the carriage and kicked it, they roared and shouted, and soon dozens of hands started rocking the carriage side to side, the sea of people pressing forward.

Someone shoved a leaflet through its cracked window.

The ground trembled under thousands of stomping feet.

The air seemed to rumble with raging breaths and spat-out threats.

*His* voice was in her head.

*"People don't have the power until they've had enough of misery. They are not brave until they unite. Then their impatience spills over, like a stream, growing into rapids, turning into blinding rage. That's how the masses awaken—from the bottom, crashing like water through a broken dam. Often violently. But often, that's what it takes to break the power that holds them in an iron grip."*

That was what Samuel wanted—people rising for the honor of their own.

Alina's heart thudded in her chest as she craned her neck, trying to see the carriage.

The general could run, but how far could he run when his enemy was the entire country? What could he possibly use as an excuse when he'd betrayed those he was supposed to protect?

And then there came the sound.

Muffled, soft, so unimpressive and unnoticeable in the uproar around.

The sound of a life ending—so mundane when surrounded by the thousands of living.

A shot.

A single shot.

It came from within an enclosed space somewhere ahead. But as the crowd kept pushing, the commotion by the carriage stopped.

And Alina's heart seemed to stop with it.

She froze.

In the square full of people, she knew that the act was over.

So quickly, in a matter of a second.

So banally.

The shot came from the carriage, and as the tight circle around it widened, someone finally broke down the door and stood staring inside.

Alina didn't need to get close to know what had happened. Cowardice didn't always mean running away. It meant not being able to face the people you betrayed.

And when the general's lifeless body was dragged out of the carriage and dropped onto the ground, his ending seemed suddenly too easy and unfair.

The crowd kept railing. Waves of people pressed onto the ones ahead. The news of the gunshot rippled through the sea of people, but they were angry, not only at the general but the power that held this country in its grip and the poor under its heel.

Only later the news would spread that it took the guards half an hour to fight through the bellowing crowd to get to the carriage. By the time they found the general's lifeless body, it was covered in frozen spit.

The crowd still protested.

The noise seemed to spread across the city.

People could forgive, but they never forgot. She knew it. The people did. So did the almighty of this world, for now staying silent in the acknowledgment of this disgrace.

It would be over soon, Alina knew.

She closed her eyes, trying to hold back tears.

It was then that she realized that she would be by her husband's side no matter what. How could she think she could shun him, push him away when her heart was breaking into pieces without him?

Harlan Krow belonged to the city. The duke belonged to the ton. And the man behind the two was truly only hers, with all his secrets and scars.

He wasn't here, at the square. She'd known that all along. She knew what he would say, too.

That the people deserved to know.

That the hundred men deserved the truth to be told.

That the general had a choice.

That this final act of judgment belonged to the people.

That Harlan Krow had laid down his arms but could still fight, only by a different means.

The crowd around railed, but for Alina, the world suddenly went quiet.

## 58

---

## THE QUIET PLACE

Alina rushed home with desperate yet happy determination. Despite the gruesome fate of the military man and the pandemonium that could follow, she felt at peace.

It started to snow outside. The carriage didn't go fast enough. And when it got to the house, Alina threw the doors open, jumped out at the gate, and dashed inside.

Yegór stood by the door, looking like a theatre performer in his new livery.

"Where is his grace?" she blurted out, shedding her coat into her footman's paws.

"Outside, my lady. In the garden. Getting snowed up like a statue," Yegór answered in Russian much to the disappointment of the butler. "I wrapped him in furs. He didn't say a word. I offered him vodka. He drank it. He might be Russian, for all I know. A strange fella."

He met Alina's reproaching gaze and cast his eyes down.

She exhaled with a theatrical eye-roll. A duke—a fella. Her servants were impossible.

"Give that back." She yanked her coat out of his hands and

walked hurriedly toward the doors to the back terrace, pulling the coat back on.

The garden seemed too peaceful and silent for a day like this. The frozen trees looked like those from a winter fairytale. Snow was everywhere, a fresh thin layer of it already covering the swept terrace and the path into the garden. Alina inhaled deeply and walked toward the table in the garden's distant corner. Soon, it would grow dark, but her Harlan Krow was already here, guarding the last light.

Wrapped in a bear hide, Samuel Cassell sat motionless at the table, the tray with an empty shot and a decanter snowed up. He looked like a mountain of a man—hatless, his hair loose, snowflakes sprinkling his pitch-black strands, the white strand unusually bright.

Alina slowed down and studied the big form of her husband, her heart swelling at the sight.

How she loved him!

Samuel could pass off as a statue if not for a small cloud of warm air escaping his mouth into the frosty air.

He raised his eyes at her as she approached.

"My love," he said quietly and smiled. His eyes on her burned with myriads of emotions—that depth that always pulled her in, making her feel like she was free falling.

She stopped in front of him. "You kept your promise."

"For you. Yes. Come." He stretched his hand to take hers and gently pulled her onto his lap. He looked tired, and she wanted to kiss his sorrows away.

"Will you forgive me?" he asked quietly, the snowflakes sticking to his eyebrows and lashes.

"For what?"

"For letting you doubt me. For pushing you away."

She shook her head. "There is nothing to forgive. I should have trusted you." She smiled, her heart melting with tenderness. "Would you like to know what happened?" She cocked her head, studying his face, trying to figure out what he thought, felt. His eyes always said it all. But right now, they were sad. And she desperately wished he'd smile.

He blinked slowly. "No. This wasn't my fight."

He wrapped his arms around her, pulling her closer.

She stroked his hair, her favorite shade of black, then picked up his white strand and kissed it. She chuckled, then took off her gloves and cupped his face. "I love you," she whispered. "I love you so much it hurts sometimes. Did I ever tell you that?"

And that was when his lips finally stretched in a smile, his eyes suddenly luminous, gazing at her in that way that made her melt.

"I love you, Samuel," she whispered and kissed his stubbled jaw, then planted little kisses on his cheeks, brows, forehead, his eyes that she loved so much.

"I love you more," he answered, his smile getting bigger.

She grinned, shaking her head. Tears burned her eyes. "You must be cold." She always said the silliest things in the most tender moments.

He shook his head, mimicking her. "Not anymore, angel." And he tucked her closer to him.

"Should we go inside?"

"Soon." His eyes burned with warmth. "Let's stay here for a moment. I like when it gets dark. I used to wait for dusk, because in the dark was the only time we could be together."

She pressed her forehead to his and closed her eyes. "I have you," she whispered. "In the darkness and in the light."

For Alina, this loudest day was the most peaceful as she sat with her husband and watched the snow fall.

They spent the rest of the evening having a long dinner, drinking wine, and talking about things that didn't have to do with what had happened that day. She couldn't keep her hands off her husband. He couldn't stop kissing her.

For the first time, she was open in her affection. For the first time, she kissed him with her eyes open.

He brought her to the study, took a seat in the chair behind the desk, and pulled her onto his lap.

"I want to show you something."

She watched his face, the long strands of hair that hung down to his shoulders and turned him from a meticulous duke to a man with a past and the scars that made him strong and powerful.

She smiled.

He took a small painting out of the drawer and, with his arms wrapped around her waist, held it for some time, studying it.

A young man, almost a boy, with bright blue eyes and shaggy blond hair gazed at her from the painting with so much happiness that it made her smile.

"I had a painter draw it from my memory," Samuel said, giving the portrait on the picture a stroke with his fingers. "Meet James Krow."

Alina studied the portrait for some time, then took it out of Samuel's hands and put it down. "I don't like when you are sad."

"I am all right, angel. It's closure."

"Will you smile more?'

He smiled as if at her request, then slid his hands to cup her face and leaned to kiss her.

"Will you look at me more often in the daylight?" he asked.

The words tugged at her heart with guilt. She traced his

eyebrows with her fingers, then his nose, his lips, just like she had done the night at the Phantom Ball.

"I can't stop looking at you," she whispered, her eyes studying his face intensely until he pulled her closer and kissed her again, deeper this time.

The knock was like a rumble of thunder.

Samuel pressed his forehead to hers, saying, "What do you say we throw out all the servants so that no one ever interrupts us."

She laughed, wrapping her arms around his neck and burying her face in it.

"And those two from your parents' place. By God, angel, I feel like they are our relatives who live with us, obnoxious and entitled."

She shook with laughter.

"Come in!" Samuel said louder, chuckling. "Oh, my, there comes your trouble," he murmured as Yegór's tall hunching figure squeezed apologetically into the room.

Alina rose from her husband's lap.

"*Sudarynia. Na minutku-s,*" the footman asked for a minute with her.

"Speak."

He glanced suspiciously at Samuel. "*Bez nevo.*" He asked to be without the duke.

"English, Yegór, please," Alina said, annoyed. "And his grace is fine."

She looked at Samuel, who looked away, smiling and tapping his fingers on the desk.

"Are you leaving Martha outside the door?" Samuel asked, not looking at the footman.

Alina looked between them, confused.

Yegór stood like a bull, his head low in a strange submission as if waiting for judgment. "So... I want... Mar-r-rtha and

I want…" He glanced up to meet Alina's curious gaze, then cast his eyes down at the cap in his hands. "We were…"

"Oh, for heaven's sake, Yegór. What caught your tongue?" Alina snapped.

Samuel behind her cleared his throat. "You would like to get married?" He finally shifted his gaze to the footman, whose eyes snapped at the duke.

Alina gaped.

Yegór nodded and cast his eyes down. "Yes," he said hurriedly and, with a nod, added, "Yor-r Gr-race."

Alina turned to her husband in surprise only to meet his twinkling eyes and a smile that was spreading on his lips.

She turned back to her footman. "And Martha?"

Yegór smiled. "She wants. Yes."

Samuel rose from his seat and walked up to Alina, wrapping his arms around her waist from behind. "I think it's a splendid idea," he murmured into her ear.

She beamed, staring at Yegór. "Yes," she said. "It is wonderful. Yes!"

She laughed happily and wanted to ask when they would like to arrange the ceremony, but Yegór, beaming and bowing, retreated. As the door closed behind him, a happy squeal and whispers came from behind the door, and the sound of two pairs of rushed footsteps echoed down the hall.

Alina turned to her husband. "How did you know?"

He pulled her flush against him. "You sleep too tight, angel."

She furrowed her eyebrows. "What is that supposed to mean?"

"The night your footman got here," he said, cocking his head at her with a mischievous smile, "the sound of the headboard hitting the wall, coming from the servants' rooms upstairs, was unusually loud." He grinned. "I assumed it was his room. And he is not sharing it with anyone."

Alina chuckled, shaking her head.

The thought of a bedroom started spreading sweet longing through her body. She fixed Samuel's shirt as if trying to distract him, then looked at the clock.

Seven in the evening.

"Do you think it is too early?" she asked coyly, casting her eyes down.

He pulled away and ducked his head, trying to look in her eyes. "For what, angel?"

She pursed her lips. "To retire to the bedroom…"

She blushed so intensely that it colored her down to the upper slopes of her breasts.

Samuel grinned and nuzzled her face to find her lips. "I thought you would never ask."

## 59

### CLOSE

"I want to make love to you," Alina said when they came to the bedroom.

With a soft smile, Samuel went to put out the sconces by the bed, just like he'd done the days before, when her voice stopped him.

"Leave them on, please."

He looked at her in surprise, not saying anything for a moment when she stretched her hand to him.

"I want to see you," she said.

He took her hand and stepped closer, brushing a strand of hair off her face. "Are you sure, angel?"

She smiled in response. "I want to see all of you. I've taken my time. I know who you are. I want to see you in the light, knowing that we don't have to hide anymore. I love you."

"Say my name."

"I love you, Samuel."

He kissed her softly on the lips. "Again."

"Samuel."

"You are working your wicked charms on me, my duchess."

"You are already quite charming, Your Grace."

He chuckled, rubbing his nose on her cheek, his soft breath grazing her skin.

They undressed slowly, peeling the garments off each other like fancy wrapping paper, kissing and gasping at each other's touches.

She let him pull her chemise over her head, then undo the ties of her drawers, letting them fall down her legs, unveiling her nakedness in the candlelight.

There.

She wanted him to see her.

She burned with arousal as she watched his gaze travel down her body, his hands following its path.

He still had his undergarments on. They'd spent so many nights together. In the dark. Unleashing their passion onto each other but hiding their nakedness.

Finally, they were out in the light.

Alina caressed his body. He was hers. Both of them. Harlan Krow and Samuel Cassell, his pain and bliss. Scars, a battlefield of them, covered Samuel's torso—deep, healed, in many languages, with no happy endings. The most mesmerizing man she'd known was etched with them. But his smile made up for all his dark past. Sadness and happiness burned in his eyes when he looked at her.

"You are mine. All of you," she whispered, feeling weak and strong at once at this confession.

She wanted to make love to him like he'd made love to her all these days. She caressed his broad chest, running her hands over the dark patch of hair in the center. Her hands slid down to his waist, caressing his latest wound as she pressed little kisses to his scars, one by one, healing the festering memories behind them.

He didn't move, letting her do what she wanted.

Her hands went down to the perfect cut of the muscles at his hips, and she slowly sank down to her knees and kissed them, making him gasp.

She was soaked with desire, raised her eyes to him, and met his gaze. The intensity of it was so strong, so overpowering that she almost moaned with need. She wanted to splay down on the floor in front of him and have him watch her as she pleasured herself. She wanted to get on all fours and let him take her. And she wanted to please him so that he forgot anything that had ever tormented him.

He said she was his angel. If anyone could make a devil lose his mind, it was her.

Her hands caressed his muscled legs, strong like columns. She kissed his abdomen and felt his hands slide into her hair.

Finally, her fingers pulled the strings of his drawers and tugged them down, letting the fabric unveil him in all his naked glory. His sex, thick and erect, was right in front of her. She looked up and met his blazing gaze, his lips parted, his chest rising and falling heavily.

When her fingers brushed the line of dark hair on his abdomen, he grunted.

When they traced the length of his hardness, he whispered, "Alina."

And when she brought her lips to his manhood and planted the first soft kiss on his length, he called out God's name.

Her gentleman-devil, who didn't believe in God, now called his name. Alina smiled, reveling in her power, and let her lips do the magic.

## 60

---

# CLOSER YET

I couldn't take my eyes off her. She'd done many things in my dreams. But seeing her on her knees, pleasuring me, set the nerves under my skin on fire.

She made love to my cock, Father.

Lovers are shameless.

She was so gentle—a sign of her naiveté—not knowing what to do but learning by my grunts and hisses of pleasure.

She kissed every inch of my hardness. She licked the sensitive tip. She took me in her mouth, making me dizzy with the erotic sight.

My angel was naughty. Her lips did wicked things.

Do angels have babies in your holy book, Father? Because I wanted to take her right then and make little angels with her.

But I could hardly hold that thought. Not when her lips caressed my length. Not when her mouth took it deeper, then let it go, sucking slowly. I wanted to teach her how to give me a quick release. But that night wasn't about the release. It was about love. And if someone tells me that my lover's tongue stroking my cock into ecstasy is not love, I shall tell them they haven't met my duchess.

Her one hand moved to the base of my shaft, wrapping around it gently like it were a precious treasure. Her other hand stroked the curls around my sex, then shifted lower, lower still to brush against my balls.

Everything around me was dissipating as I lost myself in her.

I grunted. I was ready to come. But I couldn't. I wanted more of this, of her—watching her lips slide along my flesh, sucking it like it were the source of life.

I didn't let her finish.

Not that night.

I wanted to pleasure her instead. I gently pulled out of her divine mouth and helped her to her feet.

She tasted like me when I kissed her. The taste of the devil was on my angel's lips as she curled her tongue around mine, desperate in her desire. I wanted to come all over her skin so that she knew how much I wanted her, how she made me feel, how hard I burned for her.

She was mine, and days later, it was still too much like a dream.

I held her face between my palms and gazed in her eyes for a moment.

"What have I done to deserve you, angel?"

She smiled.

I picked her up and carried her to bed, then kissed my way down her body. Her thighs were wide open for me. Her beautiful sex was right there, and I planned on devouring it until she lost her mind.

"Samuel."

I tore my mouth off her pink bud and met her gaze.

"Come here," she whispered.

And when I shifted up and settled between her legs, she slid her hand down to my cock and pressed it to her entrance.

"Make love to me," she whispered and pushed herself up onto me.

If I tell you that an epiphany came to me while my cock was inside my wife—it will offend you, Father. If I tell you that the first time I had ever praised God was when I made love to my angel, you will tell me I am a blasphemer.

But the truth remains the same.

She closed her eyes as I sheathed into her.

I paused. "Look at me, angel," I whispered. And when her gray eyes were on me again, I resumed my thrusts. "I want you to look at me when I make love to you."

There was no lust in that moment, only the heavenly feeling of profound intimacy as our flesh and our gazes met. I felt vulnerable and happy and weak and strong at once, closer to her than ever before as we made love. We climaxed at the same time, and I swear, that little brass cross that lay peacefully on her chest winked at me.

My duchess took over again. She kissed my scars and wounds. And with every kiss, she healed the dark memories, one by one.

"I want to know every inch of you," she said.

In due time she will. We have a lifetime together. Dreams.

They were all in her, the woman in my arms who that night loved my body like I was holy. I didn't know the devil could blush. But when her mouth found my most sensitive spots, kissed and licked and stroked them, I couldn't hold back. I spread her legs and took her again.

"I love the noises you make," I whispered, thrusting into her, learning her every expression, catching her every moan. But I didn't let her climax and didn't reach the peak myself. I wanted this bliss to last as long as possible.

That shawl of hers she'd given me once hadn't known as much love as my duchess did that night.

I took her again, then stopped and, being inside her, reveled in the feeling of being so close. Then I made love to her again and, without letting us reach the peak, pulled away.

I lost count of how many times I entered her.

It was sweet torture—the never-ending cycle of wanting each other and burning with need to be close.

Until my angel whimpered with need and begged for release.

An angel is too small of a word for her, Father. She is a goddess. For what else do you call a woman who takes a man full of hatred, empties him out, then fills him with love, all the way to the brim so there is no room for anything else?

We didn't talk much that night, exhausted from the lovemaking.

She fell asleep in my arms. But I couldn't close my eyes. I wanted to meet yet another dawn with her by my side. The night seemed to go by too fast, and then she would leave the bed at first light and be several feet too far from me.

It's madness, Father—how much I loved her, how much it hurt to be even inches apart from her.

I saw the thin line of dawn sneak through the curtains. She stirred, as if sensing it.

*Stay.*

She lifted her sleepy face and squinted at me, a smile on her face. "You didn't sleep again, did you?"

"I am all right." I pushed an auburn strand out of her face. "You should go back to sleep."

She shook her head, her hand sleepily drifting down my torso, then slowly sat up and looked around.

My heart fell.

She would flee again.

She slid out of bed, padded to the window, and threw the curtains wide open.

The room lit up. And there she was—my angel at the first light of dawn.

I cushioned my head with my forearm, taking in the sight of her. The bed smelled like her. My skin tingled from our lovemaking. My every muscle was sore. I was happy.

She turned and met my gaze, for the first time not shy to be all bare for me in full light.

Slowly, she walked up to the bed.

"I don't want you to get up yet," I said softly, patting the warm sheet where she'd just been, hoping she would break that silly habit of running away in the mornings.

"I am not planning to."

*God is great!*

She picked up the edge of the sheet that covered me and started pulling it. The fabric glided down my body, slowly exposing my nakedness.

"Not for a while." She smiled mischievously.

Oh, it was my lucky morning.

My body rose to the awareness under the heat of her gaze that swept across my body. My cock was hard in seconds, her eyes pausing on it as if it were a miracle.

I stilled and waited until she raised her eyes at me, shy but full of that want that could burn a man in love.

There was no mistake, Father. She pulled me into light and now stood bravely in its glory.

My manhood was begging for her again. My heart was about to burst with love.

"Come here, my duchess," I said, stretching my hand toward her.

She came into my arms, her eyes luminous with love, her lips softer than heaven, her warm body yielding into mine.

We never left the bed that morning or for the rest of the day.

The world went still around us.
It finally made sense.
It was perfect, however small.
Just the two of us.
My duchess and I.

## 61

---

# THE REVEREND

That night changed everything, Father. Who we were and who we would become. It stitched together our differences, however few were left.

Between the lovemaking, she rested her chin on her hand that lay on my chest and studied me. Days later, she does that a lot still, as if trying to figure things out. But instead of sadness, there is a smile on her face. A smile that I kiss a hundred times a day.

When she looks at me like that with her beautiful gray eyes full of love, she takes my breath away.

Oh, if I could hold on to those moments!

Love and tenderness rip my heart apart like the softest grenade in slow motion, annihilating what I know of life, erasing the world around us. The beauty of human existence is in that gaze of hers. The perils of war, the love of a mother, the laughter of a child, a man dying for his country, an injured one singing for the dead ones, former slaves becoming freedom fighters, thousands rising for the life of one.

It's devastating.

And it's healing.

It's the touch of an angel.

In moments like this, I know God exists. Perhaps we have a different opinion of what it is. But what is God if not the connection in spirit between us, in all our beauty and ugliness?

I can't say what happened the day Alina Bronskaya walked into my life. It was salvation. Redemption. Ablution. I can find many words. But one thing that she is for sure is love in its truest form.

A way to lure the devil is to tempt him with something he wants.

A way to ruin him is to make him fall in love with something he can't have.

I couldn't be the gentlemen-devil anymore, you see. If I wanted to have her by my side, I had to cross over to the light.

And that is for the better. I promised her.

There is one thing, Father, that I can't forgive myself for. For what *they* had done to *you*. For not being able to save you from their hands. More importantly—for failing to avenge you and letting the man responsible get away.

You will say it is not my fault. I will say that the only thing that brings me consolation is knowing that you wouldn't want it any other way.

There is nothing more to say except that I mourn you every day, Father. It is a day before Christmas, and I wish we could sit down in front of the crucified man of God that you had so much faith in and you could say to me, "Samuel, you can't save everyone. Not this way." And I would answer, "One person at a time, Father."

I hope Alina and I have little angels soon. I will let you know if they have wings.

Samuel Cassell, the Duke of Ravenaugh, exhaled heavily, raised his face to the sky, and smiled at the feeling of snowflakes melting on his face. It was starting to snow. His top hat was dusted with white, so was his coat. But he didn't feel cold lately. His heart burned like a furnace.

The cemetery around him was serene. Under the blanket of snow, the gray peaks of the tombstones stood like soldiers, peaceful in their silence.

Samuel lowered his head, stood up from the stone bench, and for a moment, paused his gaze on the tombstone in front of him.

*Reverend John Pearse*
*A teacher and a man of God*
*The leader of St James's Hill Parish*
*1789-1851*

Samuel leaned toward the tombstone and swept the snow off the top of it, then turned and started walking away, his dark form slowly disappearing into the white snowfall.

## 62

# FLOWERS FOR THE DEVIL

I t was Christmas Eve.

The Duke and Duchess of Ravenaugh stood in the courtyard of St James's Hill and watched the procession around the Christmas tree. This was the first such celebration organized for the orphans as well as the workers of the Hill and their families. Though being only two streets away from the rookeries, any child was welcome, and no poor soul was turned away.

Outside the gates of the Hill, dozens of men were distributing free candles and coal, bread and cheese. It was a simple act of kindness, but a Christmas miracle to some. Hot soup was served, the line a mile long, but no one dared to fight for it, and the food didn't run out. That Christmas night, it fed the hungry and homeless and saved a few lives. A bowl of hot soup. What freedom!

In the courtyard of the Hill, the gas lamps flared around the crowd, keeping it warm. Hundreds walked around the Christmas tree with lit candles in their hands. The lights flickered like stars. Carol singers hummed. Lone snowflakes fell down and melted on the smiling faces that gathered for a celebration. Nothing signified hope like the children's laughter that trilled across the court.

Samuel Cassell stood behind his wife, his arms wrapped around her, warming her. This was their first holiday together and the first time Alina felt like she had a home.

She smiled. "This is magical, is it not?" She turned her head to look up at her husband.

Her eyes were the only light Samuel wanted to see. He kissed her on the forehead. "It always feels like this when you are next to me," he said softly, his heart flaring with tenderness.

The next day, the corner of Camlet Street and Old Nichol saw a crowd. It gathered around the *Weeping Mother*. The iron statue was covered with a thin layer of snow. Around its shoulders hung a black leather coat, worn out and faded. A top hat rested on its head.

Anywhere else, one wouldn't know who the garments belonged to. But the residents of the rookeries recognized the red tassel. The name of Harlan Krow was whispered. Heads shook in disbelief. An old woman walked up and brushed the snow off the hat and the coat. Another woman kissed its hem and crossed herself.

No one knew what it meant, but one thing was certain— the gentleman-devil was not coming back.

That day, prayers were whispered, candles were lit, and someone laid a lone flower at the feet of the *Weeping Mother*.

A fresh flower in December in the poorest parts of London! A miracle!

But so was Harlan Krow.

By evening, rumor had spread like wildfire across the neighboring slums. At midnight, a group of street children brought a basket of flowers made of wire and cotton. No one dared touch those. The blooms would last a long time, through the frost of the winter. And then spring flowers and the summer ones would appear at the feet of the statue with the awkward top hat and coat over it.

They said the garments kept the *Weeping Mother* warm.

They said they warded off evil.

They said no monsters would come near when the devil himself protected the slums.

The place became a symbol of compassion.

The hungry came here by day in hope of alms.

Street children came in the evenings, smoked pipes, and talked about the future. The future! The word unheard of in these parts!

The abused came by night, timidly looking around. They kneeled before the *Weeping Mother* and prayed. To whom— they weren't sure. But they hoped that someone would hear.

And just like hope, the flowers were always there.

# EPILOGUE

## A YEAR LATER

"I've come to tell you, Father, that tiny angels don't have wings. But they do have the most luminous gray eyes. *Hers.*"

# FROM THE AUTHOR:

First and foremost, I wanted to say thank you to my friends and beta-readers: Alexander, K. M., Victoria, Julie, Lara, Linda, Casilda, and Crystal. Thank you for supporting my craft!

I hope you enjoyed the novel, reader. It's a bit dark. With all that is going on in 2022, especially so close to home, I couldn't help but talk about war and trauma.

The idea for Hindu Kush story came from the 1842 retreat from Kabul, also known as the Massacre of Elphinstone's army during the First Anglo-Afghan War. During that military retreat, over 16,000 soldiers and civilians were killed or captured. The events are used fictitiously.

The usage of Russian is very minimal in this novel. I tried to spare you the misery of constant translation. If you enjoy looking up foreign words, some words might not come up in Google as they are historical jargon. French indeed was a home-spoken language among Russian nobility for centuries. Many words were borrowed and used in Russian households daily.

As to Russian names, it's a complicated topic. The last names all have gender endings. So do middle names. In Eastern European cultures, the middle name is always the father's first name. The respectful address is first and middle name. Almost all names have a number of endearing variations and may vary drastically (as when Nikolai Sergeevich Kamenev calls his wife Anna Annushka, Olga—Olen'ka, Dunya—Dunyasha, Yegór—Yegórushka).

The Russian noble rank (countess in this case) was used with the last name as opposed to the British way of referring to the estate owned. In Eastern Europe, it was appropriate to call a titled person by the first and middle name, or the rank itself.

*Flowers For the Devil* is a novel inside a novel. The idea came while writing *Rebel's Muse* (Book 1 in *Rebels of Gracewyck* series). Valentine Bayne, the main hero, is a novelist who rose to fame with his installments about the gentleman-devil. But as he is ready to kill off London's beloved villain, Valentine falls in love and weaves his love story into the last installment of Harlan Krow, redeeming his villain through love. If you are curious to know what gave birth to the gentleman-devil, check out *Rebel's Muse*.

As always, thank you for reading.
Cheers,
Vlad
May 10, 2022

# ALSO BY THIS AUTHOR

THE BELLE HOUSE SERIES:

**THE TENDER DAYS OF MAY**
**THE TENDER TOUCH OF NIGHT**
**THE TENDER RULES OF EDEN**
**THE TENDER KISS OF FATE**
**THE TENDER ART OF WAR**

REBELS OF GRACEWYCK SERIES:

**REBEL'S MUSE (Book 1)**
**REBEL'S TEMPTATION (Book 2)**
**REBEL'S DESIRE (Book 3)**

STAND-ALONES:
**A GENTLEMAN'S WISH**
**FLOWERS FOR THE DEVIL**

# STAY IN TOUCH!

**ANNOUNCEMENTS AND FREE BOOKS:**
WWW.VLADKAHANY.COM

**FACEBOOK:** V. KAHANY BOOKS

**INSTAGRAM:** @V.KAHANY.BOOKS

**TIKTOK:** @VLADKAHANYBOOKS

**EMAIL:** VLAD@VLADKAHANY.COM